The Body in

BLACKWATER
BAY

NOVELS BY PAULA GOSLING

Fair Game
The Zero Trap
Solo Blues
The Harrowing
The Woman in Red
Monkey Puzzle
The Wychford Murders
Hoodwink
Backlash
Death Penalties

The Body in

BLACKWATER
BAY

Paula Gosling

THE MYSTERIOUS PRESS
New York · Tokyo · Sweden
Published by Warner Books

 A Time Warner Company

Mysterious Press books are published by
Warner Books, Inc., 1271 Avenue of the Americas,
New York, NY 10020.
A Time Warner Company

Printed in the United States of America

ISBN 0–89296–459–6

Map by Venner Carter

For Hilary Hale

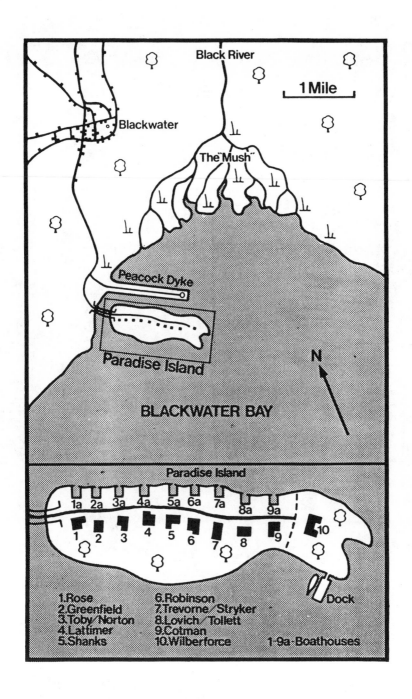

Black River

1 Mile

Blackwater

The "Mush"

Peacock Dyke

Paradise Island

N

BLACKWATER BAY

Paradise Island

1a 2a 3a 4a 5a 6a 7a 8a 9a

1   2   3   4   5   6   7   8   9   10

Dock

1.Rose   6.Robinson
2.Greenfield   7.Trevorne/Stryker
3.Toby/Norton   8.Lovich/Tollett
4.Lattimer   9.Cotman
5.Shanks   10.Wilberforce   1-9a-Boathouses

The Body in

BLACKWATER
BAY

Prologue

The killer was tired of rowing the boat, but it was the only way to do what was necessary.

It was so quiet in the Mush.

Just the frogs, the crickets, the cicadas, the rustling of wind in the reeds, a soft gurgle of water as the oars moved slowly through it, and the faint murmur of traffic on the distant highway.

The snarl of an outboard motor in the Mush at this hour would have been like a scream among the whispers of the night.

The killer rested the oars and made another sweep with the flashlight. Its beam crossed and then returned to an area of scum-streaked sand about ten feet in width. It was smooth and slightly blurred, as if the grains that made it up were in constant and minute motion.

Another two strokes brought the boat to the edge of this expanse. He very carefully shipped the oars, then regarded the corpse at his feet with considerable exasperation.

Murder was never the problem.

It was getting rid of the body that was such a pain.

A freshly dead body, after all, is simply a large and

awkwardly shaped sack of liquids and solids, heavy, ungainly, and inclined to flop at the least convenient moment.

Getting it out of the boat was more difficult than getting it in, but once the head was out, the rest seemed to slide easily enough over the side. Then, at the last moment, one foot caught in the oarlock.

The boat tipped abruptly and the killer fought to keep his balance. Sweating now, despite the coolness of the night air, he disengaged the recalcitrant foot with some distaste—it was rather dirty—and dropped it over.

The body seemed to float alongside for a moment, arms and legs outstretched across the sand as if it were a swimmer peering down. And then the sucking sound began.

Fascinated, the killer watched as the quicksand began to accept his offering, consuming it slowly at first, as a gourmet might savor a new and novel entree.

Then it became greedy.

The hands and feet disappeared. Then the arms and legs sank from sight. The head ducked next, as if accepting applause from an invisible audience. As gray-green ooze began to inch across the torso, the band of exposed flesh narrowed until, at last, the quicksand covered it completely.

There was a muffled belch, and four slow bubbles rose and broke beside the boat. A stink of decay came with them. Then the surface became as before. The streaks of mud that had temporarily arrowed toward that central point stirred restlessly and then became random.

The killer turned off the flashlight and sat in the boat, imagining the body sinking slowly and steadily into the blackness beneath, dragged down deeper and deeper into the hungry gullet of the swamp.

Until it joined the others.

After a while he picked up the oars, and with a weary sigh began to row for home. He really disliked these late nights. They played havoc with his system.

1

There wasn't anybody. I searched the yard and all along the canal to the bridge. Ground's too hard for footprints—we haven't had rain all week, and it's been hot."

"Then you admit somebody *might* have been there?"

Sheriff Matt Gabriel looked down at the dark-haired woman whose hands were twisted so tightly in her lap. "Why not? Far as I can recall, you never were the type to scare easy, or to make up stories. Anyway, we've had quite a few complaints about prowlers on the Island lately."

"And most of them were mine," she said ruefully.

"No, more than just yours. Everybody around here's been jumpy for the past few months, seems to me, but nobody can say exactly why."

"Oh?" Daria Grey stared at the dark windows as she absorbed this piece of information. "Well, I can't tell you how relieved I am to hear that," she finally murmured.

"Pardon?" It seemed an odd thing to say.

She glanced up at his puzzled tone, and smiled. The change in her face was astonishing, and Matt was shaken by it. He had forgotten how devastating that smile had been, all those years ago. And still was.

Daria had been surprised to discover he was now the local sheriff. All her previous night cries had been answered by a laconic deputy who'd given the area a cursory trudge, shrugged, and then driven away more irritated each time. Nobody had mentioned that *Matt* Gabriel was the man in charge of keeping the peace in Blackwater County. In the summer she had left home, his *father* had been sheriff, and Matt had been merely a gangly sophomore back from college, roaring around town with the local boys, apparently noticing her no more than he did any other girl.

Matt, in his turn, had been surprised to find how shy he felt standing beside her. Should he call her Daria, or Mrs. Grey? He had stayed behind, a local hero, while she had flown wide and high. She was somehow different and yet familiar. Her clothes, her hairstyle, her manner—all bespoke New York, money, success. And yet, like a ghostly presence, there was within her the old persona—the girl whose books he'd carried home from school at the painful age of sixteen and acne.

"I don't mean I'm glad crime has penetrated as far as the Island," Daria explained. "I'm simply grateful you *believe* me. You see—not everyone has, lately."

"If you mean Charley Hart..." He was puzzled by her peculiar tone of voice. Had Charley been rude to her? Admittedly, she had made four previous panic calls, and Charley had come running each time, only to find nothing and nobody. Repeated false alarms like that could get a man down. It was why he had come himself this time, but...

"Would you like some coffee?" she asked abruptly.

"Well...if you're making some for yourself, thanks, I would." He followed her out of the room. As they passed through the hall, a voice called softly.

"Daria? Who's that with you?"

"Excuse me," Daria said to the tall man, and went over to the double doors of the dining room. Sliding one back, she spoke into the shadows beyond. "It's all right, Aunt Clary. It's just me being a scaredy-cat again. I thought I heard a prowler outside and..."

"A prowler?" The soft voice was suddenly sharp, and afraid.

"It was nothing. The . . . the sheriff came right away and he's looked all around and there's nobody. We're just going to have some coffee—would you like a hot drink?"

"No, thank you. Is that you there, Matt?"

"It's me all right, Miss Shanks."

"How's your mother?"

"Very well, ma'am. Coming along to see you real soon."

"Good. She always cheers a body up."

"Yes, ma'am." It was strange, addressing an invisible presence in another room, but she would have been shocked had he set even one foot in her room after dark. Not done, her being a maiden lady and in her nightie and all, she'd say. This generation or the last, this century or the next, it was all the same to Miss Clary. Standards were standards, manners were manners, and everyone in his place, except for dire emergencies, such as fire or flood, thank you. He smiled to himself. "You rest easy, now. Get your strength back," he said gently.

"Well . . . as long as everything's all right."

"Everything's fine. You go back to sleep."

"I will, then. Good night, Daria—don't stay up too late, now."

An oblique reminder that Matt Gabriel was unmarried and she was not. Daria smiled in spite of herself. "I won't. Good night." She slid the door closed and turned to Matt. Her face did not match the light tone of her words. "Nothing to worry about now, is there?"

"Absolutely nothing," he said firmly and loudly, both of them speaking for the benefit of the invalid beyond the closed doors. They went on into the kitchen and Daria set about filling the percolator.

When Daria Grey had returned home to Blackwater Bay a few weeks before, not everyone had recognized her.

Orphaned at the age of ten, she had been sent to Paradise Island to be brought up by her father's spinster sister, Miss Clary Shanks. Daria's remarkable artistic abilities had emerged early, and after she graduated from the local high school she'd left Blackwater on a scholarship to one of the best art schools in the East. She also left behind—though she'd never seemed to realize it—several empty hearts, including Matt Gabriel's.

Daria Shanks had boarded the train as a bright flyaway girl of eighteen, full of laughter, hope, talent, and ambition. She had returned as Daria Grey—a withdrawn woman, poised but wary, quiet-spoken, and possessed (despite the shadows under her eyes) of a classic, fragile beauty.

Wariness was in her now, as she filled the percolator with fresh water from the sink tap. "There was definitely someone out there with a flashlight, but it wasn't an ordinary thief or a Peeping Tom. In fact, I *know* who it was."

"Oh? Who?"

She turned, the dripping percolator in one hand and the coffee can in the other. Her smile was bright and her chin was up—ready for the blow of his derision. "It was my husband, Michael Grey," she said. "He says he's going to kill me."

There was a long silence.

Matt stared at her, uncertain what to say. Eventually, her pale face flushed, and she looked away. "You don't believe me, do you?"

"I didn't say that," Matt said uncomfortably. "Tell me about it."

She went about the business of preparing and plugging in the percolator, then began to talk, facing away from him as if afraid to meet his eyes.

"We met at an exhibition of work by a mutual friend. Michael is an artist, too. He comes from a very wealthy old New York family, and was expected to go into the law or banking, but...well, Michael wanted to paint, and Michael always gets what he wants. When we were introduced he immediately decided he wanted me. He was very persistent, very charming, very handsome. I believe the phrase is 'swept off my feet.'" She gave the cliché a wry twist. "We were married six weeks later, and we were very happy at first. But after a few years, that changed. *He* changed."

"It happens."

She nodded. "Of course. But this wasn't the ordinary settling-in of an old married couple. In fact, it took me a long time to realize exactly what was wrong. I went through periods of suspecting the usual things—another woman, even another man, alcohol, drugs—but it wasn't any of them. It was jealousy. I had become more and more successful, you see, getting good reviews for my shows, selling lots of pictures for good prices, but Michael was not. The money didn't matter, of course, but the critics were having fun at his expense, and that *did* matter. He felt humiliated, and I felt guilty somehow. It was very difficult." She paused briefly, then continued. "After a while Michael began to . . ." She paused again. "Well, there was violence. Quite a lot of it, actually, one way or another. Eventually I left him and rented a house in a small town upstate. He . . . he didn't like that."

"I don't suppose he did," Matt acknowledged, thinking that if Daria were his wife, he'd be damned upset to lose her.

"You don't understand," she said with a sigh.

"Try me."

"I thought it would stop when I came home," she began—then suddenly her veneer of calm split wide open. "He won't leave me *alone*," she said in a thin, desperate voice. "It's been over a year and it's still going on."

"What is?"

"Michael's Game by Michael's Rules." Her voice wavered and she reached out to grip the table beside her. "Lies, accusations, hate, viciousness. No peace and no divorce, because as long as I'm his wife, I'm his prisoner. And he's a cruel jailer—more cruel than you can imagine."

"But surely you could divorce him . . ." He was trying to steady her with his interruptions, making her spell it out so she wouldn't spiral out of control. Her voice said panic was near.

"Not without a dirty fight—his words, not mine." She

clenched her fists but still could not face him. "You have to understand—my work means everything to me, it's all I have. Since his 'game' began, I haven't been able to work at all. Or rest. Or think. And that's what he wants. As long as I'm afraid, I'm in his power. He says things to me, does things to me—things that I can't prove. Nobody listens to me, and everybody listens to Michael, because he comes from a wealthy, influential family who pander to him, and because he always seems so *reasonable*. The more reasonable he sounds, the more crazy *I* sound. He's very clever. He's probably watching us now."

Matt stared at her, not knowing what to say in answer to this raw, terrible outburst.

Then Daria turned to face him and her fingers closed tightly over his wrist. He looked down at her small, white hand against the tan of his forearm, and then into her wide blue eyes. Her whole face was alight with determination, her voice harsh and insistent.

"Michael is dangerous. He's crazy. He *told* me that he intends to kill me, but only after he's had all his 'fun.' I really can't stand much more, Matt. What frightens me the most is what's happening inside myself. I've lost my sense of humor, my sense of proportion, my appetite—and I'm barely hanging on to my sanity. I feel cornered, I feel rage twisting me up, turning me harder and harder. I don't want to be like this, but I can't seem to stop it happening. I swear, if Michael goes on trying to destroy me, or if he does anything to Aunt Clary, I'll kill *him*. I will. I *will!*"

Her words rang oddly in the bright yellow-and-white kitchen, where copper pans gleamed and red-and-white-checked dishtowels hung above the stove to dry. Daria Grey was like an orchid against the gingham.

Matt Gabriel stared at her with a sense of unreality. She'd gone away an innocent girl and come back a passionate, frenzied stranger. Words like *hate* and *madness* and *kill* were strangers here, too.

After all, this wasn't New York, or Paris or Rome.

This was Paradise.

2

The Great Lakes have been called "a river of inland seas." Five of the largest bodies of fresh water in the world—Superior, Michigan, Huron, Erie, Ontario (six, if you count "little" St. Clair)—their basins gouged out by the recurring continental ice sheets, and ultimately revealed in their final form by the last reluctant, clawing retreat of the glaciers, some five thousand years ago. They form a continuous system, with no single headwater, and they flow ultimately to the sea. Eleven thousand miles of coastline encircle these magnificent lakes, some of it developed, some of it even overdeveloped, but much of it still wilderness.

Long ago, a wide stretch of this continuous coastline had been the mouth of a mighty but slow-moving river. Gradually that river mouth had silted up, creating a swampy delta rich in wildlife, mud, and mosquitoes.

During the westward conquest of the American continent, many small towns had been established around the various Great Lakes, and one of them grew up where the main highway north crossed this old river.

Although the town was well inland, the marshy presence of the river's delta was still felt. The townspeople referred to it—without affection—as the Mush. In the winter its mud flats were bleak and treacherous, in the summer they stank and brought sickness, and in the spring the Black River (for so it had been named upstream) flooded all the land around it, carrying a black stain of decay far out into the bay. It was this stain, and the frequent storms that swept darkness across it, that had caused the original settlers to translate its name from an almost unpronounceable Indian word to Blackwater Bay. The town, despite many efforts to find more euphemistic substitutes, became—by default—Blackwater. As did the county.

By the 1890s the town fathers of Blackwater decided that a system of ditches should be dredged out of the delta in an attempt to control the flooding and the mosquitoes. The engineer put in charge of this undertaking was Ernest Peacock, a somewhat eccentric local contractor with a sharp eye to the future. While surveying the area, he had noted a solid granite-based spit of land that stuck out about a mile into the lake, just beyond and parallel to the front edge of the delta. He prudently (and very quietly) purchased it from the farmer whose land it adjoined.

When the dredging operations began, Mr. Peacock directed that all the muck and sand brought up by the dredgers was to be deposited just behind this small and unremarkable peninsula. If anyone was curious as to why that particular site was chosen, it was not recorded. Mud was mud, and where it was dumped seemed irrelevant. As long as the job was done, and the river ceased to flood the farms and the town, what did it matter?

This dumping eventually created a long, high mound that hid the lone spit of land from view. The townspeople laughingly referred to it as Peacock's Mountain, and some folks thought that it might be a useful place to put a lighthouse one day.

Then they forgot all about it.

By 1909, Peacock's Mountain had compacted and solidified. The granite spit of land had acted as a breakwater to protect it from the storms of winter. Grasses and small trees had sent their roots through it, binding the loose mud together. It was lower, now, and people sometimes ventured out onto it for picnics. It had come to be called Peacock's Dike, and the view from it was splendid.

In the spring of that year, Ernest Peacock diverted his dredger (his company was still retained by the town council to keep the drainage canals clear) to a temporary duty. He had his men carve and line a small, neat canal between the dike and his land. This canal was curved back into the bay. The distant thump of the final blasting through the neck of the granite spit was the first the townspeople knew of the project. When all was done, Ernest Peacock had created a private, boat-shaped island, solid enough to be built on, and all his own.

He named it Paradise.

He then proceeded to build ten substantial cottages on it, reserving the largest one, at the tip of the Island, for his family. He sold the other nine cottages to his closest friends at a healthy profit. Unperturbed by the frustrated outcries of local citizens, who felt he had somehow pulled a highly remunerative "fast one" on them, Ernest Peacock retired to a life of lakeside pleasures, lived to the age of ninety-three, and died smiling.

To reach Paradise Island today you turn right off Highway 29 at the second junction in the town of Blackwater, follow a paved road for about a mile, then turn onto a graveled road for another half mile, passing behind rows of the ordinary and occasionally rather tacky summer houses that edge the main coastline.

And then you come to the bridge.

It is the original humpbacked bridge built by Ernest Peacock himself—a white-painted confection of solid timber and elaborate cast-iron railings. That small arched bridge looms large in local attitudes, for it is the "rainbow" that separates Paradise Island from the rest of the world, and therefore still separates Ernest Peacock's Dream from gritty reality.

On Paradise Island there are still nine of the ten original large and comfortable family cottages, each with a bit of land around it. A one-lane road runs down the Island's spine, dividing the homes from their respective boat houses, which line the back canal. There are no stores, no gas stations, nothing commercial.

The passing years have garnished the Island with many trees—oaks, elms, birches, and elderly willows with long, trailing branches that swish and sway in the lake breeze. From one end of the Island to the other, lovingly tended gardens glow with flowers. On the long lawns, rustic picnic benches stand ever ready for spontaneous sunshine lunches, and hammocks swing gently, inviting repose. Here all is peaceful. Children play freely over the lawns, each one known and (for the most part) affectionately tolerated. Nobody plays radios too loudly or argues or sulks or gives parties that rouse neighbors to fury. Island people borrow sugar and send back cookies. They borrow lawn mowers— and return lawn mowers. They also return smiles, greetings, and favors.

Those original families had treasured and protected the Island. Their heirs and assigns continue to do so. Nothing more exciting ever happens on Paradise than a new baby or a new boat or a barbecue fire getting out of hand. In short, life there is pleasant, rather slow and rather dull. And that, for Ernest Peacock and his modern-day beneficiaries, is exactly the way it is supposed to be.

Or was.

In front of Number 7 Paradise Island there are two large oak trees. Between them, on this lovely summer's day, was slung a red-and-white-striped hammock. Above it the leaves washed together in a steady whisper of an offshore breeze, their movement dappling the lawn beneath with a constantly moving scatter of bright and dark. The hammock swung gently to and fro as the occupant occasionally touched the lawn with the tip of his toe, not hard enough to unbalance himself, but with sufficient force to rock the cradle in a comforting rhythm, back and forth, back and forth, back and forth . . .

"Are you just going to lie there all afternoon?" Kate
Trevorne demanded.

"I hope so. Why, are you against it?"

"No. Just surprised."

Jack Stryker raised his straw hat slightly and peered up
at her. "Haven't you ever seen a man on vacation before?"

"I haven't seen *you* on vacation before."

This was hardly surprising, as in the few months they
had known one another, he had fully lived up to his
nickname of Jumping Jack Stryker in the pursuit of his
duties as a police detective. Indeed, it had taken the
impact of a bullet in his shoulder and a particularly grueling
case involving a cop killer to make him accept the fact that
he needed a rest. He had reluctantly permitted Kate to
drag him up to her family cottage for a two-week vacation,
and now that he was here he was determined to give it all
he had. If he was supposed to rest, then, dammit, he was
going to *rest*, and rest hard.

He resettled the straw hat over his nose, and with a brief
shrug of adjustment resumed his former position. The
rhythmic slap of the water against the breakwater and the
drone of a distant motorboat far out on the bay had nearly
sent him to sleep. Now it would take forever to get back to
his former somnolent state—perhaps even minutes.

Unless Kate had more to say, of course.

He waited for it.

"I want to go for a swim."

"So, go for a swim." He was nothing if not reasonable.
Was he stopping her? Apparently he was.

"I don't want to go alone."

"Why not? You can swim, can't you?" When he spoke,
the straw hat, resting on his chin, bobbed up and down,
letting in flashes of light.

"Yes, of course I can swim. But I haven't been in yet this
year." There was a pause. "I don't know how deep it is."

"What's the deepest it's ever been?"

"Up to my chin."

"And the lowest?"

"Up to my boobs. Only I didn't have any, then."

"Then it will probably be no deeper than your boobs now—at the very worst. Swim. Enjoy."

There was a long pause.

"It's no fun alone. And anyway..." The rest of her muttered protest was lost.

He sighed. "And anyway—what?"

Kate cleared her throat. "I'm afraid of sharks."

That called for hat removal. He stared at her, unbelieving, glanced at the bay stretching to the horizon, and then back at Kate. "Kate, that is a bay off one of the Great Lakes. It's fresh water, not salt. It's big, but it's not an ocean. There are no sharks in it."

"I *know* that," she said in a disgusted voice.

"But you said..." She had him going again.

"I only meant that when I was *little* I used to get scared that something would come up behind me and bite my leg off or drag me under. It was only an atavistic childish fear."

"Of what—an atavistic six-inch perch?"

"There are muskies out there." She was on the defensive now.

"Oh, come on, Kate—I'll grant you muskellunge can run up to seventy pounds or so, but they're only out in the deep water, in the lake itself, not here in the bay. You told me that on the way up here."

Kate stood beside the hammock sounding eight years old but looking all of her voluptuous thirtysomething in a new turquoise bathing suit. He could think of better things to do with her than go swimming.

"That's not the point..."

He swung his legs over the side of the hammock, dropped his hat onto the grass, and glared at her. "All right. All *right!*" With a swift and unexpected motion, he grabbed her up and began to run toward the breakwater. She shrieked and tried to escape his grasp, but he ran on, jumped up onto the wooden ledge of the dock, teetered there for a moment, then threw her in.

There was an almighty splash, which caught him across

the chest and rocked the small dinghy tied to the ladder that led down into the green water. Amid a boiling and churning of lake water, Kate surfaced, her short dark hair trailing in strands around her face, and outrage in her eyes. He grinned down at her.

"Are you standing up?"

"Yes, damn you!" The water lapped at the straps of her suit.

"So it's at its usual depth?"

"Yes. You're a bastard."

"And is there anything behind you?"

Her eyes widened and she whirled around, with a spiral of water coming off her head and shoulders. She stood there, staring out at the gleaming surface of the water, spangled with a thousand reflections of the late-morning sun, and unbroken by a single fin. "And isn't it a lovely summer day?" he went on. "And aren't you glad to be alive and swimming in your favorite old childhood place while your beloved rests his weary bones in the sun, saving his strength for taking you out to a sumptuous meal at the Golden Perch and returning for a night filled with erotic delights? Possibly even two?"

She turned around again to face him, and lifted a dripping hand to shade her eyes. "The Golden Perch? Really?"

He shrugged. "Why not?" Having heaved her into the water, he felt expansive. Him Tarzan, her wet.

"I thought we were saving that for the end of the vacation."

"We'll go again at the end. In the middle we'll eat beans."

"Well, then—I forgive you for throwing me in."

His smile grew wary. "No, you don't."

Her smile grew dangerous. "You're right. I'll get even."

He sighed. "And don't I know it." He left her paddling toward the dinghy and returned to the hammock, resigned to his fate. A moment of triumph, and days of waiting ahead. It could be a bucket of water over him in the next ten minutes, it could be something worse.

Much worse.

* * *

Kate turned her back on the land and began to strike out toward the horizon. Deep water was a long way out, and she had no intention of going that far—just far enough to take a good look at the Island. After a moment or two, Kate stopped her rhythmic crawl and turned onto her back, letting her legs drop slowly through the water until her toes touched the ridged sand beneath. Some years there was mud, some years weed. This year the bay was remarkably clean, for the winter storms had been many and fierce, mostly driving downland, offshore. Now, in July, the water wasn't clear—it was never clear—but the light penetrated the gray-green for some distance, as she had seen when on the bottom and rising.

She'd been making too much of going in "for the first time." As all the kids had, every year, when she was small. Maybe they still did. Well, it was understandable, she supposed. There was so *much* water, and it was mysterious under there.

Involuntarily she shivered, then turned to face the Island. Her Island. She'd come here every summer from babyhood to visit her grandparents. When she was eight, Nana and Gamp had decided to move to a small apartment in the city, and the cottage had become the whole family's summer home. The subsequent summers had gone by in a blur of bathing suits and barbecues.

Following her father into the academic life had meant Kate could continue to enjoy long summers on Paradise when she chose. Inevitably, as her career progressed, many of them had been sacrificed to study and research. And this year, because of Jack's job, there would only be two complete weeks here. She was determined to enjoy every moment of them, and hungrily drank in the details of the scene that lay before her.

Behind the green line of the trees she could glimpse the cottages, evenly spaced, white clapboard for the most part, and almost every one with a porch that stretched the width of the front—screened in summer, glassed in winter. Those cottages that did not hold permanent residents held semi-permanent ones. Nobody on the Island "rented out," as so many other communities did. These were first or second *homes*, and she could name every family in them, even now that she spent so little time here.

She began to count off: first after the bridge came the Roses, mother and daughter. Then the Greenfields, always at home but rarely seen. Then Mrs. Toby and her friend Mrs. Norton, two widows, sharing. Then the Lattimers. She frowned—the Lattimer cottage looked closed up and deserted. Of course—Kit Lattimer's wife had died last winter. Maybe he just didn't have the heart to come back alone just yet. Next to the Lattimers lived Miss Shanks and her niece, Daria.

She paused, recalling what Daria had told her in the supermarket that morning. Daria, too, had grown up on Paradise, and been Kate's summer "best friend," but Kate had hardly recognized her when they met in front of the canned vegetables.

Time has made us strangers, Kate thought, and sighed.

Poor elegant, terrified Daria.

Moving on, she noted and approved of the new green shutters at the Robinsons'. Then came the hammock and the yellow straw hat in front of her own family cottage. To the right of that came the crisp outlines of the place occupied by Larry Lovich and Freddy Tollett, then the ivy-garlanded Cotman place, and last of all, taking up the whole tip of the Island and snooty with it (or so the rest of the Islanders thought), the Wilberforce enclave.

They were Newcomers.

They'd only been on the Island for three years or so. Their sins were many. They were the only ones to fence off their land—everybody else kept their lakeside frontage clear and open. They had torn down the comfortable old Peacock place and replaced it with an ultra-modern house with two huge redwood decks, far better suited to California than the Middle West. Then they had gotten a firm in to dredge out and construct a deep-water dock for their sailing yacht. Nobody on Paradise sailed, except for the odd teenager who was into windsurfing. It was all powerboats around here. There were plenty of rude comments when the graceful Wilberforce sloop first tied up at the Point, especially when the name *Mommy's Baby* was noted on the stern. But there was something even worse than all that.

They kept servants.

Regular, live-in servants, who stayed at the Point all year round and never spoke to anyone else, belting back and forth down the narrow access road at the rear of the cottages in their fancy van with dark windows and "Wilberforce" painted on the side in gold letters, raising dust and tempers without a sideways glance.

Now some of the older permanent residents on the Island might have a woman in from across the bridge during the day to "help out," but that was the beginning and end of it. The Island was a family enclave. You hung your own clothes on the line, put out your own garbage, did your own shopping, and emptied your own dishwasher. No airs and graces here, no matter what your city bank balance might be.

Of course it was sad that old Mrs. Peacock had died. There had been Peacocks at the tip of the Island from the beginning. But it was inconsiderate of her to die leaving only one relative—a distant niece, a Mrs. Wilberforce, who'd grown up in New York and had absolutely no idea what being an Islander entailed.

The Wilberforces Did Not Mix. They refused—politely, of course—all invitations to anniversary parties, birthday barbecues, dinners at the local hotel, and other Island celebrations. They maintained their town house in Manhattan and an apartment in Grantham (Wilberforce was supposed to have connections with local industry) but were rarely At Home on Paradise. When they *were* here, they occasionally entertained, but Wilberforce guests—like their hosts—came and went by yacht, presumably to avoid contamination by the hoi polloi. In fact, there was somebody on the Wilberforce front lawn right now—somebody blond and, from this distance, apparently nude. Surely not?

Kate raised a hand to shade her eyes.

"Are you waving or drowning?" came a voice, nearly in her ear.

She shrieked as she whirled in the water, and nearly went under. Laughing down at her from a double kayak were Larry and Freddy, who had paddled silently up behind her and waited for their moment. "You stinkers!" she sputtered.

They grinned, twin white crescents breaking the even tans on their handsome faces. Larry Lovich was about ten years older than Kate, and had inherited his cottage when his parents decided to spend their retirement in a warmer climate. Kate had nurtured a teen-age crush on the handsome "older man" who lived next door, a crush that had suffered a fatal blow when Larry had brought his "friend" Freddy to live with him.

The fact that both men were delightful human beings triumphed over any gossip or disapproval their relationship might have generated anywhere else. They needn't have worried—and there was no indication that they ever had. The only thing that really upset an Islander was "show."

"When did you arrive?" Freddy asked.

"Yesterday," Kate said.

"Alone?" Larry asked innocently.

"His name is Jack Stryker," Kate said with a wry smile. "As if you didn't know already."

"These things get around." Freddy nodded sagaciously. "I hear he is a police person."

"He is a detective lieutenant in the Grantham Police Department, and he is on vacation," Kate said formally. "So please keep your murders to a minimum over the next two weeks."

Larry fixed her with a solemn gaze. "From that, do we gather you've heard about Daria's 'prowler'?"

"She said something about it at the store this morning," Kate said cautiously.

"Nobody is to say a word to Miss Shanks," Larry said quickly. "Not a *word*. She's unwell."

"Hearing that your niece is convinced she's being stalked

by a homicidal maniac is no way to get better," Freddy agreed. "She'd be upset."

"Not half as upset as she would be if it were true, and Daria actually got murdered," Larry put in. He examined his paddle, trailing drops across the surface of the bright red-and-yellow kayak. "Matt Gabriel is keeping an eye on her, of course."

"A very *close* eye, as it happens," Freddy agreed, examining *his* paddle, also. For shark bites, no doubt. "Matt is a good man."

"A very good man," Larry echoed.

"But not what you would call *experienced*," Freddy said.

"No—not in *detective* work," Larry agreed.

They both looked at Kate.

"Oh no," Kate said firmly. "Jack's on vacation. Besides, there are protocols or something. Not his jurisdiction," she said finally and triumphantly. "Like doctors. You know."

"Second opinion," Freddy said.

"Has to be asked," Larry said.

"Exactly," Kate nodded.

Both men sighed in unison. "Pity." They exchanged a glance.

"Time to paddle our own canoe," Larry said.

"On the count of three, then?" Freddy asked. "One, two, three . . ." They moved off gracefully.

"Bring him over for drinks," Larry shouted over his shoulder.

"About seven," Freddy said over *his* shoulder.

"You're not to mention it," Kate shouted.

"Would we?" they asked the world at large.

Kate looked after the departing canoe and nodded, dipping her chin into the water. "Yes, damn you, you would," she said to herself. Then smiled.

Throw her into the water, would he?

3

Daria helped Aunt Clary into a sitting position as gently as she could, and then swung the adjustable table over the bed. "There—doesn't that look good?"

Aunt Clary grunted delicately, as befitted a lady. "Passable," she said. "At least you make it *look* good," she added.

"Now don't get grumpy with me," Daria warned. "I might put itching powder on the sheets, or something, if you do."

"Highly likely," Aunt Clary said, her mouth twitching. "You always were a wicked girl."

"And getting worse all the time," Daria agreed. "Now, do you want me to cut up your broccoli?"

"It's my bottom that's broken, not my arms," the old woman said in a practical tone, her eyes twinkling affectionately. She accepted Daria's help with apparent reluctance, telling her over and over again not to fuss so—but secretly she was enjoying it. And if she lied a little bit—made out she was a bit more helpless than she really was so that Daria would stay on—well, God would forgive her. She hoped that God was a little gentler on old ladies these days—because they made so many mistakes. It was not a way she'd recommend, but if a broken hip brought her darling home again, well, it was *almost* worth it.

Not that she'd *meant* to fall—good heavens, who would? But the telephone had been ringing and she had hurried down the stairs in the dark, afraid it might be Daria ringing from New York and she wouldn't want to miss that . . . and then! The loss of balance, the flailing arms—the fall had been *terrible!* So sudden, so unexpected—and the pain afterward!

"After lunch, we'll go out onto the patio for a while," she told Daria firmly. The patio was only a few years old, and it was her pride and joy. It had been put in at the same time as the Wilberforces had been having their new place built, and she had gotten "a price" from the contractors, who'd had some concrete left over and an afternoon free. Aunt Clary always felt she had somehow scored over the Wilberforces with that patio, and she meant to enjoy it, broken hip or not!

"That's good," Daria said approvingly. "You know what Dr. Willis said."

"Old devil," Aunt Clary muttered.

"You're supposed to be as active as possible," Daria said firmly. "I know it's more comfortable for you to lie in bed, but Dr. Willis wants you to get up and walk. You have your walker, and the bone is pinned, so it won't let you down. You just have to build up the muscles now, and breathe deep. Otherwise Complications Could Set In. Pleurisy, pneumonia, blood clots—"

"Poison oak, beriberi, bubbling minge—" her aunt countered.

"What?" Daria stared at her.

"Sounds awful, doesn't it?" Aunt Clary said, as she attacked her chicken with renewed vigor. "I can hear it now, rising up through my knees, bubble, bubble—"

"You're a terrible old woman," Daria said.

"I try," murmured Aunt Clary. "Go eat your own lunch like a civilized person, instead of standing there staring at me. Go on now."

Daria smiled and went into the kitchen. With some relief, Aunt Clary removed her false teeth and set them to one side under a tissue. This was a nice soft lunch—no need to struggle with those new choppers the dentist had forced on her. Saying he was sick of repairing the old ones! What rubbish! He just wanted to stick her with another bill, that's all.

Out in the kitchen she could hear Daria eating her own meal, the sound of the fork on the plate accompanied by the occasional turning of a magazine page. As if she could be fooled! She knew the girl was upset, and she knew why. The biggest source of pain to her now was not the hip, but the knowledge that Daria was in trouble and she could do nothing to help her. Worse, that Daria wouldn't even confide in her or admit that she was in mortal terror of that dreadful, dreadful man.

Clary hadn't liked Michael Grey from the start.

All that carefully contrived tumble of black curls, those big blue eyes—as wide as a child's and as dead as a doll's—and those "thank you, ma'am" manners of a good little boy didn't fool her for a minute. Oh, she'd had his number, all right, and the boy knew it. They had been enemies from the first hello.

As for the trouble Michael was causing now—did Daria honestly believe she didn't read newspapers, watch television, or sneak a look into the scandal magazines while she waited for her permanent to take at the beauty parlor, for land's sakes?

The back-door bell rang suddenly, startling her into dropping her fork onto the bedspread. She wiped at the smear of cream sauce with her napkin and then quickly put her teeth back in. "Someone at the door, Derry," she shouted, when the bell went again. "Mrs. Toby said she might call in after lunch."

She scrunched down in the bed and peered through the lace curtains. It wasn't Mrs. Toby, it was a stranger, in a business suit and a city hat, carrying a briefcase. Insurance?

"Good afternoon," he was saying to Daria through the screen door. "Mrs. Shanks?"

"I'm sorry, she's unwell and unable to see anyone. May I help you?" Daria asked. But she didn't open the door.

"My name is Ridgeway; I've written to Mrs. Shanks—"

"Miss Shanks."

"I beg your pardon, Miss Shanks. We've written several times concerning the possibility of her selling this very fine lakefront property. We now have a client interested in this particular cottage, and he is prepared to go five thousand above the last price we quoted—"

"Get the shotgun!" shouted Aunt Clary from her temporary lair. Through the open window by her bedside she'd heard all she wanted to hear. "Call Matt Gabriel and tell him to bring the dogs!" she added. "We're not selling!"

Ridgeway's face had gone pale and he stepped back and down a step, nearly missing his footing. "Good heavens," he said thinly. "It was a perfectly good offer, we really—"

"Get the shotgun, Derry!" came the shout again.

"She's famous for yelling that, Mr. Ridgeway. Does it all the time," Daria said, trying to suppress a grin. "Don't worry, there is no shotgun. But the sentiment is genuine— my aunt has no intention of selling at this time."

"Or any damn time, you tell him. Here I am, here I stay," came the clarion call, amazingly robust considering the size of its source. "Tell him to leave Paradise Island alone, him and all the rest of the sharks and scum who've been hassling us night and day. Get the shotgun, Daria. The shells are in the sideboard."

"I don't really think there's much more to say, Mr. Ridgeway," Daria murmured, but he was moving away across the graveled rear yard, past Daria's sports car and Aunt Clary's elderly station wagon, toward the service road. He wasn't really listening anyway.

Daria went into her aunt's temporary bedroom. "Shotgun, indeed," she said.

"I swear that's what we need," said Aunt Clary, her hair practically standing on end in her agitation. Her cheeks were bright pink with annoyance—the doctor would have been pleased to see evidence of such lively circulation in a patient of her years. "They keep coming, more and more of 'em, wanting to buy. Wanting to destroy the Island, that's what—put up their ugly apartments and condo-wot's-its, charge the earth, bring in strangers, tourists, Ferris wheels, fortune-tellers and heaven knows what all, turn the place into a circus!"

"All right, all right, calm down," Daria said, but Aunt Clary was not to be soothed. This was the most fun she had had in weeks, and she wasn't going to let go of it easily.

"That's why we re-formed the Residents' Association a few years back, when the Wilberforces started building. That's when the first dogs began sniffing around *our* doors. Development potential, they said. Idyllic secluded setting, they said. Of course it is, and we want to keep it that way. Sometimes I think maybe the Greenfields are wavering (she likes her diamonds), sometimes I catch a gleam in Kit Lattimer's eye (he has the rheumatics something awful, you know, and wished he'd stayed on in Africa), but we're holding fast, Derry, we're hanging on. We *care* about the Island."

"Good."

"We don't want the Island to change. It's a family place, always was, always should be. We don't care to be rich at the expense of this lovely spot. One renegade was enough— look what happened to the tip of the Island! Tip of the iceberg's more like it—it's enough to make you spit!"

"Have you finished your lunch?" Daria asked brightly, trying to avoid the Great Wilberforce Harangue, which she had heard many times before.

"Yes, I have, thank you, it was very nice," Aunt Clary said dutifully. But she was not to be turned off-course that easily. "I mean, all it takes is one, you know. If even one gives in, the whole place will be shot to hell!" Aunt Clary banged her small tight fist down on the tray, causing the knife and fork to fly off her empty plate. She cleared her throat. "I beg your pardon for my language, but I AM NOT SELLING!"

"Good for you," Daria said, picking up the fallen cutlery. "I'll just clear this away, and then we can move out onto the patio. It's a lovely day—you can see right across to Newberry."

Her aunt looked sideways at her. "Are you going to the party tonight?"

"Now how did you hear about that?"

"I hear everything—I have lines out everywhere," her aunt declared with satisfaction.

Daria looked at the new telephone extension beside her aunt's bed. "Well, one line, anyway."

"Are you going? You ought to go, you know. You'll be expected."

"I couldn't leave you alone," Daria protested. "It's only drinks with Freddy—"

"It's never 'only' drinks, with Freddy—you take and go, my girl. You don't have to stay late; if it's dark, someone will see you back. Mrs. Crabbe from the Church Ladies' League is coming over to see me after dinner—you go along when she comes. I'll be fine."

"But—"

"You can't let him run your life, Derry," her aunt said.

Daria paused in the doorway, and then went on into the kitchen. "I don't know what you mean."

"Maybe we should get the shotgun at that," her aunt continued. "I'll keep it by me, here on the bed. I used to shoot skeet, you know. Don't suppose skeet are much different than skunks."

Daria came back to stand in the doorway. "You know about Michael, don't you?" Her face and voice revealed defeat.

"I do. Get me that shotgun and next time I'll blow his crazy head off. Put a sign on the door to that effect, why don't you? Save Matt the trouble."

"Then you heard me talking to Matt?" She came over and sank down on the chair beside the bed.

"Land's sakes, child, of course I did. Those pills might

soothe my bones but they certainly don't shut off my ears. Anyway, I'd guessed most of it already. Why haven't you come to me, told me about it?"

"I didn't want to upset you...not now ..."

"Listen, my girl, just because I'm busted doesn't mean I'm broken. I don't believe in giving in, and neither should you."

"But nobody believes me—I'm not even certain Matt believes me. I'm not even certain *I* believe me anymore," Daria wailed, tears overflowing at last. "Maybe I *am* crazy, maybe I was just hearing things..."

"No," Aunt Clary said firmly. "You're my brother's daughter and there is no craziness in the Shanks line. Never has been. Won't be. Tell you something." Daria had put her head down on her arms, and the old lady smoothed her shiny hair gently. "'When you're down and out, lift up your head and shout, "Somebody is going to pay for this!"'" she said.

Daria lifted her head, a smile starting up through the tears. "What?"

"Read it on a card in the drugstore. Liked it. What do you think?"

Daria sighed long and heavily. "I think I should never have come back..."

"Nonsense. I needed you. Anyway, home is where you belong when there's trouble."

"There wouldn't *be* trouble if I hadn't brought it with me."

"It followed you—different thing altogether. I didn't like him when you brought him here three years ago, you know. Told you he wasn't to be trusted, told you he was dangerous. Made you angry—but I was right, wasn't I?"

Daria's eyes filled with tears again. "Yes," she whispered. "You were right."

4

You believe her?" George Putnam asked.

"Until I know different," Matt replied.

"Yeah, but she's called us out there maybe four or five times in the past couple of weeks, saying there was a prowler, and never gave out *this* stuff before," George argued. "Why now?"

"I don't know. Maybe this time she was more scared."

"Or maybe she reckoned *you* wouldn't come next time unless she gave you a song and dance like this one?" George asked slyly.

Matt shrugged, yet found himself wondering if that was true. If so, it both flattered and worried him. What were all the calls about? He had to admit that, in the clear light of day, Daria Grey's story seemed even more fantastic. But her hand had trembled as she poured him a cup of coffee, and the thinness of that hand had moved something within him, like an animal turning in its sleep.

He remembered the low light in the kitchen, the distant lapping of the lake against the breakwater in front, the staccato syncopation of crickets and frogs from the marsh in back, and the dark bitter smell of coffee.

Once she had gotten the worst of her fear out into the open, Daria's voice had been soft, and she had chosen her words carefully, measuring their aptness against some inner standard of her own, wanting him to be perfectly clear on what had happened, what was still happening, and why.

He had listened because he had nothing else to do, because he was interested, and because she was so lovely that he simply could not take his eyes from her face.

George snorted. "She's nuts," he said.

Matt shrugged. "That's what she says about *him.*"

"Well, maybe they both are." George was disinclined to compromise.

"Maybe. Apparently, he's a painter, too, but not much good. I can see where her success might have twisted him up a little, can't you?"

"No," George said stolidly. "If he's so rich, why should he care whether people buy his paintings or not?"

Tilly Moss spoke up from the far side of the office. "Oh, George," she said in exasperation. "Artists are sensitive people."

"Big deal. I'm a sensitive person and I can take criticism."

Tilly and Matt exchanged a glance.

"Well, apparently Michael Grey couldn't," Matt continued. "He took it out on her, knocked her around, and so on. He finally had one big burst of fury and totally destroyed their apartment—including all the work she'd done for a new exhibition. The story was all over the papers, so I expect that's true, whatever he said afterward."

"What did he say afterward?" Tilly asked.

"Grey said that *she'd* done the smashing, and that she'd done it because she was high on drugs," Matt said. "He also said that he forgave her."

"Big of him," Tilly observed wryly.

"She says it's part of what he calls his 'game,'" Matt said. "He says and does things to her and then denies them and because there's no proof—he's very careful about that— everybody believes him, not her."

"Because he's from some swell family and she's nobody?"
Tilly asked.

"Something like that. And naturally the gossip colum-
nists loved it. He gave interviews to practically everybody,
I gather, saying how drugs had turned her from a wonderful
wife into a monster and how hard he'd struggled to get her
to stop taking them, and so on. She says the reverse was
true."

"*I* don't remember reading anything about it," George
said.

Tilly spoke condescendingly. "The New York papers, he
means, George."

"Oh, well, hell," George said. "The *New York* papers." It
might have been Sodom and Gomorrah, for all George
knew. They'd print *anything* in those Gomorrah papers.

"Of course, it's still only her word against his," Matt
went on, attempting to be objective.

"Do you *believe* her?" George asked again.

"I've got no reason *not* to believe her," Matt said cautiously.
"She looked scared as hell to me—and she's desperate to
keep Miss Clary from finding out the truth about the
'prowler.'"

"If it is the truth," George said.

"Uh-huh." He reached into a pocket and fished out a
folded envelope. "She mentioned the name of that little
town she was living in when she says Grey began to get
seriously nasty. I think maybe I'll give them a call."

It didn't take him long to get through, and the local chief
of police remembered Daria Grey with considerable clarity.

"Frankly, I thought she needed putting away," the chief
said. "I felt sorry for her, mind, but..." He paused,
choosing his words carefully. "When she came running in
that morning still dressed in her robe and slippers, I
believed her, I'll admit that. She was so pretty and so
damned scared, it was hard not to. She told us how he'd
been coming into her place at night and leaving these awful
drawings all around, and how that morning when she woke
up there was this dead rabbit on the foot of her bed with its

neck broken and a threatening sign stuck up on her wall and so on, well, it sounded real nasty. Made you want to get this guy, protect her from him, and all that, you know?"

"I know," Matt said.

"Yeah, well—when we got back to her place there was no drawings, no dead rabbit on the bed, no nasty words on the wall, nothing. What there *was* was a lot of funny pills in her bathroom cabinet, a lot of weird books on her bedside table about spooks and psychos, an empty bottle of whiskey under the bed and a lot more empties in her garbage can. When she saw this she got hysterical all over again and claimed *he'd* put them there while she was downtown with us. We checked, but his family said he was in their house in New York, asleep in bed, and had been there all night. She said *they* were lying, that they'd always covered up for him, and so on. I still wanted to believe her, so I called an old buddy who's with the NYPD and he recognized her name right away. He said to leave it alone. He said Grey was important people, old money, and that this marital thing had been boiling for months. Their feeling was that the girl was unstable and a troublemaker, probably building the whole thing up in order to get some big divorce settlement. I had to let it go at that. Chick and me tried to calm her down, but she wasn't buying it. I said she should maybe see Dr. Bean—he's our local man, he's real good with women's problems..."

Matt recognized the tone and the words—they were the kind of thing he'd said himself, to fretful women and muddled drunks and confused teenagers. See the doctor, not me. Shove your problems onto someone else, I can't deal with them. Go away.

"I'm sure it was good advice," he said neutrally.

There was a moment of silence from the other end, and then his counterpart spoke. "It was crap and you know it, but it was the best I could do. Hell, if New York couldn't tell whether she was telling the truth or not, how could I? She moved away a few weeks after that, and the house was rented to a real nice family, no trouble at all. Tell me, is

Mrs. Grey down there with you now, pulling the same stunts?"

"She's a local girl—she's come home," Matt said.

"Well, maybe that's what she needed," the chief conceded.

"Maybe," Matt agreed. This distant officer sounded like an older man, and Matt pictured him as gray and paunchy, with pictures of his grandchildren on his desk. Not a bad man, probably a good one, but close to retirement and not willing to take any chances. He thanked him and hung up with a long sigh.

"Well? What did he say?" George asked eagerly.

"He said he didn't know whether to believe her or not either," Matt said reluctantly.

"So she was saying the same things there as here?" George asked,

"Sort of."

"Well, there you are. She's nuts," George said in some triumph. Tilly glared at him and turned back to her typewriter. Matt swiveled his chair around and stared out of the window at the street.

This was a rare moment of repose for them all. The town was buzzing out there in the sunlight. For these three or four months of the year he felt useful, as the town of Blackwater and the surrounding bay area filled up with tourists. Shoplifting, bar fights, parking and traffic, emergencies of all kinds were apt to crop up any moment now—so this problem of Daria Grey's could not have been more badly timed. Usually Paradise Island was the one place he *didn't* have to worry about in summer. Why couldn't Daria have come back in the winter, when he could have given her more time, talked to her, looked after her? She needed someone to look after her.

George Putnam, twenty-two, broad of shoulder but narrow of experience, was watching his superior officer. He thought he saw a change in Matt, who was usually so laid-back and relaxed about everything, and wondered why. Suddenly he assumed a knowing expression. "Hey, this Mrs. Grey—she's pretty hot stuff, is she, Matt? Charley wondered why you stayed so long out there on the Island last night. I hear she's quite a looker."

Matt Gabriel turned and fixed his young deputy with a basilisk eye. "I grew up with her, George." That wasn't quite true—he'd been two years ahead of her in high school.

"So?" This, as far as George could see, had no bearing on the matter in question.

"She's Miss Clary Shanks's niece," Matt went on in a repressive tone.

"She's an *Island* girl, George," Tilly added.

George sank farther down in his chair until his head was resting on the back. He gazed up at the ceiling. "I only asked," he said, all hurt innocence. After a minute's solemn consideration, he spoke again.

"People change, you know," he observed.

5

The afternoon had been hot, but evening brought a light breeze that quickly freshened the heavy air. Sunset was just beginning to tint the western sky when Kate and Stryker left Number 7 and walked toward the breakwater. The slowly waning light had a pearly quality to it—a lovely day reluctant to leave. The bay was a deeper color now, neither green nor blue, but something in between, with a flush of pink reflected in the delicate scalloping of the waves.

They stood for a moment on the concrete path that ran along the breakwater, the leaves of the twin oaks whispering overhead. Stryker stroked the back of Kate's neck absently as he looked down at the boats moored below them—the white dinghy with its outboard tipped in and the gleaming mahogany speedboat with its bright red cushions now hidden beneath a tight black oilskin cover. "We should have put those away, shouldn't we?"

Kate glanced up at the sky and then across at the lights of Atticus, which pin-pricked the thin dark line of the far bayside. "It's not going to rain tonight," she decided. "They'll be all right out here."

"You told me once your father would shoot you if you left the *Dart* out of the boat house overnight."

Kate's mouth curled up at the corners dangerously. "Dad's in Nevada—if he wants to come and put his precious cruiser in the boat house every night, he's welcome. The ignition keys are right here." She patted her small handbag, slung over one shoulder. "Maybe if there's a moon, we'll do it later. Very romantic."

"You and your 'romantic,'" Stryker said wryly. They began to walk slowly back up the lawn toward Larry's cottage, from which could be heard murmurs of talk and the inviting tinkle of ice against glass. "Is this party going to be good or bad?" Stryker wanted to know.

"Oh, good. Freddy and Larry always have plenty to drink and lots of interesting bits to eat and everyone knows everyone else."

"Swell," Stryker said with a grimace. "Everybody but me, you mean."

She glanced at him. "Oh, darling—you're going to be Exhibit Number One, didn't I tell you? Everybody is going to stare and stare at the New Man That Katie's Caught. Some might even ask to count your teeth."

"All right, all right," he said good-humoredly. "You're just lucky I'm on vacation, that's all. Otherwise I'd say the hell with it."

"So would I, if it was one of your buddy-brawls," she retorted. They glanced at one another sideways and grinned.

When not on vacation, their two worlds were far apart. As an academic, Kate sought truth and meaning (although most of her time seemed to be taken up with spelling corrections and listening to her students' romantic problems). He, on the other hand, sought killers and justice (although most of his time seemed to be taken up with paperwork and kicking the coffee machine). Having attended many university gatherings, he was no longer enthused about her academic friends and acquaintances. He found it difficult to keep on his intellectual toes all

the time, and their literary bon mots sometimes took him
a while to work out. By the time he'd come up with a
good reply, the conversation had usually gone on to
something else.

Did it *really* matter who wrote *Coriolanus?*

She, having been to the bars and bowling alleys favored
by *his* colleagues, found their black humor and fatalistic
attitudes both intimidating and a little depressing. Hearing
about real blood, real guns, prejudice, ignorance, and
cruelty made her both queasy and angry. Philo Vance was
never like that.

Back-stabbing was common to both worlds, of course,
but not necessarily with the same cause or effect. Perhaps
these Island people would be different, Stryker thought.
He hoped so—but then, he'd hoped before.

He glanced down the long row of cottages. "You know,
this Island of yours is kind of eerie. How they've managed
to keep it frozen in time like this is amazing, considering
some of the commercial developments that are springing
up all along the lakeshores."

Kate shrugged. "Oh, I suppose the dam will burst
sometime soon," she said, her tone bleak. "One of these
owners will be strapped for cash, or—like the Peacock
niece—somebody will inherit who doesn't give a damn. But
the Residents' Association is very strong and they'll put up
a fight."

"You have a Residents' Association? What—all ten of
you?"

Kate grinned. "When old Ernie Peacock created Paradise
Island he sold the cottages to his friends. They had a
Residents' Association so that nobody would do anything
crazy like painting their place purple—Ernie always had
the final say on outside decorations. He was a real stickler
for what looked right, apparently. Furthermore, in the
original deeds there was a clause that said if anyone wanted
to sell, they had to offer their cottage to other members of
their families first. If no relative wanted to buy it, then
they could offer it to the families of other Island residents.

If none of *them* wanted it—or failed to come up with a buyer personally known to them—then and only then could it be placed on the open market. He wanted the Island to belong to people who cared about its traditions."

Stryker scowled. "Sounds like one of those 'keep out the undesirables' deals. I don't think much of that."

Kate scowled back at him. "Neither do we, as a matter of fact. That's not what I meant at all." He had the feeling she was a little disappointed in him, but he didn't know why. She sighed.

"Until recently it didn't really matter whether there was a Residents' Association or not, because nobody developed a fetish for purple and all the cottages *did* stay in the various families. Then the man that owned the cottage the Cotmans now own ran out of descendants." She turned and pointed to a cottage two doors up-island from the Trevorne place.

"Mr. Jarvis had to go into a nursing home, and he decided to sell to the Cotmans—I think Len had been his dentist for some years. They'd often come up for weekends, and everyone knew them already. That was fine. As you can see by the way they maintain their cottage and lawn, they clearly love the place." She turned and pointed down-island. "Then there was the Greenfield cottage. Mrs. Parmeter died intestate and there were no known relatives. I think it was old Mrs. Lattimer who knew the Greenfields, but I'm not sure, I wasn't around the Island much at that time."

"Too busy attending protest rallies?" Stryker asked innocently. It was where they had first met, he in his bright new policeman's uniform and she carrying a placard protesting the transgression of someone's civil liberties. The encounter had been a fiery one, forgotten until they had met again the previous year during the course of a murder investigation at the university.

She glared at him, then grinned. "Absolutely," she agreed. Finally she gestured up-island again, toward a high fence that blocked the end from view. "The protest rallies here began when *that* ugly thing went up. The original Peacock place was inherited by a Mrs. Wilberforce, who'd never been to the Island in her life. At first nobody said anything— she was family, if only at a distance, after all. But when she started to tear the old Peacock house *down*, everyone went crazy. It might have been badly in need of repair, but it had always been the pride of the Island. Nobody knew what to do, until Mrs. Toby remembered the old idea of the Residents' Association. They re-formed it, and it gave them a legal basis for being heard—although in the end it didn't *stop* the Wilberforces. Just made them behave better." Her arm dropped to her side and she shrugged. "Anyway, I'll inherit when my parents are gone, and *I* certainly won't ever sell."

"What about your children?"

Kate glanced at him and then at her shoes. "I haven't noticed any children running around."

"You could, if you'd make an honest man of me," Stryker pointed out. He'd been pointing it out for some months now.

"You know how I feel about that," Kate said quietly.

"Oh yes, I know," Stryker said. "If I hang up my badge and gun and start selling insurance, then you'll have my kids. Until then, we stay in devoted unwedlock."

"Let's not argue now," Kate pleaded.

"I thought it was a very good psychological moment to press my suit," Stryker said. "You're nervous about whether these people will like me or not, and so am I. But who can resist a wedding? We could announce it at the party— give everybody something to talk about. What they're going to wear, whether you'll ask that terrible woman—"

"What terrible woman?"

"You must know *some* terrible woman," Stryker said.

"I know one terrible man," Kate said. "Here we are."

He snapped his fingers. "Damn—another few yards and I would have had you cornered."

"I'm dangerous when cornered," Kate reminded him.

He smiled. "Still planning revenge, hey?"

"Damn right," Kate said, and turned away to knock on the screen door.

The Lovich cottage was quite different from Kate's place. Whereas the Trevornes had kept the original ground-floor layout (sitting room, hall, dining room, kitchen, pantry, plus front and back porch), someone quite different had been at work here. The entire ground floor of Larry's place was open-plan, save for a few supporting pillars accented with what looked like Victorian wrought-iron work, painted white. They were very reminiscent of the decorative work on the humpbacked bridge, and it was likely that Larry had either searched high and low for them or had the work copied. Either way, they were very effective.

There was a wood-burning stove—now cold—in the center of the room, surrounded by green plants and topped with a vase of beautifully arranged flowers. The wide old floorboards had been stripped back and varnished. There were many more plants placed around the room and banked beneath the windows. Green-and-white sofas and chairs were against the walls—moved from their normal places for the party, no doubt—and there were a number of very excellent paintings hanging above them. It was a room made for summer parties.

Within the first twenty minutes Stryker found himself introduced to an insurance salesman (he gave Kate a look— was this recruitment time?), a plumber, a gym teacher, a stockbroker, a butcher, an advertising executive, an industrial chemist, an electrical engineer, and an old lady who made patchwork quilts.

"Oh, and you must meet Don and Fran Robinson—he's the unofficial mayor of Paradise," Kate enthused, dragging him toward a tall dark man with a ready smile and away from a discussion of diamond versus hexagonal patches.

"I'd go for the hexagons myself," Stryker shouted to the old lady as he was propelled backward.

"Damn—another traditionalist," Mrs. Toby said to her friend Mrs. Norton.

"The world's against you, Margaret," Mrs. Norton said, holding out her glass to Larry Lovich for a refill. "Go with the flow."

"This is Jack Stryker," Kate announced in a tone slightly reminiscent of an amateur magician. "Darling, meet Don and Fran."

"Hello, Don and Fran," Stryker said happily. He was on his second martini, and neither of them looked at all like college professors. Just people—nice people. He was having a great time.

"Welcome to the Island," Don said easily. He was lean and tanned—Stryker thought he looked like one of those men who could put a strong hand to anything at all and get it under control.

"Thanks very much," Stryker said. "We came up for a few weekends in the winter, but this is the first chance I've had to see it at its best. Wonderful place, wonderful."

"We think so too," Fran agreed. She was bright and sparky, a good contrast to her husband. She came from one of the oldest families in the area, but she wore that distinction lightly. "Too bad you couldn't get up for the Fourth. Don built a raft and set off fireworks—and we had a huge barbecue."

"Yeah—I saw the burned spot on your lawn." Stryker grinned.

Freddy Tollett appeared with a tray of assorted hors d'oeuvres. Behind him came Larry with a fresh pitcher of martinis and another of Manhattans. "Eat and drink, my children, tomorrow is the first hangover of the rest of your life," Freddy said. "Hi—you must be Kate's murder man. I'm Freddy, this is Larry. Refill?"

"Thanks," Stryker said wryly. "Nice party."

"Murder man?" Fran asked rather warily.

"Jack is a police officer," Kate said, glaring at Freddy. She thought she'd made it clear that *she* reserved the exclusive right to drop Stryker in it.

"Oh, I see," Fran said in a relieved voice. "For a minute there I thought—"

"Of course we have a long history of crime in the area," Freddy went on breezily. "We had rum-runners during Prohibition, bringing booze across the lake from Canada— there are even some bullet holes in the stairway of the Ventnor Hotel, aren't there, Fran?"

She gave him a wry smile. "So they told us when we were kids." She had been a Ventnor before her marriage. "Personally, I've always suspected it was termites."

"Quite a few bottles were sunk into the Mush when Elliot Ness dropped by, I imagine," Freddy went on blithely, ignoring Kate's scowl. "A real lively little place this was, once upon a time. Now the whole county is just made up of farms and small townships and Blackwater itself—hardly anything for the sheriff to do, come winter. Of course, now and again there's a bit of excitement. Recently there's been a—"

"What are these little green things, Freddy?" Kate asked quickly.

He looked down at the tray. "Avocado and cream cheese," he told her. "With just a touch of cayenne when you least expect it."

"It all looks lovely, Freddy," said a soft voice, and Stryker moved aside for a tall dark-haired girl. "I like what you've done to the cottage—it used to be so dark."

"Ah, Daria, at last!" Kate said, nearly inhaling avocado and cream cheese in her relief at the distraction. "I want you to meet Jack. Darling, this is Daria Grey. We grew up together every summer."

"Hello," Daria said. Her voice was low and slow, but her smile was a thing of beauty.

"Hi, Matt," Don said, noticing the big man standing behind Daria. "Have one of Freddy's specials."

The big man smiled, gazed over the dazzling trayful of whirls, blobs, wraparounds, and curlicues—and then took a simple piece of cheddar on a cracker. "I'm driving," he said to Freddy, who cackled appreciatively.

"Talk of the devil. You two ought to get along real well," Freddy said brightly. "Matt, this is one of your colleagues from the big city. Jack Stryker—specialty homicide. Matt is our local sheriff," Freddy explained mischievously. "Maybe you could put your heads together on a crime or two. Got anything complicated on hand at the moment, Matt?"

Matt Gabriel and Jack Stryker assessed one another. Then Matt shoved the cheese and cracker into his mouth and chewed. "Nothing even remotely interesting," he said flatly. "Unless you count two guys fishing illegally as a crime wave."

"Only if you do," Stryker said with an easy smile.

"Hey, here are the Cotmans," Kate said. "You *have* to meet them."

A middle-aged black couple had arrived, and Freddy swept over with the hors d'oeuvres, burbling welcomes. Estelle Cotman smiled at him, looked over at Kate, and winked. Sometimes Freddy tried a little too hard.

Don Robinson frowned. "They've had to take the worst of the flak from the Wilberforces. First the dirt and noise from the construction, then a few snide snubs when they tried to be friendly, and worst of all—they lost most of their view. They're the last cottage before the Wall."

"The Wall?" Stryker asked.

"That damned redwood fence Wilberforce put across the end of the Island," Don said. "It extends right to the breakwater, and it means Estelle and Len can't look to the left across the Point the way they used to. Even if they could, there's that damn dock sticking out like a sore . . . thumb."

"I was surprised to see that had gone up," Kate said.

Don nodded. "Last spring."

"Couldn't it have been stopped?"

Don looked angry, and Matt spoke. "Technically it's off-island, because they built it six feet out and only have a temporary gangway between it and the shore. Some people always manage to get around regulations—especially if they have money."

Daria glanced up, then nodded.

"We never thought the Cotmans would hang on, but

they're good people, and they've been on the Island quite a while now," Fran put in. "We'll get that Wilberforce fence pulled down if it's the last thing we do."

"Wonder what they have to hide?" Stryker mused into his glass, and looked up to see surprise on the Robinsons' faces, and speculation on Matt Gabriel's. "Sorry—force of habit," Stryker said hurriedly. "Who's that over there?"

They all glanced in the direction of Stryker's nod. "I've been wondering that myself," Matt said. "Definitely a new face—maybe one of Larry and Freddy's city friends." He looked at Stryker. "Sure you don't know him?"

"Do you mean, have I ever arrested him?" Stryker asked, amused. "Sorry—no."

The man in question was tall and elegantly dressed in a blazer and slacks, his dark hair falling in a Clark Kent curl over his tanned forehead. Several people were directing covert and puzzled looks in his direction. Obviously at ease, he was charming Mrs. Toby by describing an exhibition of modern quilts he'd seen recently in Dublin.

Matt finished his drink. "Think I'll find out," he said, and moved away from the group. The others continued their conversation, but Daria Grey followed Matt with her eyes. She looked lost suddenly, and turned to Kate with a forced brightness.

"Aunt Clary would love to see you if you have the time, Kate," she said. Her voice was thin and it sounded as if she were fighting for control.

"I'll pop in tomorrow," Kate promised. She looked more closely at Daria, and lowered her voice. "Has there been any more trouble from . . . him?"

Daria shook her head, pressing her lips together. "No."

Kate glanced over at Matt who, while talking to Mrs. Toby and the handsome stranger, still seemed to be keeping an eye on Daria. "I see Matt is looking after you. That's good. I always thought he had a crush on you in school."

"He's . . . been very kind. Last night I told him about Michael, but I don't know whether he believed me or not.

Aunt Clary heard me talking—I guess she hadn't gone back
to sleep, after all. She reminded me this afternoon how
much she'd always disliked Michael, and got pretty worked
up about it. Some poor real estate salesman had come
knocking on the back-porch door offering to buy the cottage
and she started yelling at me to 'get the shotgun!'" Several
people turned and smiled as Daria's voice rose in imitation
of her aunt. Miss Clary Shanks was famous on the Island for
her cry of "I'll get my shotgun" every time someone
annoyed her.

Kate laughed. "Not again! She *must* be getting back to
normal!"

"Yes. She got quite pink in the cheeks. Naturally, she
scared him half to death," Daria said, attempting a small
chuckle. "I tried to explain, but he ran off. I think he really
believed she meant it."

"It's the real estate agent season again." Larry sighed.
"We've had them buzzing around here, too. Maybe *we* ought
to get a shotgun." He moved off with his pitchers and
Freddy followed him. Don and Fran were talking with the
Cotmans, and Matt was still in the group by the stove. Kate
looked more closely at her friend, who was trying so hard
to be sociable.

Daria's eyes were underlined with deep shadows, and
her skin was dull and dry. Her whole manner was one of
wariness and agitation, and when she lifted her drink to her
lips the liquid vibrated in the glass.

Kate had followed Daria's career with enthusiastic interest. They had written often during those first two years of
separation, when Daria was studying art and Kate was
taking her first tentative steps into academia. The letters
had become less frequent as their careers took over their
separate lives, but Kate, at least, had the advantage of
Daria's growing fame and then notoriety to keep her informed.

Daria's first exhibition had made news. There had been
many articles about her work and about her own attitudes
to it, all of which Kate had devoured, delighting in her
girlhood chum's success. Most of the writers had been

fascinated by the contrast between Daria's seeming fragility and the strength of her work. Kate knew that some of Daria's power actually grew from that contrast, because hidden within her apparently timid and sensitive nature had been a lion's heart and a strong determination to give the world a new visual viewpoint. They'd had so many conversations about art and literature during those formative teen years, and Kate could still remember Daria's wide eyes flaming as she formed her credo: that there was beauty in anything, in *everything*, if we only knew how to look at it.

And she had proved it, time and again. Her paintings were of garbage dumps, hospital wards, and demolition sites: broken places and shattered people. But each portrayal of human suffering and wanton destruction had been suffused with a benison of beauty that promised salvation to those who could endure and look beyond the pain of the moment.

Looking into Daria's eyes now, Kate realized that the flame of that early vision had died. She knew who had quenched it, and how—and for a moment she, too, wanted to kill Michael Grey. Daria's pain and her present inability to look beyond it were all too evident to someone who knew and loved her.

Kate had been deeply shocked by the change in her old friend and she couldn't bear it now. She spoke firmly. "Well, you're among friends here, Derry, so don't worry. Matt will do something about it."

"About what?" Stryker asked, returning his attention from another conversation.

"Shall I say?" Kate asked Daria.

"If you like," Daria said in a defeated voice.

Quickly, Kate outlined the persecution that Michael Grey had been visiting on his estranged wife. Stryker looked sympathetic, but said nothing. It seemed, on the surface, to be one of those sad but all-too-frequent stories of marital warfare and obsessive hate. When she saw that he hadn't grasped the central problem in her situation, Daria put it simply:

"I can't paint anymore," she explained. "There's no peace in me, no joy, no restfulness, and I *need* those things in order to work. He's made me *see* ugliness. He's forced me to look at one terrible thing after another. When I pick up a pen or a brush, I begin to cry, because all I can see are *his* visions, not my own. I have nothing to say. Nothing to show. Nothing. That's exactly what he wanted to do to me, and that's what he's done."

"And now he's followed her here," Kate concluded. "He's carrying on tormenting her. And the worst part about it all is that she thinks nobody believes her."

"Nobody does," Daria said, a slight edge appearing in her voice. "We artists are 'temperamental,' you see—too much imagination for our own good. And Michael is *such* a sweetie."

"Now, now." Kate smiled.

"I can't decide whether to be angry or afraid. Usually I'm both," Daria told Stryker. "It's so awful not to be able to stop him."

"He may well stop of his own accord," Stryker said.

Daria looked at him, and lifted her chin. "Do they?"

"Do who?"

"Psychopathic obsessives?"

Stryker took a sip of his drink. "Is that what he is?"

"Well, of course he is," Kate snapped.

"If his psychiatrists let him out, they must not think he's a danger . . ." Stryker's voice was mild, and his eyes watched Daria's face over the edge of his glass.

"He's also extremely bright," Daria said bitterly. "He's been seeing psychiatrists since he was a child. When he got tired of one, his mother would find him a 'nicer' one. Anything that Michael wanted, Michael always got. He has a very high IQ. He used to brag to me that he knew what psychiatrists wanted to hear. He used to think up dreams and say things to make them diagnose him manic-depressive one week and schizoid the next—he'd read all the books and performed accordingly. He said it was fun because they were so naive."

"And you fell in love with this guy?" Stryker asked.

Kate fixed him with a steely glare. "It's funny how you can fall in love with some people and not know them at all," she said pointedly. He grinned at her and raised his glass slightly.

"Sometimes it's more fun that way."

"And sometimes it isn't." Kate was not charmed. "This is a serious problem, Jack, not something to laugh about."

"I'm not laughing," Stryker said calmly. "I may be a little tight, but I'm not laughing. I've had to deal with these guys before, and I guess I know some of what Mrs. Grey is going through. A lot of it is self-made hell."

"That's a terrible thing to say!" Kate snapped, stepping nearer to Daria and slipping an arm around her waist.

"Give me a break," Stryker said. "What I meant was, the most potent weapon these bastards have is the sensitivity and imagination of the victims themselves. A little threat goes a long way—the dark and the shadows and sudden noises do the rest. You get so you jump at everything, lie awake, sure that they're watching you, go around feeling sick and choked up all the time—like you're trying to swallow a stone?" he asked Daria. She nodded, and so did he. "That's what they're after," he continued. "That's the kick. If they think you're *not* afraid, they're disappointed. The best thing to do is to take a very plain and practical attitude toward it." He took another sip of his drink. "Of course, a big mean dog is a help, too."

"But if she doesn't react, it might make him try harder," Kate protested. "Make him do worse things."

Stryker shrugged. "Then we can catch him. There's no cure for the common cold, but there *is* one for pneumonia."

"I call that cold comfort," Kate snapped. "Is she supposed to let him maim or kill her before you do anything?"

"Of course not," Stryker said. "But—"

Daria had made a noise and stepped back.

"Daria—are you okay?" Kate asked. Her friend's face was

white, and she was clutching her throat, staring open-mouthed past Kate's shoulder. "Have you swallowed the wrong way?" Kate asked. But it was not Freddy's food that had transfixed Daria—it was his window. She stared. She pointed. Her rising shriek silenced the room.

"Michael is there—outside—he's outside, watching me. Laughing at me. He has a knife... *he has a knife!*"

6

Stryker and Matt Gabriel shot out of the cottage and, with no more than a two-way glance and nod, separated and went around the house in opposite directions, meeting again at the back.

"Well?"

"Nothing."

They separated again and returned to the front. Matt went left, Stryker went right, and they ran along the front of the other cottages in either direction.

Nothing.

They came back together five minutes later and stood at the front of the Lovich place, panting. "Bastard can run faster than I can," Matt said.

"If he was there at all," Stryker observed.

Matt looked at him. "You don't believe her." It wasn't a question.

Stryker wobbled a hand as if to say maybe yes, maybe no. "I don't have all the details," he hedged. "I don't know the girl."

"I don't either," Gabriel said. It wasn't clear if he meant

the details or the girl. "This is a quiet place, normally. This kind of thing..." He paused. "Real unpleasant."

"Yeah."

Gabriel's glance was less than casual. "You get a lot of it in the city, I suppose? Nuts and kooks and crazies?"

"Way of life," Stryker agreed. "Look in the mirror every morning and wonder which side you're going to be on for the rest of the day. Doesn't always work out the way you expected, either."

"Thought I'd escaped," Matt said.

"Nobody escapes, brother," Stryker told him. "Inside the asylum or out, it's all rough country."

They went back inside.

By the time Matt and Jack returned, Daria's hysterics had abated to convulsive sighs and hiccups. She took one look at their faces, and nodded wearily. "I know," she said, in a low, shaky voice. "There wasn't anyone outside, no footprints, nothing." There were resignation and defeat in the sound of her, the way she sat, the distant focus of her eyes. "Thank you for looking."

"Here, lovey, drink this." It was Freddy, looking concerned and just a little bit excited. He held out a brandy. Behind him, Larry had a small plate of crackers, in case more solid nourishment was required.

"No, thank you." Daria stood up. She smiled, very brightly. "I think it must have been a reflection of the setting sun or something," she told them. "Sorry to make such a fuss."

Matt and Stryker exchanged a glance. "There *were* a few broken branches under the window," Matt said slowly. "Could have been broken off by someone standing there."

For a moment Daria's face held hope. Then Larry spoke.

"Me—cleaning the windows this morning," he said almost apologetically.

It was almost as if they *wanted* Michael to have been standing there, threatening her. As if, by making Daria's fear real, they could contain it. Everyone was looking at her now, making no pretense at conversation. Some glances were sympathetic, some skeptical. She stood up, and Kate stood beside her, one arm around her friend's shoulders, the other holding her wrist. She squeezed it encouragingly. Daria wiped her face, sighed deeply, and cleared her throat. Lifting her head, she smiled, rather ruefully.

"Sorry, everyone," she said. "I know Larry mixes a mean martini, and I should have come prepared. Next time I'll stick to lemonade."

A few people chuckled, and then, after a moment, conversations began again. It wasn't difficult to imagine what their subject was, but everyone was careful not to look in the direction of the small group by the sofa.

"Sorry, Freddy, Larry," Daria said. "I feel like a fool." Her words seemed brave, but Kate could feel her trembling.

"You need a rest, lovey," Freddy said. "We've left everything to you when really we should have come along and lent a hand more often with Miss Clary or the shopping or the house . . . or *something*. We're the ones who should be sorry, not you."

"No, really . . . she's fine. *She's* no trouble. It's me that's causing the trouble." The tears threatened to make a comeback.

The voice was warm and rich and unexpected, and it came from behind Stryker, so for a moment they thought he had spoken. Then he turned and they saw it was the handsome stranger.

"I wonder if I could be of some help," the man said. "We employ a private security firm, and it would be the simplest thing in the world to have someone patrolling the Island at night. The cost shared between the residents would be negligible, and it might help Mrs. Grey to sleep more peacefully."

"That's very kind of you, Hugo," Freddy said. "Very neighborly."

"I think the town budget could manage something without bringing in outsiders," Matt said, scowling. "There have been other reports of prowlers in the area lately. I'll make sure someone is out here at night from now on."

The handsome stranger looked at him, then shrugged. "Fair enough, it was only a suggestion. Sorry for your trouble, Mrs. Grey." And he faded away.

Freddy looked after him, then turned to Matt with a raised eyebrow. "Seemed a fair offer."

"You think so?" Matt said, glancing at Freddy. "I wonder if your guests would agree with you. Especially if they realized the offer came from Hugo *Wilberforce*."

Their eyes turned to Freddy, who had the grace to blush, although he brought his chin up. "Well, maybe if everyone realized that the Wilberforces aren't *all* bad, there wouldn't be so much complaining."

"Oh, Freddy," Kate said, in deep disappointment.

"He's a really nice person," Larry said, in defense of his partner's rather rash action in inviting the "enemy." "It's his *parents* who are the snooty ones, you know, not him. Hugo's been based in New York. We *did* wonder if Daria might recognize him, actually. He's a theatrical designer."

"He certainly is," agreed Matt, eyeing the perfectly cut blazer, the brilliant red shirt and the multicolored scarf around Hugo Wilberforce's muscular throat. "*Very* theatrical."

"No, I don't know him," Daria said quietly.

"No?" Freddy shrugged. "Well, he's broke, apparently. His bid for independence and artistic freedom was a flop, and he's been forced to come back and join the family business, poor bastard."

"Just what *is* the family business?" Matt asked. "I've never been able to find out."

Freddy shrugged. "Something nutsy-boltsy to do with cars or airplanes, I think he said. Or was it import-export? Copper? Steel? Nothing very *artistic*, anyway. I suppose he'll just have to buckle down like the rest of the world, and forget his dreams."

"Most people have to, in the end," Stryker said, recalling his parents' death and his aborted legal career. He kept *meaning* to go back to law classes at night, but . . .

Daria looked around for her handbag, rescued it from beneath a chair, and touched Freddy on the arm. "I think I'd better get back to Aunt Clary now. Mrs. Crabbe will be wanting to go home before it's really dark. I'm sorry if I upset your lovely party—but it seems to be surviving." Her voice was dry as her glance went around the room. It was true—from the talk and the laughter and the clink of glasses, nothing untoward might have happened at all. "Thanks, both of you."

"I'll walk along with you," Matt said. "Thanks, Freddy, Larry. Night, everyone."

There was a silence in the small group as they watched Matt and Daria go. A syncopated series of brief pauses in the various party conversations across the crowded room made it clear that their dual departure had been noted by all.

"That subdued roar you hear is the sound of a dozen matchmakers revving up," Freddy observed. He glided off to spread speculation a little further and thinner, using small bait—an old gossip fisherman's trick. Slowly the party returned to its former decibel level.

Kate waited until they were walking back through the windy dark. The earlier breeze had grown from fresh to downright sassy, and the tops of the trees were fighting back overhead.

Kate looked at Stryker's profile against the lights of the cottages they were passing. "Well? Was he or wasn't he?"

"The little man who wasn't there?" Stryker asked. "I don't honestly know. Most of the ends of those broken branches were dried—but a few were still wet."

"So he could have been there, staring at her?"

"Somebody could have been—whether it was this nasty husband of hers or not, I couldn't say."

"You're being very careful."

"I'm being very sensible. *Something* scared the hell out of her, that's for sure. I don't know an actress in the world who can make the blood actually drain from her face the way your friend Daria's did. But whether it was something outside or something inside that frightened her remains to be seen."

Before she could stop herself, Kate flared. "I suppose we'll only be certain about it when we find her *dead* some morning, is that it?"

He stopped and turned toward her in surprise. "Whoa, there, old paint. What spooked you?"

Kate was already sorry for her outburst. "I just feel sorry for her, that's all. It must be terrible to have nobody really believe you...especially when you're telling the truth."

"You're sure she is?"

"Absolutely positive," Kate said, a little too forcefully.

"Fine, then I believe her, too," Stryker said loyally. He took Kate's arm and they continued walking. "Gabriel seems a pretty level-headed type, I'm sure he'll look out for her."

Kate stared straight ahead. "Not your problem, right?"

"Not my problem, not my jurisdiction, not any of my business," Stryker said levelly. "And I'm on vacation, remember?" He cleared his throat, and spoke casually. Too casually. "By the way, is this an attempt at revenge for getting dumped in the water?"

Kate sighed. "I'd sort of thought of it that way. But seeing her face...it's too serious to play with."

"My point, exactly. Now, I did promise to make up for that, if you will recall. Dinner at the Golden Perch, and then..."

"Erotic pleasures," Kate smiled.

"Are you hungry?" Stryker asked.

"Not in the least."

"Good...then we can skip the appetizers and get right to the good part," Stryker said, opening the porch door and ushering her into the warm darkness within.

It had been a perfect summer day, closing with a perfect summer evening.

The storm broke the following morning.

7

At 7:45 A.M., the mailman dropped an envelope through Kate's back door. Similar envelopes were delivered to every other cottage on the Island. In each envelope was a photocopy of a tender made to Blackwater Town Council for the purchase and development of a certain area of land.

The envelope bore a Blackwater postmark dated the previous day.

There was nothing else in the envelope.

The Residents' Association met on the Robinson lawn immediately after lunch.

"First of all—is it true?" everybody wanted to know.

Don Robinson nodded. "It's true, all right. A company called Bobcat Investments has made an offer for the Mush with a view to developing it for commercial or industrial use. There was apparently a last-minute tender. The notice will be in the paper this Friday, and projected plans will be available 'soon' at the town hall. That's really *all* we know— and we only know *that* because some kind friend slipped us the information this morning."

Stryker had been examining the photocopied sheets with

some interest. "It might be helpful to know who this friend is. If we knew how he came by the information and why he..." Stryker trailed off as everyone turned to look at him. "Sorry," he said meekly, and thrust the photocopy into his pocket.

"How soon is 'soon'?" Larry Lovich asked, as they all turned back to Don.

"Your guess is as good as mine," Don said wearily. He'd been on the phone for most of the morning, pulling in old favors and leaning on old friends for what information he could glean. It hadn't been much. "Probably next week sometime."

They all stared at one another. "But the town meeting is this Friday," Freddy said in a stunned voice. "If they accept the bid then, seeing any plans will be pointless."

"I know," Don said. "Maybe that's why somebody leaked the information now, to give us time to make our feelings known to the council members. I can't think of any other reason."

It was another lovely afternoon, with a wide blue sky arching over the water as it chuckled and sparkled beyond the breakwater. The breeze rustled the trees overhead, and for once the mosquitoes seemed content to attack elsewhere. Far out in the bay a few windsurfers were white-winging over the beaten silver of the water, and the drone of a lawn mower was carried on the breeze from far down the coast. The sound of other people working always added tone to a summer day, Stryker thought. He was perched on the stump of a tree that had been split and killed by lightning some years before. It had been the tallest tree on the Island, had borne the name of Big Ed, and had been a boon to navigation. Now the two-foot-diameter stump, leveled and smoothed, was a boon to the backside of an outsider.

"What the devil can we do?" Mrs. Toby demanded. "Is this offer legal? Shouldn't there be a public vote or referendum? Isn't there some statute on the local books about how far ahead something like this is supposed to be announced so we can protest or something?"

"I checked with Berringer, the town clerk," Don said. "Apparently there is a loophole in the rules and these people spotted it. They waited for their chance—and made their move. The deadline for any tenders to the council was yesterday, and they got in just under the wire. Deliberately, if you ask me. If the council approves the sale, Bobcat Investments could own the Mush by next month."

"The Mush should have been declared a state park or a wildfowl reserve or something years ago," a heavyset woman said. She hadn't been at the cocktail party and Stryker didn't know who she was. "There are probably a lot of rare birds and things back there."

"We *are* a major flyway," Harry Greenfield said eagerly. "Canadian geese are very prominent in autumn, as well as several other interesting species. For example, I've spotted both a red-crested plover and a Morgan's flycatcher back there."

"They may be interesting, but I guess they're not very rare," Don said ruefully. "If you remember, a few years back the council paid the state university to make a survey, because *they* hoped it could be declared an area of scientific interest and be taken over by the state or even the Lakeshore Preservation people. But it turned out to be just full of frogs and mud and some very ordinary ducks. Not even the weeds were special."

"My God," Larry said. "That means they'll have carte blanche to turn it into anything they want."

Don nodded, his expression grim. "I think you ought to know that when I talked to Jack Fanshawe, he told me the development was going to be a real money-maker, but he wouldn't say what it was. I'm not even sure he knows. But he said that if I was worried, he could put me in touch with a buyer who'd give me ninety thousand for my place tomorrow. Cash."

There was a stunned silence.

"But it must be worth twice that," Freddy finally said in an appalled voice.

"Exactly," Kate said. She half-turned toward Stryker,

who was writing in his notebook, and raised her voice. "You see? It's just what I said this morning—even the *threat* of this development has cut property values in half."

Harry Greenfield had not been paying much attention to the discussion. "Ninety *K* isn't that bad, you know," he said reflectively. "Not what you'd call generous, but—"

"Not generous!"

"It's outrageous!"

"Haven't you looked at property prices lately?"

The voices seemed to push Greenfield back on his heels. He looked around wildly, startled at the angry response to his thinking aloud. "No, I can't say that I—"

"There are new places up the coast going for twice that," Larry Lovich told him irritably. "I went up to have a look at them as an investment. They're small and ugly and I reckon they'll be blown down in the first big winter storm. Our places are old, and of some architectural merit. Maybe they're not as modern as we'd like, but by God, they've stood up to a lot of punishment, and they'll go on standing."

"Sure they will—if the Island *itself* holds out," Greenfield countered. "But you know as well as I do we're losing frontage every winter. Look at that." He was pointing to the small pond of dark, mossy water that lay behind the Shanks section of the breakwater. The wooden facing was split and rotted in several places, and ice pressure had done the rest, allowing the lake to claw back some of the land.

"I got an order in to Lem Turkle to come up, fill in and concrete me," Aunt Clary shouted from her porch. Daria had helped her out there so she could sit in her rocker and listen in to the meeting.

Greenfield turned and lifted his voice slightly. "I didn't mean any offense, Miss Shanks—I have the same problem myself." He turned back to the others. "The point is, time is against us on the Island, anyway. It's fill and repair and fill and repair all the time. My boat house is leaking, roof *and* sides. Maybe you all can afford this constant drain on your capital—I can't," Harry Greenfield moaned. "And speaking of drain—what will draining the Mush do to

Paradise? Suppose Peacock Dike collapses, suppose we lose the canal and our boat houses end up high and dry?"

"Then we sue for damages," the fat woman said, an acquisitive gleam appearing in her eye.

"But the damage will be done, paid for or not," Greenfield said. "What's more, it's certainly not going to be very pleasant for the next few years if there's going to be a lot of construction going on back there."

"Never mind *during* construction—it's what they're actually *building* that worries me," Kate said pointedly. "Suppose they put up a chemical-processing plant or something like that back there? What then?"

"The house values will drop like a stone," Mrs. Norton said in a horrified voice. "My God, remember what happened in Lemonville? Since they built that cellophane factory you can only approach the town from downwind on a Sunday, and everyone is stuck with the stink because nobody will buy their houses."

"Do you know something we should know, Kate?" Don asked.

Kate had the grace to blush. "No," she admitted. "I just don't like the way these Bobcat people are being so darned *sneaky* about it."

"It may simply be a matter of keeping other bidders out," Larry pointed out.

"Do *you* know something, Larry?" Kate asked.

It was Larry Lovich's turn to look slightly abashed. "No. But it's quite a common thing to leave making an offer until just under the wire so your competitors don't realize you're interested in a particular package of land or stocks or whatever."

"Well, why should *anyone* be suddenly interested in the Mush?" Aunt Clary called out plaintively. Her hip might be broken, but there was nothing amiss with her hearing—she was keeping right up with the discussion. "It's just lurked around, squidging and rotting and smelling awful for years. Do you suppose somebody has discovered oil back there?"

"You mean is there gold in them there frogs?" Larry grimaced.

"Well, it's a fair question," Freddy said, smiling in spite of himself. "Maybe we ought to try to find out about that part of it. Maybe they're changing the highway or doing something else in the future that *will* make the Mush valuable. Somebody ought to check with the authorities. Anybody know any state senators or congressmen? State or county surveyors? Highway department? Waterways Commission?" He looked around, but everybody shook their head no.

"What about good old-fashioned threats?" Mrs. Norton suggested with a leer. "Do we know anything nasty about anybody on the council?"

"I know them all," Don said. "They're not bad people. Most of them would try to do what's right for the town. But you've got to remember that the town of Blackwater has never been what you'd call rich. It's barely staggered along, some years. And the incorporation of the town covers more than just the coast, you know, it goes well inland. The farmers have been complaining for years—and you can't blame them—that whatever is done in Blackwater is done with the tourist trade in mind."

"That's because the town council is made up of *businessmen*," Kate said in disgust. "Maybe they're not bad people, but do you think they're going to refuse this opportunity to unload the Mush for the sake of a few Island votes? Or, God forbid, a few birds? It costs the town a fortune to keep the Mush drained and the mosquitoes down."

Stryker looked down at his heavily bitten forearms and concluded that the town was wasting its money.

"Kate's right," Mrs. Toby said. "We're talking profits here. If they're desperate enough for money, they could build an abbatoir, a steel mill, a chemical plant, or worse. We're right under the prevailing winds—whatever it belches out will drop straight onto us."

There was a murmur of horror.

Kate rolled on. "And if it *is* something big, then the

inland real estate prices will shoot up, because the people who come to work in it will want new housing, roads, schools, shopping malls. Somebody is going to do well out of this, but not Paradise Island. We'll just sink under the sludge with all the other coastal areas that have been industrialized. There's no time to get the Lakeshore Preservation people in—I say we have to protest, and protest *now!*"

"Right!" "You said it!" "Let's do it!"

Hugo Wilberforce spoke up. Everyone had been astonished when he'd appeared for the meeting, but he seemed as angry and upset as everyone else. "Say, if you really intend to do anything in the way of an organized protest and need finance for posters and leaflets and so on, my father has told me to offer whatever funds are necessary. He's already trying to find out what he can about these Bobcat people through his commercial and banking contacts," Hugo said. "He's not a well man, he can't do much himself, but he's prepared to back anything the Residents' Association wants to do." He looked around. "Anything."

There was a silence.

"Just what are you suggesting?" Don Robinson finally said in a cautious voice.

Hugo shrugged. "I can paint a mean poster," he said.

"Oh, no—you said 'anything' in a kind of meaningful voice," Mrs. Norton said. "You mean, like a bomb?"

Good Lord, thought Stryker. It must be something in the water. That was Kate's first reaction, too.

Hugo didn't answer—which was an answer in itself.

"I don't think we ought to go off half-cocked about this thing," Don said uneasily. "There's no need for violence. If we want to protest in some way, we can stage a sit-in or something peaceful like that."

"Whatever you want," Hugo said eagerly. "If you want to do a sit-in, fine. We'll provide doughnuts and coffee and whatever else that's needed."

"Cushions," said the fat woman.

Everyone laughed, but there was little genuine amusement in it. The suddenness of the thing, the sneakiness, and the feeling that this was so inevitable—it all was overwhelming them. Nobody knew what to suggest first.

Len Cotman had been quiet up to now. His voice was soft, but when he spoke, everybody listened. "Estelle had to go to San Francisco this morning, but we talked about it while she was packing. She didn't want to leave with all this hanging over us, but it's an important concert and she had to do it. She was in tears, though. It's the poorest offer we've had yet."

"You mean you've had other offers, too?" Mr. Greenfield asked. "I must say, a lot of people seem to be interested in Paradise Island lately."

"Amen," Cotman said with a chuckle. "Some of them have even been polite."

Don frowned—there had been something in Len's voice that caught his attention. Something that rang a faint warning note. "What do you mean, *some* have been polite?" he asked slowly.

Len looked uneasy. "Oh, it doesn't matter," he said, and it was obvious he regretted his light remark. "The point is—"

"No, wait a minute, Len. It does matter," Don interrupted. "If only some of them were polite, that means the others weren't. Have you been getting hassled?"

The black man looked out over the lake, and his face darkened slightly. He was embarrassed. "Some," he admitted.

"Goddammit," Don said angrily. "You should have said."

There were murmurs of agreement and anger from the others, and Mrs. Norton put her hand on Len's arm in sympathy. Len looked at them all and smiled. He was a proud, quiet man—a highly regarded dentist, with an extensive practice in the city. His wife, Estelle, was a concert mezzo-soprano in constant demand. Between them they made an excellent income, but although they kept a luxurious apartment in the city, they considered the comparatively modest Island property to be their real home.

"It's only been in the last six months or so, Don," Len

said deprecatingly. "It never happened before. That's one reason we've been so happy here."

"But it changed six months ago?" Kate asked, as upset as Don and the others were.

Len nodded. "About that." He glanced at Hugo Wilberforce and then away quickly.

"I'm sorry, Len," Don said. "If you mean what I think you mean, I'm ashamed it should ever have happened here."

"Were there any threats?" Stryker asked suddenly, from his place on the stump. Len turned to look at him.

"A few."

"Any damage?"

"A little—windows smashed, some writing inside the boat house. Kid stuff, really. That's what I figured it to be—just kids. Nothing I couldn't take care of myself." He smiled ruefully. "I grew up in Chicago—Estelle in Alabama. We've seen a lot worse, believe me."

"You should have told Matt Gabriel," Mrs. Toby said.

"I suppose so," Len admitted, "but I didn't like to bother him."

Don looked around. "I don't like this—I usually know what's going on around here. Anybody else been having trouble?"

"Yes." Aunt Clary spoke up suddenly and strongly, startling Daria, who stood beside her. "Nasty phone calls, men coming around with briefcases, letters—lots of letters. A couple of them were . . . real unpleasant."

Daria looked down at her, stricken. "You never told me that, Aunt Clary. You never said."

"I can look after myself," Aunt Clary snapped. "Well, I could—and I will again, once this hip mends. I'll put up barbed wire if I have to, and I suggest the rest of you do the same."

There were nods and murmurs of agreement.

"Anyone else been having trouble?"

Mrs. Toby and Mrs. Norton nodded. Fran, who had been silent up until now, spoke. "We've had a few letters, Don."

He turned to her, shocked. "What?"

She shrugged. "I didn't want to bother you with it," she said.

"Damn," Don said. "Damn and damn."

"That's history—this is now," Kate said impatiently. "Can we have a vote? Are you planning to sell, Harry?"

Greenfield looked at his shoes. "I'm just weighing up the pros and cons at the moment. I've been discussing alternatives with my accountant."

"And your bookie, no doubt," Aunt Clary muttered, feeling braver now that she knew there were others who had been under pressure, too. Greenfield must have heard her, for he flushed bright red, but said nothing more.

"Well, I'm going to *attend* that council meeting," Mrs. Toby said firmly. "We pay our taxes and we have the right to be there, you know."

"That's true," someone murmured.

"It might not make any difference, but *somebody* ought to let them know how we feel," Mrs. Toby went on. "I'll think about selling when I know more about what's going to happen. That's to say, I'll think about it—but I won't do it."

"Absolutely," Len Cotman agreed softly.

There was a silence. "Larry? Freddy? You going to sell?" Don prompted.

The two men glanced at each other. "*Probably* not," Larry finally said. "But to be honest, I can't promise right now. I've had a few reverses lately—I could use a cash injection. But I certainly think I could get more than these people are offering. And if this development is something low-key, clean and quiet, like electronics, for instance, or maybe something in the luxury line like a hotel or yacht club, we'll still be in good shape. I agree with Mrs. Toby—I don't think we should panic."

"What about the agreement to offer our places to the other residents first?" Harry Greenfield demanded. "Do we stick to that, or are all bets off?"

"I don't know if those original deeds still have any legal standing," Don admitted. "I think old Ernie Peacock put that stuff in there in case somebody was forced to sell through hardship or something. It was fine if one house came up for sale, but I don't think any one of us could get together enough money to buy *all* the houses at once."

"I bet *he* could do it," Mrs. Toby said, nodding toward Hugo Wilberforce. "How about it, Hugo—your people interested in owning the whole Island? Are they behind this? Is Bobcat just another name for Wilberforce?"

Hugo looked defensive. "Absolutely not. I told you, we don't want this development any more than you do."

"What you *say* you want is no guarantee of what you'll do when the chips are down," somebody muttered.

Hugo shrugged. "Well, the land belongs to my mother, actually, but it was my father who paid to have the new house and dock built. He's a businessman, and he hates taking a loss on anything. But *that* isn't why he's so angry about this. He came here to find peace and quiet, and he feels this thing is an intolerable intrusion. He says to tell you he'd make a counteroffer for the Mush himself if he could, in which case he'd just leave it as it is. But he's simply not financially liquid enough at the moment to do it. He might have been able to get a consortium together if there'd been time, but . . ." He shrugged and looked around the group, then produced his sudden, white smile. "Bobcat got there first. But there has to be some way to stop them, to get the time we need to find another way. That's why he sent me along to see how you all felt about it."

"We feel rotten about it!" Aunt Clary shouted.

"True enough." Don Robinson nodded, a bleak look on his face. "I suggest we all go away and think it over, and then perhaps we can have another meeting and make some kind of plan."

"Fine," Hugo said. "I'll tell him."

Don looked around. "Let's see—has everyone had their say?"

"What about Kit Lattimer?" Mrs. Toby asked.

In unspoken accord, they all turned to look toward the Lattimer house on the other side of the Shanks place. The winter storm windows were still up, and the grass was knee-high around the picnic table.

Don looked sad. "I've been trying to get in touch with Kit Lattimer all morning. Nobody seemed to know where he is. I finally got through to his lawyer, who said he hadn't seen or heard from him for quite a while. He said the last time he'd talked with him, Kit had said something about going to Nevada or Arizona, or maybe even back to Africa, because of his arthritis. He never really re-adapted to Great Lakes weather after living in hot countries for so long."

"Poor soul," Mrs. Norton said. "He was always talking about Africa, wasn't he? Wanting to go back and all."

"But Ada wanted to stay here," Mrs. Toby said. "She said he'd only go back over her dead body."

"Well, she died last year, so maybe that's what he did," Larry said abruptly. "It was in the papers. Just a little announcement—I only saw it by chance. After a long illness, it said. She was never *physically* strong, you know."

There were sympathetic murmurs, but Stryker thought there was more than sadness visible in Don Robinson's eyes. There was something else. Something he wasn't looking forward to telling them. "Anyway," Don continued slowly, "the lawyer told me their last contact was when he arranged the sale of Kit's city apartment in March. He sent the proceeds to a bank in Arizona, as instructed. That's all he knows."

There was a silence.

"And the cottage?" somebody finally asked.

Don sighed. "Sold lock, stock, and rain barrel to Bobcat Investments."

There was a silence, and then Mrs. Toby spoke. "Well—there goes the neighborhood," she said.

8

Matt looked up as Don Robinson came into the office. He'd been just about to pack up and go down the street to the Muskie Lounge for beer and chili, but he settled back into his chair with a grin. "Hey, Donnell," he said, using the tall man's full name.

Don grinned. It was an old joke. "Matthew," he said.

"Oh, fancy stuff. It'll be 'mister' next," said Tilly from the corner. "How are you, Don? How's Fran and the kids?"

"All well—so far," Don said, sinking down on the chair opposite Matt. "You heard about the information we got this morning?"

"Yes, I heard," Matt said. "Somebody was real efficient—the news is all over town."

"Who do you reckon it is, Don?" Tilly asked. "I've been asking around—but nobody has ever heard of an outfit called Bobcat Investments."

"Beats hell out of me. It isn't Wilberforce—the son came to our meeting and said they were against it, too."

"No kidding," Tilly said, making a mental note to add this to her daily cache of information. Mother would be fascinated. She was a wonderful listener, and since the stroke she couldn't say much to anyone, so Tilly felt free to tell all. It was a great relief to her, for she was a natural gossip hemmed in by years of closed-mouth training by Matt's father. Being able to speak her mind about everybody and everything made looking after the old lady a lot easier, and going home each night had become almost a treat.

"We had a meeting of the Residents' Association a little while ago, and I heard some things I think you should know about," Don said. "Apparently my neighbors on the Island don't feel they should bother you about their little troubles."

"Is it something I said or something I did?" Matt asked with a smile.

"Both, probably. They like you and hate messing up your nice routine—at least, that's as close as I can get. 'He's got more important things to do' was the top and bottom of it."

"Oh, hell," Matt said in mock disgust. "I've obviously got to work on my stern-lawman image." He looked more closely at his friend. "Bad, is it?"

"Well, dammit, I think so," Don said. "Turns out various people have been getting hassled lately. Phone calls, nasty letters, that kind of thing. The one that makes me angriest is Len and Estelle—you can imagine what slant that would take."

"We've never had trouble like that before," Matt said in surprise.

"I know," Don said. "I admit there aren't many black families around Blackwater Bay, but those we have are just mixed in with everybody else as far as I've ever been able to see. My kids say there's never been any real racial trouble at school—'What the hell for?' was their attitude."

"What's Len been getting?" Matt reached for a notepad.

"Threats, slogans painted on his boat, nasty letters, stuff like that. Wouldn't ever have known about it if Kate's boyfriend hadn't spoken up and asked right out."

Matt nodded as he wrote. "I suppose Len denied it was anything much, and Jack Stryker called him on it?"

"Something like that."

"Cops down in the city get so they know the sound and smell of pain," Matt acknowledged. "Something I'm still learning."

Don looked down at his hands. "That's not all, though. I made a few private inquiries after the meeting. Others have been getting phone calls and...I guess you'd call them poison-pen letters. Makes me sick to think about it."

Matt leaned back in his chair. "Let me guess. Larry and Freddy about being gay?"

"Yes. And Mrs. Toby and Mrs. Norton. That was pretty specific—said they'd each murdered their husbands for the insurance."

Matt's eyes widened. "You're kidding!"

"Dammit, I wish I was!" Don exploded. "These people are my friends, and they were too embarrassed or too ashamed to tell me they were in trouble. Greenfield has gotten a few letters about being a Nazi because he changed his name from Grünfeldt. He managed to hide them from his wife, fortunately. And then Frannie comes out with it."

"What?"

"That *we've* had a few letters. Funny phone calls, too, while I've been out at work. Heavy breathing, somebody whispering 'Get off the Island while there's still time,' and stuff like that. She made a joke of it, but it scared her and it sure as hell scares me. I have to leave her alone there every day when I go into the city to work, and our kids go back and forth on their bikes to school and it's a long way to the highway and back. God, Matt—it's terrible!"

"Anybody else?" Matt asked.

"Miss Shanks has been having trouble, too, apparently."

Matt looked up, startled. "Aunt Clary?"

"Yes. Just threats—and name-calling. Not that anybody could hold much against *her* except being old and a spinster." Don almost smiled. "She says she'll get out her shotgun, like always."

"When did all this start?" Matt asked.

"From what I can find out, about six months ago."

"Even with Aunt Clary?"

Don saw what he was getting at. "Yeah—long before Daria came back. It was a surprise to *her*, too. Miss Shanks hadn't told her about it."

"And was there any kind of pattern to it?"

Don shook his head and looked bleak. "Your guess would be better than mine. Sounds to me like it was pretty random at first, but it's been picking up lately. The dumb thing is that nobody told anybody else about it—each one thought it was their own private problem; they were ashamed about it."

"You can understand that, if the things that were said were 'nigger' and 'queer' and 'killer' and 'Nazi,'" Matt said.

"I can *understand* it, sure, but the thought of them all just suffering like that, quietly... it just makes me want to go out and smash something, somehow. I'm an easygoing guy, pretty much. But this kind of thing is so... damn ... sneaky... and small... who'd do it?"

"What about Daria?" Tilly asked suddenly.

Both men turned to look at her.

"What do you mean?" Matt asked. "She only just got here, and anyway, she's not that kind of—"

"No, no... I meant all this about her husband trying to kill her and all—maybe she's been getting the idea it's him when it's really just part and parcel of all the *other* harassment. Maybe her husband *isn't* after her—maybe it's this Bobcat Investments bunch who have been sneaking around."

"There's something really evil going on here," Kate said, as they were getting their supper together. "You heard what Dad said on the phone."

"I did," Stryker said, getting out the cutlery to set the table. "He's just as bad as all the rest."

Kate turned to stare at him in dismay. "What do you mean by that?"

He finished laying the pieces and sat on the corner of the table, dislodging the knives and forks again. "Kate, letters and phone calls like the ones he described are against the law. Nobody is supposed to have to put up with that kind of thing. That's my job and Matt Gabriel's and every other police officer's—to protect, remember? How the hell are we supposed to do that when nobody tells us what's going on? As it is, the trail's at least six months old, maybe more, and nobody has kept anything for us to examine."

"Do you blame them?"

"Yes."

"How can you *say* that?"

"They should have complained," Stryker said stubbornly.

"Oh, sure. And they'd have been about as quickly believed as Daria was—or wasn't."

"There were threats made, Kate. Phone threats can be intercepted and traced—"

"And what kind of priority do you think funny phone calls have these days? What with murders and rapes and drugs and burglaries and terrorists and muggings and car thieves and con men and—"

"Okay, okay, I get your point. And you're right, we can't actually *do* anything unless there's physical violence. But we can often throw a hell of a scare into people and stop it. And the postal authorities *can* bring a case, if they want to. I know we're apt to ignore that kind of thing because we haven't the time or the manpower to deal with it, but Matt Gabriel doesn't strike me as the sort to dismiss Len Cotman or Freddy Tollett as a crank."

"No, he wouldn't," Kate agreed.

"Those letters could have been forensically examined— you, of all people, should know what we can do with that. I've told you some of the things we've managed to trace that way."

"Yes, I know. Daddy should have known that, too. But he only got two letters, and they were weeks apart. One was typed, the other made up of cut-up words from newspapers. He thought it was kids or some local crank. He says he didn't want to think about it at all, so he just threw them out."

"Even so..."

Kate sighed and nodded. "Even so..." she agreed, and went back to peeling the potatoes.

Stryker walked to the glass door of the porch and looked out at the bay. In the distance the thinnest of dark lines cut partway into the horizon, showing the cusp of the bay, while the rest of the sky blended invisibly into the silver haze of the vast lake beyond. As he watched, a jet took off from the Air Force base at Greenleaf, trailing a white thread of exhaust up into the sky like some aspiring spider. "You always told me it was so idyllic up here," he murmured, shaking his head. "And you believed it, too. But all the time it was full of snakes, like anywhere else."

"Only lately," Kate pointed out. "Before that, it was always just fine. Perfect, in fact."

"Hmmmm. Maybe. And maybe that's just wishful memories. You'd be surprised what we come across behind the closed doors of some nice, 'perfect' neighborhoods, babe."

"Not here," Kate said stubbornly. "Not here."

Stryker was silent for a little while longer, then he turned and looked at her with an odd expression on his face. "Next time you talk to your dad, ask him if anything odd happened up here six months ago," he suggested.

"You didn't have to tell him *everything* those letters said," Mrs. Norton reproached Mrs. Toby. "I simply didn't know where to put myself."

"I couldn't lie," Margaret Toby snapped.

"That's not the point," Mrs. Norton said.

"Well, it seems everybody else has been having trouble, too—we're not so special after all. Anyway, for all you know I *might* have murdered Haskell, and for all I know you might have murdered Bernard. Heaven knows they were both aggravating men in their way."

They eyed one another.

"Did you?" asked Mrs. Norton finally.

Mrs. Toby's mouth twitched. "Not saying. Did you?"

Mrs. Norton drew herself up and made for the kitchen. "Not saying, either."

"Are you going to put arsenic in your next batch of cookies?" Mrs. Toby called after her friend.

"Only if you go on embarrassing me," Mrs. Norton called back. After a moment, she poked her head around the corner of the door. "Bernard used to embarrass me, and look what happened to *him*."

Len Cotman went to the bureau and opened the drawer where he kept his socks and pants. He pushed them to one side and felt around for the manila envelope he'd secreted under the drawer lining. Pulling it out, he took it to the bed and dumped its contents onto the counterpane.

He sighed.

Nobody knows the trouble we've seen, nobody knows but the son of a bitch who sent these. He'd kept them carefully—salt for the wound? Maybe. It was just that burning them seemed so melodramatic, and throwing them into the garbage had seemed too easy somehow. Too dismissive.

He sensed they were important—and knew he should have done something about them from the start. It was just that you stirred up even more trouble that way. Reminded people that you were different, when they'd never made you feel it before. Taking these to Matt would have been to trumpet, "Look, we *are* different, some people *do* hate us," and he hadn't wanted to do that. He'd just wanted to be quiet and live his life. Estelle wanted that, too. Here on the Island they'd achieved it. Peace, friendship, the knowledge that they were giving as much as they were getting, and no bills presented.

He was nearing sixty, he was too old to start looking for another haven, another place of safety. And Estelle's talent had to be protected, too. Wanting to cry makes your throat close up.

But now things had changed. If the others had been getting these sort of letters, too, then he *wasn't* different. He was just another victim, as they were.

He smiled sadly.

Never thought he'd find *solace* in being a victim.

Never thought he'd be pleased to be called "nigger."

Carefully, he slid the letters back into the envelope and closed it. Then he got his jacket and went out to the car.

9

Aunt Clary was quiet after Daria had helped her back to bed following the meeting of the Residents' Association. It was partly exhaustion, and partly reflection. She waved away Daria's questions about the letters and phone calls she'd received over the past few months with the excuse that she wanted to have a little sleep before dinner. She lay with her eyes closed, listening to Daria moving about the kitchen, but she did not sleep.

It was much later, after the dinner had been consumed and cleared away and they both sat watching television, that Aunt Clary decided to speak.

"About the trouble on the Island..." she began.

"Selling the houses, you mean?" Daria kept her eyes on the television screen—they both did—and spoke into the air.

"That, yes. And all the other trouble people have been having."

"You included."

"I probably made it sound worse than it was, truth be told. But it looks like there's been more going on than I knew about. Than anybody knew about. Comes from trying to keep things nice, I guess, trying to keep quiet and smooth things over."

"Does it?"

"I think so. We've all been pretending we live in some kind of bubble where sorrow never comes, but it's not so. There's trouble on the Island, yes, but there always has been, one way and another. We've had drownings—the Peacock child, years ago—and we've had bankruptcies, and sickness, and people running off with other people's wives or husbands—all kinds of misery, over the years. That's true of any community, large or small. We're not so different as we like to think—or as maybe we'd like other folks to think. Now this prowler you've been hearing—"

"It was Michael." Daria's voice was flat.

"Could be it wasn't. You heard the others—Len Cotman, he's had things written on his boat, on his house—had to be someone creeping around to do that. Nasty letters through the door and so on have to be delivered—nobody said they came through the regular mail, did they? Somebody had to creep around to do that, too. Seems like the place has been downright alive with people creeping around, so—"

Daria took her eyes from the screen and looked straight at her aunt. Her expression was bleak. "Now *you* don't believe me either, do you?"

"I didn't say that, child. Of course I believe that Michael tormented you and all—in New York. But when it comes to what you've been seeing and hearing here, couldn't it be that—"

There was a spark in Daria's eye. "Maybe you should look at it the other way around, Aunt Clary."

"What do you mean?"

"I mean it was about six months ago that Michael began his campaign against me. Maybe all of this trouble on Paradise was a way of getting back at *me*. Maybe *he* did something that made you fall down the stairs and break your hip."

"How could he?"

"By getting on a plane to Granthem and then driving down

here and tying a string across the steps and then driving down to the corner and phoning you in the middle of the night."

"That's ridiculous. Why would—"

"To kill you, or hurt you, which would hurt me."

"I can't believe that."

"You've never fallen down those stairs before."

"Well, no, but—"

"And he has money, lots of it. He was down here with me once, remember? I used to get homesick and talk about the Island all the time—so he knows all about it. Suppose *he* is Bobcat Investments—or his family is? Maybe he found a way to destroy not just you but all of Paradise because he knew how much I love it."

"Now that's just conceit, Derry," her aunt said sharply. "How could he get his family—"

"Michael can get his family—or anyone else—to do anything he wants," Daria said bitterly. "And when he wants something, he gets it. He always has. He always will." She stood up. "He'll destroy everything I love and then he'll destroy me. Why don't you *believe* me? Why doesn't anyone *believe* me?"

"But child..."

It was too late. With a cry of frustration, and choking back sobs, Daria ran from the room and up the stairs. Her door slammed and there was a crash of springs as she threw herself on her bed. Through the ceiling Aunt Clary could hear the torrent of sobbing and crying, and felt utterly helpless. Could it be true? Michael Grey was obsessive, clearly a nasty piece of work when crossed, and his family *did* have money. The strange secretiveness of the tender to the town, the vicious letters that had been coming to people on the Island— all that *was* reminiscent of his treatment of Daria. It *was* believable. Just. Daria certainly believed it.

Was Daria right?

Or was Daria crazy?

Aunt Clary threw back her covers and with some difficulty swung her legs over the edge of the bed. With one hand on her aluminum walker she managed to get down. Slowly and painfully she made her way toward the stairs. There was no way she could have climbed them, but she maneuvered herself alongside the flight and looked up at the banister.

Old and shaky she might be, but her long sight was good—certainly good enough to see the groove that had been cut into the wood of the fourth balustrade from the top. She hadn't been up the stairs since her fall—and it wouldn't have been apparent to anyone who wasn't looking for it. In fact, it was so discreet and so level that it could easily have been part of the design—but it wasn't. What's more, caught in the roughened wood of the groove, trailing from a tiny splinter of paint, were the torn remnants of what had once been strong dark cord.

Clary felt a brief moment of triumph—she hadn't been clumsy after all!—and then she began to shake with cold and weakness and fear.

She had broken her hip—but *someone* had meant her to break her neck.

"Where are you going?"

Kate turned at the door. "I just heard storm warnings on the radio—I'm going to put the boats away."

"It's getting dark," Stryker protested.

Kate laughed. "Good heavens, I've put the *Dart* away at the stroke of midnight before now—there's the lighthouse and the marker buoys, remember?"

Stryker stood up from where he had been dozing on the sofa. "I'll come with you."

"There's no need."

"I think there is."

"Oh. Expect me to be attacked by a Bobcat, do you?"

"Very funny." He was struggling into his poplin jacket. He pulled the zipper up so fast he nearly knocked himself on the chin. "How do you expect to put both boats back in time, by the way?"

"Very easily. I'll just tow the dinghy—"

"And when you turn inland the waves will drive the little

boat straight up the *Dart*'s backside. No, *I'll* bring the little boat."

Kate leaned against the doorjamb. "Who says?"

"I says. I grant you I'm not an experienced sailor, but for crying out loud, I just have to follow you, don't I?"

"Theoretically, yes."

"Well, then—come on. It's getting darker by the minute."

Reluctantly, Kate opened the door and they emerged into the breezy dusk. There were a few whitecaps glimmering on the surface of the water, which was already looking as black as its name. The *Dart* and the smaller dinghy beyond it were bobbing up and down in a lively fashion. The air seemed a peculiar greenish-yellow, and thick clouds were obliterating the last traces of the sunset. Overhead, the oaks hissed and clacked their branches disapprovingly as a piece of old newspaper skittered across the otherwise immaculate lawn.

There was no rain, but the smell of rain coming was in the air, accompanied by the tingle of electricity.

"We should have done this earlier." Stryker had to raise his voice slightly.

"I know, but it's come up suddenly," Kate said. "Lake storms sometimes do. Other times you can feel them coming for days."

"Not this one."

"No. I guess we could call it a Bobcat storm," Kate said wryly. They reached the breakwater, and she took hold of the dinghy's rope from just beyond the cleat and began to pull it in. When it was more or less beside the wooden uprights, she gestured to Stryker to jump into it. "Go on," she said, when he hesitated. He glowered at her, then inched himself over and down, steadying himself with a hand against the rough boards of the breakwater until he felt sufficiently balanced to let go and sit.

Kate needed no such caution. While he was jerking the rope and trying to start the dinghy's small outboard engine, she coiled and threw him his mooring rope, then pulled in the *Dart* and—with a moment's pause to judge the wave action—jumped down onto it with the careless ease of experience. She stepped over the windscreen onto the plump cushions of the driving seat, roughly coiled the mooring line and dropped it on the floor, and reached into the pocket of her shorts for her keys.

For a few seconds they were both at the mercy of the waves, which were driving down-coast. They drifted past some of the other cottages until, at last, the *Dart*'s engine and then the dinghy's outboard came to life.

"You beauty," Kate purred to the big boat as it throbbed beneath her. She stood up on the seats and looked around, spotted Stryker, and waved to him to follow her. He nodded, and they both turned out toward the horizon.

Thudding through the waves in the wake of the larger boat, Stryker watched Kate sitting casually on the back of the seat, steering with deceptive ease, the wind pulling the curls back from her face and the waves splashing up around her, and had to shake his head in admiration. Damned Amazon, that's what she was. A *small* Amazon, but—

A wave caught him unexpectedly and the dinghy slewed sideways, nearly capsizing. He momentarily lost his hold on the steering handle of the outboard and had to grab for it before it swung out over the back. By the time he had recovered it, he'd gone thirty feet to starboard and Kate was well in front of him. He revved up the outboard and tried to catch up, cursing the lake, the boat, the weather, and his own ineptitude. Give me an alley and a mugger and I know what to do, he thought. But not this.

Kate, unaware of Stryker's brief diversion, was enjoying herself. They had to go out of the lee of the coast in order to pick up the channel that led back around the Point, past the Wilberforces, and into the quiet waters of the old river mouth and the canal that ran behind the Island. Once beyond the protection of the Wilberforce dock, the water was very choppy, indeed, but the *Dart* cut undaunted into the waves, her engine roaring a challenge to the weather. Kate found herself enjoying the freshness of the breeze and the twinkling lights along the Island as the cottagers turned on their lamps for evening. She checked back and saw Jack was some way behind her, but coming doggedly on in her wake. She waved, and he made a small gesture back. He looked wet and bedraggled—the waves she was breaching easily in the big boat were splashing into the dinghy and onto him. She throttled back, but found it difficult to steer, so she tried to find a happy medium to maintain way without leaving the dinghy too far behind.

At last she spotted the wink of the unmanned lighthouse at the tip of Peacock's Dike. Then came the line of red and green buoy lights that marked out the deep channel. She turned the *Dart* toward the land once more. Immediately the waves that had been parted by the sharp prow began to hammer the side of the boat, and she found it difficult to keep a steady helm.

In the dinghy, Stryker was struggling, too—with the engine and the boat, and with a sudden sensation of seasickness. The little dinghy was rocking to and fro wildly, and if it hadn't been for his having to keep a tight hold on the outboard, he would have liked just to lie down on its bottom and wait to die. As it was, he kept going. The wind was blowing him sideways and giving him earache, his arm was cramping, his fingers were cold and numb.

Suddenly, eerily, it all stopped.

He was so startled, he nearly cried out.

Then he realized that they were once again inside the curve of the coastline that ran along the bay beyond the Island. The wind was still blowing, and there was still a chop on the surface, but it was minimal compared to the white-capped monsters farther out in the bay. What it must be like on the lake itself hardly bore thinking about. He could hear the *Dart*'s engine, throttled back and grumbling with its distinctive gurgle as water ducked the exhaust, and he could see her rear riding lights. He could also see the buoy lights that marked the channel. The lights of the Wilberforce house shone out over the smooth lawns that surrounded it. There was a small beacon shining at the end of their dock, where a large sailboat was tied up. The lantern glow showed up the furled sails and the gleam of well-kept brass fittings.

It was his first glimpse of the Wilberforce enclave, and while he kept an eye on Kate and the *Dart*, he also took advantage of this opportunity to play Peeping Tom.

The rooms of the big house were well-lit now that darkness was nearly complete, and it was like looking into a stage set. There were huge picture-window walls in the rooms both above and below the redwood decks, and they revealed modern decor of a very expensive standard, with large abstract paintings on paneled walls, pale leather chairs and sofas, a huge glass dining table, and a fireplace where flames danced and flickered. That was upstairs. Below the deck he saw a large game room, complete with both snooker- and table-tennis tables, and, behind smaller windows, a kitchen. But it was a strangely empty stage set, for there seemed to be no one at home. Pots were steaming on the stove in the kitchen, candles were lit on the dining table, and a drinks tray was set out near the fireplace—but for whom?

It was just as a door opened and two men entered the upstairs room that he hit the rock.

Kate maneuvered the *Dart* backward into the boat house, throttling down and then turning the engine off to drift the last few feet. As the big boat bumped gently against the half-tires that lined the deck, she sprang out and grabbed the upper edge of the windscreen to steady herself.

The wind was beginning to send waves over the breakwater in front, but back here in the canal, protected by the Island and the dike opposite, the water was still and black, aside from the ripples still spreading from the *Dart*'s sleek sides. With practiced ease she reached out in the darkness and found the light switch. The overhead light came on, revealing the unfinished boards of the boat-house interior, the protruding nails with oddments hanging on them, the cans of gasoline and oil, the coils of rope, the orange crates that held her father's store of spare parts and old appliances he meant to "see to one of these days." The pilings that went down into the boat well were green with clinging water moss, and above the smell of hot engine and leather seats there was the peculiar and unpleasant odor of slow-moving, fetid water. Kate wrinkled her nose.

Grabbing a pair of gloves jammed behind a joist, Kate lowered the chains that hung down from above, attached the hooks to the two special cleats on the *Dart*'s decks fore and aft, then began to pull the boat out of the water. Damn it, where was Jack? She could use his strong arms just about now—the block and tackle took the strain, but it was still hard work hauling the *Dart* free of the water's grasp. At last she managed it, and locked the chain down. Now the dinghy could slide in underneath.

Turning toward the open mouth of the boat house, she frowned. Jack should have been here by now. She stripped off the gloves, jammed them back behind the joist, and then went out onto the road to listen. She should have been able to hear the outboard above the wind out here, but there was no sign of it. My God, she thought—has he gone over?

Slowly at first, then more quickly, she began to walk along the road toward the end of the Island, listening for the jaunty sputter of the little outboard. The wind was really strong now, and the noises of the Island were loud in her ears: the distant crash of the waves out front; the trees, groaning and whipping their branches together above the cottages; the clatter of a loose shutter; the creak of boats swinging on their davits within the boat houses; the crunch of her own sneakers through the gravel and dust of the road.

She began to run, peering between the boat houses.

But no dinghy.

And no Jack.

10

He felt like a damned fool.

True, the rock had been underwater, but if he'd been paying the least bit of attention he'd never have been anywhere near it. Now what?

He stood, dripping, on the narrow curve of pebble beach below the Wilberforce house, and looked at the pathetic half-sunk dinghy he'd left fifteen feet out from shore. It wouldn't sink any farther—the water was only four feet deep, at most, there. He hoped the ragged hole in the fiberglass hull could be repaired—he doubted that the outboard motor was more than junk. He didn't know much about engines, it was true, but funny noises are funny noises, and twisted propellers are twisted propellers, and life is life and night is night and wind is wind and he was getting cold.

He turned and looked at the house. From this angle he could no longer see the men in the upper room, but he had a better view of the kitchen and the big stainless-steel pots steaming on the stove, the microwave, the fancy copper-bottomed pans hanging on hooks, and the butcher-block work areas. As he watched, a woman appeared and lifted a lid to inspect whatever was cooking so merrily. She was about fifty, gray-haired and big-shouldered, with a sour expression. Her face was like a doughy, uncooked bun, with black-currant eyes sunk deep on either side of a small, pointed nose. She stirred, replaced the lid, and walked out of the kitchen again.

Back to her dressing room, no doubt, to adjust her cook's costume. Maybe she was playing another role, too, and would emerge later, dripping with jewels, as the Dowager Lady Penelope, or draped in scarves as Madame Arcati. The impression of looking at a stage set was difficult to shake as he stood there on the edge of the sweep of lawn. As was the feeling that beyond the stage there were many other unseen rooms. (Well, there had to be, didn't there? For a start he couldn't see a bathroom anywhere.)

What should he do? Walk up, knock on the door, and say something like "Just been shipwrecked, call the Coast Guard!"? Or perhaps, "Hello, I'm your neighbor up the Island and I've just had a little accident..."

Oh, swell.

Maybe a simple "I wonder if I could have a fit in your hall?" would suffice. There was a splat on his face, and then another. Rain. He sighed. Well, there was one consolation— he couldn't get any wetter than he was already. He stepped up onto the lawn and began to walk toward the house. If he was lucky, he could just find his way through the fence— there had to be a gate—get out quietly and then walk down the Island to the cottage and explain to Kate how he had run aground in the dark just because he was more fascinated by watching two men arguing than he was in keeping track of the channel. She'd be *really* impressed.

He had gone about ten yards when there was a sudden noise to his right. A scuffling in the grass, a sensation of something moving at him in the dark. He caught sight of two sleek shadows against the light from the windows.

Dogs.

Dobermans.

Two.

Running silent.
But running fast.
Watch dogs bark.
Guard dogs don't waste their breath.
They have other things in mind.

"Jesus," he gasped, and turned back toward the water. The grass was slippery and his sneakers were wet—it was more of a ski run than an escape, but he was six feet out and two feet deep before he looked back. They stood shoulder to shoulder on the edge of the lawn, watching him.

"A simple sign that says 'Keep off the grass' would have been enough," he hissed at them. They growled, low and menacing, but did not move. The rain was coming down a little harder now. The waves were pushing at his knees from behind, slithering past and foaming over the pebbles and small rocks that lay below the lawn. He started to move to his left, and they moved with him. The light was behind them, but he could just get a glimpse of the channel buoy lights reflected in their black ball-bearing eyes, and of the white of their teeth bared in what was definitely not a smile.

Their position seemed clear enough. They didn't mind in the least his standing in the water. In fact, they were perfectly happy to have him stand there for the rest of his life. But he wasn't allowed on the grass.

He had inadvertently taken a few steps forward as he considered options and the dogs growled again, reminding him that while this was a nice place to look at, it was not a nice place to visit. And people who keep guard dogs usually do so because they are not too enthusiastic about uninvited visitors, shipwrecked or not. Hadn't Handsome Hugo said something at the party about having contacts with a security firm? These dogs were no doubt their local representatives.

All right, so he'd look like the idiot he was, but shouting for attention seemed to be the only way he could get out of this. A sudden flicker of lightning forked overhead and touched down somewhere up the coast behind him, revealing the dogs in their full muscular splendor, ears up, grinning now with anticipation. Come on, they panted. Make our day.

Thunder rolled far away, growling in meteorological mimicry. If he was going to yell, he'd better start now, because the storm would soon be overhead. He looked toward the house again, cupped his hands around his mouth, and shouted, "Hey."

The dogs cocked their heads to one side as if to listen a little better to his performance.

"Hey!" he shouted a little louder. The trouble was, the wind was blowing across and away from the house, carrying his words out into the bay, instead of into somebody's shell-like ear.

"HEY!!!!!" He really put his heart into it that time, so much so that the dogs began to growl and move about restlessly. He waited a minute or two, but aside from the dogs, there was no response. He started to feel angry. "HEY! HEY! HEY!!!!!!! HELP! SOS! AU SECOURS! AYUDAME! HELLO THE HOUSE!!! HELP! DAMMIT! HELP!!"

No response.

The house looked huge from here, huge and strange and—despite its big uncurtained windows—secretive. He knew someone was home, he'd seen two men and a woman, for a start.

Well, he had a clear three-way choice: challenge the dogs (very funny), go on yelling until his throat gave out (not much longer in this rain and wind), or swim for it.

Stryker was not a particularly strong swimmer at the best of times, and the muscles of his recently wounded shoulder were still much weakened. If he opted for swimming, it seemed to him he had two alternatives: go around the Island the back way, or go around the Island the front way. Either way was wet. The front way meant fighting rough water, the back way meant mud and reeds and frogs and bugs . . .

He bagan to slide toward the front. The dogs moved, too.

At each step, he yelled again. "HEY! HELP!" Five steps

along he went under with his mouth still open. The drop-off was sudden and steep, and as deep as he went, he didn't touch the bottom, although he did take in quite a bit of water as he descended. This, presumably, was the channel cut for the dock. Rising to the top, spluttering and choking, he began to tread water, then started to move along parallel to the edge of the land in an awkward sidestroke.

The dogs kept pace.

He moved on steadily, occasionally being ducked from behind by a wave, but more or less making way. The big pilings of the dock loomed closer and closer, and he finally reached them and wrapped his arms around one, trying to catch his breath. He was relieved to see that he didn't have to swim around the dock, after all, but could pass under it, go around the boat, and continue along the front edge of the Wilberforce property. That was something, anyway.

Another flash of lightning revealed the dogs standing at the base of the dock gangway, watching him. The rain streaked their waxy black coats, running down their flanks in wavering lines and dripping off the ends of their tails. One yawned. Come on, they seemed to say, give us a chance. Don't just hang around down there—come up and let us rip your throat out—we haven't had a bite in days!

"Bastards," he muttered. What use were they? If the people in the house couldn't hear him when he yelled, how did they expect to hear the dogs barking when an intruder tried to cross the lawn? The answer was simple: they didn't expect to hear them barking, they only expected to find any such intruder spread in small pieces around their property the next morning.

He nearly went under again as a wave surged around him and thrust him hard against the piling. Time to move on. He was already tiring in the cold water, and there was quite a way to go. Taking a deep breath, he let go of the piling and swam across the space under the dock, emerging on the other side and grabbing hold of the anchor chain of the big sailboat. Its curving white flank rose above him, bumping and rubbing against the rubber guards that buttressed the dock, making a squeaking sound that set his teeth on edge.

He was about to move on when he heard voices. Two men—the ones he had seen arguing earlier?—were running down the lawn and onto the dock. He could hear their feet thudding on the boards overhead. He started to call out, then paused. Standing knee-deep on the beach and waving was one thing, but to be found apparently hiding under the dock quite another.

"What the hell are the dogs doing down here?" one voice asked.

"How should I know?" another voice snarled. "Maybe they're thinking of taking a swim."

"Very funny. We should have done this before it started to rain." The footsteps thudded overhead as Stryker moved back under the dock and took hold of a piling.

"He only told us five minutes ago."

"Bastard never knows what he wants."

"He's plenty pissed off, all right. Come on... let's get it done and get back in. I'm hungry."

"I wouldn't rush, it's bean sprouts again."

There was a pause, and Stryker clung to the piling, fighting the churning water that boiled around him with each successive wave. He started to swim into the open again and try to get their attention while standing on the beach when one of them took the decision out of his hands.

"You know, they're looking *at* something under there," said one of the men. Footsteps came back down the dock.

Shit, thought Stryker.

"Probably a dead fish, or a water rat," said the other voice. But after a moment his footsteps, too, slapped toward the lawn. Suddenly there was a beam of light, sweeping the water and illuminating the slimy underface of the boards, which glittered with waterweed and snail tracks and other unnameable encrustations.

"There's somebody *under* there," the first man said.

"Right! Hey! I'm coming out!" Stryker shouted above the slosh of the waves. He stuck an arm out into the light beam, waved in what he hoped was a cheerful, positive manner, and then slowly emerged, blinking. Beyond the glare he could make out the shapes of the men—and the dogs.

"Well, well—it *was* a water rat," said the second man. "What the hell are you doing there, fella?"

"I was shipwrecked," Stryker said, bobbing in the water beside the pilings. He tried a smile, but felt it was a less-than-number-one performance. "I was shouting for some time, but nobody seemed to hear me."

"Oh, yeah?"

"You can see my boat, over there. On the rock."

"Oh, yeah?" Neither head turned to check out the boat. The dogs growled.

Stryker's eyes were becoming accustomed to the glare of the flashlight. He could see now that both men wore guns at their hips, belt and holster slung loosely over khaki tracksuits. There was something written in red on their left shoulders, but he couldn't make it out.

"Look, I live on the Island," he began. "Sort of."

"Oh, yeah?"

"My name is Jack Stryker. I met Mr. Wilberforce at a party the other night."

"Mr. Wilberforce don't go to parties."

"This was Mr. Hugo Wilberforce."

The two men looked at one another, then one began to reach toward his belt. Toward his gun? This had gone too far. "Now, wait a minute, I'm a police—"

The guard's hand went past the holster and produced a mobile telephone that had apparently been in his back pocket. He punched a few buttons, then put it to his ear. "Brody here, Mr. H. You been to any parties lately?"

"You must have been very annoyed at Solomon and Sheba," said the blonde, gazing at him with wide blue eyes.

"I was too scared to be annoyed," Stryker said, taking another sip of the superb brandy they'd given him. "I just felt like an idiot when your men found me lurking under the dock."

"You *were* an idiot," snapped the gray-haired man, but the pronouncement was not unfriendly. "If you'd just stayed on the beach and kept shouting, somebody would have heard you eventually." He smiled suddenly. "As it is, they're probably grateful. You've given them more excitement than they've had in weeks."

"More brandy?" asked Hugo, proffering the decanter.

They were seated in the large sitting room that Stryker had glimpsed from the boat. All were dressed in tracksuits— even Stryker now wore a khaki one. It was exactly like those the guards had worn, down to the embroidered "Wilberforce" on the shoulder. His own clothes were tumbling around in a dryer somewhere in the house. The others also wore tracksuits, but theirs were of supple silk velour, turquoise for the girl (introduced as Hugo's sister Mona), red for Hugo and black for his father, Mr. Arthur Evans Wilberforce.

"You're wondering about the suits," Mona said, following his glance. "Aren't you?"

"They're very comfortable."

"They're the only clothes we're allowed to wear here," Mona said. "I think Daddy must have cornered the market. We have a roomful of them, every possible size and color, but otherwise all exactly alike. We can also wear shorts, if it's really hot, or a bathing suit." She glanced at him from under long dark lashes. "Or we can go naked, of course. It's supposed to be very healthy."

"It's all designed to make life simple," Mr. Wilberforce explained. Mona and Hugo sighed and rolled their eyes heavenward. "Having a closetful of clothes means decisions, competition, maintenance—wasted hours. Wearing these means we don't have to think about what we're going to wear in the morning. They're comfortable, attractive, and they don't need ironing. It's the same with our regime. We lead busy lives in the city—too much work, too much food, too much drink, too much everything."

"Too much fun, he means," Mona put in.

"When my wife inherited the Point, I decided to make it a haven of simplicity," Wilberforce continued expansively. "A place for rest and renewal. We have a set of rules here, and we follow them to the letter."

"Do we ever," Mona said, and leaned toward Stryker. He could smell her perfume, even above the heady fumes of the brandy. "No red meat. No newspapers or telephones—"

"Except the one in the kitchen for emergencies and ordering supplies," Hugo interrupted.

"In bed by ten o'clock, up at six," Mona went on. "Orange juice and oatmeal with bran, followed by an hour's workout in the gym, or a swim. Then a massage. Then utter boredom until lunch—lettuce and things. Then more utter boredom until dinner. Then the highlight of the day, our finest moment. *One* alcoholic drink. We can have whatever we like—but only one."

"Shouldn't even have that," muttered Mr. Wilberforce. "I've been reconsidering that rule, and—"

"Well, we have to have *something* to look forward to," Mona said with a slightly shrill edge. "I mean, I can't even wear makeup here."

"You don't need it," her father said. "Does she?" he demanded of Stryker.

"Uh—no. Of course not," Stryker said automatically.

"We can read, of course. Or watch films on the closed-circuit video. Or listen to music," Hugo said.

"Big deal," Mona said. "*You're* still recovering from New York. Wait until you've been here fifty times. I've *seen* all the videos, I've *heard* all the records."

Hugo glanced at her unsympathetically. "I paint my frustrations away, but Mona just moans."

"You know you'll feel better for coming here," Mr. Wilberforce said in a smug tone.

"That's the most annoying part," Mona sighed. "We do."

Mr. Wilberforce nodded, accepting this as tribute. "Mind you, Hugo was very naughty to slip out to that party—"

Hugo grinned. "Wow—what a devil I am. I even ate a canapé."

"—but when he returned I discovered that we *have* made a serious mistake here," Mr. Wilberforce said. "For example, our fence—"

"It's not really to keep anyone out," Mona explained. "It's to keep me in. Otherwise I'd run screaming into town and buy up every Reese's Peanut Butter Cup and Clark Bar they stock."

"We don't mean to offend people by keeping to ourselves," Mr. Wilberforce continued. "It's only because of our regime. If we're distracted—and we are easily distracted—the whole thing falls apart. Perhaps if they realize that—"

"I'll tell them," Stryker said. The brandy was beginning to have its effect. Why, the Islanders had the Wilberforces all wrong. "I'll explain about the . . . the . . . health-farm bit. Sounds very sensible to me." Anything would have sounded sensible to him, between his exhaustion and his relief at not having been shot at or turned over to those damned dogs.

"It's because you have to book so far ahead to get into one of those snobby health farms that Daddy got the idea for this place," Mona said. "We can come here anytime, with or without guests, and still get the same benefits." She added without enthusiasm, "Isn't that wonderful?"

"Needless to say, my daughter would prefer one of the fashionable spas," the old man said with a scowl. "Ridiculous places—everyone dressing up in designer clothes and wearing their diamonds in the swimming pools. No, thank you. *I* want privacy and quiet. That's why I'm absolutely against this nonsense with the fens."

"Who?" Must be someone I haven't met yet, Stryker thought.

"The marshlands . . . what do they call it?" Hugo was struggling.

"*Oh.* You mean the *swamp*," Stryker said. "We call it the Mush." He heard himself say "we" and realized he had just crossed the line from Visitor to Islander. Dammit, sucked in again.

"Doesn't matter what they call it," Mr. Wilberforce said in a boardroom tone. "It's what it *stands for* that matters."

"Here we go," muttered Mona.

"It's one of the reasons I chose to create this place. That marsh is our insurance against intrusion, our barrier against the noise and conflict of the world outside." Mr. Wilberforce said in a rising tone. "We have the bay before us, and the swamplands—"

"The Mush," Mona said, wrinkling her nose.

"—behind us, and therefore we are protected from anything that dares to despoil our peace. We have perfected the Point, and dammit, we have a right to enjoy it! All we ask is to be left *alone*."

"Now I see why you have those dogs and the armed guards patrolling the grounds," Stryker said.

There was a silence.

Mr. Wilberforce seemed to come back from a great distance. He lowered his head and stared at Stryker from beneath his eyebrows. "Not at all. They are there because of . . . things," he growled.

Hugo glanced at his sister and spoke quickly. "Father means we have a lot of valuable artwork here. Major investments, most of them."

Stryker looked around. In keeping with Wilberforce's claim to be pursuing an ascetic life, it was stark in *design*, all right: rough-plastered white walls, exposed beams, and bare floorboards. But the furniture was deeply upholstered in soft glove leather. The huge abstract paintings were full of vibrant, even violent, color. True, there were no carpets in the room. Instead, glowing long-shag rugs islanded the polished floorboards, each one clearly a unique piece from some master weaver's loom. The bookshelves held leather-bound novels, the glass in his hand was hand-cut crystal, and the fireplace was for effect only—under-floor heating warmed the boards beneath his bare feet. All in all, it was the fanciest and most expensive "plain" room he'd ever seen.

"And people," Mr. Wilberforce added darkly.

Again the glance between brother and sister. "Sometimes we have guests who are quite famous," Mona said, with an overly casual tone. "Politicians, actors, that sort of thing. They need protection."

Uh-huh, Stryker thought.

Sure.

Maybe what they needed protection from was Daddy.

When he'd first been brought into their presence, dripping and exhausted, Mr. Wilberforce had been friendly and welcoming, amused by the saga of the "shipwreck." Then there had come the soap-box outburst about the swamp, and now he was scowling into his drink. He looked up suddenly. "I got carried away, didn't I?" he asked with a boy's grin. "I do that sometimes. Sorry."

"You obviously feel as strongly about it as the other Islanders," Stryker said carefully. He had the distinct feeling he should be careful here.

Wilberforce nodded. "I do, I do. Not many places left in the world where a man can truly relax. You have to make an effort, you see, to cut yourself off these days. Some men go into the desert or climb mountains—but if they have people depending on them that's irresponsible, in my book. I thought that here I had found the perfect compromise—I can be isolated, but I can also get back to the city quickly should some problem arise. So if anyone attempts to crowd me out—well, I shall fight that. People regret crossing me. I didn't start out in life a rich man, and I've learned how to protect myself on the way up. I may have made some enemies in the process, which is unfortunate, but I have also made some powerful friends who may be able to help. Tell your people I'm on their side against Bobcat."

"I *did* tell them, Father," Hugo said.

"Doesn't hurt to say it again," the old man told him.

"Do you know who's behind Bobcat?" Stryker asked.

"Not yet, but I soon will," Wilberforce said airily. "I have people working on it."

"Will you let us know when you find out anything?"

Wilberforce nodded, but made no promises.

Stryker suddenly felt he'd been there far too long. He glanced up at the bizarrely asymmetric bronze clock over the fireplace and eventually managed to work out the time. "Well," he said, "if your bedtime is ten o'clock, then I'm keeping you up. Thanks again for the rescue."

"I'll get your clothes out of the dryer," Mona said, rising with him. "Come on."

Stryker said good-bye to Hugo and Mr. Wilberforce, then followed the blonde out of the room. One of the nicer tailing jobs he'd had, he thought to himself, as they went down the stairs, along a bare hall, and into a room that proved to be as well-equipped as any commercial laundry. It seemed a lot of equipment just to wash tracksuits and bed linen, he thought.

"You mustn't mind Daddy," Mona said, as she went to a dryer and extracted his clothes—wrinkled but dry. "He's only been on the regime for a few days, and it makes him depressed until the toxins are out of his body." She held up his trousers and shook them. "You don't want to put these back on," she said. "They'd be all itchy." She looked up and seemed to see him for the first time. She took a long breath, and smiled. "I hate itchy things against my skin, don't you?"

"Well . . . I guess . . ."

"That's why I made Daddy get these silk tracksuits for us instead of boring old cotton." She rubbed his hand along her side and over one hip. "See? Much nicer than that utility one Brody gave you."

"It's fine. I'll return it in the morning," he said, reaching for his clothes.

She held them close to her, and he stared at her, waiting. She looked into his eyes, and then smiled. Uh-oh, he thought. Game time, apparently. "Want to see the gym?" she asked abruptly.

"It's late. Maybe another—"

"It's just here." She was away and through a door before he could stop her. There was nothing to do but follow, if he wanted his trousers back.

The gym was as well-equipped in its way as the laundry. There was some equipment there that even the Police Athletic Association couldn't afford. Mona was moving fast, past the gleaming steel-and-leather structures, and through another door. He had no option but to follow, but he was beginning to wonder if his old chinos and sweatshirt were worth it.

"This is where we come for our massages," Mona said, leaning against a leather-topped table. "Greta has a light hand with soufflés but a strong hand with us."

Ah, thought Stryker. The lady in the kitchen *does* play other roles in this little setup.

Mona put her hands on either side of her and hiked herself up onto the massage table. To do so, she had to put his clothes down, and he snatched them up before she could grab them again.

"Very nice," he said. "Well, thanks again for—"

"I love a massage, don't you?" she asked, lying back on the leather and stretching luxuriously. "Daddy says I'm half cat because I love to be petted."

She was very beautiful and very sexy and he wished to hell he'd stayed under the dock, dogs or no dogs. He judged her to be about nineteen, educated by Hollywood, but not very bright, and very, very bored. She looked at him from under her long lashes. "Don't you love to be touched and stroked all over? Everywhere?" She ran her hands over her body, sliding them between her thighs, and arching her back. "Mmmmmm," she murmured.

"I prefer a cold shower," he said, rather more loudly than he'd intended.

She opened her eyes wide. "You've *had* a cold shower," she said. "Out there, in the rain. You didn't look like you enjoyed it very much." She sat up and dropped one leg over the edge of the table. Then she raised her other knee

and rested her chin on it, reaching out to tug at his
tracksuit waistband. "We don't have to give up *everything*
when we're here, you know," she murmured.

"Maybe you should," he said. "Abstinence makes the
heart grow stronger."

She glared at him. "You sound like Hugo," she snapped.
And then she pouted. He supposed that was inevitable—
once it had been Marilyn, now it was Madonna.

"Look," he said weakly. "I'm an engaged man."

"Oh, pooh," she said.

Well, it was a point of view.

"And I've just been shipwrecked," he added.

Fortunately, that struck her as funny. "Aren't you going to
say you're old enough to be my father?" she giggled.

He drew himself up. Tucking his clothes under his arm,
he turned toward the door. "I was saving that for an
emergency," he said, and walked out. Her giggles followed
him all the way down the hall.

When he finally reached the road, he was more exhausted
than he'd been when the guards dragged him out of the
water. It was hard to say which had been the more
frightening—the dogs or Mona Wilberforce. But he certainly felt a lot safer now that he was on the far side of the
redwood fence.

11

"But why should they have guard dogs there?" Kate asked for the tenth time.

"I told you—the place is full of valuable stuff," Stryker said, stifling a sneeze as he lay soaking in the hot bathwater.

He had returned to the cottage a weary man, expecting to be welcomed with open arms—but had instead been greeted by the sight of Don Robinson and Len Cotman starting to swing their boats out into the canal in order to join Kate in a search for his drowning or drowned body. When they saw him, they looked relieved and began to reverse back into their respective boat houses. He noted they were both in their pajamas. Their wet pajamas.

He tried to explain to them, but they just grinned and said they were glad he was okay, and ran back indoors, as if this kind of thing were a normal occurrence on the Island. Perhaps it was.

After a quick call to the Coast Guard to cancel her previous somewhat hysterical plea for assistance, Kate gave him a top-of-the-voice lecture on boatmanship and taking orders, followed by tears of relief, a painfully enthusiastic rubdown (no velvet glove), and then the promise of supper after his bath.

Now she sat on the edge of the tub, hearing once again the stirring tale of his bravery and resourcefulness in Evading the Monster Mutts. He left out the part about evading the Dangerous Damsel.

"What were these paintings like, then?"

"Very big, very abstract. Like that thing in the English Department foyer—you know, the purple-and-orange one that looks like the floor of a casualty ward on Saturday night."

Kate glared at him. "That was painted by a departing professor of art in 1959. He now lives in California, has a show once a year at which his pictures are snapped up by millionaires and corporations for ridiculously huge prices."

"All art prices are ridiculous," Stryker muttered, having once spent six months taking part in an art-fraud investigation.

"I am told by Dr. Stark that the god-awful thing to which you refer so scathingly is now insured for over two hundred and fifty thousand dollars," Kate said rather smugly.

"Then somebody's getting ripped off," Stryker said. "Why the hell don't they sell it and use the money to put a new roof on the department? That leak in the corner of your office has been dripping for over a year now, you told me. You showed me the mushroom, for crying out loud."

"I'm very proud of that mushroom—it's a symbol of life triumphant over adversity." She threw the sponge at him.

"It's a sign of lousy building maintenance," Stryker grumbled. "Anyway, that's obviously why they have these damned dogs."

Kate eyed him. "And the men with the guns? Why are they there?"

He explained about the Reese's Peanut Butter cups.

"She sounds like an idiot," Kate said, going toward the door. "They all do."

"Well, they're a bit nuts, I agree, but they seemed okay," Stryker said. "They were damned nice about me creeping around under their dock."

"Well, why not? For goodness' sake, you had a perfectly legitimate reason for being on their grounds, didn't you? Stupid, but legitimate. You were a shipwrecked mariner in distress."

"That's for sure," Stryker said, rubbing his aching muscles.

"Well, then." She turned at the door. "Are you certain that's all that happened while you were there?"

He concentrated on soaping his foot. "What else would have happened?"

"I don't know—you seemed kind of funny about it."

"I told you—they gave me one of their tracksuits and a glass of brandy. They insisted on drying my clothes for me, and then I came back. I'm sorry I didn't ring you, but they don't have a phone, and I didn't think that I would be so long. Okay?"

"Mmmm." She regarded him thoughtfully. "You seem to have picked up quite a sunburn today."

"I am aware of the state of my nose," Stryker said, with as much dignity as he could muster, being nude, exhausted, and under attack.

"In fact, if I didn't know you better—and come to think of it, I don't know you better—I'd say you were blushing. I have an instinct, you know."

"Yeah, I know. An instinct for melodrama, and for imagining mystery where there is none. You're as bad as your friend Daria."

Kate had come back into the bathroom and was busy at the washbasin. "You mean you still don't believe her, is that it?"

"As I've said all along, I am reserving judgment until— yeeoww!" The water she dumped over him was icy cold. She stood over him, holding the pitcher she used for hair-washing, and smiled an equally icy smile.

"Never underestimate the power of an instinct," she said, and walked out.

During the night, the storm continued to hover over the Island. Lightning flickered almost continually at one point, and thunder echoed back and forth across the bay, each clattering crack louder than the one before. The waves kicked up over the breakwater, but despite Stryker's conviction that he had swum through hell, there was more sound than fury in the storm. When it was at its peak, the ground actually shook with the reverberations of each successive roll of thunder. The rain came and went in showers as clouds dispensed their various contents.

Kate lay in bed, watching the lightning through the windows, enjoying the feeling of warmth and safety within the cottage. Stryker slept beside her, oblivious to the noise, save once—when a particularly loud and sharp crack seemed to rip the air apart. He sat up, said "Whoa!" and then fell back onto the pillow again, sound asleep. Kate waited for further comment, but none came.

She sensed a certain reticence in his story of shipwreck and rescue, and suspected it had to do with the girl, Mona. Blondes named Mona were a *known* menace—she'd had one in a class once, who had rendered half the male students non compos mentis. And that had been more than sunburn on his cheeks, she was sure of it. Perhaps she would change her attitude toward the Wall—if it kept pert little blondes inside, it was definitely a good thing.

The dinghy sounded repairable, but the outboard might be another story. She'd have to see it first. Tomorrow she'd walk along to the Wilberforce gate and claim it. She would also take a good hard look at this Mona creature.

No matter what Stryker said about them, she was still suspicious of the Wilberforces. During the entire time the old Peacock cottage was being demolished and their big new house was being constructed at the end of the Island, the Wilberforces had apparently been unwilling to compromise in respect of the other residents, whose lives they were undoubtedly making difficult and downright unpleasant. They had indicated—or their lawyers had—that they had no wish to mingle or communicate in any way with the peasants who clustered around their gate. The Island road was a public right-of-way, and they had as much right to use it for access as did anyone else.

They did "apologize" for the inconvenience.

Since the house had been completed they had lived in splendid isolation. They themselves didn't even *use* the access road now. They left that to the servants. The Wilberforces themselves always voyaged to and from their property on their boat. And they never spent long periods here, according to the other residents. Visits of more than two weeks were rare.

So maybe the story about a retreat for rest and rehabilitation was true. But she didn't have to believe it if she didn't want to, did she?

She turned over and looked at Stryker. His nose was blistered at the tip, and his hair had dried every which way. There was a bruise forming on one shoulder—the same one that bore the scar of a recent bullet wound—and his hands looked raw and sore. He had quite a noble face in repose, she decided. Too bad he was such a stubborn bastard. She socked him gently on the unbruised shoulder, but he only muttered and flailed back feebly at her, missing by a mile. He didn't wake up at all—the response was automatic, if weak. A cop's reflexes stirred him, even in sleep.

Too bad they weren't working so well when he was awake. He thought the Wilberforces were "nice," and neither he nor Matt seemed to be taking Daria seriously, especially now that everybody else had admitted having been bothered one way or another by—presumably—the advance guard of Bobcat Investments, whoever they proved to be. And what were they going to do about *that?*

"Oh, the hell with it, as Granny used to say," Kate mumbled. "I'll cry tomorrow, as Scarlett said. All's well that ends well. It's always darkest before you fall off the mountain... No smoke without matches... there's many an Armenian streetcar... said the camel..." Her voice faded. Eventually, with the thunder still sulking and muttering in the distance, she curled against Stryker's solid sunburned back and fell asleep.

* * *

In the morning the dawn light was clear and strong—the air cleansed by the storm. Few clouds were in the sky, and the day seemed to burst upon the sleeping Island in one glorious flare. Its brightness touched the windows of the cottages, the scatter of garden furniture on the lawns, a few toys left out, and the thick golden pelt of the Robinsons' dog as it sniffed its way along its morning circuit. Its identity and license tags jingled merrily as it trotted beside the breakwater, and its bright eyes missed nothing, because it was a young and healthy dog who found everything in life extremely interesting.

Particularly the dead man lying on the lawn in front of the Lattimer place.

That was new.

That called for a bark or two.

12

What the hell is that muttering? Who's giving a party at"—Stryker squinted at the alarm clock beside the bed—"at seven-twenty in the goddamn morning?"

Kate was already struggling into her slippers, one of which had sneakily scuttled under the bed during the night. She lurched to the dormer window and bent to one side to peer through the glass toward the source of disturbance.

"It's down past the Robinsons'—people in their bathrobes . . . I can't really see what's going on. Oh, there's Matt Gabriel with Don Robinson . . . and a young man who looks familiar—now, that *can't* be George Putnam. The last time I saw . . . well, I guess it must be. He's got some yellow tape . . ."

Stryker lay on his back staring at the sloping ceiling as she described a scene that, with each added detail, was growing more and more familiar to him. No, he thought. Please, no, I'm on vacation . . . .

"They're all looking at something on the ground, covered by a tarpaulin. Matt is lifting up a corner of it. Oh. Jack, I think . . . oh, no."

"Let me guess. It's a body." Stryker spoke in a flat voice. Kate turned and stared at him. "How did you know?"

He rubbed his eyes and sat up, swinging his legs over the side of the bed and sitting there, hunched and scowling, elbows on knees, head on hands. "Because I don't hear any music, so it's not a circus parade. And I don't hear laughter, so it's not somebody's dog doing tricks. And I don't hear anybody shouting, so it's not a snake-oil salesman or a politician asking for votes. That leaves disaster. In my experience, it takes quite a disaster to bring people out in their pajamas at seven in the morning. Probably somebody drowned in that storm last night. It *could* have been me," he finished in a pointed tone.

Kate was still looking out the window, her tense figure outlined by the early-morning light. Suddenly she relaxed. "It's a man," she said.

He was scratching his head vigorously, and missed it. "What?"

"I said, it's a man."

"You sound relieved."

Her voice was small. "I was afraid it was Daria."

He was silent, staring at the wall, then he lay back down and pulled up the quilt. "I'm going back to sleep."

She came over to the bed and knelt on one side. He felt the mattress dip, but ignored it. "You can't just lie there."

"Why not?"

"Because . . . because . . . don't you want to find out what happened? Don't you want to help?"

He turned his head slightly, and spoke over his shoulder. "Kate, you said Gabriel was there, didn't you? And a deputy?"

"Yes, but . . ."

"Gabriel seemed like a nice, intelligent guy. I'm sure he can handle it. The last thing he'd want is me horning in."

"But you know all about murder."

"You don't know it's murder. More likely an accident. Or even suicide. Murder isn't as common as all that, and you know it. If I *only* worked Homicide, I'd be pretty bored, even in the city. No, this is Gabriel's business, not mine. I'd only be in the way, and a pain in the ass, besides. How would you feel about Betty Crocker coming in and watching you bake a cake? Come to think of it, why *not* bake a cake or something? Pancakes. Coffee. Orange juice." He reached back blindly, and grabbed her pillow to put over his head.

"But—there's a *dead man* on the grass..."

"GO AWAY!"

"Huffy, huffy," she said. She put on her robe and gave her hair a quick brush, then descended the narrow stairway. Opening the front door, she went out onto the screened porch and looked down the lawns toward the crowd, which had thickened considerably in the past few minutes. The morning air was fresh and cool, and the lake glittered silver to the horizon. The trees whispered softly overhead. A fat robin struggled with a worm underneath the picnic table.

And there was a body on a neighbor's lawn.

How incongruous, to wake to death on such a beautiful morning, in such a beautiful place. But then, as Jack had once told her, murder is never a convenient caller.

The group on the lawn was relatively quiet. The faces she could see looked serious, even horrified—but not grief-stricken. Not a friend or relative, then. No one to comfort, no help to offer. Just a stranger lying dead. Drowning? Heart attack? Murder? She yearned to go and find out, but something held her back—a kind of loyalty to Jack, who had stated his position, damn him, and left her caught between wanting to know all about it but having to be professionally aloof on his behalf. It was infuriating.

She was brushing her teeth when the tentative knock sounded on the back porch. Sticking her head around the bathroom door, toothbrush still in place, she looked down the length of the porch and saw George Putnam standing nervously on the back step.

After a few minutes' conversation through the screen door, she went back upstairs and poked Stryker in the shoulder.

"Wha'?" he mumbled. "Breakfast ready?"

"No. Matt would like you to come over."

He seemed to stop breathing for a minute, then sighed. He pushed her pillow off his head and opened one bleary eye. It was not a happy sight. "Very funny."

"His deputy is downstairs. They'd like your advice."

"My advice is everybody go home and go back to bed. If the guy is dead, he'll still be dead this afternoon."

"Jack." Her voice was tight with annoyance. She had grown to accept his casual attitude toward violent death. In its way, she understood it to be a defense. Every cop she had met was the same—although at least Jack's partner, Tos, still had an embarrassingly delicate stomach. But this was on her Island. This was death on Paradise!

"Please, Jack—get up."

"You did this, didn't you?" he said accusingly. "You went out and killed somebody and left the body lying around so I would have to get out of bed at some ungodly hour and say what a great job you've done."

That didn't deserve a response. Kate turned and went back downstairs, leaving him to mutter and lurch around looking for his pants. He staggered down the stairs a few minutes later and glared at the deputy, who was now standing on the front porch, watching the crowd. "Well?" Stryker growled. "Have I got a minute to brush my teeth?"

The deputy whirled around and regarded him with some dismay and a little awe. "Sure. He's not going anyplace."

"My sentiments exactly," Stryker grumbled. He raised his voice as he went through the dining room. "I don't suppose there's any . . ."

"On the table," Kate said, from the kitchen. "And you don't deserve it."

He picked up the coffee cup and swallowed a scalding mouthful. "What the hell did *I* do?" he asked. There was no reply. Muttering a little more, he had a quick wash and brush, then went out to the deputy. He held out his hand. "Jack Stryker."

"Deputy George Putnam, how-do." George looked at the older man with admiration. "Are you really in Homicide?"

Stryker glanced toward the kitchen, whence came sounds of banging pots and pans. "At the moment, I seem to be in hot water," he said. "Come on, let's have a look."

The small crowd was an obedient one—staying well back on either side of the strip of lawn, about thirty feet wide, which had already been marked off by yellow tape.

George and Stryker excused themselves through and, walking carefully, approached Matt Gabriel and the covered mound at his feet.

"Sorry to drag you in on this, but I'd appreciate your opinion," Matt said. Like most of the men present, he was unshaven. His thick brown hair was tousled over his forehead. Stryker wasn't certain what he envied most, the man's height or the abundance of his hair. He himself was just over regulation stature, and his prematurely silver hair was receding steadily, year by year. Standing beside Gabriel, he felt like the old wizened cowboy who holds the young gunslinger's jacket for him. Gabriel, however, was looking bemused rather than superior. "It's a messy one," he told Stryker.

"Oh?" Stryker hunkered down and lifted an edge of the tarpaulin that had been laid over the corpse. "Jesus," he breathed. "Looks like a shotgun blast right in the chest."

Matt signed. "Yeah. And at point-blank range, too. Not much spread at all. Really tore him apart inside."

Stryker considered, turning his head one way and then the other so as to gauge the damage. "Not a hell of a lot of blood," he commented.

Matt shrugged. "He's been lying face-up to the rain. I figure most of it got washed away."

Stryker stood up. "You know him?"

"Never saw him before, far as I can remember."

"Anybody else recognize him?"

"No." Gabriel's voice was strange.

"Any identification on the body?"

Gabriel nodded. He looked absolutely miserable now. "Wallet in his hip pocket. Driver's license says he's Michael Grey."

Stryker looked down again at the face of the dead man.
Both Kate and Daria had called Michael Grey "handsome"
—and certainly the features of the dead man were regular
enough. The blind eyes were blue, startlingly so, considering the blackness of his thick and curling hair. The nose and
chin were strong, the cheekbones high—movie-star materi-
al, all right—except for the mouth. Even in the slackness of
death there were lines around the full, sensual lips that
showed they had been all too frequently twisted in a sneer.
There was a gold earring in the corpse's left ear, several
gold rings on each carefully manicured hand, a Rolex
Oyster on one wrist, and a strange bracelet on the other.

Stryker bent down again and looked at it. It was made of
tiny links forming the bodies of two snakes, repeatedly
entwined, each grasping the other's tail. Each tail bore a
rattle. The bracelet, too, was gold.

Robbery was certainly not the motive here. Stryker
straightened up, took a breath, held it, let it out. "Have
you spoken to Daria? Has she come out, seen it?"

"I spoke to her—but I couldn't bring her out. Not with
all the people standing around. I reckoned there was time
enough for that later."

"How did she take it?"

Gabriel added puzzlement to his expression. "She was
very calm."

"Did you ask her?"

"You mean, did I ask her if she shot him? No."

"You'll have to ask her."

"I know that."

And that's where I come in, Stryker realized. The poor
bastard can't bring himself to do it. "Does Miss Shanks own
a shotgun?"

"Daria says no."

"We had a guy in the office, day before yesterday,"
George Putnam put in. "Complaining that the old lady told
Daria to shoot him when he was making a perfectly ordi-
nary call."

"He was trying to get her to sell her house," Matt said. "That's not 'ordinary' to an Islander."

"Well, he said she told Daria to 'get the shotgun.'"

"Miss Clary has always done that, she says it all the time. That doesn't mean anything," Matt said in annoyance.

"Daria says there isn't one."

"Well, she would, wouldn't she?" George said stubbornly.

Stryker looked from one to the other. "Well, was there a shotgun, or wasn't there?"

Matt sighed. "A lot of people up here have shotguns. Don Robinson says he thinks there was one on the Shanks place, once. He didn't want to say it, but he's a truthful man. Says if it's still around it's an old one, probably rusted up. Aunt Clary's brother had one years ago to hunt duck, and she never throws anything away."

"And her brother was Daria Grey's father," George put in.

"I see. So you think maybe Daria Grey got out her father's old shotgun and shot her husband, is that it?" Stryker said brusquely. There seemed no point in pussy-footing around it any longer.

Gabriel sighed and looked out over the lake. "Doc Willis is on his way over. He'll do the death certificate, and then the body'll have to go over to the hospital at Hatchville. County medical examiner'll do the autopsy. Thing is, should I call in the state cops, or what?"

Stryker knelt, briefly lifted and then replaced the tarpaulin, and looked up at the giant towering over him. Glancing around, he saw people's feet—not in the usual polished shoes or beat-up sneakers he might expect to see in the city, and not even in deck shoes, or sandals, which were more likely out here—but in bedroom slippers. Wet bedroom slippers, at that. It lent a novel note, he felt, to an old situation. He stood up and moved closer to Gabriel, speaking quietly. "I don't know. Do you have a choice?"

"As a matter of fact, I do."

"Well, state has really good forensic people, of course— they could give you a lot of backup that way."

"They could also give me a lot of crap," Gabriel said. "Asking them for help is more or less stepping off the plate and letting them bat, right?"

"I'd say so. But then, I was always a picky bastard."

Gabriel nodded. "So I hear."

Stryker raised an eyebrow. "Oh?"

"I phoned somebody I know down in the city the minute I heard I had a body out here."

"Oh?" Stryker said again.

"Well, hell, I don't know you, do I? For all I knew—"

"All right, all right. Who did you talk to?"

"Guy named Bannerman? I went to college with him—"

Bannerman was the medical examiner in Grantham, and a friend. Even roused from a sound sleep Bannerman had probably said nice things about him, Stryker thought gloomily. Whereas if Gabriel had talked to Captain Klotzman, he might have thought twice about dragging Stryker into this. Damn, why couldn't he have called Klotzman?

"Bannerman said you're kind of choosy and go your own way, which the brass doesn't like, but your record runs interference for you."

"Did he mention I was an awkward son of a bitch?"

Gabriel smiled. It was an effort. "That, too."

"And you still called me out here?"

"Look, I'm good with drunks and traffic and lost kids. I've had a fair few deaths to deal with, but they were mostly car crashes and heart attacks. I've had some killings, but never one that needed real working out, as you might say. I'm not proud—I'm willing to learn."

"I'm on vacation."

"I know that, and I'm sorry to be asking. Your choice."

Stryker stuck his hands into the back pockets of his chinos and stared out over the water, watching a gull dip and curve against the early-morning sky. "Only when you need me," he finally said. "I'm a little washed out at the moment."

"Fair enough." Gabriel nudged the tarpaulin with a booted foot. "Don Robinson called me. His dog found this, and he put the tarp over it. Kept everyone off until I got here, and they've all been pretty good about staying back. Do you think you could help us do a quick once-over of the scene?"

"You'd be satisfied with that?"

"I think so. I mean, there's not a hell of a lot of subtle details about a shotgun in the chest, is there? We've had two weeks hot and dry. There was enough rain to wet the surface last night, but it's nowhere's near soft enough to take a footmark, especially with this grass so long."

Stryker agreed. "Outdoor sites are a bitch, and this is worse than most, because it's unprotected. We can look over the ground, sure. And we might find a bit of this or that—but it was windy last night, which means a lot of stuff blew off the grass and a lot of other stuff blew onto it, which could confuse the hell out of us. We have great forensic teams in the city, and I really admire their work. But in a situation like this you have to be practical. We can take samples from his clothes—stuff like that. But figuring angles or hunching around looking for matchsticks is a job for a lot of men with a lot of time. You've got to go one way or the other. The fact is, he's dead as hell. 'When' he was killed is presumably during or after last night's thunderstorm. It was light until nine-thirty or so, and nobody noticed him then. Also, the ground is wet underneath him, so presumably he was killed after the rain had started. I don't think we need to be any more precise than that right now. The coroner might be tighter on the time, but it isn't always as easy as Quincy makes out. As for clues—people watch a lot of television, so they know about leaving clues. We can crawl around a little, but unless we're incredibly lucky it won't tell us who did it, or why, which I guess is probably more to the point. I assume you looked for the shells?"

"Went over the lawn real quick before the people came out. Nothing."

"Gun?"

"No sign."

"Well, in that case I'm afraid you'll never get the coroner

to agree to suicide," Stryker said. "Unless we come up with something to indicate otherwise, it's murder, and Daria Grey is your prime suspect, whether you like it or not."

Matt's eyes were bleak, and his voice was rough. "Daria has been begging for help right along. She *said* he was tormenting her. That he'd been threatening her for months. She told everybody he was making her life hell, but nobody would believe her."

Stryker looked down at the mound under the tarpaulin. "I guess habits die harder than people."

"What do you mean?"

"I mean he's still a threat—to whoever killed him."

13

Daria Grey was sitting by her aunt's bedside, completely still, hands folded, head down. She said nothing when Stryker and Matt Gabriel entered the cottage, but Aunt Clary had no hesitation in letting them know how she felt.

"Have you sent for the garbage truck yet?" she demanded. "I hate to have trash lying on my lawn."

"Aunt Clary, please," Daria said. "That won't help."

"We'd appreciate it if you would come out and make a positive identification, Mrs. Grey," Stryker said. He glanced out the window. "Most people have left now. It will just take a minute."

Aunt Clary's bright-blue eyes swung to him, and he felt momentarily pierced. "And who might you be, young man?"

The "young" man was some compensation for her irascible tone. He guessed the source of her anger was a simple one—she was afraid for her cub. "My name is Jack Stryker."

"He's a police lieutenant down in the city, Miss Shanks," Matt Gabriel explained. "He's had a lot of experience with murder."

"Murder? What do you mean, murder? Didn't you say

that fool boy finally shot himself?" Aunt Clary demanded of Daria.

"The man lying on the lawn has been blasted in the chest by a shotgun from nearly point-blank range," Stryker said harshly. "But we found no shells and no gun in the immediate vicinity. Logic makes that murder, not suicide."

Aunt Clary was annoyed. "And so naturally you think Daria shot him, I suppose? Damn fools."

Stryker looked at the girl. "Did you shoot the man on the lawn, Mrs. Grey?"

She lifted her head and looked him straight in the eye, which impressed him not at all. "No, I did not shoot him," she said in a flat, even voice.

Though he made no sound and did not move, Stryker sensed Matt Gabriel's relief. The question had been asked. Whether they should believe her or not remained to be seen. "Can you tell me what you did last night?" he asked her.

"After the residents' meeting, Mrs. Toby and Mrs. Norton came in for a cup of tea, but they didn't stay long because Aunt Clary was tired. I spent a while sitting with my aunt, then I went up to bed."

"Did you make any phone calls?"

"No," Daria said.

"Yes," Miss Shanks said at the same moment. Then, "Oh," when she realized what Daria had said.

"Well?" Stryker asked patiently.

Miss Shanks spoke first, with a sideways glance at her niece. "The phone rang about ten o'clock. Daria answered it."

"Oh, that," Daria said uneasily. "It was a wrong number."

"I see," Stryker said. "Then it wasn't a call from your husband?"

Daria's chin came up. "No, it wasn't. Just a wrong number."

"But he has been telephoning you, hasn't he?"

Daria glanced sideways at her aunt. "He did phone me

in New York a number of times. But I got an answering machine, so he stopped."

"Why would that stop him?"

"Because he wanted to hear me cry," she said simply. "Because it wasn't satisfying to leave a message and not know that I was upset by it. He wanted to *know* I was afraid."

"I see. But he didn't call you last night, or come here to see you?"

"No." Her voice was strained, and he had the feeling she was lying. Her aunt had stirred slightly at the girl's denial, but she had not spoken. That phone call. According to her and to her aunt, it was the only unusual thing that had happened last night. He'd be willing to bet it had been Michael Grey. But, short of calling her a liar, there was nothing he could do to prove it. He wondered what the position was with the local telephone system, and whether he could get at any records—then realized that was up to Gabriel. Even though he didn't want to be doing this, even though he was desperately trying to stay out of it for the sake of a little peace and quiet, the automatic impulses born of training and long experience were difficult to suppress. "Did you hear anything at all during the night?"

"The storm." It was an obvious answer.

"Nothing else?"

"No."

"Did you get up during the night at all? Look out of the window, perhaps? To have a look at the storm?"

"No."

"And neither did I," stated Miss Shanks firmly.

"Could you have?" Stryker asked, interested.

"My aunt has suffered a broken hip. It was pinned in place. She *can* stand, with a walker, but it is still painful and difficult for her," Daria explained. "That's why I've come back—to help her convalesce."

"And not to get away from your husband?"

"That, too, yes. And I thought I had, for a while. Then it started up again."

"Show him the picture," Miss Shanks said.

"Picture?" Matt and Stryker said, almost together.

Daria was staring at her aunt in dismay. "How did you know about the picture?"

Her aunt pointed toward the window beside her, which overlooked the rear porch. As with the Trevorne cottage, the front and rear enclosed porches had been later additions, creating the oddity of a window that looked into another room. In the Trevorne cottage the rear porch held a long trestle table to accommodate the large family dinners that had sometimes been held when relatives visited on weekends. In the Shanks cottage it was used for storage—presently for most of the furniture that had been moved from the dining room in order to accommodate Miss Clary's rented hospital bed. "I saw you pick it up, and I saw your face when you looked at it."

"When was this?" Matt asked.

"This morning," Daria said reluctantly.

"Can we see it, please?" Stryker asked.

"I tore it up. It's in the trash—under the sink."

Matt went out, but Stryker looked at the girl. "Why did you do that?" he asked. "You've been trying to prove that your husband was harassing you, haven't you?"

"Yes, but—"

"But you knew he was dead, so it didn't matter?"

"I *didn't* know he was dead—not then," Daria protested, with the first sign of animation she'd shown since they arrived. "I came down and went straight out to pick up the newspapers and the mail. The picture was underneath them. It was just—too awful to keep, that's all. I didn't want Aunt Clary to be upset." She glanced at her aunt, but the old woman was determinedly engrossed in a loose thread on her blanket. "It wasn't until a few minutes after that I heard the commotion of the lawn out front and went to see."

Gabriel returned with four pieces of crumpled paper, holding them wrapped in paper towels. He stood at the sideboard and fitted them together. When he had finished, he looked at the result and his fists clenched at his sides. Stryker stepped over to stand beside him.

The technique was beautiful—the subject was not. Apparently the late Michael Grey had been a fine draftsman, but a seriously perverted human being. The drawing was of a naked girl—very clearly Daria herself, despite the distortion of her agonized features—spread-eagled on a table and being literally cut to pieces by a group of hooded beings. At the head of the table was a throne on which sat a man, watching and smiling.

"Is this man your husband?" Stryker asked, pointing at the watcher.

"Yes. A self-portrait," Daria said thinly.

"I can't see it," complained Aunt Clary, leaning to one side and trying to peer between them.

"I think that's just as well, ma'am," Matt Gabriel said, gathering up the pieces and putting them into his jacket pocket. He was still handling them with paper towels, Stryker noted, and it was not because they were particularly stained—although there was a smear of tomato sauce on one piece.

"And that was on the porch this morning?"

"Yes."

"Was the outer door locked when you went to bed?"

"Yes. I lock all the doors and windows at night."

He glanced at the woman in the bed. "Did you hear anyone on the porch during the night?"

"No." She shook her head on the pillow. "I had a sleeping pill—I have one every night now. I didn't even know we'd had a thunderstorm last night until Daria told me about it."

"Do you own a shotgun, Miss Shanks?" Stryker asked abruptly.

"I told you, she doesn't," Daria said to Matt.

Stryker was gazing at the old woman, who was trying to avoid his eye. "Ma'am?" he asked again.

"My brother Clay had one," she finally admitted very slowly. "But it's out in the boat house, if it's anywhere. He never took it with him when he married—Daria's mama didn't hold with hunting. Probably just all rust by now." "Why didn't you tell me?" Daria protested.

"I only just remembered," the old woman said fretfully. "If they look they'll find it, so there's no point lying about it." She looked at Stryker and Matt Gabriel. "But it wasn't Daria shot him, you can be sure of that. She never. She *never*." Tears appeared and overflowed.

"Aunt Clary, please . . . it's all right," Daria said, getting up and wiping her aunt's cheeks with a tissue. "Don't be upset. Matt doesn't think I killed Michael, not for a minute. Do you, Matt?"

"Of course not," Matt Gabriel said loudly.

Too loudly.

And the silence after he spoke was even louder.

14

Matt Gabriel and Jack Stryker sat on Aunt Clary Shanks' steps, looking out over the lawn to the lake beyond. The tarpaulin still lay on the ground, but the body had been removed to the Hatchville Hospital morgue. Dr. Willis had pronounced the man to be "dead as a goddamn doornail, as any fool could plainly see." He was extremely annoyed at being called away from delivering triplets. He said he'd never delivered triplets, and now he probably never would have another chance. The county coroner would do an autopsy as soon as he could get around to it, but according to Willis, there had also been two drownings, a lightning strike, and a two-car pile-up with three dead during the storm. "Expect your boy here will be well down the list," he said, not without a trace of malicious satisfaction. (Triplets! And only four more years until retirement.)

Daria Grey had come out and they had peeled back the tarpaulin from the corpse's face—there was no need to reveal it further. Daria had gone white, nonetheless, but had not fainted. Her voice, when she'd managed to speak, had been no more than a whisper, audible only to Stryker and Matt Gabriel.

"Yes," she said. "That is Michael Grey."

When Matt had taken her arm and guided her back into the cottage, her steps had been as stiff as a puppet's, and the muscles in her face had been rigid with the effort of not screaming or weeping.

Stryker rubbed his face, wondering if he should worry about shaving or just let it go and see how far he could get toward a beard by the end of his vacation. That would go down well with Captain Klotzman, who was of the old school and considered beards the natural accompaniment to sandals and sedition. "How many men do you have in your command?" he asked.

Matt snorted. "In my 'command'? Are you kidding? We're full strength at the moment—which means eleven of us altogether. In winter we're down to five. George is my first deputy days, Charley Hart nights. I have Glen Hardwicke and Frank Boomer as permanent patrolmen, and in summer we take on some extras, usually college boys. Then there's Tilly Moss. She answers the phone, does the filing, and types up the paperwork because nobody but her can read our writing."

Stryker looked at him. "That's *it*?"

"That's it. You see, Blackwater County is kind of lopsided. The indigenous population is only about five thousand, but we have maybe three times that in the summer—mostly concentrated along the shore here. The rest is marsh, dunes, hills, forest, and farmland. Not much crime happens—the people come here to relax. I've got a few more men I deputize for crowd and traffic control during the special holiday weekends and the Town Carnival on Labor Day—four or five old-timers my father trusted, and a couple of younger men I know myself."

"They all local?"

"Yes, sure. Why?"

"You're going to need a lot of help if you want to keep this thing under control," Stryker said. "On a city homicide I have my sergeant and two detectives directly under me, plus about fifty to a hundred detectives I can put on duty for interviews, plus uniformed men to handle traffic and crowds, plus a forensic department, plus—"

"I get the idea," Matt said.

"Yeah." Stryker kicked the grass with the toe of his sneakers. "Thing is, you've got a lot of ground to cover on this. If Daria didn't shoot her husband—"

"She didn't," Matt said stubbornly.

"We'll see." Stryker sounded equally stubborn. "If I were you, I'd test her hands and face for powder traces. There's a fair amount of blow-back with a shotgun. I'd test the old lady, too."

Matt turned and stared at him. "Are you nuts?"

Stryker's control snapped. "Look, do you want my help on this or not? If it weren't for Kate nagging me, I wouldn't be here at all. I'm just as happy to forget the whole thing—go back and have my breakfast. Jesus Christ, you either do the job or you don't do it. And at this moment in time *everybody* is suspect—including Kate and me, by the way. All right, so the ID says it's Michael Grey. Daria claims it's him, but maybe she only wishes it was. Suppose it isn't. Suppose the guy is an old enemy of mine from the city, or an ex-lover of Kate's, or a burglar somebody else caught and shot and now is too scared to own up about. There's a lot of possibilities besides the obvious. All I can tell you is what you know already—just eliminate. Question and look and listen and keep eliminating until—as good old Sherlock used to say—what remains, no matter how unlikely, is the truth. Do you *want* the truth, or are you just interested in protecting Miss Big-Eyes in there?"

Matt stood up. "Go to hell."

Stryker stood up too. "My pleasure," he said, and started to walk away. He got as far as the Robinsons' lawn.

"Hey!" Matt caught up with him. "Look—I'm sorry. I want to do it right," he said awkwardly. "I've only been sheriff for a few years now—my father was sheriff here, and his father was sheriff before him. Kind of a family business, I guess you'd say. See, when I got out of college, I didn't really know what I wanted to do with my life. I drifted around for a while. Then, when my dad died, I decided to run for sheriff. It's mainly a peace-keeping job, and I figured I could handle it until I thought of something I wanted to do more. But, apart from some quickie state police courses when I first took over, and watching my old man most of my life, I've never really been trained for it. Contrary to general belief, I got my degree in philosophy. If you want to know about Wittgenstein, I'm your man. But as far as serious crime goes, I'm almost a virgin."

"No homicides?" Stryker asked in genuine surprise.

"Oh, sure. Some drunken killings, a few domestics, all pretty straightforward. Like I said before—nothing needing *real* investigation."

"This may be straightforward too," Stryker said, turning to face him. "The problem lies in the fact that you don't like the straightforward explanation much. You know, if she did it and you could get her to admit it, I don't think there would be a real problem. Her lawyer could make a case for provocation—plea-bargain it down to manslaughter, whatever—and probably get her off with a light sentence or even a suspended sentence and probation, depending on the judge. The trouble comes because she won't admit she killed him, and you won't, either."

"Because I don't think she did."

"Based on what?" Stryker crossed his arms and looked up at the big man.

Gabriel shrugged and turned to look out at the lake. "Because I just don't think she did, that's all."

"I see. There's sound, objective reasoning for you."

"I think that if she did, she *would* admit it. Given the background of his harassment, she would probably feel she was justified, and wouldn't be ashamed of it."

"Ah. The philosopher speaks. That's better, but still not hard evidence. So you are going to proceed on the assumption that a woman who has been harassed, threatened, and tormented by a possibly psychotic husband is *not* guilty of shooting him when you find him lying dead practically on her own front lawn?"

"I guess."

Stryker took a long deep breath, and then let it go. "Well, at least we know where you stand." He walked away a few steps, considered his shoelaces for a while, and then came back, his hands jammed down deep in his pant pockets. "Well, you'd better get Tilly to round up your part-time deputies, and add a few more. The press is going to get on to this pretty soon, because it's just the kind of thing they love, and summer is a slow-news time. Twenty-four hours from now Paradise Island is going to be overrun with serpents carrying a lot of nice apples to exchange for interviews, photographs, and quotes. Unless you've dealt with them before, you have no idea how cunning they can be—one casual comment can be twisted to make the nicest person sound like a real horse's ass. Believe me, I've done it and it's been done to me."

Matt looked around. "I guess we'd better close off the bridge."

Stryker nodded. "That will do for openers. In addition to fending off the media, there's going to be a lot of people to question and a lot of information to collect if you're going to insist on looking for a killer *other* than Miss Big-Eyes."

"Stop calling her that!"

Stryker stepped right up to him and poked him in the shirt button. "Look—my first advice to you is to *start* calling her that, or something like it, or you are going to get yourself tied up in a real bastard of a knot. Professional or casual, you're the law here, and the law is supposed to be objective, or the hell with the whole thing. You don't like it? Tough shit. You want my help on this, even a little bit? Then bite the bullet and do the job right. Or turn it over to the state police. Or let it go and pretend the guy was hit by goddamn lightning. I guess, being sheriff, you could do that. Depends on what kind of a sheriff you plan to be. Let me know what you decide. I need a shave and breakfast."

He turned away and went back to the Trevorne cottage. He stopped at the steps and turned back. "And don't let anybody else walk on the goddamn lawn." He slammed the porch door behind him as he entered.

Kate came running out of the kitchen. "What happened? Who was it? Are you going to—"

Stryker stopped on his way to the bathroom and glared at her, in the style of the late Jackie Gleason. "Don't start up with me, Alice—just don't start up with me." He marched on to the bathroom and slammed that door, too.

"Have you calmed down now?" Kate asked, as she set the waffles and bacon on the table and began to pour the coffee. She sat down and opened her napkin with a flourish, quite prepared to carry on arguing, but he was past that.

"The dead man is Michael Grey."

"Oh."

He speared a waffle and transferred it to his plate. "What do you think?" he asked.

"I think that you think that Daria killed him."

"You win the fuzzy pink dog," Stryker said, pouring syrup.

"But I don't agree with you."

"It would only be news if you did," Stryker said wryly.

"What does Matt Gabriel think?"

"He's keeping an open mind. In other words, he has a few holes in his head. The wind whistling through is confusing him."

"My goodness," Kate said in surprise. "I thought you liked him."

"I do. But he won't accept the obvious explanation."

"You never do, either."

"When an elephant sits in your lap, it's kind of hard to pretend it's a kitten," Stryker said. "As things stand, the case is purely circumstantial. Frankly, with the best will in the world, I don't think Gabriel is capable of making it into anything else—mainly because he doesn't want to."

"Well, he likes Daria. They're old friends."

"It's not that—it's simply that he's not equipped for any real investigation. He has two full-time deputies, named

George and Charley, a couple of other regulars whose names I can't remember, some college boys working during summer vacation, a woman named Tilly who handles the office work, and a few old buddies he calls in occasionally when he needs them. That's it and that's all."

"Yes, but—"

"He told me that if she did it, she would admit it and accept what was coming to her."

"Yes, she would."

"Oh? Well, how about this? How about her having planned this all along, set it up beforehand to look like that? She carefully tells us how her husband has tormented and threatened her, keeps begging for protection, keeps 'seeing' him—and then kills him in 'self-defense.' How about them apples?"

"That's diabolical."

He sighed, and picking up a piece of bacon, nodded. "And she, of course, is an angel."

"You don't like her."

"I neither like nor dislike her, she's a stranger to me. But I have to ask myself questions, Kate."

"Then ask yourself this: if what you say is true, why doesn't she admit doing it?"

"Maybe she will—eventually."

She glared at him for a few minutes, watching him cut bacon and waffles, drink coffee, sip orange juice, scratch his shoulder, wipe his chin, chew, stare out the window, spear another waffle from the platter, reach for the butter. "Maybe you'd better just let Matt get on with it," she finally said.

"Hey—who was it who dragged me out of bed this morning?" he protested.

"Yes, but... you're on vacation."

"Oh, you remembered finally, did you?" He was cross again.

"Well..."

He pointed an accusing finger at her. "Now *you're* scared, like Matt Gabriel. You think she did it, too."

"I do not!"

"Then why the sudden haste to get me off the case before I even get on it? Are you worried I might find evidence to prove it was premeditated murder?"

"No, I just think you need a rest." She began to gather up the dishes.

"I am not through eating yet. Sit down. *Sit down!*" he bellowed. She sat. He poured syrup onto his third waffle. "Now, then. Because he doesn't want to upset her, Gabriel hasn't searched her place for a gun yet. Her aunt says there's one in the boat house, which we will look for. She denies killing her husband—"

"Well, of course she—"

"*Shut up!*" He banged the table. "You have to make a decision right now, Kate. Do you want me to find out who killed this man or don't you?"

Her face lit up. "Then you *don't* think she—"

He raised his voice over hers. "Because it will mean I won't be around much for the next few days. Let's hope it's a few days, anyway. It could be the whole two weeks, come to think of it, if we solve it at all. The way things look at the moment, I'll have to help Gabriel question people and all the rest of it because the guy just doesn't have anybody and he's so tied up with worry about your friend Daria that he's not thinking straight, yet. If ever. Furthermore, it could boil up into a mess because I have no jurisdiction and he'll have to swear me in as a temporary deputy, I suppose, and there could be a legal problem there, and then—"

"But you'll be able to finish it quickly because you know—"

"AND THEN—at the end of it—we may find out Daria Grey did kill her husband, after all," he concluded.

"Oh."

He finished his last piece of waffle and his last piece of bacon and sat back. "Your choice," he said.

15

Stryker glared out at the lake. Kate had swept out of the cottage carrying a frozen casserole and sympathy down to Daria and Aunt Clary, refusing to discuss the situation further. It was up to him, she said.

Which meant she wanted him to go on but wouldn't say so in so many words—he'd known her long enough to read *that* one.

Well, he was prepared to go on—but not without help. He threw himself down on the couch, picked up the phone, and punched out a very familiar number.

"Hey, amico, how's it going?" he asked.

"I got hay fever," came the sepulchral tones of his recently wounded partner, Toscarelli. "It's not enough I have to go in the hospital for physiotherapy every day with that sadistic bastard, Sonderstrom, I also have hay fever. I never had it before, and now I get it, when I could do without. My mother keeps feeding me every three hours, I've gained at least twenty pounds. My nose runs, my gut rumbles, my legs ache, and I'm beginning to look forward to watching 'As the World Turns' every afternoon. Yesterday I was looking at knitting patterns. How do you think I'd look in a yellow-and-black-striped turtleneck?"

"Depending on the direction of the stripes, either a very fat bee or a very tall banana."

"You're right—maybe I'll go with beige after all," Tos said morosely. He and Stryker had been partners for years, the Odd Couple of the Grantham Police Department: Toscarelli huge, muscular, and as leisurely as a benign bear; Stryker shorter, thinner, faster, and usually in trouble. Toscarelli looked after him like an Italian Jewish mother, constantly reminding him to put on his coat, eat his lunch, and visit the dentist twice a year. Stryker had always behaved as if this constant gentle harassment was irritating. However, having been without it for some weeks, due to Tos's nearly dying in the line of duty, he found himself a little lost. What was more, he wasn't accustomed to *worrying* about Tos, he was accustomed to his *being there* when needed.

Like now.

"I didn't expect to hear from you," Tos said. "Aren't you supposed to be on vacation?"

"While I was trying to get a tan, somebody got both barrels of a shotgun in the chest," Stryker said.

"That was inconsiderate," Tos said. After a moment, he spoke again. "You're not serious?"

"I am."

"Honest to God, the minute I turn my back! What is it with you, some kind of jinx?"

"I'm beginning to think so," Stryker muttered.

Hearing the warning tone, Tos attempted a distraction. "How's Kate?"

"Kate is the reason I'm calling," Stryker said. "This guy that was killed was the husband of an old friend of hers, and she wants *me* to prove it was a mysterious stranger that did it rather than her friend."

"What's the matter—they haven't got cops up there?"

"They have a sheriff and a few deputies."

"A *sheriff?* Does he wear a white hat and ride a horse and everything?"

"No."

"How about a six-gun and a badge?"

"He's got a badge and a thirty-eight, just like you and me. He's all right."

"Does he play a guitar and sing to—"

Stryker broke in. "Look—this whole thing is a pain in the ass, all right?" he snapped. "I would ignore it entirely if Kate wasn't on my back about Daria Grey, who she insists is innocent."

"And is she?"

"How the hell should I know?"

"You're a professional detective, you're *supposed* to know," Tos pointed out expansively. "You're supposed to get hunches and gut feelings about such things. Strange moments of intuition and brilliant insights—"

"Jesus, are you sure *your* mind isn't acting up?"

"I do get these weird headaches," Tos acknowledged.

Silence.

When Stryker didn't respond to this opportunity for further badinage, Tos's voice changed. "Bad one, is it?"

"They're never fun," Stryker said wearily. "And this is worse because it's . . . well, it's pretty up here. Slow and peaceful and nice. People shouldn't get blown away here."

"Or anywhere."

"Or anywhere," Stryker echoed bleakly.

"Well, hell—let this hick sheriff get on with it, then," Tos said. "It's not your responsibility, for crying out loud. Kate should know better than to pressure you."

"It's not Kate entirely," Stryker sighed.

"Oh, come on, not that old crap about helping out a fellow officer in distress," Tos said.

"More like that old crap about helping out a fellow human being."

"You're too good to live," Tos said, not without an edge of sarcasm. "Which is probably why you're going to die young of exhaustion, ulcers, and baldness."

"I'm not going bald; I am wearing my hair out from the

inside due to my constant and brilliant thinking," Stryker said.

"Now why did I never realize that?" Tos asked.

Another silence.

"Well, are you going to help me or not?"

"What do I have to do?" Tos asked cautiously.

"A little research, that's all."

"I'm a sick man," Tos protested. "I've hardly got enough strength to drag myself slowly and painfully to the dinner table five times a day—"

"All it needs is some computer time and maybe a trip to the library for a little photocopying. An hour or two tops."

"I suppose it would mean missing 'As the World Turns.'"

"We all have to make sacrifices in the name of friendship."

Tos sighed hugely. "All right. Tell me what you want."

Stryker gave him the list: background on both Michael and Daria Grey, on the Wilberforce family, and anything he could pick up about Bobcat Investments.

"Is that *all*?" Tos asked in a snide voice.

"I can always ask Pinsky," Stryker said.

"He's too busy."

"Oh?" Stryker sat up a little. "You talked to him?"

"I had a word."

"What's he working on?"

"You're on vacation, you don't want to know."

"I want to know."

"You don't. Pinsky is fine. Neilson is fine. Peters is fine. Jake Chase is fine. Kaminsky is fine. Captain Klotzman is fine."

"Sorry to hear about Klotzman."

"Yeah, me too. According to Pinsky, everything is running like clockwork down there."

"You mean they've realized they don't need us?"

"That's it."

"I knew this vacation was a bum idea."

"Listen—the way I figure it, we should quit the force and start up a little chicken farm somewhere. What do you say?"

"I say go to the library and start checking out those names."

"You don't change, Jack. You don't *grow*," Tos said in a reproachful voice.

"Grey, Daria and Michael—New York papers. Wilberforce, Arthur, Hugo, Mona, and Mrs., plus any others you come across up to first cousin—New York and Grantham papers. Bobcat Investments—Chamber of Commerce, Hall of Records, whatever it takes." Stryker reached into his pocket and extracted a scrap of paper. "You can fax it to me through the sheriff's office." He read out the number.

"Some sheriff. He doesn't have a white horse but he has a *fax*," Tos muttered. "You know what that whirring noise is?"

"No."

"That's Wyatt Earp, spinning in his grave," Tos said, and hung up.

16

M y old lady says I can come out and play detectives with you and the other guys," Stryker said, coming up behind Matt Gabriel. "Is that okay with you?"

Matt turned. "I thought you were on vacation."

Stryker made an expansive gesture. "I don't mind handing out free advice now and again. What the hell is my great expertise and brilliance for anyway, if not to share with others?"

"I don't know," Matt said. "What do you think it's for?"

"Keeping me on the streets," Stryker said. "What have you done so far?"

"Taken photographs, done a sketch or two."

"I see George is starting to look for clues," Stryker observed. They watched Putnam, who was crouched on all fours peering under the breakwater.

Matt smiled grimly. "I haven't seen George this excited before. It's giving me a whole new insight into his character. If I didn't know where he was last night, I'd say he set the whole thing up himself in order to fulfill his fantasies of being a Great Detective."

"I've got one like that back in the city," Stryker said.

"Guy named Neilson. Sharp dresser, smart mouth, general pain in the ass. But he's beginning to shape up."

"I wouldn't call George a smart dresser."

"No."

"He has got a mouth, but it's usually full of doughnuts."

"Ah. I've got one of those, too. Maybe George is a Great Detective, after all." George stood up suddenly, holding up a small rock. He seemed to find it fascinating. "And maybe not," Stryker concluded.

When George had finished his minute but fruitless search of the breakwater, they went over the lawn on their hands and knees, the three of them abreast. This activity proved to be of vast interest to the Islanders, some of whom had re-emerged from their various cottages and stood around watching.

Freddy Tollett was the first to snap. "Looking for clues?" he asked brightly.

"No," Matt said. "George dropped his contact lens."

George guffawed at this, and they had to wait until he had finished before they resumed their slow progress toward the house. They reached the steps without discovering anything except a few leftover firework sticks and four ring-pulls. They stood up. "You can take the tape down, George," Matt said.

"You may now consider your immediate scene-of-crime forensic obligations at an end," Stryker said. "What do you plan to do next?"

"I've got all my usual temporary deputies coming in as Tilly catches up with them—not easy, because they scatter a bit in summer. I've managed to get Glen Hardwicke and Frank Boomer onto the bridge to stop any newspaper people from coming over, but they're getting bored because nobody's showed up yet."

"They'll be along," Stryker said confidently.

Freddy had come over to stand near them. "Nobody on the Island will call them," he volunteered.

"Maybe not. But that body is a mess," Stryker said. "If the doctor doesn't talk, a mortuary attendant will, or one of

the ambulance drivers—it won't take much longer. And if
you don't think it will be a problem, you're wrong. It's not
so much the newspaper guys, they can be reasoned with
most of the time. It's the television bunch. They're like
wasps—they swarm. They'll want pictures, all they can get,
and interviews, too. They love getting local reaction, and
very few people can resist a chance to get on TV."

"Islanders will resist it," Freddy said firmly.

"Want to bet?" Stryker said.

"Sure." Freddy grinned. "Bet you a dinner at the Golden
Perch." He was resplendent in ice-green slacks and shirt,
with a dark-green paisley scarf at his throat. Stryker, who
was in wrinkled chinos and a pale-blue "Pigs Are People,
Too" T-shirt, looked like somebody's gardener.

"Hate to take your lobster," Stryker said. "But it's a bet."

"Speaking of interviews, we're going to have to interview
everybody on the Island," Matt said slowly. "Including the
Wilberforces."

"Oh, Lord," Freddy said. "I don't suppose anyone has
even told *them* about the murder. Our usual grapevine
doesn't extend beyond that wall."

"Well, we can bring the news," Matt said, looking at his
watch. "After lunch."

"Let's hope they're not the kind to shoot the messenger,"
Stryker said. "And what's this about 'we'?"

It was sometime during lunch that Stryker began to feel
unreal. Back in the city, given a homicide showing this
degree of violence, taking place in a neighborhood of
similar standing, involving people of like degree, the police
would be running around like crazy getting interviews,
taking forensic samples, talking to people, fending off the
press, and in general falling over one another to get the
damn thing solved.

Here everything stopped for tuna-fish sandwiches.

"I talked to Daria," Kate said, as she poured him a cold
beer and set out the corn chips. "She's very upset."

"Funny, she didn't seem upset when I saw her," Stryker

said. "In fact, she was as cold as a flounder about the whole thing."

"Well, she's shy," Kate said, reaching for a sandwich.

He stared at her. "*Shy?* What the hell does 'shy' have to do with it? Her husband is shot dead practically in her lap—"

"I didn't mean shy in that way," Kate said. "I mean, she's not very good about showing her feelings. I think that's why nobody believed her when she said Michael was threatening her—she was probably trying not to be silly about it."

"In my business, we allow for silly," Stryker said.

"Well, Daria's different."

"This whole place is different," Stryker said. "We're talking about murder now, really violent murder—and you'd think nothing had happened at all. Maybe somebody spilled something, or dressed improperly for church—it all seems to be on that level. The only person excited about it is Gabriel's young deputy, George Putnam, and he's just the opposite. He goes haywire every time I say something like 'fingerprints' or 'procedure' or—"

"The Putnams aren't Island people," Kate said, idly spinning a corn chip on the table. "And Georgie was always a baby about things, he'd cry at the least little—"

"*Jesus!*" Stryker said, leaping up and going out into the kitchen for another beer. "I thought this place was okay, but it's worse than the university. Talk about ivory towers—your precious 'Island' has them all beat. It's only a little spit of land with a few cottages on it stuck out at the end of a humpbacked bridge that goes over an itsy-bitsy canal. A *canal*, mind you, not the Straits of Gibraltar or anything."

"You don't understand," Kate began.

"Too right," he agreed, returning. "Nobody here takes anything *seriously.*"

"Oh, yes they do, of course they do," Kate flared. "But we don't show it, we don't get riled."

"No, you get shot at, instead. You get murdered."

"Michael wasn't—"

"An Islander, right, I got that part. So doesn't his getting murdered here count for anything?"

"He wasn't a very nice person."

"Oh, say, let's hear it for the nice guys," Stryker said with great disgust. "Only nice guys deserve justice, naughty guys deserve zip. Great little code of justice you have there."

"If Daria *did* kill him it would be understan—"

"*Aha!*" He pounced. "So you're beginning to wonder, too."

Kate stood up and took the empty sandwich platter from the table. "No, I'm not. But isn't there such a thing as justifiable homicide? If she—"

"No," said Stryker. "There isn't."

Kate paused in the doorway, platter in one hand, empty beer bottles in the other. "There isn't?"

"No, there's isn't. Not if you're talking law. Are you talking law?"

"I don't know what I'm talking," she said irritably.

He nodded. "I noticed."

There was a clatter of dishes in the sink, and then Kate returned to stand in the doorway, hands on hips. "Do you know, Daria even asked me if I thought Aunt Clary had done it?"

"Yeah, I wondered that too," Stryker said.

"*What?*"

"Oh, I know, I know. But working on the literary theory that the least likely person 'dunit,' you must admit old Miss Shanks is a prime candidate. She *can* walk, you know. She can't run, or dance, but she can walk if she has to. And she is pretty damn devoted to Daria—that sticks out a mile. Suppose Michael crept into the house during the night and she was awake, hey? Suppose she watched him creep around, then followed him out and shot him during the storm?"

"Oh? Where's the gun, then?"

Stryker gestured out toward the front of the house. "That's a pretty big lake out there. How far do you reckon an old, crippled, and very angry lady could fling a shotgun? Ten feet? Twenty? Or there's the canal, out back, nice and murky with a real muddy bottom."

"Well, why aren't you looking for it then?"

He leaned back and balanced a corn chip on his nose. "Oh, we will, we will. Sometime or other. Next week, or next month, maybe. Depends on whether the wind blows east or west. Life is like that, here on the Island of Dreams—"

"Jack, for heaven's sake—"

He shrugged. "Just trying to fit in," he said. "Just trying to belong."

"Okay, so that's the situation," Matt Gabriel said, addressing the small group of older men gathered in his office. The remains of his lunch lay in various wrappers on his desk. George was too excited to eat, apparently, for the little Styrofoam box holding his congealed hamburger was still unopened, and only a few fries had disappeared from the packet. George sat on the forward edge of his desk, trying to look stern and official, but only managing to appear constipated.

"It's murder," he pronounced.

"I said that, George." Matt pointed out.

"Right," agreed George. "Right."

"I don't know that my wife would want me working on no murder," said one of the older men. "A shotgun, you say?"

There was a degree of restlessness apparent among the others, too. "Not exactly traffic duty, is it, Matt?" another said. "More like you need professional help, seems to me."

Matt sighed. He had expected more enthusiasm. Some enthusiasm. Something. "I'm not asking for help in the investigation," he said. "But there will be a lot of people trying to get onto the Island, and I need them kept off."

"Sightseers?" somebody asked.

"Yes. Well—the dead man is the husband of Daria Grey, and she's kind of a celebrity back east."

"If she wasn't before, she will be now." George grinned.

"Anyway, I'm told there will be a lot of interest—" Matt continued.

"Who told you that?" somebody wanted to know.

"Jumping Jack Stryker," George said dramatically.

A burly man with a large nose laughed harshly. "Who the hell is Jumping Jack Stryker when he's at home?"

"That's just a silly nickname, George," Matt said.

"Well, that's what somebody said he was called down in the city," George said. "Said the papers called him that."

Matt turned back to the men. "Lieutenant Stryker is a Grantham police detective who happens to be vacationing on the Island. I've asked him to advise on the case, that's all."

"What do you need him for? Not his territory."

"No, I agree. But you wouldn't think much of me if I walked around pretending to be something I'm not, and I'm not experienced in homicide investigation," Matt said firmly. "Personally, I think I would be a damn fool to ignore the fact that the guy is here and knows the right way to go about things."

"Ain't you supposed to call in the state police on something like this?" a bald old-timer asked.

"No. Tilly checked it out, and our local bylaws say it's up to me. If I want to investigate it myself, then I can. And I do. Who the hell needs state police tramping all over everything and everybody here?" Matt said. "We're not hicks, we can handle our own troubles."

"Yeah!" somebody at the back said.

"Damn right!" came another voice. "I got hauled over by one of them state police assholes once. Big hat, big sunglasses, and big mouth, that was him. They think they own the goddamn world."

Matt took a cautious breath. As he had hoped, the chauvinistic approach had wrought a change in the atmosphere. Reluctance to become involved had extended to a reluctance to let anyone else take over what was their own particular crime—however unpleasant it might be. If Matt wanted to ask some smart city cop for advice, that was one thing. But those state police assholes—never!

"Right," he said. "What I need now is—"

The telephone rang. Tilly, who had been listening to all this with some amusement, answered it. She listened a minute, then called out to Matt.

"It's Glen Hardwicke, calling from the Rose place. He says there's about six reporters and a television van wanting to go onto the Island, and he and Frank can't hold 'em off much longer on their own."

It was the word *television* that did it.

Matt could hardly hand out the badges fast enough.

17

The "posse" arrived just in time.

Glen Hardwicke was arguing with a man carrying a camera and a huge bag of accessories, while behind him the television van was trying to edge past the sawhorse barrier and cross the bridge. Frank Boomer kept stepping in front of it, and then got edged away by the photographer and the other reporters. Each time he moved sideways, the van moved a couple of inches farther forward.

It was nearly at the apex of the hump.

Matt posted three more men to maintain order. He had issued them with shotguns, but only with birdshot shells, in case somebody actually had to fire off a warning. They outstared the driver of the television van and his three cohorts—including a lady interviewer with a very steely eye—and made him back down the bridge to the mainland. He drew over to one side of the dirt road and, opening a brown paper bag lodged on the dashboard above the steering wheel, he extracted, peeled, and began to eat a banana.

Matt then organized three patrols of two men each to walk along the breakwater and the road to stop anybody getting the bright idea of coming around by boat. Or rather, if they got the idea, to abandon it. None of the reporters, who were from Hatchville and the city, had thought of it yet—but it was only a matter of time.

When he'd set his perimeter guards, Matt felt happier. He strolled along the road to the Trevorne cottage and knocked on the back-porch door. Kate appeared behind the screen. "Hi, Matt."

"Kate. Jack around?"

"He's *very* busy," she said pointedly.

"Oh. Sorry."

"He's trying to balance a corn chip on his nose and then flip it into his mouth without dropping it," she added with considerable sarcasm.

"I—"

She raised her voice. "He seems to think that's more important than finding out who killed Daria's husband."

Stryker appeared behind her. "You mean more important than proving Daria *didn't* kill him. That *is* what we're supposed to be doing, isn't it?"

"No," said Matt.

"Yes," said Kate.

"Just so we all agree," Stryker muttered.

They walked slowly down the road to the bridge, where an even bigger media crowd had accumulated, some of them quite determined. But the guards, who personally knew everyone who should be on the Island, were holding the line against all those who shouldn't.

There was a lot of shouting. Gabriel's men were grinning. The reporters were not. There was a good deal of discussion about freedom of the press. According to the guards, it did not include freedom of the Island. According to the reporters, it did.

There the matter seemed to rest, at the moment.

"This is mild," Stryker said, as they paused behind the Roses' cottage, which was the first on the Island after the bridge. "This is nothing."

"It'll do," Matt said. He turned and walked over to the back porch of the cottage. Parking space being both necessary and limited on the Island, all the cottages had had the small space between the house and the road graveled over to provide room for—usually—two cars. The road itself was only just wide enough for one car at a time, and when two had to pass, it involved one scrunching over onto either the edge of somebody's graveled patch, or the sometimes treacherously soft ground that edged the canal. The road, though narrow, was straight—and ran the length of the Island. When leaving a cottage, a quick glance to right or left usually was enough to ascertain that the way was clear. You edged your car out, judged your chances of making it to the bridge unchallenged, and then made a run for it. Sometimes you made it, sometimes you didn't.

The Roses only had one car—a very old Buick sedan, which Mrs. Rose ran out once a week to do the shopping. Very heavy and getting on in years (rather like the car), Mrs. Rose never washed the car, so it was usually dusty. The rain the night before had rinsed it clean, however, and it sparkled in the sun, the hundreds of little orange rust spots making a colorful contrast with the chrome and the baby-blue paintwork.

Two Roses bloomed in the cottage, the mother and the daughter. Mrs. Rose was an American Beauty—now overblown and heavily perfumed. Miss Roberta Rose was more of a bud—at the age of thirty-four she was still tightly furled and showing very little color. According to her mother, Roberta was "delicate." As a result she could only *just* manage the part-time job of Blackwater town librarian, poor thing. The fact that she also managed all the cooking, cleaning, and maintenance of the old cottage seemed to be lost on the older woman, who took it as her due, and moaned about her "poor bones." One could have sympathy with Mrs. Rose's bones—they supported a body that weighed at least two hundred fifty pounds.

It was Mrs. Rose herself who came to the door, dressed in a brightly flowered muumuu. Stryker recognized her as the fat woman who attended the Residents' Association meeting. "Now look what's happened," she announced.

"What?" Matt asked warily.

"They took off 'Oprah Winfrey' and put on a movie about the Foreign Legion," Mrs. Rose said, opening the door and stepping back so they could enter the clean but cluttered back porch. "What do I want with the Foreign Legion, I ask you?"

"This is Jack Stryker," Matt began.

"Kate's man," Mrs. Rose said. "Saw you at the meeting— wondered who you were."

"How do you do?" Stryker said politely.

"Always thought Kate hated men," Mrs. Rose said, looking him up and down with a judicious eye.

"She never mentioned it to me," Stryker said.

"No? Well, she probably found something about you she could tolerate," Mrs. Rose said. She turned and went through the kitchen into the sitting room, where she switched off the television set and dropped into a reclining chair that groaned under the impact. "This is about the killing, I suppose. Never come to see me, otherwise, would you? Hey? Sit down, sit down. Hear he had his head blown clean off."

"Not exactly," Matt said.

"Left a shred or two, did they? Enough to clap a hat on?"

"More or less. Is your daughter at home?"

"Sorry. Roberta's at the library, counting the books again, probably. Can't be more than a couple of hundred, but she takes all day about it. Had to make my own lunch, fortunately." She laughed heartily. "All *she* gives me is salads and lectures, salads and lectures." She clasped her hands across the high round of her stomach and regarded them with amiable expectation. "Well, come on. Grill me."

"You don't seem very upset, if you don't mind my saying so," Matt observed.

"I don't mind your saying so," Mrs. Rose said. "Why should I be upset—got nothing to do with me, has it?"

"You're not afraid that there might be a killer on the Island?"

"Hah!" She seemed genuinely amused. "Don't be ridiculous, Matt Gabriel. You mean you think one of the Island people is going around knocking off strangers? No way." She leaned forward. "Unless he was a real estate man. Was he?"

"No."

She leaned back again. "Well, then. We got no call to kill anyone else, any of us. As for outsiders dropping their dead around the place—why should that scare me? Makes me cross, sure—I hate a mess same's anybody else. But scared? *Absolutely* not."

There didn't seem any way to dent her impervious cheer. She was a woman accustomed to getting her own way. The thought that someone might have the temerity to point a gun at her—much less pull the trigger—simply didn't enter her mind. And, in accordance with the general view, if it wasn't Island, it didn't really count.

The body had lain well up the Island. Mrs. Rose hadn't even been one of those who had come along to view it out of curiosity. As far as Mrs. Rose was concerned, it was vaguely interesting, but not her problem.

"Did you hear anything during the night? Aside from the storm?" Matt added quickly, as he could see she was forming some smart remark concerning the thunder.

"I heard a shot," Mrs. Rose said.

"What?" Both men leaned forward.

"I said, I heard a shot," Mrs. Rose repeated with some satisfaction. There, now she'd startled them, all right.

"What time was this?" Stryker finally managed.

"Oh, about three o'clock," Mrs. Rose guessed. "When the storm was really rolling. I expect it was the one you're interested in—wasn't more than the one, was there?"

"Weren't you curious about it?"

"Nope." She looked at them calmly. "It was chilly and I was comfortable—why haul myself out of bed at look for something I couldn't see anyway? Black as your hat out here at night. Mind, if there had been another shot or two, I might have stirred myself, but it was just the one. Way I know is, it went off just after the first crack of thunder—and you don't get thunder like that cracking twice. Anyway, it was different. My husband used to take a shotgun out on the Mush in winter for duck—I know the sound."

"And you did nothing about it?"

"Now, what would you have had me do, Matt Gabriel?"

"You could have rung me."

"Well, the way I thought about it was this—if it was an accident and somebody was hurt, then the person who pulled the trigger would be calling for help. And if it was on purpose, well, I was better off in bed, anyway. I wasn't about to go running out into the rain in my nightgown, if that's what you had in mind. Make a fine target, I would." She laughed at them and herself. "Land's sakes, boys—I'm no heroine. Oprah Winfrey, now, she might have gone out there and told the person off, probably scared the hell out of him, she's the girl could do it, but not me. No, sir."

There was a thud from the back porch, and Mrs. Rose, without seeming to draw breath, suddenly shouted out, "Roberta? That you? We got visitors."

Stryker jumped a foot when she yelled without any warning. He stifled the temptation to touch his head to see if his thinning hair had been blown out of place by the blast of her voice. He looked at her in some admiration and wondered if she had entered any hog-calling contests when younger. She still would have a hell of a chance at the blue ribbon.

"There are people all over the bridge, and men with—" Roberta had started speaking as she came through the kitchen, but trailed off when she reached the doorway and saw the two men sitting on the sofa. "Oh," she said. "Hello."

If God had decided to give Adam a small-town librarian instead of that airhead bimbo Eve, He would have produced Roberta Maybelle Rose. And, given Roberta Maybelle Rose, it is almost certain that Adam would still be happily ensconced in the Garden of Eden, for at first glance she

appeared the type who would have followed every rule to
the letter. She was thin, she was tall, she was buttoned up
to the chin, and she wore glasses that owed absolutely
nothing to fashion. Her hair was drawn back tightly into a
bun on the nape of her neck, and not a touch of makeup
showed on her face. Her nails were cut short, her ears
were unpierced, and her full skirt reached nearly to her
ankles. This latter piece of apparel gave her the spurious
attribute of being fashionable, in a hippie sort of way, but
only for the moment. When skirts went back up, hers
would remain where they were, locked down tight.

Women who looked like Roberta Maybelle Rose always
made Stryker want to kick something. She had good bones
and a clear complexion and the eyes behind the glasses
were dark gray and very fine. Although she dressed to hide
it, she had a normal, even graceful figure, and her hands
were lovely. The something he wanted to kick in this case
was her mother, for it was obvious who had imprisoned
Roberta Maybelle Rose in a cage of useful and obedient
rectitude.

"Roberta, you know Matt, and this here is Kate's man,
Lieutenant Shriker."

"Stryker," Stryker said.

"How do you do," Roberta said, coming forward and
extending a slender ivory hand. As he took it, Stryker had a
closer look at the eyes behind the lenses of the spectacles,
and experienced a considerable shock. Roberta Maybelle
Rose had hidden depths. His spirits rose immediately, and
he wondered what form her escape from her mother took.
Whatever it was, he applauded it.

"Miss Bertie, did you—" Matt began.

"He wants to know if you heard any noises during the
night," Mrs. Rose boomed. "Like a shotgun going off or
anything."

Matt sighed. "Did you?" he asked.

"No. I slept pretty soundly last night," Roberta said
demurely. "Did you hear anything, Mother?"

"I heard the shot," Mrs. Rose said proudly.

"Really?" Roberta seemed startled. "Usually your sleeping pills put you out like a light."

"Well, the storm made me restless," Mrs. Rose said, avoiding her daughter's eye. "What with the lightning and the thunder and all—enough to wake the dead, it was."

"It didn't wake me," Roberta said virtuously. "Not for more than a moment or two."

"Have you noticed any prowlers lately?" Stryker asked.

"No," Roberta said.

"Lots of funny noises in the night near a lake," Mrs. Rose said helpfully. "Birds, wind in the trees, frogs jumping in the canal out back, things like that. Mind you, being first off the bridge, we hear everybody going to and fro—there's a couple of loose boards that rattle every time a car goes across them. And footsteps—we hear those, too. Mostly kids."

"But you haven't seen anyone?"

"No." They both agreed on that, anyway.

"We missed you at Freddy's party," Matt said conversationally.

"Oh, Roberta wanted to come, but I was having a lot of pain, so she stayed with me, and we watched TV. She's a good girl," Mrs. Rose said. "Knew a storm was coming day before yesterday. Storms coming always affect my bones, you see. A regular weather vane, that's me!" She laughed heartily, and Roberta smiled too.

Just.

"Aside from the shot, Mrs. Rose, did you happen to hear anyone driving over the bridge during the night?"

"My bedroom is in front," Mrs. Rose said regretfully. "Only hear the bridge during the day, really."

"My room's at the back, and I didn't hear anything," Roberta said firmly. "I slept soundly the whole night through."

18

Stryker started to chuckle as they left the Rose household and turned right toward the next cottage. Behind them, at the bridge, there was still a good deal of shouting and horn-blowing, which they studiously avoided noticing.

"Sounds like Roberta Rose could have had a close call last night," he said.

Matt Gabriel looked at him. "What do you mean?"

"Her mother woke up."

"So?"

"Didn't you see her eyes when her mother claimed that she'd heard the shot? She was absolutely horrified. If you ask me, she dopes her mother up and sneaks out at night."

"Roberta?" Matt was startled. "Are you kidding me?"

"No, I am not kidding you," Stryker said. "Although I may be kidding myself. There's something in her eyes that is definitely not beaten or cowed. Are you sure it's the mother who holds the upper hand in that setup?"

"She's always been a real dominating woman."

"Hmmm. I wonder."

Matt considered this as they crunched across the gravel.

"Guess maybe it takes an outsider to notice things," he conceded doubtfully.

"Or to draw the wrong conclusions," Stryker said. "It was just an impression I got, that's all. But under all that official spinster getup, Roberta's an attractive woman. Somebody besides me must have noticed it."

"You think she was out last night?"

"I don't know. Interesting thought, though, isn't it?"

The Greenfields were an older couple, he a semi-retired stockbroker, she a dedicated collector of jewelry and assorted other goodies. Their place, far from being the rustic retreat that other Island properties seemed to be, had been "done" by an interior decorator. Indeed, "done" many times over, as Mrs. Greenfield, along with being a collector, was also a woman of changing tastes.

At the moment she was in a French Provincial phase.

The rear porch at the Greenfields' was not a catch-all for odd objects, as so many others were. It was a country bower, full of fernery and greenery and pots of herbs and flowers. The kitchen was paneled in limed oak with designer wormholes, wearmarks, and scuffs. The L-shaped sitting/dining room was a glory of reproduction French country antiques, on mock Aubusson carpets. Since picture windows were not a feature of Gallic country homes, the two that bracketed the front entrance (from an earlier Scandinavian modern phase) were festooned with sheer silk and overhung with brocade. The front porch was laid to greenery, too, but here the ferns and other plants were more exotic, and complemented the delicate scrollwork of the white-painted porch furniture.

You could hardly see the lake at all.

Stryker remembered Greenfield from the meeting on the Robinson lawn the day before. He was a nervous man, with thinning hair brushed ruthlessly straight over his pink scalp. His skin had a pale translucence that was quite unique among the tanned Islanders. His white shirt and khaki Bermuda shorts were smoothly and impeccably ironed, his long socks had proper turnovers below the knee, his shoes (two-toned) were highly polished. Indeed, he himself seemed highly polished, as if he were kept in a cupboard and brought out only for company. Mrs. Greenfield also demonstrated the delights of careful grooming. She had a mound of blond hair carefully swirled and tucked, a taut face that hinted at some excellent plastic surgery, bright eyes and equally bright lipstick. She had kept her figure, with a considerable struggle, and was proud of it. Her white dress fitted flawlessly and was accented with a matching set of jewelry consisting of earrings, necklace, bracelet, and two brooches, all in gold and jade. She smiled a lot.

Both looked as though they had expected a visit from the *Good Housekeeping* photographic team, rather than the police.

Greenfield had also been one of the people who had come out onto the lawn that morning, and had observed all the procedures. He was, he said, very impressed.

"I'm sure you will arrest the killer in no time," he said, with a wide, encouraging smile that did not extend to his worried eyes. "I'm sure there will be no problems at all."

Mrs. Greenfield nodded agreement, and toyed with her bracelet, turning it around and around her wrist.

"May I ask if either of you heard anything out of the ordinary during the storm last night?" Matt asked.

"No, no, nothing at all. The air conditioner tends to obscure any small noises from outside. Of course we heard the thunder, but nothing else," Mr. Greenfield said earnestly.

Mrs. Greenfield nodded agreement, and plucked at an earring, which seemed to be too tight.

"And have you noticed any prowlers in the area recently?"

"No, no, nothing like that," Mr. Greenfield assured them. "In any event, we have an excellent alarm system which we switch on every night when we go to bed, and we feel quite secure here in our little hideaway."

Mrs. Greenfield nodded agreement, and went back to turning her bracelet. She smiled.

"I know you moved here about six years ago," Matt said.

"Do you know Daria Grey or Michael Grey? Or Miss Shanks?"

"We know very few people on the Island, other than to say good morning or good evening," Mr. Greenfield said. "Of course, we're members of the Residents' Association, we support it with enthusiasm, but other than that we don't mix much. We've met Miss Shanks, of course, but not her niece. And I don't believe we ever met... the victim. We lead a very quiet life here. Very quiet."

Mrs. Greenfield smiled and hesitated. And then she spoke.

"We read a lot," she screeched. She had the face of an elegant matron, and the voice of an irate baseball fan. Stryker wondered briefly if there was something in the lakeside air that affected the voices of certain women. He hoped Kate's low, firm tones wouldn't escalate into a steel-wool scrape like this woman's. Or a bellow like Mrs. Rose's. The screech went on. "I like romances, but Harry prefers Westerns and books about how to play the stock market, Harry's very good at that, you know. And we watch TV, of course, and play Scrabble and—"

"A very quiet life," her husband interrupted. "Really, I'm afraid we can't help you at all."

"I'm surprised they bothered to move out here," Stryker said, when they had finished questioning the Greenfields and were out in the open air again. He took a deep breath. "They obviously don't swim or go boating or fishing or water-skiing or anything else. They don't even seem to look at the scenery. That house must be hermetically sealed. You could hear the air conditioner going all over the place. And the antiques and the curtains and the plants—"

"Yeah," Gabriel said. "They're a funny couple all right."

Stryker looked at him. "Meaning?"

"Mrs. Greenfield drinks, Mr. Greenfield gambles—stock market, horses, ball games, cards, everything and any-thing. When he wins she gets a few nice trinkets and a redecorating budget. When he loses he sells her jewels and

she changes from vodka to cheap jug wine. He's lucky most
of the time, as a matter of fact. But they redecorated that
house two years back now. And that jade is not her best."

"So you think maybe he's on a downer?"

Matt shrugged. "Haven't been many vodka bottles in the
garbage—or so I hear."

"And do they always *look* like that?"

"Oh, yes. Always," Matt said. "Good times or bad, they
keep up the front."

"Any children?"

"No, just themselves."

"You know a lot more about *their* secret lives than you do
about the Roses'," Stryker observed.

"They're new," Matt said. "When you're used to something, you hardly bother to look at it. But people have been
wondering about the Greenfields ever since they moved in.
Maybe some of them make up stories or exaggerate—people
do. But I know the guy who collects the garbage out here,
and he told me about the bottles. And I know the local
banker and a few others who can verify the gambling.
Those are facts."

"Six years. You said they moved in six *years* ago."

"That's 'new' on the Island. Over the bridge we get a
fairly normal turnover of folks buying and selling, but not
here. The Cotmans ten years ago; the Greenfields six years
ago, the Wilberforces about three or four years ago, and
that's it. All the others have been here— or their families
have been here—since the first cottages were built on the
Island, which was back before World War One, I think.
That's part of it, you see. Part of why it's so different from
the rest of Blackwater Bay. From the rest of the world,
seems to me sometimes. That main canal can't be much
more than forty feet across, but you'd think it was a mile or
two. Show you what I mean—here."

He raised his arm and made a wide gesture toward the
next cottage along their route. "This belongs to Mrs. Toby
and Mrs. Norton. Been Tobys in that place from the start,
and right along. When Mrs. Toby goes, Mrs. Norton—if

she hasn't gone first—will either have to jump in the lake or move in with one of her daughters, because another Toby will get it. Probably Tony Toby, over in Hatchville, but Mrs. Toby never says. Could be Ambrose Toby down in the city. Could be Clarence Toby, who's out in Colorado somewheres, although that's not too likely. She plays them off, one against the other, just for fun. They all want it, but she's good for quite a few years yet, so they'll just have to wait. They all visit, of course. That's the scourge of living by the water—everybody drops in. Weekends you can hardly get down the coast roads for visitors' cars stuck every which way. Come on, let's get it over with. Feeling strong?"

"Do I need to be?"

Gabriel looked at him and grinned. "Yup."

"Rock cakes, snickerdoodles, peanut crumblies, chocolate chips, or molasses thumbprints? Take your pick. Take one of each, why don't you, then you'll know what to take again."

"I just finished lunch," Stryker said weakly, eyeing the platter of cookies that was being thrust under his nose.

"Rubbish," countered Mrs. Norton. "Bet you had a lettuce leaf and a sliver of chicken. Kate can talk you under the table on Shakespeare, but I never heard she could cook."

"She cooks very well." Stryker heard himself on the defensive, and winced inwardly. Kate would not thank him for it, preferring to be known more for her views on Byron than her recipe for jambalaya.

"Come on, choose, I'm not going away until you do." Mrs. Norton stood before him, skinny and adamant, with flour on her apron and fire in her eye. The house was filled with the fragrance of more cookies baking. Chances were if he didn't start eating now, they'd soon be crushed under an avalanche of nuts, raisins, and crumbs. He selected a flat, dark-brown cookie with scalloped edges and a circle of jam in the center.

Mrs. Norton nodded approval. "Molasses thumbprint.

Old recipe, handed down from my mother's side. Now, how would you plan to eat that? she asked.

"I beg your pardon?"

"Myself, I bite off each of the scallops around the edge, then keep on spiraling in, saving the jam for last bite. Other folks, they just charge in from the edge, willy-nilly. No organization at all." She regarded him with interest, waiting for his reply.

He looked at the cookie and cleared his throat. "I think probably I would tend toward your method—if I wasn't in a hurry or really hungry," he said cautiously. He studiously avoided Matt Gabriel's eye. He needn't have bothered—Gabriel was having his own problems concerning whether Mrs. Toby should have used the red or the blue calico for the flower centers on her latest quilt.

Entering the house had been like transportation to an earlier and better time. Indeed, if it hadn't been for the large television set in the corner, Stryker could have been ten years old and in his grandmother's farmhouse upstate. The faded ivory wallpaper was scattered with posies, the bird's-eye maple furniture was upholstered in needlepoint, and each chair was headed with a lace antimacassar. There were Godey's prints and ruby pressed-glass vases full of flowers. There were souvenirs from all the best resorts on the Great Lakes, including a china model of the hotel on Mackinac Island. There was a stuffed owl under a glass dome, and there was a great quantity of threads and cloth scraps obscuring the flowered wreaths on the peacock-blue carpet. (He knew what Kate would say about that carpet. She would say Maud Silver.)

But these two ladies were nothing like that doughty little fictional detective. Mrs. Norton was tall and thin, and Mrs. Toby was short and round. Mrs. Norton lived to cook, and Mrs. Toby lived to sew. Each had won prizes at state and county fairs for years and years past—through an archway he could see the sideboard in the dining room was literally covered with ribbons and little silver cups and curling rolls of testimonial.

"I like the snickerdoodles myself," Mrs. Norton said, shoving the platter under Matt's nose. With a smooth motion born, Stryker felt, of long experience, Gabriel went for two peanut crumblies and two snickerdoodles. And, as an afterthought, a chocolate chip cookie. For dessert.

Satisfied, if only temporarily, Mrs. Norton put the platter within easy reach of both of them—on a cobbler's-bench cocktail table—and settled back in her rocker.

"Was it him or wasn't it?" she demanded.

"Wasn't," said Mrs. Toby, stabbing a patch with her needle.

"Was," retorted Mrs. Norton. "Was. Had to be. Was it?" This last was directed toward Matt.

"You mean the victim?"

"I don't mean Moby Dick," snapped Mrs. Norton. "I mean the dead man who was lying on Kit Lattimer's lawn this morning. Can't remember if we've ever had a murder on the Island before."

"Haven't," said Mrs. Toby. "Downright disgrace, if you ask me."

"Well, I *am* asking you, ladies," Matt said easily. "See or hear anything last night, during the night, during the storm, anytime lately? What can you tell me?"

"What did you have in mind?" Mrs. Toby asked. "You want gossip, you want information, you want—"

"I'll take anything," Matt said. "Jack and I are—"

"The traditionalist," Mrs. Toby said, glancing at Stryker. "Thought I should stick to hexagons."

"Only if they're suitable," Stryker said quickly. "Only if the design seems to . . ." he paused. What the hell was he saying? "I don't know anything about it," he said, and bit off the last scallop of his molasses thumbprint.

"Have another cookie," said Mrs. Norton kindly, nudging the platter toward him with her toe. "She doesn't know anything about homicide, either."

"Know who I'd shoot first," said Mrs. Toby darkly—but her eyes were twinkling.

"We could really use your help on this," Matt persisted.
Stryker looked at him in perplexity—what the hell was he
after? Gabriel wasn't stupid. These two were nuts, obviously, and lived in a world all their own. Or did they? "Who is
Roberta Rose sneaking out to see at night?" Matt asked
abruptly.

"Charley Hart," Mrs. Toby said promptly, picking up
another patch from the basket at her side. "He usually
parks the other side of the bridge around midnight, and she
goes over. Spends about an hour. He lives with his mother,
too. They commiserate." She lifted her eyes from her work
and met Stryker's gaze for the first time. "No nonsense,"
she said firmly. Stryker took this to imply that there was no
sexual activity taking place. At least, not right there in the
police car. "He keeps his radio on, just in case he's needed,
of course," she added.

He sat back on the sofa, feeling the prickle of the
needlepoint against his neck. So that was it. He regarded
Matt with slightly more respect—obviously the cookies and
the sewing advice were a passport into the inner sanctum of
the local oracle. But Matt had not been pleased to hear
about Charley and Roberta Rose.

"So Charley was at the bridge last night?" he demanded
angrily. The news that his night-duty deputy was regularly
taking an hour off was bad enough—but that he might have
been within range of a major crime and not known anything
about it was too much.

"I don't think he was there *last* night," Mrs. Toby said
doubtfully. "What with the storm and all. He doesn't come
every night, anyway. Just some."

"Damn," Matt said. It was obvious from his expression
that Charley was in for a talking-to.

"Does seem a shame," Mrs. Toby agreed calmly. "Still,
the thunder pretty well covered everything."

"Did you hear a shot?" Matt asked.

"No," both ladies said.

"Then I'd guess Mrs. Rose was mistaken," Matt mused.
"She guessed she heard a shot around three in the morn-

ing. Said it made kind of a double crack of thunder, is why she noticed."

"Wind can blow sound around," Mrs. Norton conceded. "It was blowing down-island last night, wasn't it?"

"Then why didn't *we* hear it? We're right next door!" Mrs. Toby said righteously.

Mrs. Norton glared at her. "Because we both sleep like stones once we hit the pillow," she snapped.

"Clear consciences," Mrs. Toby said, subsiding complacently. "I still say she just wanted to get her oar into it. Always was one for getting into things, was Clara Biggs, even from a girl. Good thing Roberta never inherited her tendencies, is what I always say."

"But she *might* have heard something," Mrs. Norton persisted.

Mrs. Toby looked at her. "You think so?"

"Benefit of the doubt," Mrs. Norton decided.

"All right," Mrs. Toby conceded. "She might have. *I* didn't." She reached for another patch.

By the time Stryker had eaten nine cookies and Gabriel fifteen, they had learned the following:

Nobody had ever met Mr. Rose—Clara Biggs had gone off to Grantham alone and had come back with a wedding ring, Roberta wrapped in a blanket, and a mysterious "pension" that was sent from Des Moines, Iowa, on the tenth of every month. "*Claimed* her husband had crashed while testing some new kind of plane."

Marianne from the Golden Perch was going to marry the man who sold them their tartar sauce and ketchup.

Len Cotman had been losing patients because some woman was telling everyone he'd made a pass at her friend while she was "under the gas," which had to be an out-and-out lie.

Farley Biltmore, the young man who managed the Texaco station on Route 14, said he was going to shoot the man who sold ketchup to the Golden Perch, and had bought a new shotgun last week. (Stryker glanced at Matt, who shook his head, grinning.)

Hugo Wilberforce had lost all his own money backing some weird off-Broadway show about a serial killer, and his daddy had forced him to come home.

Larry Lovich had also lost a lot of money recently—by investing in an art gallery whose owner had absconded with funds, paintings, and Larry's reputation.

Tom Berringer, the town clerk, had a wife who was suspicious of his fidelity, and he was trying to keep her happy by buying expensive presents he couldn't afford.

The Wilberforces had a "foreigner" working for them who was always asking Harry Peters, the grocer, for things he didn't have and couldn't get if he wanted to, which he didn't. Like what? Stryker wanted to know. Like chicken feet, for instance.

Fran Robinson was pregnant again.

Cissy Greenfield had joined the Alcoholics Association, (nothing was Anonymous in Blackwater Bay), and had gained five pounds.

Some woman in Hatchville was claiming that Freddy Tollett was the father of her unborn child, and couldn't be talked out of it. Mrs. Norton snorted. "I expect Freddy doesn't know whether to be flattered or insulted."

"Probably depends on who he's talking to," Mrs. Toby said mildly.

Clary Shanks was taking a long time to get better from that broken hip, and Dr. Willis was worried about her, said he wanted her in the hospital so he could do some tests, but Clary said she knew all she wanted to know about her insides and wouldn't go.

Tilly Moss was thinking of marrying Frank Boomer once Frank's divorce came though, but was worried about her invalid mother. ("My God," Matt said, "I'm beginning to think I live in another town. Nobody ever tells me *anything*.")

The Ventnor Hotel had been sold to the Japanese.

Darius Ventnor, the Water Commissioner, was not going to stand at the next election because he had gotten a "call" and was going to go to Divinity School as a mature student, which just went to show that God wasn't all that choosy after all.

Kate's father had shaved his head for a bet and his wife had made him take her to Nevada until it grew out some. ("Kate never told me about that," Stryker said. "They never told Kate" was the swift reply.)

And Nell Norton had poisoned her husband. ("Now you take that back, Margaret Toby." Mrs. Norton had giggled. "Or I'll tell them about you!")

More giggles. More tea. More gossip. More cookies.

"How much of all that was true?" Stryker asked, as they shut the door of Old America behind them.

"Maybe half." Matt grinned.

"Four o'clock," Stryker said, glancing at his watch as he brushed cookie crumbs from his T-shirt. "At this rate, I think we ought to have the thing all tied up by Christmas."

"Not fast enough for you?" Matt asked.

"Not nearly."

"What do you suggest?"

"A little honesty might help."

Matt looked down at him and then walked across the road to spit into the canal. He gazed at the sky, scuffed the ground, and all in all did every Gary Cooper thing he could think of. Finally he returned. "About what?"

"About why you're pretending to be so dumb, for one thing. This is cold-blooded murder. This is nasty stuff. You want my help, fine, but I don't think I can stand the pace. What the hell are you stalling for? Or do I guess?"

"You'd guess it's because I think Daria Grey shot her husband, right? You're worried I'm stalling my ass off in the hope it will all go away. You think I'm wandering from house to house having leisurely conversations with the down-home folk while I'm trying to think of a way out of all this."

"One or two of those, yeah." Stryker crossed him arms and glared at him. "And I can't figure it. If she was guilty, and *I* was sweet on her, I'd be kind of worried that what she did to one husband she'd do to another, so maybe it ought to be cleared up before I got in too deep."

Before Gabriel could form an answer, a young man of about twenty came trotting up to them. He was carrying a shotgun, carefully broken, in the crook of one elbow. "Hey, Matt."

"Hey, Ted."

"Tilly sent me over with this." He handed Gabriel a brown envelope. "Where do you want me?"

"Best go back to the bridge and relieve somebody. Glen Hardwicke's been there the longest, seems to me." Gabriel tore open the envelope and peered inside. The deputy went back toward the bridge, squaring his shoulders slightly. He had a fresh haircut and looked very vulnerable around the back of the neck.

"So you think I ought to be doing a few more things about all this, is that right?" Matt asked, pocketing the brown envelope.

"Yes, that's right."

Gabriel began to walk along the road toward the next cottage. It was the last one—Kit Lattimer's—before the Shanks residence. It looked empty—shuttered up and asleep. "Like what?"

"Jesus. Like look for the gun, for one thing! Like find out where Michael Grey was staying, where he's been eating, whether he came by car or bus or camel. Can't George do some of this interviewing? Can't Charley get out of bed and help out? Can't you—"

"George is busy," Matt said.

"Doing what?"

"Swimming. And cursing, sounds like."

"What?" Stryker stopped and stared at him.

Matt had gone on walking and was about four steps ahead of him. "Hey, George," he said, raising his voice slightly. "That you, or have we been invaded by the Martians?"

Stryker took a few more steps and was then able to see into the gap between the Lattimer and Shanks boat houses. Seated on the weather-beaten gray wooden docking that edged the canal on the Island side was a large black object. It pivoted, and he saw that it was George Putnam in a gleaming wet suit, ribbons of muddy weed trailing from oxygen tanks on his back. He had pulled off his face mask, leaving an oval of clean skin surrounded by greenish-brown mud.

He smelled like a Paleozoic creature that had just emerged from the primeval slime.

"I suppose you think that's funny," he said, clearing his throat and spitting. "I will probably die some god-awful death from swimming in this crap and it will be your fault."

"I told you to start with the grapple," Matt said, grinning.

"I started with the goddamn grapple. Something grabbed it and took it away from me. That made me mad."

"It would," Matt agreed.

"So I went down."

"I see that."

"Found the grapple."

"Good."

"Also found about forty assorted beer bottles, an old tire, two anchors, a baby doll—that scared the shit out of me—and an old outboard motor. No shotgun."

"You sure?"

"Halved it, quartered it, dragged it. No shotgun."

"Guess you'd better start out front, then."

George struggled upright. "I should have started out front in the first goddamn place," he complained. He reached down and dragged off his flippers and, trailing and dripping slime, he walked across the road, danced—cursing—over the gravel, and squished across the patio of the Shanks house toward the lake.

Matt watched him go, then turned to Stryker. "Now, let's see, what were those other things you mentioned? Oh, yeah." He counted off on his fingers. "We think he's been staying in a motel about five miles this side of Hatchville, under the name of Allan—Daria gave me a photograph of him and I'm having it duplicated so somebody can run over there and get a positive identification from the clerk."

"But how—"

"Oh, Tilly phoned around with a general description to all the hotels and motels and so on. Saves time and shoe leather and she knows just about everybody, anyway, so they talk to her. He's been eating in various places, between here and the motel, mostly. She's getting a list together. What else did you ask me? Oh, yeah, the car. He's been driving a dark-blue Chevy Camaro, New York plates, we got the license number from the motel, but haven't located it yet. No keys in his pocket, but I figure it to be somewhere near. We'll get it. Tilly's phoning New York to see if they have a record of ownership on that." He took a breath and wiped his face with his forearm. "Anyway, while George is messing around in the lake out there, I guess we'd better execute this search warrant Ted brought over and go through Miss Shanks's house and boat house."

"You got a search warrant to look for the gun?"

"For the gun, sure. What do you think?"

Stryker smiled wryly. "I think I should learn to stop shooting off my big-city mouth. After you, Sheriff." He started to follow Matt into the Shanks cottage, then stopped.

"Haven't we missed one?" he asked, looking back.

"Lattimer's. But it's empty, remember? Kit's sold up and moved to Arizona."

"Oh, really?" Stryker said. He walked over to the rusty garbage can that leaned against the Lattimer garage. It was half-hidden by long-uncut grass, and the lid was askew. He lifted it and pulled back slightly, his nose wrinkling in distaste.

"If this guy is living in Arizona, how come he puts his garbage out here?" he asked.

19

The back door was unlocked.

Matt was surprised, but Stryker only smiled.

They went into the Lattimer cottage slowly. The shades had been left drawn on all the windows, but the sun outside was bright enough to penetrate, giving the kitchen a shadowy illumination even through the fabric of the blinds and curtains.

Matt's flashlight was necessary, however, when they had passed through the kitchen and reached the sitting room, for the shutters were over the front-porch windows, and there was only a small window at either end of the room itself. When the beam clicked on, both men gave a start.

It shone onto a hideous, grimacing face, staring at them with glittering eyes.

"Shit!" Stryker exclaimed.

Matt gave an uneasy laugh, and moved the beam around a little, revealing the fact that the face belonged to a nearly life-size statue standing in the corner of the room. The sculpture was of dark wood, primitive in execution, and the eyes were of some kind of shell or stone. They glared, but did not see.

"When Don told me that Kit had sold up, I guess I thought he'd moved out already," Matt said in a rather shaky voice. "I heard that his selling this place came as a shock to everybody—but it wouldn't have if there'd been a moving van here. Looks like he either sold the place intact—or they've given him time to clear it out. Interesting, isn't it?"

"That's one word for it, yes," Stryker said. "Do you suppose the electricity is still connected?"

"Let's see." Matt went to the wall and clicked the switch. Light flooded down from above. "Well, it appears to be, at that."

"Jesus wept," Stryker said, gazing around him.

"The Lattimers were one of the original families on the Island. Kit grew up here," Matt explained. "But he spent most of his adult life in Africa, working for some mining company. He met Ada out there, I believe. Just after he retired, his mother died—his dad died when he was still young—and so they decided to come back here."

"Looks like they brought half of Africa with them," Stryker said. There seemed to be items on every horizontal surface, including the floor—although there were some gaps, and in a few places the rug was matted down, as if something heavy had stood there for a long while. He went over and inspected an arrangement of African weapons arranged on the wall—spears, clubs, bows, darts, and shields. He picked up and then hurriedly replaced a particularly alarming example, a heavy, highly polished ball of wood fastened on the end of a longish handle—and shook his head. "Just think—all this weaponry hanging here, ready at hand, and Grey gets it from a shotgun." He ran a tentative finger along the thin and surprisingly sharp edge of an assegai blade. He looked at his hand—even that light touch had made a delicate but bloodless slit in his skin. "This would have done the job much more neatly—and quietly. I suppose using a mechanical weapon like a shotgun shows some kind of cultural 'progress.'"

He moved along and examined a pair of hide drums sitting on a table. Delicately he tapped the face of one and was rewarded with a hollow echo from within, accompanied by a tiny rising of dust. "The natives are restless tonight," he said portentously.

Matt sighed. "Look, why are we—"

"Upstairs," Stryker said. "I think we'll find it upstairs."

Reluctantly, Matt followed the older man up the stairs, which rose against the far wall. After opening three doors, Stryker spoke. "Aha!" he said softly. "The lair of the beast."

Daria had been working in the kitchen, clearing up after the lunch neither she nor Aunt Clary could eat, making preparations for the dinner that would also doubtless end up in the garbage.

"Daria?" Aunt Clary's voice was just audible from the dining room. Daria wiped her hands on her apron and went through. She'd helped her aunt into the shower after lunch, put her into a fresh nightgown, combed her hair, and given her a new library book, which still lay unopened on the coverlet. During all that time her aunt had said nothing about the horror that had descended upon their lives. Now she appeared ready to do so. "Sit down, child."

Dutifully, Daria sat down in the chair beside the bed.

"This is a terrible thing," Aunt Clary began, then made an impatient gesture. "As if I needed to say that." She was silent for a moment, then took a deep breath. "I have to ask you, my dear—"

"No, Aunt Clary, I didn't kill Michael," Daria said. She felt quite calm saying it. "I wanted to, but I didn't."

The dull voice came from a Daria that Clary didn't know and could not gauge. She was an old woman now, and she felt her helplessness in the face of the girl's obvious suffering.

Daria spoke slowly, as if she were exhausted. "I thought I had gotten away from it by coming here, and I just wanted to forget. But he wouldn't let me."

"Those times you called the police—"

"Michael *was* outside, Aunt Clary. He *was*."

"Oh, Derry . . ."

At that moment there was a knock on the back door. Daria's head came up with a jerk and she turned in her chair. "It's Matt and Jack Stryker," she said in a defeated voice. "They've come to arrest me."

"Nonsense," Aunt Clary said, but her voice shook.

"I don't know if it's much consolation, but we've found where your husband was hiding out," Matt Gabriel said.

"There, you see?" Aunt Clary said, avoiding Daria's eye. "He *was* sneaking around, after all."

"And doing it from the Lattimer house," Matt went on. "That's how he could come and go so quickly, be here one minute and disappear the next."

"He was a neat ghoul, though," Stryker said. "He put out his garbage."

"*That* doesn't sound like Michael." Daria frowned, trying to comprehend this sudden verification of Michael's presence. "But if he was hiding next door, watching me . . ." She looked from one to the other. "You see? I felt him watching me all the time, and I couldn't understand it. But I was right. I was *right!*" Her voice started to waver upward.

"It's all right, child," Aunt Clary said. "It's over now."

"That would be so like him," Daria went on compulsively, trying to explain what was already clear to them all. "Watching in the dark, sneaking around, wanting to have power over me, over everything, wanting to *know* everything, *see* everything, hug the secrets, play God . . ." The words were coming faster and faster, she was running now, her mind spinning with relief and the need to justify all her fears. Like a hypochondriac whose tenth X ray finally reveals a tumor, the relief of being proved right momentarily outweighed the horror of the truth. "He was such a terrible man underneath all that charm, nobody understood that, nobody saw it, nobody would *listen* . . ."

"Daria!" Aunt Clary's voice was sharp, adult to child. "That's enough!"

Daria stared at the old woman, who was suddenly upright and bright-eyed in the bed. Then she looked from Matt to Stryker and, wrapped in a kind of astonishment, sank into a chair. After a moment, she covered her face with her hands.

"I'm sorry," she whispered. "I'm sorry."

"Knowing where he was sleeping doesn't tell us anything about who killed him," Stryker said uncompromisingly. "It's still a murder that we're investigating here. And we have to look for the shotgun."

"You mean you want to look here," Aunt Clary said in some disgust. "You mean you still think my girl did it."

"It won't take us long," Matt said, avoiding Daria's eyes. "We'll try not to disturb anything too much. It's routine, just part of the routine—"

"You'll be searching everybody else's place, too, then?" Aunt Clary asked pointedly.

Matt flushed, and it was Stryker who spoke, addressing his remarks to Daria, telling her straight. "There's no point in pussyfooting around this, you know. Your husband has been murdered practically in front of your own house. Suspicion naturally falls on you first. It's simple statistics, Mrs. Grey. Husbands kill wives, wives kill husbands. We can't ignore that—people would say Matt wasn't doing what was necessary, that he was biased. If we search the house and don't find the gun, well, that's good for you, not bad. We've got a warrant, it's all legal, and nobody can say otherwise."

"I'm sorry, Daria," Matt said. "I have to do my job."

"I know that, Matt," she told him with as much dignity as she could muster. "I understand."

"You won't find any gun," Aunt Clary said firmly. "You can look all you like, but you won't find it."

She was right. They searched the house from top to bottom, in closets, boxes, trunks, under beds, behind bureaus, high shelves, low cupboards, everywhere it was possible to hide a shotgun. Then they searched the boat house. But they didn't find it.

George did.

20

I damn near missed it!" George shouted triumphantly.

He'd laid his treasure out on the concrete walk, and stood over it as proudly as if it were a twelve-point moose instead of a twelve-gauge shotgun. "I started way out, thinking it would have been thrown, but it was dropped instead. I found it right up against the breakwater—it had gone straight down."

"Where, exactly?" Stryker asked.

George turned and pointed to a place about ten feet along—almost directly in front of the empty Lattimer cottage. Stryker and Matt exchanged a glance, then concentrated on the gun itself. It was not new—a Remington, walnut stock, double-barreled, a working gun with very little engraving on the plates. Stryker hunkered down and leaned over to examine it more closely. The name "Shanks" was cut into the base of the stock in lettering much like that found on a school desk.

Matt, kneeling beside him, started to swear.

"Not exactly rusty, is it?" Stryker murmured reluctantly.

The gun, although of an older and out-of-date design, was polished and looked in good working order.

"Guess there won't be any fingerprints on that now," George said regretfully. "Been in the water since last night."

Stryker lay down on the grass and sighted along the gun, at an angle to the sun. "How did you pick it up?" he asked George. "Where did you feel it, first, and where did you grab it?"

"I didn't grab it—I was real careful," George said defensively. "We do a lot of underwater searches around here, you know. I was wearing a mask and using a light, and saw it before I touched it. Picked it up with a snaphook through the trigger guard, carried it up the ladder that way."

Stryker glanced up. "Good man," he said, in a gratified and slightly surprised voice. "You were well prepared."

"Matt taught me," George said.

"Out of a book," Matt said wryly.

Stryker grunted and stood up. "Well, you're probably right about the fingerprints. Even if the water didn't wash them off, the killer probably wiped them. Whoever cleaned this did a damned thorough job, from the look of it. Still, he had to have used oil at some point, and sometimes . . . sometimes . . ." He dug in his pocket and pulled out a small pad and a stub of pencil. He scribbled for a moment, then tore off the sheet and handed it to Matt. "Do you think you can get me these things quickly?"

Matt read down the list. "I reckon."

George came over, still dripping slightly, and peered past Matt's shoulder to read the list aloud. "One forty-gallon plastic garbage can, some picture wire, a glass dish, cotton balls, rubber gloves, sodium hydroxide, distilled water, and a tube of Hubbard's Holdfast Superglue. What the hell is this stuff for?"

Stryker grinned. "I read books too," he said. "If there are latent oil-based prints on that gun, maybe we can smoke 'em out."

Four hours later in Matt's garage, Stryker coughed, straightened up, handed Gabriel the small bottle of sodium hydroxide, and clapped the lid on the garbage can.

"Could take quite a while," he said. "And I might not get anything at all."

"But if you do..." George began.

"If I do, then we'll know who last held the gun," Stryker said flatly. "We won't know who fired it. We won't even know if it's the gun that killed our victim."

"But the odds..." George said.

"No odds," Stryker said. "It's a shotgun, not a rifle."

"Oh, shit," George said. "I forgot. No ballistic evidence from a shotgun. Non-rifled barrel, isn't it?"

"That's right. Of course, if we'd found any shells we could compare striker marks—that might tie it in. I'd say it might be useful to look for those shells. And maybe at any other shotguns in the neighborhood."

"Jesus, every farmer in the county has at least one shotgun," Matt said. "And a lot of the summer people come back in the fall to shoot duck. We can't get warrants for them all."

"No," Stryker agreed. "It's really the shells you want. Otherwise—we're no better off as far as courtroom evidence is concerned. All we know is, we found a gun near the scene of a killing that *could* have been the murder weapon. Anything else is conjecture based on circumstantial evidence."

"Wouldn't hold up in court," Matt said, clearly relieved.

"No—but it will hold up in the newspapers," Stryker said. "They've hanged people in print on a lot less than that."

"Speaking of prints," George said. "What if you *do* find some? We'll need to have others to compare, won't we?"

There was silence.

Then Gabriel sighed and picked up the battered suitcase that held the entire Blackwater Bay Forensic Investigation Unit. "I'll do it," he said wearily. "I'll go and do it right now."

"Go with him," Stryker said to George. "I'll clean up here." He began to collect odds and ends, but turned as Gabriel started up the car and began to back out of the garage. "Hey!"

Gabriel stopped and Stryker went over to lean in the window. "Not just fingerprints. Palm prints, too."

"Okay," Matt said, without even bothering to ask why. He backed up a bit more, but Stryker came after him again, before he got more than a few feet.

"Do everybody on the Island," he suggested. "Get 'em all mad. That way she won't stick out so much." He straightened.

"Okay," Gabriel said heavily. He lifted his foot from the brake and began to ease the car farther out into the alley.

"But hey!" Again the car stopped, and Gabriel waited with the engine throbbing, looking out the window at Stryker, his face blank with resignation.

"Do *her* first," Stryker said.

21

Matt stared down at the cardboard containers of fried clams, hot sauce, cole slaw, and french fries that were supposed to be inside him and not spreading slow stains across his blotter. Both George and Tilly had gone home to eat, and he was waiting for Charley Hart, grateful—for once—that his night deputy was late.

The reaction of the Islanders to being finger- and hand-printed had been mixed. The Roses had been suspicious and hesitant, Mrs. Toby and Mrs. Norton had been amused, the Greenfields had been exasperated by the messiness of it, the Robinsons had been friendly and interested, Kate Trevorne had been businesslike. Daria and Aunt Clary had been tight-lipped and cold. There remained only Len Cotman, Larry Lovich, Freddy Tollett, and the Wilberforces.

There was some consolation in that fingerprints might reveal the source of the letters Len Cotman had brought in yesterday—if the sender was someone actually on the Island. Matt's mouth twisted in distaste as he thought of what had been in the letters. He had waited until Len left to read them—the embarrassment of the man had been so great it would have been impossible to do it in front of him.

Dr. Cotman was a man of great privacy and dignity, and it must have cost him dearly to reveal that not only had he gotten these letters, but had kept them. A secret scourge? He didn't seem the type—and yet, what other reason could he have had? All the others had thrown their letters away, hot with shame and anger.

Not Len Cotman.

Why? If he had intended to show them to Matt with some thought of finding out the culprit, why had he waited so long? Or had he *known* who sent them, and thought keeping them would be some kind of weapon to hold over the sender?

Matt sighed and shook his head. He was making it all too complicated. The simple answer was usually the right one. And the simple answer was that the hate letters to the Islanders and the murder were totally unconnected. The simple answer was that Daria Grey had killed her husband— out of fear or out of greed or out of malice.

The other simple truth was that, guilty or innocent, she had very little time left.

The stop-press coverage in the evening papers and on the local radio and television newscasts would blow wide open tomorrow, because of the previous furor over the Grey marriage, because of her growing fame in the art world, and because of Michael Grey's money and madness. Irresistible reasons for innuendo and conjecture, all of it. Especially the funny part about the dumb hick sheriff who insisted on solving the case himself.

There had already been pressure calls from the state police and from some quick-triggered PR man on the Governor's staff who was worried about "image." He'd stalled them all, claiming that nothing was "clarified" yet.

Well, that was true enough.

If he wanted to, he could make certain nothing was *ever* clarified enough, drag the case out for weeks, months, even years, and never close it. No evidence, no proof, no case that would stand up in court, he could say. And nobody would be in a position to argue with him as long as he held on to the reins.

Turning it over to the state police would close off that option. They were interested in a quick arrest, and would clap Daria Grey in jail without the flicker of an eyelid. They might even drag her to trial, in which case it was anybody's guess what might happen.

He could protect her from that, but not from the rest of it.

The pressure from the media would grow and grow, and short of a solid ring of deputies, somebody, somewhere, would break through and get to the Islanders. Maybe even to Daria herself.

And the fingers would always point to her, the questions and suspicions would remain. Could she bear it? Could he?

If he lost a future election, some other sheriff would be perfectly free to reopen the case, drag it all out again, or turn it over to the state police at any time.

Perhaps arresting her would be some kind of protection. But once in, would she ever get out? Only if he found out that someone else had killed Michael Grey—and that meant luck and long hours of investigation.

He just wasn't sure he could go on with it.

Just after he'd come in from the Clamshack laden with what he had expected to be his dinner, the coroner had called. He had only had time to give the body a quick preliminary glance. He assured Matt that a written report would be sent to him by the end of the week. While the cause of death *seemed* perfectly obvious, he would not commit himself until he was able to do a full autopsy and had the laboratory reports back. A matter of days, not hours, as some television programs would have it. Maybe even a week? Yes, if it was necessary. No, it couldn't be hurried—as it was, his usual assistant was on vacation and he'd have to dictate his notes to be typed up by some temporary secretary who wouldn't know how to spell half the words, so it would have to be corrected and redone, and the laboratory was understaffed due to vacationing technicians, and—

"What about the *time* of death?" Matt had interrupted. "Can you give me any idea on that?"

"Not really." The coroner was a precise man. "I did take rough vitals—but he was lying in the open, remember."

"Make a guess."

The coroner, too, wanted his dinner. "Well, all right. Say no later than two o'clock. But that's only a guess. The full investigation may reveal—"

"That will do for starters," Matt said. "Thanks."

He'd hung up the phone and stared at the cardboard boxes on his blotter. He'd already begun to lose his appetite for clams, fries, and criminal investigation.

There was a step outside, and Charley Hart appeared. He let the screen door slam behind him. "Hey, Matt."

"Hey, Charley."

Charley was excited. "I woulda been here earlier, but I only just heard about the killing," he said, dropping into Tilly's rocker and offering his excuses at the same time. He was a skinny blond man, usually fairly diffident, but now seemingly charged with new energy. "I can't hardly believe it!" he said, slapping his hat on his knee.

"What time did you park by the Island last night?" Matt interrupted.

Charley was startled into momentary silence, and then his face began to go red. "What do you mean?"

"Look, I don't give a damn about your love life," Matt said. "Although the thought of having Mrs. Rose *and* your mother—"

Charley straightened. "We're beginning to think they might cancel each other out," he said defensively. "Like, if they were busy arguing between them . . ."

"You and Roberta might get a little peace?" This rather shrewd insight on the part of a normally timid Charley Hart startled Matt into a brief pause for reflection. "Yeah. But, if they ever got *together* . . ."

"We'd move to California," Charley said flatly.

"So what time were you out there last night?" Matt repeated the question. "You *were* out there, weren't you?"

"Well... yeah, as a matter of fact." Charley's initial enthusiasm had waned somewhat. "I drove over and waited, but Roberta never came out. It was raining, you know. She would have got wet."

"What time did you get there and how long did you wait?" Matt asked patiently.

"I got there about ten to twelve, and I waited until about twelve-thirty, but I didn't see anything or anyone," he said very quickly.

"Did anyone go on or off Paradise while you were there?"

"Not over the bridge, they didn't."

"Did you hear any boats?"

"With all that thunder? Give me a break. Anyway, I had the windows closed."

Matt sighed. "You and everyone else," he said.

22

Have you got any secrets?" Larry asked Freddy, as they were being fingerprinted. "Did you live somewhere under another name? Do you have a wife and twelve children in Holy Cross, Alaska?"

"I'm afraid not," Freddy said with evident regret, as Stryker efficiently rolled his fingertips over the paper. "You know every boring detail of my entire life from the day I was born—"

"February tenth, 1942, it was raining and your mother kept playing bridge until the pains became too frequent..." Larry pronounced the litany.

"Until the day we met."

"September thirtieth, 1975. Washington, D.C.—a magical encounter," Larry sing-songed in a parody of Broadway.

"It was pouring with rain—rain has figured largely in my life—and there wasn't a damn bit of magic in it. We were both trapped in a doorway, introduced ourselves, and we've been together ever since," Freddy said uncompromisingly.

"And it don't seem a day too long?" Stryker asked, handing Freddy one of the special wipes to clean his fingertips.

"Everything seems a day too long as you begin to approach fifty," Larry said.

"You mean a day too short," Freddy corrected him briskly as he dropped the stained tissue into the wastebasket.

Larry sighed. "So true." He looked at the cards with their fingerprints neatly boxed along the top, and dropped the air of pseudo-ennui for something more practical. "What will happen to those now? Are we to be held forever accountable in the files of Blackwater Bay?"

"Unless you want them destroyed when the case is closed," Matt said. "That's your right."

Larry looked at Freddy. "Do we?"

"I don't know—what are you planning for the future? A little light thieving?" Freddy was interested.

"I've always fancied myself as a cat burglar," Larry mused. "All in black, like Cary Grant in *To Catch a Thief.*"

"Hmmm," Freddy said. "I suggest you note the operative word in that title—'Catch.'"

"Better destroy them, Matt," Larry conceded. "I may go wild in my old age and decide to murder Freddy. It wouldn't be fair if you had an advantage."

Matt reached for the cards and made a notation in the corner of each one. "Right—they'll be destroyed. That's assuming, of course, that the case will finally be closed."

"Not going well?" Freddy asked sympathetically.

"Not going at all," Stryker said.

They needed the flashlight to walk along the back road. Stryker, accustomed to a city environment where it was half-dusk the whole night through, no longer marveled at how anyone could sneak around Paradise Island at night. The phrase "couldn't see your hand in front of your face" could be taken literally here, once everyone was asleep. He'd tried it earlier himself. Held up against the starry sky, his arm and hand were visible, but otherwise not. There were no streetlights here, no city glow, nothing beyond the individual light of each cottage.

No wonder Michael Grey had been able to sneak into the

Lattimer cottage at will. It was only Daria's supersensitivity that had made her feel his presence—she couldn't have seen him at all.

"We don't need to do Len Cotman's," Matt said as they crunched along the road behind the cottages. "I took his yesterday, when he brought in the anonymous letters. And his wife's still away, of course."

Stryker looked at him in surprise. He could just make out the taller man's features against the light from the Cotman cottage. Inside, they could see Len in the kitchen, stirring something on the stove. "He kept them? That's terrific."

"I don't know that 'terrific' is the right word. I wouldn't have kept them if they'd been sent to me," Matt said glumly. "They were god-awful. Not just nasty—but sick."

"They often are," Stryker said. "Somehow the conviction that nobody will know who wrote them frees the sender to dredge the absolute depths. According to one of our department psychiatrists, they are 'cathartic'—which is great for the sender, but not very good for the receiver. I've been a cop for almost twenty years, and I still get shocked sometimes by how rotten some people are. We had a case of incest a few years back that still stages repeat performances in my nightmares."

"I suppose something as complex as the human brain must be capable of equally complex depravity," Matt observed, as they approached the Wall.

"Yeah. That same psychiatrist told me that some people are twisted by poverty, some by their parents, some by society—and some are just plain no-good rotten."

"Nice to have a professional opinion now and again."

"Right. Watch out for the dogs."

Gabriel looked around. "What dogs?"

"The ones on the other side of the gate that are waiting to tear your throat out," Stryker said. He explained about the other night and the initial reception accorded a poor innocent shipwreck victim. "Be particularly careful of the female," he concluded, as he pushed the doorbell. "She's in heat."

"Which one is the female?"

"You'll have no trouble recognizing her." Stryker grinned.

"Absolutely not," said Mr. Wilberforce. "It can have nothing to do with us—nothing at all."

They were in the large sitting room, their reflections visible in the black expanse of the window wall. The images were insubstantial and slightly distorted, with dots of light breaking through from outside: buoys and channel markers and a few distant cottages up-coast set diamonds into their mirrored transparent selves. Their ghostly reflections moved as they moved, glanced in as they glanced out, always caught the eye of their beholder, and seemed to be listening intently to all that was said within.

"This is the first we've heard of it," Hugo said in a rather apologetic tone. He glanced toward the stiff figure of his father, who had turned his back and was staring into the fire as if it were speaking to him. "It really is a shock."

"I think it's kind of exciting," Mona said from the depths of the largest sofa. "I've always wondered what the people on the other side of the fence are like. I thought they were simple native folk who wove blankets and baskets and things." Her tone was arch, but her eyes were as business-like as a slaughterman's, assessing the height, weight, and breadth of Matt Gabriel. Stryker was no longer of interest to her now that someone taller, younger, and thicker of hair had appeared. He didn't know whether to be relieved, amused, or miffed. It felt like a combination of all three.

She stretched herself, catlike, and purred. "I don't mind you taking my fingerprints—or anything else that looks interesting."

Mr. Wilberforce turned. "I said no and I meant no," he snapped. "I believe I have the right to refuse?"

"Yes, sir, you do. I also have the right to apply for a court order forcing you to cooperate in the investigation should I feel it necessary."

"Obtain it, then," the old man snarled. "Or try. There's absolutely no reason to think any of us could possibly be responsible for the murder of some man we've never met or heard of in our lives, and so there is absolutely no need for you to take our fingerprints or involve us in any investigation."

"Actually," Hugo said slowly, "I have heard of him. And met him. Well, been introduced to him at a party. In New York. Until the other night, I had no idea he had any connections down here."

Stryker looked at him with new interest. "You knew Michael Grey? Why didn't you say so before?"

"I said I had been introduced to him at a party," Hugo said carefully. "You know the sort of thing—'This is Tom, this is Dick, this is Harry, and this is Michael.' I didn't 'know' him at all."

"Do you know anything about him?" Stryker asked.

"Dammit, Hugo!" his father exploded. "When will you learn to keep your goddamn mouth shut?"

Hugo shrugged. "They could reasonably expect I might have met him," he said. "What's the point in hiding it?"

"Jesus Christ." Mr. Wilberforce was disgusted. "Offer yourself up like a Christmas goose, why don't you?"

"Anything you could tell us—" Stryker began.

"Will be taken down and used against him?" Mona bounced with pleasure.

"—might be of help," Stryker continued, ignoring her.

Hugo shrugged again. "The night we were introduced someone warned me that he was a loose cannon. Even before he went over the edge on this thing with his wife he was into playing power games. He angeled a play by friends of mine—and apparently thought his investment bought him the right to interfere. The producer actually gave him his money back before the play opened, which was very rare—and lucky for Grey, really, because the play was an absolute flop. He was a pretty boy—and a general pain in the ass, I gather. The night I met him he was absolutely charming, so it took a while before I could believe the gossip. Apparently it took his wife even longer."

"Why didn't you introduce him to *me*?" Mona pouted. "I love men who are beautiful and dangerous."

Hugo eyed her with irritation—it seemed obvious that she had somehow evaded her father's single-drink edict. "I should have, at that. It might have taught you a lesson."

"I'm always willing to learn," Mona said, smiling at Matt, who actually flushed as he turned away.

"We're considering having her sent to Switzerland to be finished," Hugo said pointedly. "Or neutered."

Mona stuck her tongue out at him.

"Is there anything more specific you can tell us about Grey?" Stryker asked. "Acquaintances, activities?"

"Not really," Hugo said. He seemed genuinely to regret his inability to contribute anything. "I was absolutely amazed to meet his wife the other night. I'd seen her picture in the papers during all that fuss, of course, but—well, she's changed considerably. Grey is a fairly common surname, and as I said, I had no idea he had any connection with this area. New York is rather a long way from everywhere else—in more ways than one. *His* area of New York, anyway. His family is *very* well-placed, both socially and financially. We're definitely nouveau riche by comparison."

"I hardly think that's relevant," Mr. Wilberforce said sharply. "And your mother wouldn't appreciate the comment."

"My mother appreciates very little that doesn't have a designer label," Hugo murmured, sipping his pale drink. "Are you gentlemen sure you won't have something?"

"Nothing, thank you," Matt said. "We really would appreciate it if you would cooperate by allowing me to finger—"

"I said No and I meant No, dammit," Mr. Wilberforce said loudly. He returned from his communion with the fireplace and glared at them. "I think it's time you left."

Matt and Stryker looked at Hugo, who raised his shoulders and his eyebrows simultaneously. "He's in charge," he said.

"Damn right," Mr. Wilberforce said, and stared at them until they accepted his edict.

"Oh, Daddy, you're a brute," Mona pouted, as they left the room with Hugo. "I *want* my fingerprinties taken. And my toeprinties, too."

"Jesus," Matt muttered under his breath.

"I think she took a correspondence course in how to be pretty awful, but only completed the awful part," Stryker muttered back.

Hugo looked at them with considerable amusement. "Personally, I blame the parents," he said with a crooked grin. "I gather that at the age of eight I tried to drown Mona in the swimming pool. They stopped me. It's been a source of regret to all of us ever since."

He handed them over to Brody, who escorted them to the gate in the fence, but gave absolutely no sign that he recognized Stryker. In fact, he didn't speak at all, just opened the gate and waited for them to pass through. The two Dobermans eyed them peaceably from their kennel, not even bothering to growl.

"I thought you said the dogs were fierce," Matt said to Stryker.

"Only if you step on the grass," Stryker said. "I guess they're really just garden dogs."

23

The Paradise Island media war broke out at nine minutes past eight o'clock the next morning. First casualties were a three-man team from the Hatchville television station, who had managed to discover the service road that ran along Peacock Dike to the unmanned lighthouse and placed themselves opposite the Shanks back door, awaiting the first appearance of prime suspect Daria Grey, wife of the deceased, possibly as she took in the papers or the milk. Or made a break for it.

Frank Boomer and Glen Hardwicke removed them before Daria appeared, Glen and Frank sustaining heavily bruised shins in the process.

By nine o'clock there appeared to be a regatta taking place just offshore, with many small boats patrolling back and forth in front of Paradise Island. Sunlight glittered off the massed camera lenses that instantly and synchronously started to focus on anything that moved. Several excellent shots were taken of Larry and Freddy's two Abyssinian cats, the Robinsons' dog, and the blue jay that lived in Mrs. Toby's willow. The only casualty in the media fleet was entirely self-inflicted, and due to a combination of over-enthusiasm and the sudden wash from another boat. The victim gamely swam ashore, but was then escorted firmly and rapidly along the breakwater and off the Island by Harry McGruder. The sodden photographer's camera was emptied before being returned, lest others be inspired to try a similar appeal for access on humanitarian terms. His wet footprints dried slowly in the sun, and after a while his Budweiser baseball cap sank forever out of sight somewhere in front of the Roses' cottage, where it had drifted following his unexpected immersion.

In the continuing scrimmage at the bridge, one rather small cub reporter had three ribs broken by a television team as they rolled a sound van backward onto the grass, squeezing him against the bridge supports until he was forced to dive into the canal.

And Mr. Isiah Naseem, delivering the morning papers and milk, nearly had his eye put out by a reporter's pencil as an impromptu interview was attempted through his van window. (He had already refused four good offers to smuggle someone onto the Island in the back of his van. His loyalty was being strained to the limit, and possible blindness did not add to his normal good humor.) He drove over the reporter's foot. Twice.

It soon became clear to the media that this was a tough setup, and so by noon, reinforcements arrived from Grantham and other large cities. They were not only tougher, but they had bigger expense accounts. Stringers for all the wire services also ambled in, along with many amateur video experts who hoped to offer their wobbly shots to the highest bidder.

Nobody got a foot in.

Paradise won the war but lost its peace.

And just after noon, when Matt Gabriel indicated he would prefer that the Greenfields didn't leave the Island, it got even noisier.

"But my wife's nerves cannot stand all this intrusion and confusion," Harry Greenfield shouted in inadvertent rhyme.

"I can't stand it," shrilled Cissy dutifully. "It's driving me *crazy.*"

"I'm surprised you can even hear it inside your cottage," Stryker observed.

They were standing on the Island side of the bridge, with the Greenfield car throbbing beside them. Eager reporters watched from the other side, noting down every word they could manage to lip-read at a distance. Some of them even got a few right.

"Don't you realize that once you leave, you'll be hounded from pillar to post?" Stryker continued. "At least here on the Island you're protected. Over there, they're waiting to pounce." He eyed Greenfield. "Of course, they pay well per pounce—if that's of interest to you."

"Of course not," Greenfield huffed. "All I have to do is drive past and say nothing. Once we're away from here—"

"Do you have a permanent home in Grantham?" Stryker asked. He knew they did—an apartment on the east side. "Are you listed in the phone book? Are you prepared to fend off a constant stream of calls and callers..."

"Maybe we'd better stay, Harry," screeched Cissy. "Maybe it would be better."

"I think you should listen to your wife, Mr. Greenfield," Matt said.

"I listen to my wife all day long," Greenfield growled.

"But Harry," screamed Cissy, "all we have to do is keep the doors closed and the shades drawn and the phone unplugged unless we want to call out and—"

"All right, dammit," snapped Greenfield. He shrugged off Cissy's importuning hand. "All *right.*" He got into the car and reversed along the road and back into the parking space behind their cottage. Cissy, with a delicate smile, fluttered her ringed fingers and followed on foot.

"Better the devil you know," she screaked, with a dimpled glance over her shoulder. She seemed more pleased than disappointed at the change in plans.

"I wonder who will be next," Matt said. "I can't really prevent anyone from leaving now. After all, they don't have to use the road—they all have boats of one kind or another. Fran Robinson took Freddy Tollett over to the Canadian side in the *Flash* around ten this morning to get in some supplies. None of those little boats could catch the *Flash*. Fran had a shopping list from Miss Shanks and Mrs. Norton, both. It seemed only sensible to let them go."

"I don't think any of them intend to desert," Stryker said. "You told them to let Don Robinson through early this morning."

"Well, he had to get to work, didn't he?" Matt said reasonably. "Len Cotman went, too—he had appointments. But it wasn't such a gauntlet run at six A.M."

"What will it be like when they come home?" Stryker mused.

"You're about to find out," said Kate, coming up behind him. "Did you invite Tos up here?"

"No—I only asked him to get some information for me," Stryker said. "Why?"

"Well, he just called. He and Liz will be here this evening."

Stryker eyed her, trying to calculate whether she was angry or pleased. "You could have told him to stay away," he said.

"I *thought*," she said, "that it would be nice to have someone to talk to for a change." Her voice was neutral.

"Now, Kate—" Stryker began.

She grinned. "Besides—he sounded absolutely desperate to get away from his mother and sister. They're stuffing him like a Normandy goose and 'poor bambino'-ing him to death."

"And Liz?"

"I'm *always* glad to see Liz," Kate said, knowing he was, too.

"I shall await their arrival with interest," Stryker said.

Matt looked from one to the other. "Just who—"

"Sergeant Toscarelli is my partner in crime, Liz Olson is Kate's," Stryker explained rather unsatisfactorily. "The two of them seem to be falling in love. The sight is rather like watching two—"

"Now, Jack..." Kate warned.

"Like watching two ocean liners trying to moor at the same dock," Stryker finished, feeling a maritime simile was appropriate to the locale.

"And what will they be driving?" Matt asked, getting out his notebook. "So I can tell whoever is on duty that they're allowed through."

Stryker looked at Kate and raised a questioning eyebrow— between them, Tos and Liz owned several idiosyncratic conveyances. "A reconditioned army Jeep. Red. With white sidewalls," she said. "Probably with the top down."

"I hope the Island can take it," Stryker added.

Matt glanced over the bridge at the milling reporters, who—lacking any fresh target—were now arguing among themselves. "I hope *they* can."

"Playing 'The Ride of the Valkyrie' at full volume was *his* idea," Liz said, pushing her windblown blond locks back from her face. "Also the air horn."

"I got it off my dad's old truck," Tos said with some modesty. "I thought that little guy with the mustache jumped highest, but her money is on the woman in the yellow cat-suit. Anybody care to make a decision? I got fifty cents on it."

"Jesus wept," Stryker said, eyeing them with some dismay. "I know it was a head injury, Tos. But—"

"He said it was diversionary tactics," Liz said, throwing her cape back in order to search for a comb in her capacious handbag. Liz always wore capes—this one was made of natural linen with a bright Mexican print of lizards and mushrooms. "He said if we came in like that, nobody would wonder who we were, just *what* we were. A traveling circus act, perhaps."

Kate regarded her friend with deep affection. At six feet, shapely, blond, and blue-eyed, she was an impressive sight, especially in a tight T-shirt and shorts that revealed many,

many inches of smooth tanned skin. In that getup it *was* unlikely that any of the reporters guessed she was a feared and respected professor of Romance languages at Grantham University. Beside her, at six feet four inches, in magenta Bermudas, a purple-flowered shirt that hung partially open to reveal a broad, furry chest, and with the savage scar on his forehead only partly concealed by a crumpled khaki sun hat, "Tos" Toscarelli was *almost* a distraction. He certainly did not in any way resemble a police officer.

"This *is* a case of murder, folks," Kate reminded them.

"Oh, I'm getting used to murder," Liz said negligently. "Aren't you?"

"No," Kate said pointedly. "I'm not."

Liz glanced up and immediately changed gear, lowering her sunglasses and gazing over the top of them, her blue eyes questioning. "When was the last time you had a drink?" she asked.

"Not as recently as you," Kate said with a grin.

"It was a hot day and a long drive," Liz said firmly. "Large people are particularly vulnerable to dehydration, you know. All these square inches of skin. One has to keep one's liquid intake high."

"One is keeping something high," Kate agreed. "Come on in. I've given you the bedroom with the roses."

Liz stared at her in horror. "But it has twin beds."

"We pushed them together. It also has the strongest floor," Kate said, as they went inside.

Stryker and Tos looked at one another.

"What did you get?" Stryker asked.

"Plenty," Tos said. "And all of it confusing. That's why I thought I'd better come up."

"Balls," Stryker said. "You wanted to get in on the action."

Tos looked down at him, his eyes unreadable behind the dark sunglasses. "Do you have any idea what it is like to be sick while in the clutches of an Italian mother?" he asked.

"No, but—"

"Besides, you need me," Tos said smugly.

Stryker glared at him. "Have you any idea what it's like to be a cop in the clutches of a Jewish mother?"

"Did I bring you chicken soup?" Tos asked innocently. They crossed the gravel and entered the cottage. "By the way, you need a haircut."

24

"What's wrong?" Liz asked, sitting down on the edge of the bed and regarding her friend with some concern.

Kate was staring out at the lake and the dozens of little boats that still patiently crisscrossed in front of the Island, filled with (by now) irritable, seasick reporters, their cameras loaded for prey. She had almost become used to them, as you become accustomed to a nagging headache or trains that pass by all day. If you don't listen, you don't hear. A slight crossing of the eyes and you can look but not see. A matter of practice.

"Well, I feel like Harriet Vane," she complained.

"Ah. As in *Busman's Honeymoon?*"

"Yes. I mean, I know I wanted Jack to help Daria, I *know* it's my fault he's involved—"

"But you don't have to like it." Liz sipped at her gin and tonic and untied her cape. She leaned down thoughtfully to scratch a mosquito bite on her ankle.

"No. But I also feel..."

"Well? Out with it, I only have a few days to spare from

my rigorous summer schedule of sunbathing, sleeping, and eating," Liz said.

"He seems to be *enjoying* it!" Kate burst out.

"He didn't look so damn happy to me."

"Well, he did after visiting the Wilberforces." She told Liz about the "shipwreck." "He came back that first time all aglow with brandy and beaming like a lighthouse. Never a thought about how worried I was that he might have drowned, oh, no. *He* was fine. *He'd* been royally entertained by the rich folks who live on the Point. He'd penetrated their defenses and was feeling pretty clever about it—almost as if he'd done it on purpose. And if he did . . ." From the tone of her voice the consequences would be pretty terminal. "Anyway, he went down there again last night, supposedly to take fingerprints. He and Matt Gabriel came back looking like guilty schoolboys. They didn't get the fingerprints, but they got *something*."

"Possibly a dose of the clap," Liz said.

Kate turned. "*What?*"

Liz grinned and rummaged again in her capacious handbag. "Tos isn't the only one who can use the photocopier in a library. When he told me what Jack was after, I thought I'd get a few bits and pieces, too. I know what you're like. I ought to, after all these years. I figured you might feel like doing some detecting of your own. I mean, why not use non-public resources? University libraries aren't quite like public libraries."

"That's for sure," Kate agreed.

"Yes, well—ours is even less like them than most." She produced a sheaf of paper. "This first one is from the Anthropology Section."

On the top of the stack was a very revealing picture of Mona Wilberforce in bed, smiling at the camera. According to Liz's note on the top, it was from a magazine called *Wow!* Under the photography was the headline "Mmmmmmmmmmona!" The story that followed concerned lovely socialite Mona Wilberforce and her bizarre determination to seize and devour everything male from shy Sea

Scouts to "distinguished older men." (She claimed that a walker could be an asset to the erotically inventive mind.)

Apparently Mona's voracious sexual appetite was due to her deep belief in the life-extending power of what she called "sexual exaltation." She believed sexual activity happened "out of time," so that every moment of physical stimulation bestowed an equal moment of further existence.

"Whether you want it or not," Liz commented over Kate's shoulder.

Apparently, Mona was grateful to her daddy for giving her the money to do "everything and anything" she wanted in order to explore the mystic properties of sexual union between "friends or strangers."

"What about door-to-door salesmen?" Liz demanded. "Has she no respect for tradition?"

Mona was just twenty-three. She looked much younger, but was wise beyond her years, the article continued. The writer (obviously male) described her as "bold, beautiful, and eagerly female." In conclusion—having exhausted his stock of adjectives, innuendos, and (presumably) hormones—the reporter wondered whether Mona would ever prove her theory to her own or anyone else's satisfaction. "She certainly proved it to mine," he said smugly.

"Is she really like this?" Kate asked faintly.

Liz grinned. "Oh, come on. I don't think *anyone* is really like that," she said. "The guy made up the whole thing—it's the kind of dreck you find under every center spread in these flesh-books. As a matter of fact, I'd be willing to bet good money that little Mona is a steel-assed virgin—I've had girls like that in my tutorial groups. So have you. They *think* they're being sexy. Actually they're still just playing Daddy's Little Girl, so they scream when a guy actually lays a hand on them." Liz shrugged. "But she obviously cooperated on this, because I didn't find a retraction in later issues. Or reports of a lawsuit, either."

"And this was in our *Anthropology* Section?"

Liz laughed. "Yes, indeed. Don't you remember Professor Soskivitch's endowment?"

"Oh, Lord," Kate gasped, sitting down in the rocker under the window. "Soskivitch and his 'Theory of Self-Destructive Societies.' So it goes on?"

"Much to the delight of the student staff," Liz said with a chuckle. "I gather they fight to index the purchases."

The late Professor Soskivitch had left a considerable sum of money to enable the university library to maintain and extend the huge specialist archive of "Sleaze and Sensationalism" that he had amassed over the years. (His wife had another name for it—and him—when she discovered it in the closet of the guest bedroom.) He wanted to enable future anthropologists to prove his theory that certain kinds of publications provided a measurable index of progressive cultural decay.

"If he'd ever met Mona I bet he'd have felt his collecting days were over. On this evidence she's proof *positive* of cultural decay. In satin sheets," Kate said. She grimly put the article to one side. "Well, I bet that's one Tos didn't get."

"There's more," Liz said.

"On Mona Wilberforce? What on earth has she left to say?"

"Oh, nothing more on her specifically. But on the family."

"In the Soskivitch archive?"

"No, but just about everywhere else. If you ask me, it should all come under 'Psychiatry.'"

Kate looked at the next photocopied item. "My God. Mama is even worse!"

"She's not sexy," Liz observed.

"No, just wacky, apparently," Kate murmured. The article concerned Mrs. Arthur Wilberforce's generous offer to endow the Grantham Museum with enough money to open a permanent display of Psychic art. Not psychedelic, she insisted, but *Psychic*—inspired by Messages from Beyond. She couldn't understand why the museum's directors were being so *cautious*—wasn't absolutely *everybody* interested in the Other World?

"How could I have lived in Grantham all these years and missed the Wilberforces?" Kate asked, shuffling through the other things Liz had unearthed.

"We obviously don't move in the right circles," Liz said.

"On the contrary," Kate observed. "We obviously do."

"... 'gives every indication of artistic schizophrenia,'" Stryker read aloud. "'The savage subject matter and the delicate rendering of each detail reveal an artist whose demons have been successfully disguised as angels, and whose views of the world are made bearable through the filter of flawless technique.'"

"And you said she seemed like such a nice girl," Tos said.

"If I hadn't read the name at the top of the article, I would have thought this review was about Michael Grey, not Daria," Stryker said.

Tos laughed. "Oh, well—*his* reviews are much more to the point." He shuffled through his folder of photocopies and produced a very small clipping. "This one says, 'When I see crap I shall shout crap.'"

"Succinct," Stryker agreed.

"Here's another. 'If Michael Grey thinks being married to a genius imbues him with genius, then he has only his biology teacher to blame. Talent is not an osmotic commodity, and juxtaposition is no guarantee of acquisition. He can stand close to Daria Shanks Grey forever—but he will never touch her for sheer brilliance. If he hopes for success, I would suggest a career in industrial-box design.'"

"Jesus," Stryker said, holding out a hand for that one. "I'm glad nobody does reviews on police investigation."

"You mean something like, 'Stryker draws a strong line between good and evil, but his value judgment is variable, and his perspective is faulty'?" Tos suggested innocently.

Stryker glanced over at him. "You sit there in that shirt and say that to me?" he said. "In *that* shirt?"

"What's wrong with this shirt?"

"Don't ask me, my perspective is faulty. Where are the reports on Grey beating up his wife?"

"Here. A real range of opinion. The *New York Times* refers to it as a 'marital dispute' and mentions 'artistic pressures.' The *Village Voice* calls Grey a 'no-talent shithead who decided to do a portrait in blood of his gifted and beautiful wife.'"

"I love unbiased reporting, don't you?" Stryker said. He spent another ten minutes on the Greys, then looked up at Tos. "I don't understand this at all."

"I told you it was confusing."

"If I took these reviews or samples of her work into court as character witnesses, they could really undermine the defense," Stryker said, swinging his feet up onto the sofa and dropping the first group of photocopies onto the floor. "Apparently all she paints is beggars, dropouts, criminals, whores, and garbage dumps. Almost every review talks about her 'two personalities' or her 'artistic schizophrenia.' If I was on a jury I would look at those pictures and think yes, maybe this girl *is* capable of cold-blooded murder. Wouldn't you?"

"Absolutely," Tos agreed. "I'd also say that her husband had a pretty good case for wanting to strangle her—*if* you only showed *his* artistic reviews as character witnesses. All the critics say she's brilliant and he's a klutz."

"Yeah. But then there's a lot of *other* stuff about both of them. Society stories of his generosity and charm, her gracious and sweet personality, how attractive and delightful they both are, right alongside the police report of him beating her unconscious and the claims of his family that *she* drove him to it in private with her vicious and cruel tongue. Jesus. What are we supposed to believe? Who's telling the truth?"

"Me," Kate said, coming down the stairs with Liz. "We're all at *least* two people, Jack, and creative artists are more divided than most."

"Sure, I'll give you that," Stryker conceded. "And I can

see that even a schizophrenic has a right to be damned scared of a psychotic in the same ward."

"They wouldn't *be* in the same ward," Tos argued.

"Just in the same marriage," Stryker said.

"Well, I've got a new suspect for you," Kate said. "How about Mona Wilberforce?" She had the dubious satisfaction of seeing Jack Stryker appear disconcerted, and glanced at Liz. "See?" she said.

"See what?" Stryker asked in a belligerent voice.

Wordlessly, Kate handed him the article from *Wow!* Tos leaned over for a look.

"We have decided she shot Michael Grey because he turned her down," Liz said. "Probably the first man in the world to do so. It threw her into a tizzy, and *bang!*"

"Then I should be dead, too," Stryker muttered.

Both women leaned forward. "What?" Kate demanded. "What was that?"

"No wonder they call this Paradise Island," Tos said without thinking.

"And what does *that* mean?" Liz asked sharply.

Both men leaned back. "Where did you get this rubbish?" Stryker counterattacked, throwing the article aside.

"From the university library," Liz said. "I thought you might be interested in an objective, scholarly point of view."

Tos was still looking at the picture. "This is scholarly?"

Liz explained about the Soskivitch Collection. Leaving the *Wow!* article to one side, to avoid bloodshed, they began to compare the two stacks of "evidence." The discussion carried on through dinner and after. When Kate went to make coffee around nine o'clock, they felt they had earned it.

"The consensus is that the Wilberforce family is a collection of nuts," Stryker said, leaning back and putting his feet up on the arm of the sofa. "Right?"

"Right," Tos said.

"Wrong," Liz said. They both looked at her. "*My* opinion

is that they only *appear* to be nuts. It's all over the top. Too bad to be true."

"Oh, come on," Stryker said. "Look, you haven't actually met them, have you? I have, and I assure you, they *are* crazy."

"Even Mona?" Kate asked, returning with the coffee.

"*Especially* Mona," Stryker growled. "Despite his relatives, Hugo *seems* okay."

"They said Dr. Crippen could be charming," murmured Kate.

He ignored this. "I haven't met the mother yet, but the old man is a crackpot of the first water. One minute he smiles, the next minute he stabs. How he's gotten to be rich is a mystery."

"It wouldn't be to Machiavelli," Liz pointed out.

"Hah!" Kate said. "I should think it's his percentage on what Mona brings in—"

"Listen, let's leave the Wilberforces and get back to the Greys," Tos said hurriedly. "Allowing for the fact that Liz and I haven't met *them* either."

"We've *all* missed our chance to meet Michael," Kate observed.

"The consensus is that the Greys might both have been lying, both telling the truth, or one or the other lying and one or the other telling the truth," Liz said. "Which leaves us no further on. *She* could have set up a situation where killing him seemed excusable, or *he* could have been tormenting her as she claimed, or—"

"Some consensus." Tos took his coffee mug and stirred cream into it. "Any cookies around?"

"Your cookie days are ended," Liz scowled. "Here beginneth the diet."

"The hell with *that!*" Tos said, outraged.

Liz glared at him, then shrugged. "Okay, the hell with that. Just thought I'd make the gesture. Are there any cookies, Kate?"

"Snickerdoodles, raisin-and-oatmeal, brownie bites, or molasses thumbprints," Stryker said, knowing that Mrs.

Norton had made a "delivery" that afternoon. This demonstration of expertise earned him a long, hard look from everyone. He shrugged a shoulder. "Some of us have it, and some of us don't," he said negligently.

When they had all made their selections, Stryker leaned back. "And what about Bobcat Investments?" he asked Tos through a mouthful of oatmeal-and-raisin.

"Ah," Tos said edgily. "I was afraid you were going to ask me that." He put down his coffee cup and delved once again into the folder to produce a single sheet of paper. "This is the best I could do—it's a rabbit warren."

Stryker took the paper. "What do you mean?"

"It's all there, 'all' being a laugh and a half. Bobcat Investments is part of a small conglomerate called Elysium, which in turn is owned by a holding company called Roha, which is based in the Cayman Islands. Finding out *their* pedigree takes more clout and more time than we've got."

"You say Elysium is a conglomerate," Stryker said slowly. "What are the parts of the whole?"

Tos produced another slip of paper. "Sorry—that's here. As far as I can tell, they're in names only—Aphrodite's Secret, Nectare, and Goddesse." He recited the list with a twist of wry.

"Address?"

"Of Elysium?"

"Of any of them."

"All the same—a post-office box. We would have to go to the postal authorities to find out who pays the bills on it, and whether the mail is collected or forwarded, and if forwarded, to what address. Which in turn, could be another blind."

"Why should it be?"

"Why shouldn't it? They seem to be going to a lot of trouble to be invisible—or at the very least, hard to slap with a subpoena. It could be a long and winding trail."

"Great."

"But why would what sounds like a cosmetic company go into land development?" Kate asked.

"Your guess is as good as mine. As far as I can tell, they haven't really gone into anything beyond fancy names, so—"

"Jesus—what's that?" Stryker raised his head, startled. A thin but piercing shriek was rising and falling in the distance.

"It's the siren calling up the volunteer firemen," Kate said. She took a breath and looked suddenly pale. "Do you smell smoke?"

25

It's the Lattimer place!"

They had all tripped over one another getting out the front door, and now stood on the lawn looking down the Island. Smoke was coiling out of the upper windows of the empty cottage, forming itself into rippling curtains that were then torn and blown away by the breeze. Sparks twinkled in the updraft, challenging the stars overhead.

"My God," Kate said, horrified. "What if it spreads?"

They ran toward the cottage, joining the other Islanders who had spilled out of their respective doors. As usual, they all looked to Don Robinson to take charge, but before he could say anything, Mrs. Rose came lumbering up, out of breath and barely able to speak.

"They won't be able to get through," she gasped.

"Who?"

"The fire engines . . . the bridge is blocked by all those reporters' cars, and there's hardly room for them to move back . . . it will take a while . . ."

"Come on," Stryker said to Tos. Let's see what we can do down there."

"I always knew I'd end up back in Traffic," Tos grumbled,

and followed his partner back to the road and toward the bridge.

"What about buckets?" somebody suggested.

"I've got a couple of fire extinguishers in the boat house," somebody else said. They milled and wavered, unsure what to do.

Fran suddenly shouted. "Uncle Paul!"

Everybody stared at her as if she were insane, but after a second Don's face brightened. "Sure. They should still work. Here—Freddy, Larry, Len—come with me."

Perplexed, the other men followed the tall figure back toward the Robinson boat house, while Fran explained to the women. "Don's Uncle Paul Osius was an inventor, and one of the things he patented was a portable pump for fighting forest fires. He left his prototypes to Don—and they're still out there under all the junk in the boat house. At least, I hope they are."

Daria and Aunt Clary appeared on their porch, Aunt Clary muffled in a blanket and dragging herself along in her aluminum walker. Mrs. Toby and Mrs. Norton went over to help her down the three steps to the lawn.

"The smoke is coming through our windows," Daria said, her eyes pink-rimmed and tearful. "The rooms are filling up with it."

Without anyone's noticing, the wind had shifted. Not a great deal—just a few degrees—but enough to mean trouble.

Six cottages lay up-island of the burning Lattimer place— and all of them, including the Wilberforce enclave, were suddenly very vulnerable.

"Well, dammit," Liz suddenly said. "We can't just stand here. Buckets will do until something else comes along, won't they?"

A sudden lick of flame burst out of an upper window, lighting their upturned faces. Immediately everyone scattered, galvanized by the realization that a third of the island homes were literally "under fire."

Back in the Trevorne cottage, Liz and Kate rummaged in the kitchen and on the back porch, finally producing one plastic bucket and one large Dutch oven. "Now all we have to do is move the lake onto the land," Kate said grimly.

They ran back and looked around. Everyone had returned with something—but they were mostly women. They stared at one another, holding their buckets and pans.

"Bucket brigade," Liz said.

A line was quickly formed between the lakeside and the now crackling Lattimer cottage, but the problem of lifting the water from the lake was still with them. Realizing that her height was an advantage, Liz jumped fully clothed into the dark water and began handing up buckets of water to Kate, who leaned down over the breakwater's edge to receive them. She then poured the water into the first receptacle that was held out to her and handed the bucket back to Liz. The pans and buckets of water began to move down the line, but their progress was slow and spillage was great. Within a few minutes, however, both Liz and Kate began to feel their muscles flutter. Water is heavy, and lifting it over your head (Liz), or dragging it up with your back bent double (Kate), was not a task for the unfit. Brute strength was needed.

Then Hugo Wilberforce and his security men arrived, apparently drawn by the noise and the increasing glow— the midsummer dusk was giving way to the night, and the light of the burning was more and more apparent. Hugo took in the problem at a glance, jumped in beside Liz, and directed one of his men to do the lifting from above.

Liz dragged herself up the ladder, water streaming from her shorts and blouse. She joined Kate on the bucket brigade. Everyone was helping—including Aunt Clary, who was leaning on her walker and handing the empty receptacles to the Wilberforce security man at the breakwater. Even the Greenfields had appeared. Their impeccable appearance was soon reduced by sloshed water and flying soot, so that in the wavering light they were more or less indistinguishable from the others.

It was upon this dramatic scene that Mona Wilberforce

arrived, having followed her brother. Despite the late hour and the coolness of the evening, she was wearing a bikini.

Kate looked up. "My God," she said.

"What?" Liz peered out through the straggling strands of her dripping hair. "Oh. Miss Satin Sheets. Well, I have to admit—some nice workmanship has gone into that." They continued to shift the water-filled receptacles to one another and on down the line, all the while staring at the vision before them. Mona danced up and down, wringing her hands.

"Oh, I didn't bring anything...I should have brought something..." she simpered.

"You brought your arms, didn't you?" Liz asked uncompromisingly. "Here—get in line."

"Oh...oh...all right." Mona gingerly inserted herself between Liz and Mrs. Toby. "Hello," she said to the older woman. "I'm Mona Wilber—eeeech!"

Liz had handed her a dishpan full of lake water, and a good deal of it had slopped over, soaking the pretty bikini.

"Sorry," Liz grunted.

Mona glared at her, but handed the nearly empty dishpan on to Mrs. Toby, who received it and its meager contents with a wry glance. "You could have mailed that in," she said to Mona, who pouted, but managed not to spill much of the next container.

Then Don and the other men appeared, lugging two objects that trailed hoses and flapped with unbuckled straps. Freddy Tollett was carrying a couple of cans of gasoline.

"I hope there's some life in these," Don said. "I put in new spark plugs, just in case—that's what took so long." He threaded the starting rope through the appropriate pulley, took a deep breath, and pulled.

Nothing.

Everyone groaned.

"Try again," Larry said.

"I am, I am," Don said. He tried again. And again.

On the fifth pull, the little red engine snarled into life, and everyone cheered. Don handed the starting rope to

Larry and told him to start the other one. Then he bent down and lifted the engine onto his back. Freddy grabbed the straps and fastened them around Don's chest.

Hugo appeared at the top of the ladder, streaming water as Liz had done. "Here," he said. "I'll carry the other one, if you can get it started."

It took a little longer, but Larry got it going. When Don and Hugo were both rigged out—a matter of only a minute or so—Don directed Larry and Freddy to drop one end of his take-up hose over the breakwater and into the lake.

"Uncle Paul had a special long hose put on, remember, Fran?"

"He said we might need it one day—boy, was he right!" Fran shouted over the noise of the two small engines.

Hugo shouted. "I'll go out back and draw from the canal."

"Good idea," Don shouted back. "We'll hit it from both sides."

When the hoses were arranged properly, Don put the pump into gear, and a fierce stream of lake water spouted from the hose that he held before him. He directed it at the Lattimer cottage. Despite the small size of the pump, the force was sufficient to break an upper window, letting the water in and onto the flames. From the back, another jet of water appeared, breaking through the back-porch windows and running alongside the framework of the cottage. It was nothing like the force of water that the fire department could have supplied, but it was *something*.

Then, after a minute, the water from the rear was suddenly directed away from the Lattimer fire and onto the Shanks cottage.

"No!" Don shouted. "Keep in on the windows!"

There was an indistinguishable response from the rear. "Jesus, we're only holding it, why doesn't he—" Don began angrily. Then somebody yelled.

"It's jumped to Miss Clary's roof!"

The spectators, bedraggled and soaking, now saw that a few sparks had indeed caught on the roof and clapboard siding of the Shanks cottage, which stood only twenty feet away from the Lattimer place. It was clear Hugo thought it better to save what was whole than limit the damage on what was clearly lost.

"That was smart," Liz said to Kate.

"I never noticed," Aunt Clary said. "We might have gone up too, Derry." She began to shake. Daria put an arm around her.

"It's all right, Aunt Clary," she said. "Look. Mr. Wilberforce has soaked it all down now. The water's running down from the roof and over the side—it will put out any other sparks that cross over." She spoke confidently, but mentally crossed her fingers.

The Lattimer cottage itself was still containing the fire, but it was only a matter of time before the outer fabric of the building would begin to go. Even as they watched, two of the shuttered front porch windows burst outward, followed by a rolling ball of flame that licked out and up over the porch roof, attacking the cottage from the outside.

The women shouted and screamed, falling back before the sudden wave of heat and smoke that came across the lawn.

"It's been so dry," someone said. "That rain the other night didn't really damp things down."

"And that place is filled with junk," another voice reminded them. "All that horrible, ugly stuff Kit brought back from Africa... shouldn't wonder if something in there set it off."

Aunt Clary snorted. "Next they'll be saying it was voodoo, I suppose."

"Voodoo is West Indian," Kate murmured vaguely, as if it mattered.

"But originally African," Liz said in a similarly automatic tone. They glanced at each other and grinned ruefully. "There will be a test at the end of the class," Liz said in a resigned voice.

"It's terrible," Mrs. Rose said, coming up to them. She, like all of them, presented a comic figure—clothes plastered with lake water or, worse, canal water (25 percent organically pungent mud, 3.5 percent weed, 9.33 percent oily pollution), and face streaked with sweat and smoke. They were all coughing now, as the smoke spread around them in a pall. The fretful evening breeze, which earlier had threatened destruction to everything up-island from the Lattimer place, had abruptly died down. While this relieved some of the worry, it meant that the smoke could settle around its source. "We've never had a fire on the Island," she went on in a hoarse choked voice.

"Except for wild barbecues," Fran said, joining them.

"Hell, *they* don't count," Mrs. Rose said.

"But where are the firemen?" Aunt Clary asked in a distraught voice.

"If they're not here yet, it's not for lack of trying," Len Cotman said. "Listen to that."

From the bridge end of the Island there rose a great noise of honking and sirens. The scene there was of barely contained chaos. Jack and Tos had been working with the deputies—directing, pushing, or dragging the many cars and vans of the reporters onto lawns and sandbanks and ditches so that the fire engines could get through. In the end it was a fender-scraper, but they got them over the bridge.

Of course, once the fire engines had cleared the bridge, the newspaper and television men tried to follow.

"Is it the Shanks place?" one of them shouted.

"None of your business," Glen Hardwicke countered, re-forming his line of deputies.

"But this is news!" they protested. "The public has a right to know!"

"Some of the public also has a right to keep its trouble to itself." Hardwicke's voice was bland, and he did not move out of the way. He did, however, heft his shotgun a little, as if to test its weight.

The argument became quite heated, but when they saw that Hardwicke and the other deputies had things in hand, Jack and Tos returned to the scene of the fire. Joining the others on the lawn, they stood watching as the firemen completed the dousing that Don and Hugo Wilberforce had begun.

The Blackwater Volunteer Fire Department was literally a motley crew. Summoned from all directions and all occupations, they answered the call in whatever they were wearing at the time. The chief was the only one in full gear. The others—despite the hold-up at the bridge—were still struggling into their oilskins or slickers.

They were all ages from eighteen to fifty-two but they were fairly well drilled in what had to be done. Two of the bunch (one in surfing shorts and the other in a dress shirt and bow tie), nicknamed Daz and Dooga, were performing their usual double-act of Young Frankenstein and Igor ("Yes, Master") while dragging hose reels across the lawn. Lem Turkle and Farley Biltmore (pajamas and swimming trunks, respectively) were fitting hoses to nozzles and outlets in perfect synchrony, despite the fact that they hadn't spoken to one another in six weeks due to an altercation over a stolen base in a Tigers-Indians ball game.

Harry Peters, the grocer, had been serving at the delicatessen counter when the siren went off, and still had his apron on over his boots. Isiah Naseem, caught in the bath, had grabbed the first thing at hand, and thus—in his wife's new Yves Saint-Laurent jumpsuit—was the most stylish firefighter in the Great Lakes area.

All of them were inordinately cheerful, considering their present occupation, which said much for the rarity of real fightable fires in Blackwater.

"I thought it would be down to the ground by now," Stryker said, running up with Tos close behind him. "It took such a long time to clear the way for the engines, and that fire was moving fast."

Kate explained about Don's Uncle Paul and his portable pumps. Fran, listening, grinned. "For once, keeping the boat house full of everything Don ever bought, found, or inherited paid off... the Robinsons have always been pack rats." Her grin faded. "Oh, hell—now I'll *never* get him to clear the place out. Every time I suggest it, he'll just say, 'Remember Uncle Paul's pumps?'"

"And I'll be right, too," Don said, coming up. "Undo these straps, will you, Frannie? These things are supposed to be portable, but after a while they weigh a ton."

They all turned to the task of undoing the soaked and recalcitrant webbing straps. Hugo came up, followed by one of his security men, who was carrying his pump. They placed it on the grass. "That's a hell of a useful item," Hugo said, gazing down at the pump. "Where did you get it?"

Again there were explanations. Hugo raised an eyebrow. "Your Uncle Paul still around, is he?"

"No, he's passed on," Fran said sadly.

"Ah," Hugo said. "Shame. That thing takes good advantage of a bad situation—and that's often a way to make money." He looked around with a smile, apparently unashamed of possessing the family streak of venality. Even so, from the faces that smiled back at him, it was obvious he was making it difficult for the Islanders to maintain their dislike after his performance during the past hour. Hugo looked down at his filthy tracksuit and tried to wipe a smear of oil from his forearm. The effort only spread it. He glanced back at the Lattimer cottage.

"Well, things seem to be under control now—I think I'll go home and have a shower."

"Thanks for all your help," Don said. Whatever the man's family might be like, he had behaved like a good neighbor and more in the past hour. His actions had spoken for him, and Don, for one, was grateful. The Robinson cottage might also have gone up if things hadn't been kept under control until the firemen arrived.

Daria spoke up too. "We really appreciate what you did, Hugo," she said. "Aunt Clary's cottage would have caught fire if you hadn't been here."

"Glad I was around, then." Hugo smiled at her.

"Well, I think all the men were just *wonderful*," Mona said, strolling over. She had been watching the firemen—

most of them young and strong and stripped for action. Now she stroked Tos's muscular arm, which just happened to be beside her, and gazed admiringly across the group at Don Robinson, who was managing to look fairly magnificent in a tousled, rangy way.

The men stirred and grinned.

The women glared.

Somehow the lake water that had bedraggled every other female present had produced on Mona's skin a kind of shimmering gleam. As there was a great deal of skin on display, she seemed to shine in the waning light of the dying fire. She didn't even have the decency to have pink eyes from the smoke, Kate was annoyed to see.

"And who is *that*?" Fran asked her through gritted teeth.

"That," answered Liz, in a low, strangled voice, "is Miss Mona Wilberforce."

"Ah," Fran said. "Maybe that big fence of theirs isn't such a bad idea, after all."

"I mean, it was so exciting—the way you all took charge and everything," Mona was chirping.

"Ah, shucks, ma'am, it warn't nuthin'," Stryker said in an ironic tone. He pretended to dig his toe into the lawn.

"Well, it *was!*" Mona insisted, ignoring Stryker's sarcasm and somehow managing to reduce her hips and expand her bust in one breath, putting the fragile straps of the bikini under severe strain.

"I thought I told you to wait in the car," Hugo said to his sister in an exasperated voice, exchanging a resigned glance with Stryker, who grinned.

"But it was so *exciting*. I wanted to *see*." Mona pouted.

Aunt Clary Shanks was gazing at Mona and her posturings openmouthed. Mrs. Toby leaned over. "It's not polite to stare at the afflicted," she said. "Close your mouth, Clary."

"If you ask me, I think it's a thyroid condition," Nell Norton observed.

"Wouldn't they have to cut her throat to cure that?" Liz asked Kate sotto voce.

Kate barely stifled a laugh, and Mona shot her a poisonous glance.

Hugo took hold of his sister's arm. "Come on, brat—it's time for your carrot juice." Then he turned, gathered up his two men with a glance, and they all walked away, Mona casting glances over her shoulder.

"So that's the Wilberforces," Mrs. Rose said.

"Only two of them," Kate said.

"Well, the girl is a tramp, but *he's* a handsome sonofabitch, isn't he?" Mrs. Rose opined admiringly.

"Mother!" her daughter said in a shocked voice.

"I've got eyes," Mrs. Rose said. "I can see."

They watched the Wilberforces and their escorts disappear around the edge of the Cotman place.

"Interesting, what he said," Freddy Tollett observed in a deceptively mild voice. "About making money by taking advantage of a situation."

Larry Lovich looked at his friend. "Why?"

"Well," Freddy said, glancing around. "If it's so advantageous to *use* a situation, it must be even more advantageous to *create* a situation." He paused delicately. "Or am I just being a naughty little thinker?"

26

I can tell you two things about the Lattimer place," Volunteer Fire Chief Mark Clowes said. He was surprisingly young for the job. Tall, dark, and handsome, he appeared to be a typical all-American—until he opened his mouth. Then his strong Nottingham accent betrayed his British birth. "One—it's unsafe, so I want nobody poking noses in there, just for the minute, if you doon't mind. We're going to pull down the unstable walls when things cool off a bit. Someone could get hurt, otherwise. Me, most likely."

Stryker and Matt Gabriel nodded solemnly. Beyond Clowes' shoulder stood the smoldering husk of what had been the Lattimer cottage. In the pearly light of pre-dawn, it had a peculiar asymmetric appearance, since the roof had fallen partly in. It was no longer white, but surfaced with the smoked-on shadows of flames. The clapboard siding above each empty window frame was charred to an alligator texture. Steaming heaps of unidentifiable furniture and oddments littered the lawn. The stink of the burned building and its contents was everywhere, embittering the fresh early-morning air.

"What's the other thing?" Matt asked.

The fire chief sighed. "It was definitely arson," he said.
"You're sure?" Stryker asked.

Clowes looked at him. "It's as plain as a wen on a
whippet's tail. You can sniff bloody kerosene everywhere in
the house. Lou Buncie found two burned-out petrol tins
lying in the middle of the sitting-room floor, where they had no
right to be. Doesn't take an expert to make that out, does it?"

Matt glanced at Stryker. "You were right," he said regretfully. "I should have listened to you."

Clowes raised an eyebrow. "Right on what?" he asked.

"He *predicted* arson—or something—yesterday," Matt
said. "I thought he was crazy, but I guess he wasn't."

The fire chief had shed his oilskins once the fire was out.
He stood before them in boots, pants, and suspenders, his
lean muscular body streaked with soot and sweat. Midsummer was a hot time to barbecue a house. There was a tiger
tattooed on his right upper arm—a souvenir of his wilder
youth. Mark Clowes had worked on one of the big mer-
chant ships that crisscross the world's oceans and, like
many before him, had sailed down the St. Lawrence Sea-
way straight into the heart of North America. He had fallen
in love equally with the place and a girl, and now had a
thriving business restoring and redecorating the historic
homes of Blackwater. Fighting fires was as close as he
came, these days, to adventure. He did not, however, take
kindly to someone's setting them on purpose.

"Those who set blaze to folk's homes are bloody mad,"
he said angrily. He glared at them for a moment, and then
he raised an eyebrow. "This wouldn't have anything to do
with your murder, would it?" he inquired.

"It would." Stryker was angry too. Knowing—or guessing—
ahead of time hadn't provided even an ounce of prevention
or protection. He cursed himself for having been so hesitant about insisting on a guard. Matt had thought he was
overdramatizing—he'd almost thought so himself—and now
the Island, Kate's precious Paradise, was despoiled by fire
as well as violent death.

"Destroying evidence, like?" Clowes persisted.

"Something like that," Stryker said.

The fire chief glanced over his shoulder. "Well, they did a good job, then. There's not enough left in there to fill a miner's lunch pail." He turned back, real anger in his eyes. "If you were so bloody sure something was going to happen, why didn't you bloody do something about it?"

Matt and Stryker spoke together.

"I did," they both said.

And then stared at one another in surprise.

"I told my deputies to keep an eye on the place," Matt said. "For all the good it did."

"And I stole something," Stryker admitted. "Arrest me."

"It does seem to fit," the medical examiner said reluctantly. "He's been lying on it since yesterday, just waiting for me to turn him over."

"And we just zipped up the body bag and sent him along face-up," Matt agreed.

"You would have found it the minute you got to the head," Stryker said, taking the plastic bag containing the knobkerrie back from the ME.

"I've been so goddamned backed up here—you have no idea what it's like." The county medical examiner was perfect casting for Humpty-Dumpty, ovoid in shape from his bald head to his tiny feet, a wide black belt cutting the line midway and having a struggle with it. He'd arrived to find Stryker and Matt Gabriel waiting for him, and had been resentful at their presumption in coming along personally, as if he'd been derelict in his duty.

"Pretty much like it is in the city, I'd guess," Stryker said. "Death seems to run a lot faster than the rest of us—Bannerman is always telling us to get off his back."

"There's a regular order to these things," the ME said. His name was Furzell, and he was already regretting his lavish breakfast, as sour acid rose in his throat. He reached into his jacket, which he'd hung on the coatrack, and extracted his pills. Some days he could sneak bacon past his ulcer, and some days he couldn't. No telling in advance. Damned annoying. "We do them in order, as they come in—"

"Sure," Matt said in a conciliatory voice. "It was only that we had this thing and wanted to check it with you. Get your opinion and all, before we proceeded."

"Yes. Well." Furzell crunched the pills and washed them down with a paper cup of water from the dispenser. "I'll have to do exact measurements—"

"But you think this could be the murder weapon?" Stryker interrupted.

Furzell glowered at him. "Not easy to say until I open up the head and do some analysis. But if it was used first, then, yes—it probably was."

"I still don't know what made you think of it," Matt said, eyeing the knobkerrie in the plastic bag. Stryker had laid it on an adjacent autopsy table and it looked incongruous and primitive against the modern gleam of the stainless steel.

"Well, it was the only *clean* thing in the Lattimer place," Stryker told him. "You could write your name in the dust on everything else—but that African club was *shiny*. It bothered me. I went back to get it, sure—but I promise you I didn't know then that it was the actual murder weapon. Just a guess."

Furzell managed to belch in a tone of annoyance, an ability born of long practice. "It would explain a few things that bothered me," he said, implying his expert eye hadn't *really* been fooled for a minute by that gaping shotgun wound in Michael Grey's chest. "I told you there were anomalies."

"Yes, you did," Matt said gravely. "You certainly did."

A few minutes later, Matt and Stryker emerged, blinking, into the hot sunlight of the Hatchville County Hospital parking lot. The cloying smell of formaldehyde still filled their nostrils. It took a moment or two for the scent of frying onions from a nearby White Tower and the tarry tang of baking asphalt to clear their sinuses.

"I have a feeling you've made an enemy there," Matt said with a grin. "Story is that Furzell needs two hours of sleep behind his desk before he can get going each day. He's not used to being second-guessed before eleven A.M."

"Okay. I'll just add him to the list," Stryker said. "Kate is always telling me that every time I'm right, somebody loves me a little less."

They reached the car and opened the doors to let the heat out before getting in for the drive back to Blackwater Bay. Matt reached in and flicked on the air conditioner, then straightened and stared across the car roof at Stryker. "So it wasn't that the rain had washed away all the blood from the shotgun wound—"

"—but that the shotgun wound was inflected *after* death. There was never any actual bleeding in the wound—just a bit of drainage," Stryker finished. "If that clown in there does his stuff right—"

"He's supposed to be pretty good—"

"After eleven."

"Right."

"Then he may well find that the murder was done with Lattimer's African souvenir. And if that's so, then anyone— man, woman, or child—could have done it. No great strength was needed. That knobkerrie was made and *weighted* to kill, nothing else, and nothing less. Forget your forty-five Magnums and your fancy knives—that simple primitive weapon was scary as hell to hold. The minute I picked it off the wall I felt it was still sort of. . . I don't know. . . eager for death. That's why I put it back so fast. It was only later that I began to think about it."

"That isn't what scares *me*," Matt said. "That club may feel evil, and it's evil that someone bashed Michael Grey over the head with it, sure. But it could have been in self-defense, during a fight—"

"He was struck from behind," Stryker pointed out. "The *back* of his skull was crushed in, very neatly, with no break in the skin, no bleeding. Grey had thick hair, he was lying on his back in the grass, and that shotgun wound sort of drew the eye. That's why we missed the head injury—and why the medical examiner hadn't noticed it yet, no matter what he says."

"Okay, okay, but that still isn't the worst of it to me. It's the thought that once Michael Grey was dead the killer wasn't satisfied. He—"

"Or she."

"—or she thought about it. Stood over him and *thought* about it. Made some kind of plan, took it even further, dragged him out onto the lawn, waited for the lightning, counted for the thunder, and then blasted him full in the chest with a shotgun."

"Well—there was the storm, all handy. There was Aunt Clary's old shotgun in the boat house—there was Daria under pressure—and there was Michael Grey."

"But then it couldn't have been Daria," Matt said triumphantly. "Why would she set up Grey's death to implicate herself?"

Stryker shrugged. "Double bluff?"

"Oh, come *on*—Daria?" Matt's disbelief ran deep.

"If you care about her, don't insult her by thinking she's stupid," Stryker said quietly.

"But it was so cold-blooded. Jesus—I can't believe *any-body* could be that . . . that . . . calculating."

"Or that desperate?" Stryker asked. "I can."

They got into the car, and Matt started the engine, then leaned back without putting it into gear. He stared blankly out at the car in front of them. "How would Hugo know about Aunt Clary's shotgun, anyway?"

"I gather it was pretty common knowledge. I think even I might have known about it—Kate was always telling me stories about Paradise. And it was talked about at the party, remember?"

"Yes, but—"

"As it happens, we don't know that it was used to shoot Grey at all," Stryker said, snapping his seat belt. "We only know it was found near the scene of the crime. *Any* shotgun could have been used to inflict that postmortem wound. There's no ballistic evidence with a shotgun, remember?" He shifted in his seat. "By the way, the Shanks gun was wiped as clean as that knobkerrie. I checked this morning—my makeshift little experiment didn't fume up a single print on the stock or the barrel. It was polished up like new. Sorry."

Matt put the car in gear and reversed out of the parking bay. He drove through the outskirts of Hatchville and then turned toward the main highway. "What time did you go into the Lattimer place to get that thing off the wall, anyway?"

"About seven, I guess. Tos and I slipped in while the girls were making dinner. Why?"

Matt shrugged. "So much for me telling my patrols to keep a special eye on the place."

"Listen, short of standing men around it shoulder to shoulder, or installing some kind of an alarm system, there was no way you could have kept me *or* the arsonist out of the Lattimer cottage. Anyway, your men know I was helping out—they probably saw me but thought nothing of it."

"Well, they should have noticed—"

"Oh, hell, Matt—never mind me. Why would they have taken any notice of an *Islander* wandering around, either? They were only supposed to notice *outsiders*, not the people who were supposed to be there. I gather from Kate that Islanders wander in and out of one another's places all the time—it would only be a matter of walking along casually and then ducking in at the right moment."

"Well, nobody came over the bridge, that's for sure."

Stryker gazed out at the flat fields that bracketed the highway. Under the blast of the sun the waving carpets of grain and the tall stalks of corn seemed to shimmer. "By that I assume you've decided it had to be someone on the Island who set the fire?"

"What else?"

Stryker shook his head. "Again, short of men standing shoulder to shoulder around its entire perimeter, there's no way you can keep Paradise secure. It's not a real island. A guy in a wet suit could have just waited his opportunity between patrols, climbed the breakwater and crossed the lawn or the back road in about forty seconds or so."

"Why a wet suit?"

"Black doesn't show up in the dark the way naked skin does." He paused. "Unless the skin is black, of course."

"Are you talking about Len Cotman?"

"Not particularly," Stryker sighed. "It was just an idle observation." There was a short silence, and then he spoke again. "Thinking of Paradise as an island is an illusion. In fact, if you ask me, everything about the place is an illusion—maintained by the people who live on it and the people who *wish* they lived on it. It's the old illusion that there is a 'right' side of any given tracks. Something to aim for, maybe."

"Or at," Matt murmured.

"Yeah, or at," Stryker agreed. "Envy is right up there with the big ones, like greed and hate."

"She didn't kill him," Matt said in a flat voice.

"Maybe, maybe not. I'm not going to come to any conclusions without more evidence."

"Meaning I shouldn't, either?"

"Whatever you like." Stryker stared out at the passing fields. "Dammit—I just wish that when Tos and I went in there last night for the knobkerrie we'd also picked up those sheets and other things from the bedroom. I'd planned to go back this morning."

Matt flicked the turn signal and glanced up and down the intersection, then turned onto the road that led to Blackwater. "Good thing I went back last night, then, isn't it? Before the place burned down, I mean."

"Oh, sure you did," Stryker said sarcastically. "I wish."

Matt shrugged. "Okay, then I didn't."

Stryker turned in his seat to stare at him and then, slowly, grinned. "Son of a bitch," he said. "You sneaky bastard."

Matt smiled sadly, but didn't take his eyes from the road. "I guess that makes two of us, doesn't it?"

27

I can't think of anything that would help you," Daria
said quietly. "Michael was one of life's enthusiasts—he was
'into' all kinds of things. I don't suppose property development is any more odd than some of the other things were.
He tried to invent a perfume once—"

Tos and Stryker exchanged a glance. "Did he now?"
asked Stryker.

Daria didn't notice their interest. Her eyes sought the
lake, the pictures on the wall, the small objects in the
room, hands, feet, colors. Objects seemed to fascinate her,
as if each were being seen anew. Dr. Willis had insisted
that Aunt Clary go into the hospital for a few days—the
shock of the fire and all the stress surrounding the murder
had exhausted the old woman. With no more phantoms to
haunt her, and no one to care for, Daria's thoughts seemed
to scatter. She said she wanted to help, but she was
distracted and remote.

Kate had tried to get her to move in with them temporarily, as had Mrs. Toby and Mrs. Norton. But Daria
insisted on staying in the family cottage. "I've nothing to
fear, now Michael's dead," she said. Matt Gabriel had

stared at her and wondered if she realized how much she did still have to fear—from him, and the system he represented. The pressure was mounting on him to make an arrest, and she was still the prime suspect, despite all the inconsistencies he and Stryker had uncovered.

"What was the perfume called?" Tos asked.

"I don't think it had gotten as far as a name," Daria said. "He had a friend with a laboratory who specialized in creating scents, and he used to go over there and play around. That's all it was—that's all Michael's enthusiasms ever were—playing around." There was no bitterness in her voice, just a great weariness.

"Did they ever—"

"I think you should—"

Stryker and Kate had spoken at the same time. Kate glanced at him, then continued.

"I think you should get Dr. Willis to have a look at you, Daria," she said. "You've lost so much weight since you came back, and—"

"I'm all right, really," Daria said. "I'm beginning to feel hungry again. A little, anyway."

Kate didn't look happy with this reply, but she leaned back in her chair and said nothing more. They were all sitting in her front room. The tangy smell of barbecued ribs came from the kitchen, where Liz was busy clattering and stirring. On any other summer afternoon they would have been out on the front lawn, happily charring their food on a grill—but there was still the buzzing flotilla of reporters eager for pictures circling in front of the Island, and the wet black stink of the burned-out Lattimer cottage hanging over everything. Kate had lured Daria over for the day, but now she regretted it. It was impossible not to ask questions, or to pretend that everything was normal, and Jack seemed intent on learning all he could. Nobody could relax.

"Did they ever make anything else but perfume in this lab?" Stryker asked.

Daria frowned. "I don't know what you're—oh. You mean drugs?"

"Yes. Did Michael ever mention anything called Elysium, for example? Or Aphrodite's Secret? Or Nectare, or Roha?"

Daria was silent for a moment, then spoke. "No—none of them sound familiar. Of course, I wouldn't be all that surprised if his friend did make designer drugs, but they never offered me anything. Michael knew how I felt about drugs. And about Monty."

"Monty?"

"His friend with the laboratory—Monty Carpenter. 'Doc' Carpenter, they called him sometimes. It was a big joke with Michael and his friends—'Doc' knows best." She didn't smile.

Stryker glanced at Tos again—and this time Daria caught the exchange. "If you check I expect you'll find he'll have some kind of criminal record," she acknowledged. "That would have added to the excitement for Michael."

"But you're not aware of any kind of interest in property?"

Daria shrugged and lit a cigarette. Kate was startled, as she had never seen Daria smoke before. But, of course, this was Daria as she had become, not Daria as she used to be, or even had been while living in terror of Michael. This was the New York Daria, the successful painter, the Widow Grey. This was someone new.

"His family owns all kinds of property all over the place. Some of it could be around here, I suppose." Daria sounded unconvinced. "You're thinking of this Bobcat thing, are you?"

"I'm trying to think of anything I can," Stryker said frankly. "If you didn't kill your husband—"

Daria glanced at him through her cigarette smoke. "I didn't," she said evenly.

"Then someone else did. You knew him, we didn't. Who else am I going to ask?" His voice was reasonable, not aggressive. He was only too aware of the protective attitude of both Matt and Kate. Their eyes were on him, not Daria, and they were waiting for him to go too far. They *expected* it.

He smiled. "You can't think of any enemies?"

Daria laughed then, a short sound of genuine amusement. "My God, I can think of hundreds." Her attention caught at last, she leaned forward and looked him straight in the face. "You have to understand—Michael never did anything in moderation. He said moderation was for people who were afraid of life. That made him interesting, exciting, and totally single-minded. Like a steamroller. So if people got in the way of his enjoyments—they were flattened. Even destroyed, if he thought that would be fun."

"You make him sound like a monster," Tos said with a note of disbelief.

"He was," Daria agreed, leaning back. "A handsome, delightful, charming monster. If you did everything he wanted, didn't compete, told him he was wonderful, catered to his least whim, fed him and nourished him and soothed him—all things that many women would have been perfectly happy to do—why, then he loved you. Otherwise..." She shrugged.

"And you were an otherwise," Kate said.

Daria grinned—the first time in a long time anyone had seen her do so with any degree of naturalness. Suddenly Stryker saw what Matt Gabriel saw in Daria—what, presumably, Michael Grey had seen in Daria. He loved Kate, of course he did—but this woman was unique. He had no wish to possess her, or to love her, or to control her—but he would have been perfectly happy to go on *looking* at her for a long, long time. Relieved of the strain and the fear, it was quite a face.

"Yes," Daria said to Kate. "I was an otherwise all right."

"An Island girl?" Liz asked, from where she leaned in the doorway, brandishing a spoon. "I'm told they're always on Paradise, no matter where they happen to be standing."

Kate and Daria looked at one another and laughed.

"So that's why you're such a pain," Stryker said to Kate. She stuck her tongue out at him. He turned again to Daria.

"Did Michael ever mention Hugo Wilberforce?" he asked.

"I don't think so. In fact, I was surprised when somebody said Hugo Wilberforce was a New York artist. All right, his field was stage design—but the art world is a small one, even in New York, and *I* never heard of him."

"He says he met your husband at a party—says your husband backed a play for a friend of his."

"That's quite possible." Daria nodded. "We certainly didn't always attend the same parties. But I don't remember a play . . ."

"Maybe it happened before you met him," Kate said.

"Or after you broke up with him," Stryker suggested. "During the period you claim he was crazy."

"I don't 'claim' he was crazy, he *was* crazy," Daria flared, her cheeks flushing pink.

"Jack . . ." Kate began. "Can't we just let it go for a little while?"

"No," Stryker said. "If we let it go on much longer, Matt may have to arrest Daria, whether he likes it or not. Obviously we don't want that to happen."

Daria looked at Matt. "Why?" she asked.

Matt felt her eyes rather than saw them, wanted to suggest running away to Mexico, wanted to pretend none of this was happening. "Official pressure," he said briefly.

"Oh," Daria said in a small voice. "Because everyone still thinks I did it, you mean."

"We don't think you did it, Daria," Kate said quickly.

"I know *you* don't," Daria said. Now she was avoiding Stryker's eye again.

He sighed in exasperation. "Look, I don't want to badger you, but I have to know all I can about Michael Grey," he said earnestly. "There's always a *reason* why someone is a victim, and the more we know about him, the more chance we have of finding something that will lead us to the killer. Maybe someone hated him. All right—that's a mine field, because you say practically everyone hated him if they knew him long enough, but it would help if you could think of a few *names* that might help us make a connection.

Other women, perhaps? Old flames? New flames? No? Well, then, maybe someone wanted something he had. His money? Drugs?" Daria was shaking her head. "Still no? Okay—how about that he was in someone's way? Or that he knew something he shouldn't—about this 'Doc,' maybe? Or Wilberforce? Michael Grey's death must benefit *someone*. Who?"

"Me," Daria said. "Just me."

"My God," Liz said in some sympathy. "Theories and more theories. Maybe the guy was just in the wrong place at the wrong time, for crying out loud, did you ever think of that?"

"Hey—" Tos said. "I'ma hungry—go cooka the din'."

"Hey, you shutta you' face, I'ma tella you when din' isa ready for eat or not," Liz mocked him good-naturedly.

Tos beamed. "She's learning Italian," he said.

Everybody laughed but Stryker.

After dinner, while the men were loading the dishwasher and the women were watching the local television news, Stryker spoke in a low voice. "She might be right, you know."

"Who?"

"Liz."

Tos looked alarmed. "Jesus, don't ever tell her that."

"No, seriously."

"Right about what?" Matt asked, handing him the rib platter.

"About Grey being in the wrong place at the wrong time."

"The wrong place being—"

Stryker licked barbecue sauce off his wrist. "The Lattimer cottage, of course. If that knobkerrie turns out to be the actual murder weapon, then it stands to reason he was killed inside the place and then carried outside during the storm, right?"

"I suppose so," Matt agreed.

Tos straightened up from jamming cutlery into the dishwasher basket and rubbed his back. "Where's the soap powder?"

"Over there." Stryker pointed. "To my way of thinking, Michael Grey wasn't the only person who could have been using that empty cottage for his own purposes. According to the motel manager, he came back very late each night, but he always came back, right?"

Matt nodded, and stepped back so Tos could pour the powder into the dispenser. "Right."

"But someone *was* sleeping in that bed." Stryker grimaced. "I wonder what blood type those semen stains will show?"

"Some local teenagers, probably," Matt said. "They seem to have a sixth sense about empty houses."

"Maybe Grey got off on watching Daria." Stryker hesitated, then came out with it. "Or maybe Daria used to sneak out and..."

"Forget it," Matt said angrily. "She was terrified of him."

"Anger can be an aphrodisiac," Stryker said quietly.

"Fuck off!" Matt snapped.

Stryker grinned. "See?"

Matt glared at him. "Very cute."

Stryker's grin faded. "I'm not trying to be cute, Matt. I'm trying to remind you that all things are possible—especially the things we don't want to believe. Don't tell me it hasn't occurred to you that she may have arranged to meet him there in order to kill him?"

Matt turned away, his fists clenched. From the other room came the voices of the women, talking low and giggling. "Of course it has," he said through his teeth. "She's... she's a complicated person, and she's smart, I can see that. I've realized from the beginning that she could be lying about it all—his threats and so on—and I know she has the *brains* to work out a way to kill her husband and get away with it. I just don't think she has the heart for it. I can't believe she's that cold, that... rotten."

"I'm not asking you to believe it—I'm just asking you not to forget it," Stryker said gently.

"There—that's done," Tos said with some satisfaction, as he closed the door of the dishwasher and began to rotate the dial to start it up. "Oh, damn." He'd spotted a stray dish on the far counter and went to retrieve it. As he stepped back he put his hands on his hips and glared at the other two. "Do I have to do *all* the cleaning up?"

Stryker glanced at him. "Only while you're wearing that apron with the flowers on the pocket."

Tos looked down at his unfortunate pose, and the apron he'd automatically tied around his waist. He ripped the apron off and threw it on the floor. "Shit. Do you think it's too late for me?"

"I *was* beginning to worry." Stryker grinned.

"I'll beat this thing," Tos said, inserting the dish into the rack and turning on the dishwasher. "I'll give up watching the soaps, I'll tear up the knitting patterns, I'll work out in the gym, I'll go back on the pistol range, I'll..." He paused. "Do I have to give up my bunny slippers?"

Matt was looking at the two of them bemusedly.

"I think it would be better if you put those away," Stryker said in all seriousness.

"I just got them broken in," Tos said sadly.

"Yeah, well...I know it's hard," Stryker agreed. "But Captain Klotzman wouldn't appreciate them. And if you had to take part in a lineup, well..."

Tos sighed. "Okay. They go, too."

Matt said, "What the hell are you two *on?*"

"Are you wondering about Lattimer?" Tos continued smoothly, starting to wipe down the counters with a damp cloth. Then he looked down at what he was doing, muttered something, and threw the cloth into the sink.

"Well, it's kind of funny that nobody seems to know where he is," Stryker said slowly. "Don Robinson said Lattimer's lawyer 'thought' he'd gone back to Africa, but that sounds a little loose to me. They sent the money from his house sale to Arizona. And if everybody on this Island is so tight with each other, why didn't he say good-bye to anyone? What kind of insurance settlement did he get when his wife died? Was it enough to set up this Bobcat thing?" He turned to Matt. "Was he the kind of man to do something like that?"

"It's possible," Matt said, relieved to turn away from any questions about Daria. "He was kind of a bad-tempered guy, but everybody put that down to his arthritis. He and Ada didn't mix much—she wasn't all that well, either— apparently she died last year."

"Of what?"

"Don't know, to tell the truth. It was in the city—maybe you could find out."

"Anything else?"

Matt smiled. "He used to walk around in bush gear. You know—khaki shirts with epaulets and a pith helmet. The kids used to like him, though—he'd tell them stories about Africa and show them his collection. He was real proud of all that stuff he brought back from Africa—always claimed it was worth a fortune."

Stryker pounced. "Then why did he leave it behind?"

Matt shrugged. "Well, hell, it's only been a few months— maybe he planned to send for it when he got settled down over there."

"*If* he's 'over there,'" Stryker said. "I think we ought to spend some time tomorrow finding out whether he actually left the country or not. And how much he got for his cottage from Bobcat Investments. Remember, that money was remitted to some bank out west, not to Africa."

"You're thinking the sale to Bobcat was really just a transfer thing?" Tos asked. "That *he's* Bobcat? And that Michael Grey found out about it somehow? Maybe ran into him in the cottage and—"

"How would he know who Kit Lattimer was?" Matt asked.

"How would Kit Lattimer know who *he* was?" Stryker countered. "Maybe it was a case of shadows in the dark— hit first and think afterward."

"But why? And why would Kit Lattimer sneak in and out of his own place?"

"I don't know. Maybe he doesn't want to face the other Islanders, but he can't resist getting some of his treasures back. Weren't there some funny marks on the carpet—maybe places where things had been removed?"

"Now that you come to mention it..." Matt began.

"Hey—instead of Lattimer, maybe one of the *other* Islanders is hard up for money. Maybe this person has been slipping into the place and helping him- or herself to the odd piece of ethnic artwork and selling it. Lattimer was right—it can get high prices, these days. Maybe Grey surprised *him*," Tos suggested. "Or her."

Matt looked from one to the other. "Then why the business with the shotgun?"

"Because whoever it was might have figured that Daria would get off with a suspended sentence for self-defense," Tos said. "That's what Jonas did."

They looked at him. "Who the hell is *Jonas?*" Stryker demanded.

"He's the boyfriend of the sister of the woman who runs the beauty parlor in Dempster Place," Tos said. "He knew she was—"

"'As the World Turns'?" Stryker interrupted.

Tos closed his eyes. "'The Brave and the Brazen,'" he finally admitted through clenched teeth. He opened his eyes. "But it still *works*, doesn't it?" he asked.

28

The next day started hot and got hotter.

As there had been no further developments in the murder investigation—or, at least, none had been announced—many of the reporters had vacated their stand at the bridge. Of those that remained, many were short-tempered and bored.

It made stopping them just a little bit more difficult.

There was a rare appearance by the Wilberforce guards as they frog-marched a particularly bold pair who had beached themselves on the Point and—although held offshore by the dogs—had busied themselves taking pictures of the Wilberforce enclave. If they couldn't get one story, why not another? They had learned why not the hard way. The guards were not particularly gentle as they pushed them over the bridge, nor were they talkative.

Watching their stiff backs retreating down the road, Glen Hardwicke spat into the canal. "No wonder nobody likes them," he observed. "Not a decent word or look out of either of them."

Harry McGruder was also gazing after them. "You know, that tall one looked familiar," he said. "I seen him somewheres before."

"Probably in the Dirty Duck," Glenn said, referring to the town's lowliest bar.

"No—not there. They never go there. Somewheres, though."

It was while they were engaged in this conjectural exchange that one of the female reporters managed to slide past them in her sneakers and slip around the front of the Rose cottage. She was later discovered poking around the burned remains of the Lattimer place and muttering into a small tape recorder. She, too, was returned to the far side of the bridge.

The sun shone out of a clear sapphire sky, but nobody emerged to enjoy it. And, by late afternoon, it was too hot to enjoy. No breeze blew from the bay—all was still and heavy.

Trapped inside by the circling media, the Islanders had nothing to do but turn up the air-conditioning and watch old movies on television.

Nell Norton heated things up so much while compulsively baking that she and Margaret had words—something that hadn't happened since November 1985 (a disagreement about turkey stuffing).

Freddy and Larry took their motorboat out of the water and scraped weeds off her bottom until the heat in the boat house drove them back inside, where they broke out the chilled white wine and soda and decided to review their video collection of old Garbo movies.

The Greenfields were silent in their sealed and icy home. Their blinds were drawn, as always, and the air conditioners hummed loudly in almost every window. At two o'clock Cissy took out the garbage, then went back in and shut the door.

Fran Robinson tried to find yet another project to absorb the children, who could not understand why they weren't allowed out during their summer vacation. In despair, she finally piled them all into the *Flash,* and with a burst of speed that nearly swamped one of the newsmen's rented boats, shot out into the bay and toward the fun and games on Canary Island. She'd been saving the outing for later in the year, when everything else palled, and now would have nothing to hold over the kid's heads when they got out of line. She thought it was worth it.

Mrs. Rose—deserted by Roberta, who had marched past the reporters without answering a single question (a feat of remarkable self-control)—made herself a huge gooey ice-cream sundae and sat back to wait for Oprah Winfrey to appear on her television screen and dazzle her with other people's lives and problems.

Len Cotman and Don Robinson had left just after dawn to go into the city, where—oddly enough—there was a breeze that cooled the air a little. For a while they could forget what was happening on Paradise, instead of longing to be back there.

Kate, Daria, and Liz sat around Kate's living room and talked about art, music, literature, politics—anything except the one thing they wanted to discuss. Kate and Liz had agreed on this policy before Daria arrived. Daria seemed grateful.

Aunt Clary lay back in her cool hospital bed and fretted, until Daria called her and told her where she was, whereupon she rang every half hour just for company. The woman in the next bed, she reported, must have sleeping sickness or something, because she never spoke—just snored.

Nobody knew what the Wilberforces were doing.

Stryker spent the morning with Matt while Tos pursued some errands in Blackwater. Tos and Stryker went into the city, making phone calls, sending faxes, checking records, and pursuing one false trail after another.

Matt spent the afternoon with the town council, preparing for that evening's public meeting. The council members were of the opinion that no special preparations were necessary. Matt informed them that it was wishful thinking

on their part, and that he had it from several sources that
there would be a big turnout that evening.

He was right.

The meeting of the town council was scheduled to begin at
seven-thirty. By seven-fifteen P.M. there was hardly an
empty chair in the place.

"Is it always like this?" Liz asked, obviously impressed by
the display of civic participation that was taking place before
them.

"No," Kate told her. "According to Dad, the council
meetings never draw more than ten, maybe fifteen, in the
summer, and then only if it's raining." They stood on the
sidewalk, watching people filing into the old town hall.

Daria stood between them, her hair covered with a scarf
and wearing the glasses she used when painting. They had
huge lenses and provided a very effective disguise—even
the deputies hadn't recognized her in the shadows of the
rear seat when they'd driven off the Island. "I can understand all the Island people wanting to come—Aunt Clary
would be here if she could be—but what about these
others?"

"I bet half of them are reporters," Tos observed. "Well, a
third, anyway. Probably fed up with trying to get over that
bridge and looking for a story. Somebody must have told
them about the plans for the Mess."

"The Mush," Kate corrected him absently.

"Whatever."

Stryker took Kate's arm. "Guess it must be a lousy night
for TV," he said. "We'd better go in if we want a seat."

They found places along the left-hand edge, but had to
split up. Liz and Kate sat in the third row, with Daria safely
bracketed between them. She had insisted on coming for
Aunt Clary's sake, although she was well aware of the
whispers and the stares of townspeople who recognized her
despite the "disguise." Tos and Stryker had to sit farther
back, in the seventh row. Larry Lovich smiled at Kate as he
moved along to make room.

"Quite a turnout," he said. "Even the Adcocks are here."

"Where?" Kate asked, turning in her chair. "Oh, my God, so they are."

"Who the hell are the Adcocks?" Liz asked.

"They're cucumbers," Freddy said.

"What?"

"They repeat on us," Larry explained. "It's the kind of thing you have to expect in a resort area. It's just that some are more than others."

"More what?" Liz wanted to know.

"Just...more."

Kate tried to help. "The Adcocks have been coming to Blackwater for years now. They met here when they both worked at the local hotel during their college vacations. They came back on their honeymoon. And they keep coming back every year."

"Like the mayflies," Larry said in a distant voice.

"I think that's kind of sweet," Liz said.

"It is. Or it would be for ordinary people. But the Adcocks are enthusiasts."

"About what?"

"About *anything*," Larry groaned.

"About *everything*," Freddy moaned.

"Take a look for yourself," Kate suggested. "Third row back, on the aisle."

Liz turned. Seated at the indicated spot were a family of four. They were hard to miss. The father sported a beard. The wife wore glasses. They and their two daughters all had masses of thick wavy hair that sprang from their scalps with gusto and was only partially under control. They all had bright smiles and clear eyes. They were all dressed in neon-colored cycling gear, the complete kit, head to toe. They fluoresced together, and stood out among the cotton dresses and shirts that surrounded them like parrots in a chicken house.

"Last year they wore only L.L. Bean and slept in a tent on Rockfish Point," Larry sighed.

"The year before it was ethnic Peruvian. They tried to

teach old Mrs. Peach how to make guacamole and tacos,"
Freddy recalled. "She's seventy-six and runs the oldest
guest house in Blackwater. She's real proud of her chicken
fricassee and dumplings. Guacamole nearly did it for her.
Apparently the avocado stones kept slipping out of her
fingers and she said she felt inadequate to the occasion."

"They're both high school teachers. They speak to their
children in foreign languages in order to Widen Their
Horizons and prepare them for 'an international life.' This
year it's Esperanto—I guess they're covering all the bases."

"They only eat organic food. Mr. Adcock brings his own
sourdough starter and insists on baking his own bread."

"One year they ate only citrus fruit and shredded wheat."

"They've stayed in nearly every guest house in town."

"Are they so awful?" Liz asked in astonishment.

"Oh, no, they're perfectly pleasant people. They're intelligent and kind and thoughtful."

"Well, then..." Liz was perplexed.

Freddy tried to explain further. "They rise at five A.M.
every day and go jogging. They slump not, nor do they
smoke. They are very clean. They are the American Dream.
They are driving us all to drink."

"If once, just once, they would have a fight..."

"Or a head cold..."

"Belch in public..."

"Or fall off their bicycles..."

Liz looked at them all. "You're crazy."

"Exactly," beamed Freddy. "And they're not. You see?"

"But why are they here?" Daria asked plaintively. "Why
is everybody in the whole of Blackwater Bay *here?*"

"Money," Freddy Tollett said.

"I thought only the Islanders had been told about the
offer," Liz said.

"Didn't you know? It was in the local paper this morning."

"I owe your boyfriend a lobster dinner—somebody talked,"
Freddy said in a meaningful growl.

"And *they* don't like it," Larry whispered, as the town
council members filed into the room and glanced edgily at

the watching crowd. "Look at them—not a clear eye in the carload. If you ask me, they figured this to go through very cozily and quietly. I wonder how much each one'll make out of it?"

"Ssshhh, that's slander," Kate hissed.

"No, it's logic," Larry said grimly. "Pure logic."

Freddy grinned. "And experience," he said.

The Blackwater Town Hall had been built in 1928, in an attempt to bring "character" to the town. It was in what could be called "Cape Cod" style—if you had something against the Cape. Most locals referred to it as "the Shoebox," which was apt. The use of a shoehorn would also have been appropriate on this particular evening. Crowded onto plastic chairs, the gathering became restive as the council members crouched low over the table and conversed in whispers. Despite the opened windows along each long wall, heat was beginning to build up inside. The doors had been propped open out of desperation, but the oppressive warmth of the day still lingered. The evening was still and there was very little relief to be had from this feeble attempt to achieve further ventilation.

Finally, the town clerk stood and faced them. He was a small man, finicky of manner, a former undertaker by profession. "Good evening," he said, looking straight ahead while his fingers, seemingly with a life and intent of their own, fussed and straightened the papers on the table before him. His eyes were focused on the clock over the door at the rear. "It is heartening to see so many of our citizens eager to participate in local government—"

"Somebody's got to make sure you don't bury the wrong body, Berringer," came a voice from the back.

The clerk managed a weak smile. "There are a great many things on the agenda this evening..." His eyes became unfocused as he began to drone on about sewage-pipe renewals, the question of a second stoplight near the school, et cetera, et cetera, et cetera. The crowd, attentive at first, grew restive again.

When he, perforce, came to the question of the tender to

purchase the marshy area known locally as the Mush, the listeners could contain themselves no longer.

"That's what we want to know about," came one voice.

"What are these plans?" came another.

"*Where* are these plans?"

"Are they going to turn this into another Lemonville?" asked someone.

Mr. Berringer looked uneasily around him, as if startled out of a reverie. He seemed suddenly to become aware that people were not looking at him with what he would term proper respect, nor were they behaving as he would expect them to behave while attending a town council meeting.

They sounded impatient.

Possibly annoyed.

Some of them had even gotten to their feet.

He looked down at his fellow council members, somewhat at a loss.

"Sit down, dammit," snarled Fred Mortimer. "Boring them to death isn't going to work."

Berringer sat down. "We always list the agenda—" he began.

"The hell with the goddamn agenda," snapped Mayor Merrill Atwater. "Let's get to it and get it over with, fast."

"But..." Mr. Berringer had always been a stickler for everything in its place. Considering his former occupation, it was an exemplary trait, but in this instance it was obvious that strict attention to proper procedure would not suffice.

Mayor Atwater stood up. He was a huge, overdeveloped man for whom clothing seemed a waste, as his body always seemed to be on the verge of escaping from it. Already his shirt had lost a button, spreading the collar wide to show a tanned and muscular chest. He took a breath, lost another button, and bellowed. "All right, everybody, just calm down, please. Seeing as how you're all so interested in the Mush, we'll take that first."

The volume of his voice startled them into silence, and its message caused those who had stood to sit down again, momentarily pacified.

"Right." Atwater took another breath. The remaining buttons held, but there was an ominous sound of cloth parting from behind his shoulders. In the audience, his wife sighed. It was all very well being married to someone who strongly resembled Conan the Barbarian, but expensive and time-consuming. She'd often wondered if Lois Lane had had the same trouble with Clark Kent's shirts, what with gathering them up from doorways and phone booths and then having to get down on her hands and knees to search for the buttons...

"Now, as you all apparently know, we have had an offer from a development company to purchase the Mush. It's a fair offer, considering that the land will require a great deal of—"

"How much?" someone asked.

Mayor Atwater scowled. "A reasonable offer—"

"How *much*?" asked another voice.

Atwater glanced at the town clerk, who mouthed something at him. The mayor cleared his throat. "I believe the offer is six hundred an acre—"

"I heard it was eight hundred," Larry Lovich shouted. "Or was that six hundred to the town, and the other two hundred to the council members?"

Considering Atwater's size (huge), temper (uncertain), and occupation (he ran a local martial-arts center), Larry was showing considerable bravura.

Surprisingly, Merrill Atwater did not look angry—just very, very disappointed. Larry flushed as Atwater focused on him. "Everything is up-front and in black and white," he said. "It's the town that will benefit, not the council. I don't know about you folks, but I'm damn sick and tired of budgeting for mosquito control every winter, and then paying out all summer for insect repellent."

There was a murmur of assent and some laughter. "The tourists call this Scratch City," somebody said.

"Exactly," Atwater said. He had been elected mayor only four months earlier. He had campaigned on a friendly, one-to-one basis, looming up suddenly on street corners

and doorsteps, shaking hands with knuckle-rupturing enthusiasm and talking about a "positive image" for Blackwater Bay. As the previous mayor had dropped dead during a
council meeting—some said out of pure pique—and the job
was poorly paid and largely ceremonial, he had beaten the
only other candidate—Berringer—and had so far made no
enemies. So the people listened as he went on about the
Mush. "And, come late August, it stinks when the wind
blows in from the lakeside, doesn't it?"

"It damn well does," said old Mr. Bishop in a surprisingly deep voice. "I live next to it, by God, and I know."

"Ah," murmured Freddy. "Adjoining land—that's *his* interest declared."

Behind them, Don Robinson leaned forward. "Look
around," he whispered. "There's about a dozen here who
own substantial tracts of land adjoining the Mush."

Liz looked at Kate and raised a questioning eyebrow.

"If the development is good, their land goes up in
value," Kate whispered. "If it's lousy, they're wiped out,
the same as the Islanders."

"And to think I could have stayed home and read a
book," Liz whispered back. "When does J.R. come in with
his bid for the oil rights?"

Larry Lovich suddenly paled, and turned to look at Don
Robinson. Don grinned and shook his head. "No oil," he
said. "I told you—they looked and tested for everything.
It's just mud, weeds, and bugs."

Just as Atwater was about to continue, a loud voice came
from behind them. "What's the connection between Bobcat
Investments and Elysium?"

"Oh, God," Liz said, scrunching down in her seat. "That
was Tos."

"No, it came from over there," Kate said.

"He can throw his voice," Liz said. "He's been practicing
ever since he got back from the hospital. Somebody gave
him a book about it . . ."

Kate sighed. "You can't really *throw* a voice—people
have to be looking at you to create the illusion."

"It was Neilson," Liz said, ignoring this piece of information. "He also gave Tos a book on juggling, and he's already broken four of his mother's plates and nine of mine."

The question about Elysium, whether from Tos or someone else, hung in the air and seemed to confuse Mayor Merrill Atwater. He looked down at his fellow council members, two of whom had gone dead white. "What's Elysium?" he whispered.

Suddenly a man stood up in the front row and turned to face the audience. He was a handsome, well-dressed older man, almost actorlike in demeanor and appearance. "I wonder if I might be permitted to speak?" he asked Mr. Berringer. Atwater sat down abruptly. Berringer waved a hand at the stranger, either asking for help or granting permission. The stranger made the latter interpretation, and turned to face the gathering.

"My name is Daniel Cater," he said in a rich brown courtroom voice. "I am a lawyer representing Bobcat Investments, and I think I can answer all your questions if you'll permit me to speak."

"Who is that masked stranger?" came a shrill voice. Kate turned to look back. Tos looked very, very innocent. He was gazing at the ceiling.

Cater smiled, and went on. "The area you call the Mush is a disaster that we plan to turn into a triumph. To in-fill the site would cost millions. To clear and deepen it is a much more economic proposition."

"My God, there goes the Dike," muttered Don.

"If our tender for purchase is accepted, Bobcat plans to turn the so-called Mush into a luxury marina development, including a hotel with a top-class restaurant, a yacht club, various other leisure facilities, and mooring for over a hundred boats," Cater announced dramatically. He clicked open a large briefcase and produced drawings, which he proceeded to unfold and hold up.

"There you are—isn't that beautiful?" he asked, looking around.

The sheet of paper he held up showed a line drawing of

an admittedly beautiful marina, filled with sailing and motor craft, and surrounded by a series of long, low buildings that blended perfectly into the wooded background. Those in the front could see most clearly, and began to comment. There was a great scraping of chairs as those in the back stood up and began to move forward to get a better view.

"Can you imagine the money such a development will bring to Blackwater Bay?" Cater continued. "The increase in property values? Other businesses will flock to the town, it will grow and prosper..."

The crowd was beginning to chatter, and the buzz of their conversation had a tone of approval. Cater had brought them exciting news.

There was the scrape of a chair from the opposite end of the front row. Hugo Wilberforce's voice rose over the whispers and talk of the crowd, which now filled the center aisle between the two ranks of plastic chairs.

"If this marina is going to make us all rich, why has Bobcat Investments offered such a low price for the cottages on Paradise Island?" Hugo asked.

There was a sudden silence. Hugo stood there quietly, waiting for an answer.

Cater was unfazed. "It seemed to us that, of all the properties bordering on the development area, Paradise Island was going to suffer most from the noise and dirt of the development. After all, a project of this size cannot be accomplished overnight, and—"

"How much is it going to cost?" Hugo asked. "And how long is it going to take?"

Cater gave him a disarming grin and shrugged his shoulders. "How long is a piece of string?"

"Try a ballpark figure," Hugo suggested with an equally disarming grin.

"Go get 'em, Hugo," Freddy murmured.

"Costs are related to time..." Cater hedged.

"Two million? Eight million? Twenty million?" Hugo persisted.

"Certainly millions," Cater agreed. "But we have estimates on all the buildings—"

"Does Bobcat *have* millions?" Hugo asked. "Or did those low offers represent the best they could do at the moment? Where does Bobcat Investments get its money? Where does it *keep* its money? We have many friends in the financial community and yet we have been unable to find any concrete information concerning this company. Our own company lawyers have been equally unsuccessful in doing so. I would like to know—I think we all would like to know—just *who* is offering to buy land from this town? Names, please, Mr. Cater."

"I assure you, they would mean nothing—" Cater began.

"The name Coloron Chemicals means something to me," Hugo said casually. "Does it ring a bell with you, Mr. Cater?"

"Oh, God," Larry gasped. "It was Coloron who built that cellophane plant in Lemonville."

Cater was trying to calm things down. "I assure you, Coloron Chemicals has nothing to do—"

"Hey!" someone shouted from the crowd that had gathered around Cater. "Look at this!"

A hand waved a large folded packet of paper.

"Here!" Cater said, making a grab for it. "You had no right to take that—" He stopped, looking around in puzzlement. "I have no idea what—"

But it was too late. "I got it from his briefcase," the owner of the hand and voice continued. "Look—" The paper was being unfolded, revealing another set of plans and blueprints. Other hands reached for it and it was held up, passed along. Cater was pushed aside and there was a thud as his briefcase—carelessly left open on his chair—fell to the floor.

"Here's a *letter* from Coloron Chemicals—" someone shouted, holding up a piece of paper.

"Here's a proposed contract for permission to landfill—" came the first voice again. "They're offering to pay Bobcat hundreds of thousands to dump *garbage* into the Mush—"

The voices rose to shouts, and Cater in vain tried to answer each challenge as he backed toward the table around which sat the now beleaguered Blackwater Bay council members. People were shouting, shoving, banging on the council table. Berringer looked as if he were going to faint. Mayor Merrill Atwater had hold of one of his fellow councilmen by the shirtfront, and was shaking him like a rat. Two others were trying to separate them, while a third was frantically gathering up council papers and clutching them to his chest.

"My God, it's a riot!" Liz said, as they were jostled by people hurrying forward to see for themselves.

"Yes, isn't it?" said Kate in an odd voice. She pulled Liz back against the wall. "And Hugo started it."

"Well, he must have had some information we didn't," Daria began in a frightened voice.

"He sure did," Kate agreed.

Stryker and Tos came up to them. "This looks bad—I think you'd better get out of here," Stryker said. "We're going to give Gabriel a hand—"

"Fine," said Kate meekly. "We're going."

"Hey, wait a minute," Liz protested, as Kate dragged her back up the side aisle. "We'll miss all the fun." For a moment they were wedged together in the rear corner of the hall.

"Come on," Kate said. "There they go."

"Who?" Liz asked.

"Hugo and his minions," Kate said. "I guess you couldn't see. As soon as Hugo mentioned the magic words 'Coloron Chemicals,' those new plans were produced. Someone *said* they came from Cater's briefcase. But the guy waving it around was one of Hugo's security guards, out of uniform. Remember? They were with him at the fire, too."

"You think *they* set the fire?" Liz asked, squeezing through the crowd after Kate.

"I don't know. But it was the *other* Wilberforce security guard who began shouting about the garbage dumping and so on—don't you see? It was all *staged*. All Hugo had to do was mention the *name* of that dreaded chemical company. He can't be accused of slander—he never said they were behind Bobcat—he just asked Cater if the name meant anything to him. He can always claim he just asked a simple question—it wasn't *his* fault people just jumped to that conclusion."

They emerged into the cooler air of the street and took deep breaths. Other people had followed them, getting away from the fracas. Some were waving and shouting and laughing, others looked frightened and worried. Car doors slammed. Someone whistled. A few yards away the Adcock family had mounted a custom-made double tandem and were cycling away, their eight legs pumping in unison.

"But why would Hugo do that?" Daria asked.

"I don't know," Kate said. "Maybe just to stop the meeting so the sale couldn't be approved. But if he was so interested in stopping the sale, why didn't he stick around for the fight?" The Wilberforce Rolls swept past, with the two guards in the front, one driving, and Hugo in the back. Kate grabbed Liz's arm and headed for the car. "Come on. I want to see where he's going."

"He's probably going home," Liz protested as she was dragged along. Daria followed reluctantly—glancing back all the while as if wanting to return to the fray.

"Maybe he's frightened by what he started in there," she suggested.

"Did he look frightened?" Kate asked.

"No," Liz admitted, glancing at her reflection in a darkened store window. "But *I* sure as hell do."

29

There, I told you, he's just going back home," Liz said, as the Rolls turned off onto the gravel road that led eventually to the Island.

"Maybe so," Kate said. "But he must have had a *reason* for causing all that kerfuffle and then running out. Oops." She braked hard, as two vehicles came toward them down the narrow lane. Slowing to a crawl, they edged past one another between a gate labeled *Endoline* and another labeled *Seaspray*. The vehicles behind the headlights proved to be two of the television vans that had been laying siege to the bridge.

The maneuver successfully completed, Kate pressed down on the accelerator, only to have to slow down again as yet another vehicle—this time a plain sedan—came toward them.

"Maybe he came back to watch the traffic jam," Liz suggested as, ahead of them, the Rolls edged past a station wagon with WZYX—WE KEEP YOUR EAR ON THE NEWS printed on the side in large red letters. Inside, a woman was talking into a radio microphone held in one hand while trying to steer with the other. Kate waited for her to come by their car, too, and as their open windows passed one another, they heard her say something about "mayhem at the town hall."

"Sounds like the boys are having fun," Liz commented, as they approached the bridge, which was looking strangely deserted. When they slowed to cross it, one of the deputies stood in front of them, rifle up.

He came around to Kate's window. It was Charley Hart. "Say, Kate, that snot-nose Wilberforce guard said there was some kind of riot at the town hall—was he right?"

"Things were getting a little lively," Kate admitted. "Why?"

"Well, all the reporters shot out of here a few minutes ago—seems to me I might be doing more good down there than here. Aha—like I thought." The radio in the police car on the other side of the bridge had begun to crackle. He ran back over the bridge, where another deputy was standing outside the car with the radio mike in his hand, nodding.

Kate drove over the bridge slowly, and came to a halt beside the police car. "Bad?" she asked.

"Seems pretty bad," Charley said, throwing his rifle into the back seat of the police car. "Matt says there's a lot of strangers stirring things up, getting people excited. He needs a hand."

"Then you'd better lend it to him," Kate said. "We'll be okay here."

"Right. We'll be back soon as things cool down, because once the reporters realize—" He didn't have to say any more.

As they drove down to the cottage, Kate glanced back in her rearview mirror. "I wonder," she said, as the taillights of the police car disappeared around the first bend.

"Whether that was what Hugo was after?" asked Liz.

"Yes."

"Well, if it was, he succeeded. Paradise Island is now open to wolves, bears, tigers, reporters, and anyone else who cares to come ashore," Liz said. "Nice one, Hugo."

* * *

They dropped Daria off behind her cottage. She had elected to drive over to the hospital to see Aunt Clary while she could. Once the "riot" died down, the reporters would remember her, and the murder, and the whole ugly horrible mess would continue. This might be the only time for weeks she could move around on her own and not be noticed or followed.

She took the long way around the town, taking back roads that were deserted, grateful for the darkness and the quiet. The commotion at the town hall had frightened her badly. If she was charged with murdering Michael, would the trial be like that? She had kept her chin high when people looked at her in the town hall, but it hadn't been easy. She was so tired. All the months of fighting Michael, of being afraid, of trying to find a way out of her misery had taken their toll. As the lights of the large white building appeared on her left, her impulse was to pass the hospital and keep on driving. She felt her leg muscles tense. The highway lay straight and empty before her. And her life was her own—at last.

Now that Michael was dead.

She looked up at the windows and imagined Aunt Clary lying there, fretful and alone. With a sigh, she turned in and found a parking space.

Her life wasn't really her own.

Not yet.

Kate and Liz leaned against the redwood fence and listened.

"They are, you know," Liz whispered. "They're letting them out of the kennel."

Beyond the fence they could hear the guards talking to the dogs, and the clank of a metal gate swinging back. There was a snick of toenails on pavement, then the swish of pads on grass. No barking.

"How very inconvenient," Kate whispered back. "But why would they do that?"

"He said something about watching until morning," Liz hissed after a moment. "Maybe..." She turned to say more, and found that Kate had sidled down to the water's edge. She followed, shoving the plastic-wrapped packet she was carrying into the pocket of her dark jacket.

They had both paused to put on dark clothes, giggling in their respective bedrooms, and feeling very, very clever. Now, with the sound of the guards and dogs coming from the other side of the fence, they did not feel so brave.

"Hey," she whispered, coming up behind Kate, causing her friend to emit a brief startled yelp that seemed to echo out over the lake. They both froze, listening, but the voices of the guards continued on the far side of the fence—their words unclear but their conversation apparently not interrupted by a sudden suspicion that two idiotic women might be creeping about in the night, spying on them. There was the sound of a door closing, then silence. Or was that someone or something breathing on the other side of the fence? About knee-high? Liz was suddenly aware that they were trespassing on the Cotman property, and spying on the Wilberforces. She felt remarkably silly. And remarkably vulnerable.

"This reminds me of the night we crept up on the Delta Chi house to see if Roy Highland was two-timing you," she muttered.

"He was, and he married her," Kate whispered back.

"Whatever happened to him?"

"I think he's selling office equipment or something like that."

"I wish he were here."

Kate turned to look up at her friend, whose tall figure was outlined by the thin light of a new moon. "Why?"

"He was a gutsy bastard," Liz said. "And he'd been in the Navy, remember?"

"What's that got to do with it?"

"Well, they're trained to *do* things, aren't they?"

"Then you'd better wish Ted Niforos were here. He was

bigger than Roy. Or Steve, or George, or Howard, or Harry, or Bob—"

"I wish all the strong, brave, and beautiful men we've ever known and loved were standing right here, with *clubs*—"

"But not Jack and Tos."

"God, no," Liz breathed with a certain degree of horror. "If *they* caught us doing this, they'd probably kill us."

"Or laugh themselves silly."

"They'd have a point," Liz said. "This *is* pretty stupid. I mean, we're not schoolgirls anymore—"

"In my heart I am still sweet sixteen," Kate averred, fluttering her eyelashes.

"And in your head you are still sweet seven and a half," Liz retorted. "Come on, let's go back to—"

"Shhhh. Listen."

They listened. A sudden breeze stirred the trees overhead and carried to them, from far off, the faint wail of a police siren.

"I can't—" Liz began.

"They've put the dock lights on! They're taking the yacht out!" Kate whispered. "They're leaving!"

"Good. Now we can go back and make fudge or something," Liz said, relieved. "This creeping and crouching is playing hell with my back."

"Wait here," Kate commanded, and before Liz could grab her, she'd kicked off her shoes and slid over the breakwater and into the lake.

Liz hung over the breakwater. "Kate, don't be silly—" But it was useless. Kate's dark seal-sleek head was already halfway to the long white yacht that rode beside the Wilberforce dock. Liz straightened slightly, rubbing her back, then stiffened again with horror as she saw—simultaneously—two men start down the dock, and Kate start to climb hand over hand up the front anchor chain. All three of them were clearly visible to one another—if they had looked the right way.

"Oh, my God—" Liz choked. She jerked back behind

the fence and then moved forward again until just one eye was peering at the scene before her. It was all right—in a manner of speaking. The guards had boarded the yacht from the other side, while Kate had gained the deck from this side, and was now hidden from them by the superstructure. The guards didn't appear to have heard anything. They climbed aboard and disappeared into the main cabin. After a moment, the yacht's lights came on, clearly outlining Kate's figure as she edged along the deck toward what were most likely the saloon windows of the large vessel. If the men chanced to look out, they might see her. Liz held her breath but, again, nothing happened.

At least Kate now knew that someone was actually *on* the boat, and that she was in imminent danger of being discovered. But she didn't seem inclined to do anything about it.

"Oh, shit," Liz said. Hugo and another man were coming down the lawn toward the dock. The other man—presumably Hugo's father—carried a briefcase and wore a suit. Hugo was still in the casual jacket and slacks he'd worn to the town meeting, although he'd changed from his Gucci loafers to ordinary deck shoes. Kate had seen the men too, and slid down until she was flat on the deck.

"Come on back now, Kate," Liz whispered in the moonlight. "Just come home like a good girl and we'll pretend this never happened. I won't tell anyone, I *promise*."

But Kate lay still, waiting until Hugo and the older man had boarded the boat and disappeared within. Liz saw the pale oval of her face turn toward her, and the quick wide wave of her hand, palm out. Then Kate flattened herself down again as the saloon widows were suddenly unlocked and thrust open above her head. Voices came across the water, their words indiscernible to Liz. But Kate was listening—it was obvious in the tense line of her body as she rose to her knees and tilted her head.

"Eavesdroppers never hear good news," Liz muttered. "Come on, Kate, give it up."

One of the guards appeared back on deck. He looked

around, and Liz ducked back. When she braved another look, she saw him carefully and deliberately cast off first the rear line, then the foreline. Looping the latter over his arm, he jumped back aboard as the yacht shivered into life, the low throb of heavy engines barely audible over the lap of waves against the breakwater and the rustle of the trees that hung above Liz's head.

"Now's your chance, Kate," Liz urged, wanting to shout, wanting to scream across the water. "Jesus, woman—jump!"

But Kate did not jump.

Kate arose, slowly and deliberately, and went forward as the guard went back along the deck on the far side. As he bent down to coil the rear mooring line, Kate slipped down onto the foredeck and opened a door. No light shone from it. She seemed to bend down, to look and listen intently. After a long moment, she went through the door and disappeared from view. Slowly, slowly, as the yacht cleared the length of the dock, the door closed behind her.

Then, as Liz watched helplessly, the long, graceful boat slid out into the darkness beyond the end of the dock. The running lights and the small squares of the saloon lights grew smaller and smaller. The low, purposeful throb of the engines grew fainter and fainter.

And then it was gone.

30

Meanwhile, back at the town hall, the situation had worsened.

Berringer was down.

Mayor Atwater was shouting at old Mr. Bishop, and ducking, as the elderly man tried to clip him in the head with his cane. When Matt Gabriel seized the old fellow from behind, he narrowly missed a concussion himself, on the backswing. He passed the whirlwinding Mr. Bishop over to a deputy and turned to the task of discouraging two women who were apparently intent on tearing Mr. Cater's clothes off. Cater was dancing a fine tango of evasion around the now deserted council table.

Tos had already carried two unconscious people out of the hall and laid them gently against the stone garden wall to recover in the night air. One had fainted from heat and excitement, the other had been knocked unconscious by a flying half-full beer can. Now Tos was engaged in an earnest discussion with Mrs. Toby and Mrs. Norton, whose adrenaline was up. They were all for setting fire to the place as a token of protest. Tos maintained that he liked a good blaze as well as the next man, but as it was a hot night he was against it. As he spoke, he edged them toward the open door.

In the front of the room, his back against the low apron of the stage where the annual Christmas and Easter concerts were held, and where the Blackwater Bay Players had recently presented *Arsenic and Old Lace* to excellent reviews, Stryker was trying to decide whether or not to throw the chair he was holding at the man coming toward him. The man was definitely not a local. He was very fat and had both momentum and somebody's money on his side. His eyes were bloodshot with rage or drink and he looked as if he would take some stopping.

Stryker looked around—then threw the chair.

Even before it struck the fat man's shins, Stryker was down on his hands and knees crawling toward his new objective—Cater's briefcase, which had fallen to the floor and inadvertently been kicked under the council table, where it lay open and inviting and totally unprotected. Halfway there, someone stepped on his hand. Repressing a scream, he persevered, and was rewarded by reaching his goal without further interference.

Sitting up under the table, with the open briefcase wedged between his outstretched legs, be began to read.

Matt Gabriel turned to George Putnam, who had an androgynous teenager under each arm, and shouted, "If we don't get this stopped in the next five minutes, we're going to have to call out the state police or the National Guard!"

"State police!" shouted one teenager.

"National Guard!" shouted the other, and they began to fight again, flailing at one another around George's midriff.

George dropped them and they lay, stunned and winded, at his feet. "Girl Scouts," croaked one.

"Yeah," croaked the other, and threw up on George's shoes.

It was patently obvious, from the sudden eruption of the

violence and the unfamiliar faces of many of its contribu-
tors, that the riot had been instigated on purpose. Furthermore, what George was wiping off his shoes gave testimony
that free alcohol had been the greater part of the deal.
However, fired by indignation and the rare excitement of it
all, many locals had joined in. It was these who had most
readily responded to Gabriel's requests for calm and retirement from the scene. The remaining knots of people shouting,
arguing, shoving one another and kicking things were
mostly strangers and, like the two teenagers, were at least
tight, if not downright drunk. Severe measures were called
for.

Gabriel unsnapped his holster, extracted his .38, and
fired into the air. There was immediate silence, except for
the clatter of falling plaster.

"I appreciate your coming, folks," Gabriel said. "But the
party's over. Anyone in here after I count to sixty is under
arrest."

He only needed to count to thirty before the only people
remaining in the hall were he himself, George, Charley
Hart, assorted part-time deputies, Tos, Stryker, and the
fallen town clerk.

Berringer opened an eye and peered around cautiously.
"Is it over?" he croaked.

"Oh, yes," Stryker said from under the table, in a
conversational tone. "I think you could say that."

Shakily, Berringer got to his feet and looked around. All
of the council members had long since fled. Even the
mayor had disappeared. Berringer reached for the aban-
doned gavel and crashed it down onto the table. Underneath it, Stryker winced.

"Meeting adjourned," the town clerk whispered, and
scurried out.

It didn't take Matt and Tos long to go through the papers
in the briefcase—Stryker had sorted out the pertinent
ones. They looked at one another.

"That's it, then," Matt said, grinning. "It was Lattimer, after all."

"Knowing it doesn't get you any closer to doing anything about it," Tos said. "We couldn't find him anywhere."

"Not yet, but we will." Matt was confidence itself.

"Maybe," Stryker said.

"What do you mean?"

"I mean it's pretty odd that all traces of his existence stop cold as of last March," Stryker said.

"Oh, hell—so he changed his name, went underground, whatever. But it's only a matter of time before we dig him up."

Stryker glanced at him. "Interesting choice of words," he said.

They snapped the briefcase shut. Matt signaled George and Charley to come with them, and left the closing up of the town hall to the other deputies. As they emerged, they were attacked.

"Illegal search and seizure," Cater shouted. He'd been lurking outside, and was apparently electrified by the sight of his briefcase in Stryker's hand. "I want everything returned immediately. You had no right—that is private property, and you had no warrant—"

"Arrest me, Sheriff," Stryker said.

"Any minute now," Gabriel said soothingly. "I've got the words already in my mouth."

"Do it, do it, do it!" shrieked Cater, all pretense of smoothness and polish gone. His hair was a tangle, his tie was awry, and one bow of his spectacles was missing, so that they hung lopsided on his nose. There was a bruise on the side of his jaw, and one sleeve of his jacket hung by a few threads.

"All in good time," Matt said.

"Give me back my property!" he shrieked, running after them.

"Can't. Evidence," Matt threw over his shoulder.

"Inadmissible! Inadmissible!"

When they drove off he followed them, driving close

behind them down the highway, onto the coast road and even over the humpbacked bridge. He parked bumper to bumper behind them, leapt out and continued his attempts to snatch his briefcase from Stryker's grasp, but somehow Tos was always in the way.

Now, as they crunched over the gravel, went up the two steps, and pounded on the rear door of the cottage, he suddenly seemed to realize where he was. Apprehensively, he backed off into the shadows.

Lights came on in the kitchen and then on the porch. Curtains were pushed aside, and then the door was unlocked and opened.

"Good evening," said Mr. Greenfield. He was dressed in dark-brown wrinkle-free slacks, a tan and equally unwrinkled shirt, and wore a gold-and-scarlet paisley silk scarf tucked in around his neck. He looked, as always, a flawless model of the perfect gentleman. His smile wavered and died as his eyes fell on the hovering figure of Cater, but he said nothing further.

"I was surprised not to see you at the town council meeting," Matt said conversationally. "Pretty well everyone else was there."

"Well, I..." Greenfield shrugged. "There was a good ball game on television, and I didn't want to miss it."

"Uh-huh," Matt said. "The meeting got pretty exciting."

"Oh?" Greenfield shifted uneasily.

"Yes. Seems that the Bobcat offer wasn't as straightforward as some people thought."

"Well..." Greenfield said.

"I wonder if we could come in and have a few words," Matt Gabriel said.

"Well..." Greenfield still hesitated.

"Who is it, Harry?" came a screech from within. Greenfield winced.

"Can't we talk here?" he asked. "My wife isn't well—"

This claim was instantly belied by the appearance of Mrs. Greenfield, immaculately dressed as always, with every hair in place and an overbright spark of friendly interest in her eye.

"Maybe you'd like to come down to my office," Matt suggested. "I have a feeling you can help us straighten out a few things."

"I don't see that..." Greenfield began.

"What things?" Mrs. Greenfield asked in her rusty-gate voice.

"Oh... town business," Matt said, feeling a bit sorry for Greenfield, who had shied away from his wife like a skittish horse, and was beginning to look a little haunted.

"What are all of you doing here?" Cissy squawked, looking around. "What's this all about? What's going on?"

"It's nothing, dear. Go back inside and I'll..." Greenfield urged, actually beginning to push her gently back toward the kitchen. This only had the effect of making Cissy plant her feet more firmly and glare at him truculently.

"I want to know what's going on, Harry," she brayed.

Stryker cleared his throat. "We have reason to believe that you, Mr. Greenfield, a Mr. C. Lattimer, and... a certain other person, are the sole stockholders of a company called Elysium—"

"Oh God—" Greenfield said.

Cater could contain himself no longer. "Don't say anything, Harry," he advised. "You've done nothing illegal—"

"What's Elysium?" Mrs. Greenfield demanded shrilly, the bright spark in her eye turning to fire. "And who's this certain other person? Is it a woman, Harry? Is it some tramp?"

Greenfield looked down at the briefcase in Stryker's hand, and then at Cater. "You damned incompetent fool," he snarled. "All you had to do was show them the marina— couldn't you even do that? I told her ... I *told* her ..."

Suddenly he bolted. Pushing Stryker back onto Gabriel, he leaped down the steps, legged it across the gravel, and turned toward the bridge, running fast. The sound of his footsteps receded before Gabriel, caught off-balance and dumbfounded at the unexpected turn of speed which Greenfield had shown, started after him.

Mrs. Greenfield's eyes narrowed as she looked at Stryker and the others. She looked down at the briefcase and then at Cater, whom she obviously didn't recognize. She took a deep, deep breath.

"Harry! Harry! Come back here, you son of a bitch!" she screeched at the top of her voice. And for a moment—just a moment—even the frogs in the Mush were silenced.

31

Mona Wilberforce's first glimpse of Liz Olson was an unfortunate one, as Liz's reflection in the large plate-glass window was distorted and partial, lending even more inches to her already considerable height, but obscuring her face. Mona, outstretched on the large sofa, was eating greedily from a long-hidden box of chocolates while watching a definitely proscribed soft-porn video. She had chanced to glance up between wriggling pleasurably at the advance of the devil-masked and impressively naked villain and biting into a particularly succulent coconut cream.

She screamed.

Liz, tiptoeing into what had seemed an empty room with a television set eerily flickering with an arcane occult ritual, was startled into screaming herself.

The "virgin" in the video also screamed.

This female cacophony was followed by a moment of reflective silence. Then Mona sat up. "Who the hell are you?" she demanded.

"I am the Defiler, the Master who demands service—" droned the villain from the video.

"And I'm your Avon Lady," Liz said, coming across the

room and glaring down at Mona. "Where's that damned yacht going?"

"Out," Mona said. "How the hell did you get in here?"

"I have a way with animals."

"Nobody has a way with those dogs."

"Well, they seemed all right to me. I just fed them a little something in some ground-round steak. They wolfed it down and never noticed the barbiturate seasoning. Don't you ever feed the poor things?"

"You've poisoned our dogs!" Mona shrieked unconvincingly. "I'll have you arrested!"

"Do it, do it, do it!" shouted the nude celebrants on the video as they gathered around the stone altar with its writhing sacrifice, who now looked more eager than frightened.

"Oh, for crying out loud, turn that thing off," Liz said in disgust.

"Won't," Mona said, folding her arms across her chest.

Liz regarded her. Mona's expression was childishly stubborn, but—like the "virgin" on the altar—she looked more excited than afraid. Liz had seen students who looked like that too often in the past to be fooled. She walked around the sofa and turned off the television set, then came back to stand over Mona.

"I'm not here to play games with you," she said.

"Oh? What a shame. I like games," Mona said, gazing up at her with an oddly calculating expression.

"So I've heard."

The kitten-face became coy. "What have you heard?" Mona asked. "Who's been talking about me? Was it nice things?"

"Give me strength," Liz muttered.

"Who are you, anyway?" Mona demanded again. "What do you want?"

"I told you—I want to know where that yacht is going."

"I don't know. Out somewhere. Down to Grantham to pick up Mummy, I guess. Who cares?" Mona pouted.

"I care," Liz said.

"Why?"

"Let's just say I have an interest in some of the cargo."

Mona's eyes flashed with a brief moment of what could have been intelligence, but then it disappeared under a fresh veneer of little-girl lewd. "You mean Jeff? Or is it Walt? I knew Walt was screwing someone on the Island, but I didn't think he could handle a woman like you."

"It's not Walt, whoever he is," Liz said impatiently.

"Then it must be Jeff," Mona concluded.

"Not Jeff. Look—"

"Well, it can't be Daddy, and it's certainly not Hugo because Hugo doesn't like girls," Mona went on conversationally. She looked at Liz speculatively. "So why are you interested in our boat?"

Liz was becoming exasperated. "Because my friend is on it and I want to know where it's taking her."

"I told you—I don't know where it's going. Hugo and Daddy often take the boat out and don't take me. I'm surprised they took your friend."

"They didn't take her along... exactly," Liz said.

"Oh? You mean she stowed away? What fun. Why would she do that?" Mona asked interestedly.

"God knows," Liz said. "The point is—"

"Maybe she wanted to make you jealous," Mona suggested.

"Don't be ridiculous."

"I'd be jealous if somebody went off and left *me* behind," Mona said. "Of course I'm glad when Daddy and Hugo go off, because then I can do anything I want to do." She giggled. "As you saw when you came in. I am a naughty girl, aren't I?"

"For heaven's sake—" Liz said in despair. Talking to this girl was like trying to catch a fish with your bare hands.

Mona stood up beside Liz. "I'm sorry your friend went off with them, but they won't be back for hours and hours."

"Why not? Where are they going?"

"I told you, I don't know," Mona snapped peevishly. "So it's no good asking." She eyed Liz again. "Would you like a drink?"

"No, thank you. I just want—"

Mona continued, half-smiling. "Do you live on the Island? You must be new. Nobody ever mentioned you before, and they would have, because you're so tall and really beautiful..." Her little hand, with its coral fingernails and gold rings, reached out to stroke Liz's arm.

Liz stepped back as if stung. She considered the alternatives open to her. And then she slapped Mona Wilberforce clear into the middle of her daddy's custom-made carpet. Mona shrieked with fury, and came up fighting.

Liz had the advantage of height, weight, and outrage, but for a moment or two a natural viciousness gave Mona the edge. She went for Liz's eyes, but Liz's reflexes were good, and she was clawed only on one shoulder as she turned to the side and swept her arm across to backhand her adversary. Then she grabbed her and held her at arm's length.

"I'll give you your due," Liz grunted. "You try everything, and you try damned hard."

"Get out! Get out of my house!" Mona screamed as she writhed and twisted in Liz's grasp—but twelve years of tutoring hysterical undergraduates through temper tantrums, broken hearts, and drug trips had put steel in Liz Olson. She simply held on until Mona momentarily tired, and then she threw her down and placed one knee—quite gently—on her midriff, holding Mona's little manicured hands hard against the carpet on either side of Mona's pretty little blond head.

"Where is that yacht going, and when is it coming back?" she asked through gritted teeth.

"I don't know, I don't know!" Mona screamed—but for a moment, just a moment, her eyes strayed toward the clock over the fireplace.

"I *thought* you were playing for time," Liz said, and pressed the knee into Mona's stomach a little harder. "And time is what we don't have. I am just over six feet and I weight one hundred and forty-nine pounds. If I bring all that to bear on this one knee, the pressure per cubic inch will—"

"Get off!" Mona screamed. "Help! Help! Greta! Greta! Come and help me!"

Liz was taken aback. She'd seen Hugo, his father, and the two security guards go off on the yacht. Who the hell was Greta? She was trying to think of another threat that might have some influence on this sneaky little bitch, when she caught sight of a new reflection in the picture window. From her position on the floor, she only caught half of it, but it was enough. A woman was coming into the room, a very broad, very muscular woman in an apron and rubber gloves. A few wisps of foam clung to the gloves—obviously Greta had been washing the dishes—but the rolling pin she carried was dry.

Liz took a breath, swallowed, and then smiled.

"Good evening, Greta," she said. "Can we talk?"

"What is all the screaming? Who are you?" Greta demanded, glaring at Liz.

Mona giggled. "She says she's the Avon Lady, Greta."

"We don't want any," Greta said.

"Now, look," Liz said, getting to her feet. "I just want to know where that boat is going."

"What boat?" Greta asked, bearing down on her.

"Get her, Greta. Make her squirm," Mona said, getting to her feet and excitedly bouncing up and down like a spectator at a wrestling match. "She *hurt* me."

Greta flashed a glance toward the girl, then returned her ball-bearing eyes to Liz, who was backing away. "You shouldn't have hurt her," she said. "She is delicate—"

"She's a vicious little bitch," Liz snapped, with far more bravado than she felt. "And about as delicate as a rhinoceros."

"You shouldn't have touched her," Greta went on implacably. Liz glanced behind her, and saw that there wasn't much space left between her back and the fireplace. She began to sidle to the right, and Greta matched her, step for step.

"Now, look," Liz began. "My friend is on that boat..."

"Who's your friend?" Mona asked suddenly, all coyness

gone from her high, thin voice. "And why is she on the boat?"

"It doesn't matter," Liz said, still sidling. The stairway up which she had come looked very far away—and Greta stood between her and escape. "The point is—"

"You shouldn't have touched her," Greta repeated, and lunged.

"Oh, shit," Liz said, and lunged back.

"He's going to run out on Peacock Dike!" Charley shouted as Matt and George ran down off the humpbacked bridge.

Greenfield's figure was clearly visible on their right, speeding along the service road that led to Peacock's Dike. He seemed to hesitate for a moment, then turned off the road and disappeared into the darkness beyond.

"No," Matt said, as Stryker and Tos came panting up behind him. "He's going into the Mush."

"Does he know what he's doing?" asked Tos.

Gabriel shrugged. "He's lived here six years. He goes into the Mush a lot—bird-watching. Or, at least, that's what he said he was doing. I guess what he was really doing was planning this Elysium thing."

"What are you going to do?" asked Stryker.

Gabriel sighed. "Go after him, I guess."

"Do you know your way around the Mush?" Tos asked.

"Well . . ." Matt began.

"I do," Charley Hart said. "I hunt frogs in there all the time." He looked at them and flushed in the glow of their collective flashlights. "Little sideline I got, supplying the hotel and all."

"Christ, if I'd known their frog legs came from the Mush—" George choked.

"They're good frogs," Charley said defensively. "The river is pretty clean, you know, and the Mush filters—"

"You can give us a lecture on amphibians later, Charley," Matt said. "Right now, I want Greenfield."

"Okay," Charley said reluctantly. But he didn't move.

"Well?" Matt asked impatiently.

Charley was looking at Stryker. "I looked over your shoulder at the town hall," he said. "When you was packing up them letters."

"Oh?" Stryker asked. He hadn't noticed the nondescript deputy in all the noise and confusion.

"Look, the bastard is getting away from us," George said, hopping from one foot to the other. "Isn't anybody interested in catching him?"

Stryker looked at the deputy sympathetically. "I'm sorry, Charley."

Charley looked chagrined. Then, in turns, his plain and earnest face became sad, worried, puzzled, and—eventually—angry. He went white, then flushed beet-red. His hair seemed to rise up on his head. His lips drew back and he straightened up, sheep into wolf.

"I'll get him for you," he snarled, starting off down the service road toward the Mush. "I'll get the bastard."

32

We're nearly there," said Walt, sticking his head into the saloon. "Maybe fifteen minutes more."

"Fine," said Mr. Wilberforce. "Let me know when you sight the freighter, and we'll come on deck."

"Will do," Walt said, and went back to the wheel.

"How many more this year?" Hugo asked his father.

Mr. Wilberforce consulted his electronic pocket organizer, which beeped cheerfully at him. "Four, if the weather holds. They don't like to risk it once the autumn storms start."

"Neither do I," Hugo said. "But four more should bring the bank balances up nicely. We don't want to be greedy, do we?"

His father smiled. "As a matter of fact, we do."

Both men laughed.

Hugo was topping up their drinks when Walt appeared once again.

"The freighter already?" Mr. Wilberforce asked.

"No." Walt looked worried. "It's Miss Mona on the radio."

The men looked at one another in surprise. "I'll come," Hugo said. A few minutes later he returned, scowling.

"According to Mona, we've got a stowaway on board."

"A *what?*" Mr. Wilberforce was dumbfounded.

Hugo went toward the door that led to the cabins. "I'll just make a little check, shall I?"

It didn't take long.

Hugo returned to the saloon, holding a gun and pushing Kate in front of him. She glanced over her shoulder, aware of a great change in him. No charm now, only frigid anger and a hardness along the mouth and jaw.

"There's no need to be so cross," she said with a little laugh. "It was a dare, that's all. I was curious to see the inside of your boat, and somebody bet me I couldn't get on board. I was just about to leave when the engines started up and the next thing I knew we were out on the lake. I was too embarrassed to come out and 'fess up, so I was just going to wait until you got back, or docked somewhere, and then I was going to slip off—"

"Who the devil is this?" Mr. Wilberforce demanded of his son.

"This is Kate Trevorne, one of our neighbors on Paradise," Hugo told him.

"And what's all this rubbish about a dare?" Wilberforce asked.

"Just a silly thing," Kate said. She found it was difficult to keep the tone light when you were telling out-and-out lies that were obviously not going down very well. But she continued doggedly. "You see, we went for a drink after the meeting at the town hall... quite a few drinks, really... and I said what a beautiful yacht this was and how I'd never been inside a really luxurious—"

"When I left the town hall a riot had started," Hugo interrupted. And he did not lower the gun.

"Yes, you made sure of that, didn't you?" Kate said, and then could have bitten her tongue. So much for the Famous Trevorne Dare Ploy. It was just what Jack always told her—she was too eager to show how clever she was. He maintained she'd probably be bragging on the scaffold.

Maybe she was, at that.

"I don't know what you mean," Hugo said.

"Well—I meant that you asked some pretty tough questions of that lawyer," Kate said hurriedly. Maybe there was still a chance. "You had him up against the wall—we were really grateful to you. And then when your man produced those plans for the chemical plant—"

"My 'man'? I don't..." Hugo began blandly.

Mr. Wilberforce sighed heavily. "Oh, cut the crap, Hugo. She's on to it. What did Mona say? How did she know this woman was on board?"

"Apparently some friend of hers—"

"Of whose? Of Mona's?"

"No, a friend of Miss Trevorne's here, drugged the dogs and broke into the house and attacked Mona—"

"Good Lord," Mr. Wilberforce said. "Are the dogs all right?"

"I have no idea," Hugo said. "But Mona managed to get away from this woman, eventually. I gather Greta helped. They locked her up in the gym and then Mona radioed us."

"Perhaps she's growing up at last," Mr. Wilberforce said with every evidence of satisfaction. "Did you say it was a *woman* who got into the house?"

"Yes."

"What did you tell Mona to do with her?"

"I didn't tell her to do anything," Hugo said with a puzzled expression."

"Well, I'll take care of her when we get back. *You'll* have to kill this one," Mr. Wilberforce said, opening his briefcase and rustling through its contents.

Hugo's mouth dropped open. "*What* did you say?"

Mr. Wilberforce seemed annoyed. "I said kill her—but do it outside. I detest loud noises. Throw the body overboard when you've finished. I'll radio Mona to keep the other one locked up until I get back. I'll deal with *her* myself, in the usual way." He looked up, only then seeming to sense Hugo's astonishment. "What's the matter?"

"You... you... can't just *kill* people," Hugo stammered.

"Why not?" Mr. Wilberforce asked him curiously.

"Well, because... Jesus God, Father... you can't..."

"I can and I have," Mr. Wilberforce said. "Why the devil do you think I told you to break up that town council meeting? I couldn't possibly have permitted that marsh to be developed. There are nine bodies out there—or what's left of them. It would be very inconvenient if they were discovered."

"No," Hugo said. "No—you can't be serious."

"Well, of course I'm serious. This is *business*," Mr. Wilberforce said. "I am always serious about business."

"But... killing... you said... you said..."

Mr. Wilberforce looked at his son reproachfully. "Hugo, it is a simple matter of profit and loss. They don't *all* have the money they've said they'll have, you see. And I'm not running a soup kitchen, after all. If they'd lie to me about the money, then they'd probably lie about keeping their mouths shut. Oh, no. I'm no fool. There's only one way to keep people's mouths shut when they let you down, and that is to kill them."

Kate stood there between them, hardly able to believe her ears. "But I *don't* know too much. I don't know *anything*," she said wildly.

"You may not have a moment ago, but you do now." Wilberforce's voice was bland and he smiled at her. "But I did have to explain to Hugo, you see. He's only just returned to join the family firm, and he doesn't understand all the ramifications, yet, of our latest venture. I was going to get around to such details, of course, but there hasn't been time..."

"There's been time," Hugo said hoarsely.

Wilberforce went on as if his son hadn't spoken. "There are some people who are strong enough to face facts without window-dressing, and there are others who are not. I was going to explain to Hugo when the time was right . . ."

"When I'd gotten in too deep to pull out?" Hugo asked, his face white.

Again Wilberforce ignored him and continued to address Kate. He was smiling, he was being charming, he was certain she was coming around to his point of view. "It was unfortunate you were here, but there it is—you know too much." Above the professional chairman-of-the-board smile his eyes were empty and she knew, suddenly, that he was totally without conscience, a sociopath, and as such could not be reasoned with or appealed to for mercy.

Kate stared at him. "Then it was *you* who killed Michael Grey?"

Wilberforce raised his hands in a gesture of dismissal. "Now why on earth would I kill Michael Grey?" He seemed genuinely perplexed.

"Because he found out what you were doing," Kate said. "By the way, what *are* you doing? Smuggling?"

"No," Hugo said, but it was unclear whether he was answering Kate's question or his father's demand.

"Something like that," Mr. Wilberforce said, turning to rummage in his briefcase. "In fact, that particular murder was very *unfortunate* as far as we were concerned. It brought far too much attention to the Island—newspapermen, police, everyone asking awkward questions, and so on. Why, they wanted to take *my* fingerprints, of all the nerve! I couldn't allow that. Certainly not."

He sounded like an outraged homeowner complaining about the unwelcome attentions of a wandering mongrel.

"I assure you, young woman, if *I* had killed that man, I would *not* have left him lying about the place. I have a passion for neatness, and I have always disposed of things in an orderly manner. I couldn't let someone like that interfere with my business."

"Drugs, I suppose," Kate said in disgust.

Wilberforce's head came up with a snap. "Certainly *not*," he said waspishly. "Our great and noble country is being *destroyed* by the drug trade. I would never have anything to do with such a disgusting business—even though I understand it is extremely profitable."

"People," Hugo said weakly. "He's smuggling in people. From Hong Kong, mostly. Rich men who can't get into the States any other way. Undesirable—except for their money, of course." Hugo's voice was strangled, and his face was glossed with an overlay of perspiration. The gun in his hand trembled.

"Really, Hugo, there's no need to tell her any *more*. Get on with it. And not in here, please. You know how I hate loud noises."

"I can't," Hugo said. "I won't."

Wilberforce sighed heavily. He produced a gun from his briefcase and stood up. "Very well, then—I'll do it myself," he said petulantly. "You know, Hugo, when you came back from New York you were broke and broken. You accepted that I knew what was best, and that the theatrical world was not for you. You said if I cleared your debts you'd do anything for me. Anything. So I cleared your debts and welcomed you back into the family, and now you refuse the first request I make of you. I am very disappointed, you know—I thought I could *count* on you."

"Not for . . . murder," Hugo managed to say.

"Obviously not," his father said, and sighed again in exasperation, a doting father tried beyond endurance by an intransigent son. "You disappoint me, Hugo. But then—you always have." He gestured with the gun. "Come along, Miss Whatever—out on the deck with you."

Kate looked at him, then took a deep breath and screamed as long and as loud as she could. Mr. Wilberforce jumped and then glared at her.

"You said you hate loud noises—was that loud enough for you?" Kate asked nastily. She'd hoped to startle Hugo into helping her, but he stood there staring at his father, immobile with shock.

"You are a very unpleasant young woman," Mr. Wilberforce said.

"I try my best," Kate said, as he took hold of her arm and propelled her from the saloon onto the deck.

"What do you think of your father now, Hugo?" she shouted over her shoulder. "Still want to give up stage design and join the family business?" She began to shake with anger and fear and cold. Out on deck, the wind of their passage was considerable, and the blackness around them was all the more complete because of the brightness of the saloon lights. Wilberforce's back was to the cabin, the outstretched hand with the gun obscured within his silhouette. But she knew it was there. And she knew, with complete and final conviction, that he was going to use it.

The moon was high now, but intermittently obscured by thin, racing rags of clouds. She looked around her, at the gleaming mahogany of the deck where she would soon lie bleeding, at the glinting ebony of the lake at night, at the furled sails tied around the boom and the lurching whipsaw of the mast against the starry sky. What a stupid place to die, she thought, as if anywhere were wise. I thought I would be old, in bed, brave and beautiful, with my long hair in braids on either side of my face and my thin old hands folded on the counterpane...

There was a long moment in which she lived for several years, ended by the appearance of Hugo in the saloon doorway.

"I'm sorry, Father," he said. "I can't let you do this."

"You have no choice in the matter," his father snapped.

"I do, you know," Hugo said, and tried to grab the gun from his father's hand. Wilberforce cursed as he struggled for balance. They staggered across the deck, fighting for the gun and supremacy.

"Help me!" Hugo shouted to Kate. "Get the gun!"

Kate danced around them, trying to catch hold of the flailing arm with the gun in it. Suddenly the deck tilted and the two of them fell against her, still cursing and struggling. She felt the rail hit the back of her knees and then she was arching through the air. She hit the water on her back, and the impact knocked the wind from her lungs.

She seemed to go down forever, but she never reached bottom.

Then she began to rise, but it also took forever. Her lungs were in agony, and the darkness of the air and water were one, so she didn't know she was near the surface until she broke through it, and did not realize she could breathe for a second or two, until she felt the wind on her face. Then, gasping, she opened her eyes.

The Wilberforce yacht was about a hundred yards from her and moving away. She could see the two Wilberforces—father and son—struggling. Then there was a muffled shot, and they both went down out of sight onto the deck. She was safe from bullets—but where, pray, was the satisfaction in that?

The yacht was continuing on its way. It grew smaller and smaller, until the lights were no brighter or bigger than the few stars she could glimpse overhead. She could no longer hear its engines but, oddly enough, she could still hear its bell, tolling over the distance, like some ritual farewell. She kept treading water automatically as her brain began, slowly, to comprehend her true position.

The yacht had been under way for well over an hour when Hugo discovered her. That, the incredible coldness of the water, and the longer chop of the waves told her that she was no longer in Blackwater Bay, but out in the great lake itself. Out in the deeps, where the big fish swam and hunted, out in the shipping lanes, where a bobbing head would be invisible to any casual lookout high above, and where the churning propellers of the great freighters could cut her to ribbons. Bodies often drifted to shore chopped up like that—and chewed by fish. She was miles from any shore, and she was not a strong swimmer. Already her muscles were beginning to flutter and her body was growing numb.

"Oh, Jack . . ." she whispered, and went on whispering in a litany of pleading, until a wave filled her mouth with water and she choked.

All Kate's life, her worst fear had been to drown.

Time and again, through childhood and beyond, nightmares had jerked her awake as bedclothes wound around her face made her dream of death and water closing over her. She would awake, gasping, thrashing, terrified by the thought of endless depths beneath her, and the things that swam there, and the weeds that could entangle her legs and drag her under...

Horrified, she suddenly knew that they had not been nightmares, but premonitions. She *was* going to drown after all.

Alone in the middle of this vast body of water, struggle as she might, she would lose in the end. Her clothes would weigh her down, her strength would ebb, and eventually, inevitably, she would give up and slide beneath the waves for the last time.

As if to confirm her destiny, as a promise of things to come, something cold and slimy passed by in the blackness beneath her, brushing lightly against her right leg.

Kate began to scream.

She went on screaming until the water filled her mouth.

33

"All we need now is the Hound of the Baskervilles to appear," griped Stryker as he pulled his foot out of the mud for the sixty-fifth time, steadying himself against George Putnam. "If this isn't the Great Grimpen Mire, I don't know what is."

"The what?" George asked, after four steps needing in his turn to be extricated from the slimy grip of the swamp.

They were all well and truly in the Mush.

In fact, all of them were covered in the Mush.

It was a matter of some amazement that there was any mud *left* in the Mush, so much of it was now distributed over them.

The only one who was relatively clean was Charley Hart, who alternately strode and hopped before them, moving along invisible lines of firm ground, nimbly skipping from one hummock to another, and—unlike the rest of them—never once sliding down into a morass of weeds, reeds, and startled frogs.

Somewhere ahead, Charley shouted, "Stop, you stinking bastard, I want to shove your head under the mud and watch you bubble."

"I don't think that approach is going to bring Greenfield to a halt, do you?" Matt wheezed. "You know, it would have made a lot more sense to surround the edge of the Mush and wait for the guy to come out."

"*Now* he thinks of it," George said, slipping and sitting down suddenly. He stayed still for a moment, trying to catch his breath. "Why is it that whenever that happens, I land on a rock?" he asked nobody in particular. "The whole damn place is squishy and soft and sloppy and yet—"

"It's a law," Stryker said, reaching out to grab some reeds and then slowly sliding down them as he sank to his knees. "Hey! I believe I've fallen into some quicksand here, guys."

"Christ!" Tos said, reaching for him.

"No," Stryker said after a moment. "I've touched bottom, after all." He looked at Matt. "Any alligators in here?"

Matt grinned, only his teeth and eyeballs visible in the moonlight. "Not that I've heard." He shone his flashlight around. "Unless they've moved in recently."

Their flashlights did not provide much illumination because they, too, were covered in mud, and they, too, stank.

Everything stank.

The farther they went into the Mush, the more mud and water they stirred up, the richer and more malevolent the stink became, until it seemed almost visible, a kind of phosphorescent miasma of botanic putrefaction hanging over them.

And it was hard work. The mud sucked and dragged at them, weighted them down, squelched and bubbled and gurgled as they pulled one foot and then the other out of it, staggering and lurching. They had to pause frequently to get their breath.

At one such moment, Stryker looked up at Tos. The big man's face was a mask of dark smears where he'd scratched at mosquito bites, and his once flamboyant Hawaiian sport shirt was a solid monochromatic black, the thick encrustation lending it and his shorts a sculptural quality. Stryker grinned, his teeth so white in his own muddy face that they seemed to glow.

"Aren't you glad you came?" he asked.

* * *

They didn't so much capture Greenfield as fall over
him.

The older man, exhausted by his hopeless flight from
implacable Charley Hart and the others, had simply col-
lapsed near the edge of the Mush, hands outstretched
toward solid land.

When they rolled him over they saw he wasn't dead, but
he certainly wasn't in the peak of health, either.

By now, dawn was starting to lighten the sky, and birds
were beginning to sing their territorial songs over the Mush.
Mosquitoes, too, were humming in clouds over the mud
and water that glistened in the pale light.

Charley stood over their fallen quarry, a kind of disappointment evident in the slump of his shoulders. No fight
here, no satisfaction. "I say leave him," he said. "The hell
with it."

"Now, Charley, you know we can't do that," Matt said.

Charley turned away. "Well, I ain't gonna carry him
back," he growled.

"Jesus—you mean we have to go *back* through all that?"
Tos asked in deep and sincere horror.

"No—we're better off going straight ahead," Matt said,
gesturing. "Once we're on the solid bank we can move
easily, and we're not that far from the schoolgrounds, as a
matter of fact. I can just about make out their flagpole
through the trees. We've kind of come in a circle around
the edge of the Mush."

"Well, we'll have to carry him," George said grimly. "Or
drag him." He wiped his forehead, then looked at Stryker.
"I'll tell you, though—it might have been muddy and it
might have been hard, but it was worth it. I never hunted
down a murderer before."

Stryker sighed and stood up. He'd been kneeling beside
Greenfield, who had been whispering to him. "And you
haven't caught one now," he said.

George gaped at him. "What the hell are you talking
about? I thought he was behind this Bobcat thing."

"He was," Stryker agreed.

"But—"

"We can discuss it later," Matt said. "I want to get this man to the hospital and I want to get this goddamn mud off. Let's move."

Between them, they got the limp figure of Greenfield up and onto their shoulders and began to make their way across the last yards of the Mush and onto the solid bank. Charley Hart, who had less mud and more energy than the rest of them, went ahead to summon help.

As they staggered along, Tos turned his head to look at Stryker, who was beside him. "Hey," he said suddenly. "This isn't Sherlock Holmes, it's Orson Welles."

Stryker was puzzled. "What do you mean?"

"I mean he just whispered something."

"What did he say?"

"He said 'Rosebud.'"

34

Roberta Maybelle Rose sat with her feet neatly together, her hands folded in her lap, every hair in place, every button on her dimity nightgown buttoned tight, her flannel robe closed over her maiden breast, and swore savagely.

The stream of blasphemy and filth poured from between her lips like vomit, but not once, not in any way, did anything else in her expression or her demeanor match what she was saying.

Charley Hart could only stand and stare.

He was a broken man.

"I kind of thought there was someone else..." he said to Matt Gabriel. "I thought maybe Berringer, because she was always talking to him, or even the mayor ..."

Roberta Rose's eyes flicked to him. "It was all of them," she said derisively. "It was everyone, anyone...whatever was necessary. *You* were only necessary now and then."

"And each one thought you were their secret," Stryker said.

She looked at him then.

And smiled.

"Of course," she said.

Stryker turned away and walked to the front windows of the Rose cottage. The morning seemed to be holding its breath.

Out on the horizon he could see the long, slim shape of the Wilberforce yacht coming toward the shore. Must have gone out for an early-morning sail, he thought.

"Which of you killed Michael Grey?" he asked Roberta Rose.

"I don't know what you're talking about," she sniffed. "And I don't wish to say any more."

Her mother, who seemed to have shrunk to half her previous size, spoke from the depths of her armchair. "You've said far too much already," she whispered.

Roberta glanced at her with disdain. "Oh, shut up," she said.

Stryker turned around. "Did you hit him with that club?"

Roberta said nothing.

"Greenfield told us you did," Matt put in.

For a moment her eyes flickered, then she lifted her chin. "Nonsense," she said. "He said no such thing."

"He told us that Grey discovered the two of you in bed at the Lattimer house and threatened to tell Harry's wife about your affair. He said while they were arguing you hit Grey from behind with that African club, then told Harry to use a shotgun to make it look as if Daria Grey had killed him. You thought he was still alive, but he wasn't. *You* murdered him with the club—Greenfield only mutilated the body."

"That's a lie."

"We have traces on the sheets that the forensic lab will have no difficulty identifying. Semen, skin cells—they'll stand witness."

"That's another lie—it all burned down."

"Indeed it did. But not before we removed the things we wanted. By the way, where are the spare gas cans your mother always keeps in the trunk of her car?"

"Up your ass, if you're lucky" was the reply.

In the corner, Mrs. Rose moaned and hid behind her handkerchief. Not even Oprah Winfrey could help her now. Her precious daughter was disappearing before her eyes. Roused from sleep and challenged, Roberta Maybelle Rose had at first been confused and shocked. But gradually, as Matt Gabriel and the others had questioned her, she had dropped her petals, one by one. What was revealed—the canker in the bud, the maggot at the heart—was a stranger.

And what would Mrs. Rose do without a daughter to look after her?

"You have been involved with the entire Bobcat-Elysium scam from the beginning," Stryker went on. "There was a certain mark, a small scratch, repeated on all the letters that went out to the Islanders about the Bobcat offer. It had to be a scratch on the glass bed of the photocopier to have been exactly the same over and over again. It was small— but it was clear. I had Tos go around the town getting some letters photocopied. That scratch was on the library photocopier. It was also on two of the hate letters that Len Cotman kept—because you are so efficient you photocopied the newspaper headlines you cut up to make the messages. Couldn't destroy library resources, could you? A proper Marian the Librarian to the end."

She hissed like an angry cat, but said nothing.

Stryker continued calmly. "As a matter of fact, I think the whole operation was your idea. We know Greenfield is a gambler, but he's not an ideas man. And Lattimer had the money to back the scheme through his South African investments, but he's a sick man, and not capable of detailed planning. Those are the only three names in Cater's file, Miss Rose. It was the names that gave me the connection— the 'green fields' of Elysium, the 'Bob' from Roberta, and 'Kit' Lattimer turned into 'Cat'—all games with names, Miss Rose. Word games—something a librarian might come up with during the long, quiet hours she spends bored and confined in her library. Something someone might come up with who knows a lot about plots, and who already leads many secret lives—and you do, don't you?"

"What I do is no concern of yours or anyone else's,"
Roberta Maybelle Rose spat.

"Oh, baby..." her mother moaned.

The girl turned. "And certainly no concern of yours,
Mother, with your fat body and your constant complaining.
I was going to be free of you at last." She turned back to
Stryker, and her mouth twisted in a sneer. "It was going to
be so easy to panic everyone, to jolt them out of their little
world by making them think a chemical company was going
to take over the Mush, to drive their prices down and pick
up the cottages dirt cheap. Then all we had to do was offer
the Island to a development company and take the profit."

"But the man said it was going to be a marina," Charley
said.

She didn't look at him. "Cater was supposed to say that
to get the sale through. *Then* we would have leaked the
information about the chemical company's interest and got
the prices down. But he fucked up, and let it all out too
soon."

"Roberta!" Mrs. Rose said.

"What's the point of pretending anymore, Mother *dear?*
I'm so sick of namby-pamby Roberta Maybelle Rose that I
could spit. I'm not that person, I never was—and she isn't
useful anymore."

"I can't b'lieve it," Charley Hart kept saying. "You was so
sweet to me, out in the car, when we talked about—"

"Does he have to stay?" Miss Rose asked Gabriel. For a
moment there seemed to be a possibility of kindness within
her—but it was only a moment. "He makes me want to
puke," she said. "Can't stop whining, can you, Charley?
God, I *hate* whiners." She glared at her mother.

Stryker turned away again, disgusted by the cruelty and
hatred that was being revealed. When he had first
encountered her, he had suspected Roberta Rose had found
an escape from her dull life—but he had not suspected how
many escapes she had managed, or how many people she
had lured into those secret lives of hers. She played the
sweet persecuted daughter for Charley Hart, whose patrols

interfered with her clandestine nighttime forays; she played
the sensual animal for Greenfield, whose obsessive neatness disguised a man hungry for sensual excitement and
passion; she played the woman offering a means of revenge
for Kit Lattimer, who hated the Island and all it stood for and
willingly put up the seed money for its destruction. God
only knew what she had offered to Berringer, or to any of
the others on the council. It might come out—or they
might keep their secrets.

The Wilberforce yacht had moored now. No doubt they
were all going in to eat their muesli and do their daily
exercises—nice to know there were still something healthy
in Paradise.

"I don't think there's any more point in talking here,"
Stryker said to Gabriel. "You might as well arrest her and
get someone to take down a full statement. Somebody
should contact the Phoenix police and ask them to talk with
Lattimer. As it happens, the Bobcat business broke no
laws, and he's not technically involved in Michael Grey's
murder, but his evidence—"

There was the bang of a door and Tos appeared.

"Jack—I think you'd better come..." he said. "Kate
is... Kate is... she might be..."

"What?" Stryker demanded. "She might be what?"

But Tos couldn't say it.

"I'm sorry," Hugo said weakly. His torn shirt showed a
hastily improvised bandage around his shoulder and chest.
"I got the gun away from him and made Walt turn back,
but we couldn't find her... we circled for a long time..."

They stood on the Cotman lawn, looking at the flat
impersonal line of the horizon. Stryker was pale and stiff,
his hands clenched to fists and his anger only just held in
check.

"I *tried* to stop her..." Liz said. She was bruised,
tear-streaked, and stricken with remorse.

Stryker shook himself. "She's not dead," he said flatly.

"But we were right out in the lake," Hugo protested. "It's been hours. Even a strong swimmer . . ."

"She's not dead," Stryker insisted. "I'd *know* if she was dead."

Liz went to him, put her arms around him, but he didn't notice. Tos shook his head helplessly.

"Well," Len Cotman said in a brisk, practical voice. "If she's not dead, then we'd better go and find her, hadn't we?"

Stryker looked at him gratefully. "Yes," he said.

"We can take the yacht," Hugo said. "The course Walt set will still be on the chart table."

Matt Gabriel frowned. "I don't know that I should let you—" he began.

"He's not going to escape, Matt," Daria said softly. "He stopped his father, he looked for Kate—"

"He *says* he looked for her," Matt interrupted.

"We can take more than that damned yacht," Don Robinson put in. "And we can keep an eye on your prisoners, too, Matt. Come on."

And so it was that while Mr. Wilberforce, his daughter, Greta, and his two "security men" were being guarded by Charley Hart and Frank Boomer until the Customs and Immigration people drove up from Grantham, and while Glen Hardwicke was sitting by Harry Greenfield in the hospital, and while Tilly Moss was making coffee for an ungrateful Roberta Maybelle Rose as she sat snarling in the cell behind the sheriff's office . . . all the boats set out.

Don and Fran Robinson came in the *Flash*.

Mrs. Toby and Mrs. Norton came in the *Stitch in Time*.

Larry and Freddy came in their speedboat, the *Dun Cruisin'*.

Tos went with Stryker in the *Dart*.

Daria and Liz went with Len Cotman in the *Aria*.

George came in the police cruiser.

Matt and several of his part-time deputies went on the Wilberforce yacht with Hugo.

As Stryker opened the throttle he was sure he would find Kate. (Everyone else was sure they would find a body. But nobody said so out loud.)

The Coast Guard met them halfway and joined the search.

A Navy helicopter came over from the air base and made wide sweeps of the area.

But Stryker (and Tos) didn't find her.

Don Robinson didn't find her.

And neither did Len Cotman and Daria and Liz; Larry and Freddy; Mrs. Norton and Mrs. Toby; Matt, Hugo, and the deputies; nor the Coast Guard or the Navy find her.

George did.

"Worst case of seasickness I ever saw!" marveled George, as he dragged a moaning, prune-wrinkled, soggy and limp Kate from his boat and onto the grass in front of the Wilberforce house.

She moaned again and threw up some lake water.

"She's been doing that all the way back," George said, grinning. "Reckon the water level must be down a foot with all she's got in her."

Stryker knelt down and took Kate into his arms. "Katie," he murmured.

She threw up all down his back. "Oh, God," she gurgled. "Put me down."

He put her down, and looked up at George. There was a lot of noise from the engines of the returning boats, and people were shouting and waving at one another and pointing to the Wilberforce beach. From the kennel the dogs, awake again and infuriated by all the people who were clambering over their lawn, were barking wildly. Stryker had to raise his voice.

"Where did you find her?" he asked. "How did she survive?"

George laughed. "She was clinging to the buoy that marks the wreck of the old Peacock dredger that sunk in '25. It's a danger to shipping, being on the edge of the lanes, so they anchored a special buoy to it, bell and radar, and there she was, sitting with her legs wrapped around it, rocking back and forth, back and forth, and puking up as regular as clockwork."

"Sell the cottage to Bobcat Investments," Kate groaned. "I never want to see Blackwater Bay or the lake—or even a pond—ever again."

"But Kate," Stryker said, as amused as he was relieved. "This is Paradise."

"Then let me speak to the Snake," Kate said, and passed out.

35

In the red-and-white-striped hammock slung between two oak trees in front of Number 7 Paradise Island, Stryker swung back and forth and listened to the water lapping against the breakwater. In the distance the Robinson children were playing with their dog, and from Freddy and Larry's place came the sweet sounds of Mozart, overlaid by a slightly shrill argument about oregano.

A few feet away from the hammock, Tos lay in the sun, lavishly overflowing a deck chair, his bare stomach growing pinker by the minute.

Out on the bay, a water-skier who was being towed by a large speedboat from up the coast suddenly fell backward with a splash, and some passing gulls screamed with laughter. From the Lattimer property there came the subdued roar of machinery and the shouts of men clearing up debris. Occasionally, borne on the fitful afternoon breeze, there came an elusive aroma of cinnamon and cloves. Mrs. Norton was baking again.

"When do you think you'll hear from the bank?" Stryker asked Tos.

"He said he'd call back tomorrow, but it looks like it will

be okay. We can probably move in next month," Tos murmured.

Tos and Liz had decided to buy the Greenfield cottage. Cissy Greenfield was determined to realize all the cash she could to finance her divorce and her new life.

Kit Lattimer had died in Phoenix, eaten up by bitterness and cancer. He had asked for his ashes to be scattered in Africa.

There was still a twenty-four-hour guard at the bridge, but the reporters had pretty much departed, holding their energies and their fire for the trials of Harry Greenfield and Roberta Rose, at present languishing in the Hatchville jail. These trials were being looked forward to by every citizen of Blackwater Bay, for whom there had not been so much excitement since Prohibition.

Mrs. Rose went in every day to see her daughter, but Roberta refused to talk to her. Mrs. Rose had written a letter to Oprah Winfrey and expected a reply any day now. She was certain Oprah would be interested in putting her on a program about Ungrateful Daughters.

The Wilberforce family had been taken away by the Federal authorities. It was not certain whether Mr. Wilberforce would ever face a homicide charge. There were so many details to clear up concerning the people he had brought into the country illegally and allowed to *live* that it would be months before they could even consider mounting a trial for the ones he had *murdered*—and his mental condition was clearly unstable. The entire case was being hushed up from high up—so nothing of the secret of the swamp had appeared in the newspapers as yet. Stryker was privately certain it never would.

Nothing had been heard of Mrs. Wilberforce following her sudden departure from Grantham to Paris. Interpol would interview her when she was located—it was simply a matter of following the trail of her American Express Gold Card purchases. It was possible she knew nothing of her husband's crimes—unless she had been informed by Some-

one from Beyond. Mona and the Wilberforce employees
were being charged with complicity in illegal immigration.

Whether Hugo would be charged with anything remained
to be seen. While he had started to take part in an illegal
immigration operation, the actual crime had never been
completed. (Two very indignant Hong King drug importers
had been removed from a Tanzanian ore freighter by the
Coast Guard.) Hugo's attempts to save Kate and his ignorance of his father's homicides were being taken into
consideration.

In any event, the house at the Point was up for sale, too.

Kate was trying to convince Daria to buy it. She said that
if the redwood deck were glass-covered, it would make an
ideal studio in which to paint. Daria said that luxurious as it
was, it gave her the whim-whams, and that if she did buy
it, she would have it torn down and replaced by a replica of
the old Peacock place on the site, which would take every
penny she had inherited from Michael, and be money well
spent. She and Aunt Clary and Matt argued about it every
day.

"You know, I think maybe it would be a good idea if you
and I bought the Lattimer land and used it for our chicken
farm," Tos said thoughtfully. "We could sell a lot of eggs to
Mrs. Norton for baking cookies, and when production
really got going—"

"No," Stryker murmured.

Tos sighed. "You have no vision, Jack. You don't look
ahead, you don't see the Big Picture. Why, we could stamp
each egg with a little sign that said, 'This egg was laid in
Paradise.'"

Stryker peered at him from under the straw hat. "Look,
we only have three days left before we have to go back to
work. What with Liz's broken ribs, and Kate nearly drowning,
we'll be lucky if *we* get laid in Paradise."

"Now, now—there's no need to get touchy."

"Well, dammit . . ."

The cottage door opened. Kate stood there, with a spoon
in her hand. "Dinner will be ready in ten minutes. Tonight

we are having baked Virginia ham with pineapple and candied yams, buttered corn on the cob, fresh green beans with baby onions, and scalloped potatoes au gratin, followed by a choice of apple or banana cream pie for dessert." She shut the door.

After a minute, it opened again, and Liz appeared. "Actually, it's hot dogs and potato salad, we've run out of mustard, and the buns are burned." The door closed again.

Beneath his hat, Stryker grinned wryly.

"Ah, Paradise," he said.